"When ya gonna shoot him?" said a voice beside him. The ranger turned and looked into the wide-eyed face of an old townsman, leaning near him, squatting with his palms on his knees. The townsman nodded toward the rise of dust far away, then back to the ranger. "I mean, he shore ain't getting no closer."

The ranger studied the stream of dust in the distance until a dark speck rose up out of the narrow tip of it, ascending above the thick brown cloud, climbing the rising land toward the foothills beyond.

Then he leaned forward into the butt of the rifle, aimed it, locked in on the tiny dark speck, followed it as it climbed higher, then eased his finger back against the trigger until the slam of the butt stock jarred him to his bones.

The sound of the shot cracked along the front of the buildings, jarring them as well, and echoed off through the swirling heat . . .

Montana Red

—◆—

RALPH COTTON

A SIGNET BOOK

SIGNET
Published by the Penguin Group
Penguin Putnam Inc., 375 Hudson Street,
New York, New York 10014, U.S.A.
Penguin Books Ltd, 27 Wrights Lane,
London W8 5TZ, England
Penguin Books Australia Ltd,
Ringwood, Victoria, Australia
Penguin Books Canada Ltd, 10 Alcorn Avenue,
Toronto, Ontario, Canada M4V 3B2
Penguin Books (N.Z.) Ltd, 182-190 Wairau Road,
Auckland 10, New Zealand

Penguin Books Ltd, Registered Offices:
Harmondsworth, Middlesex, England

First published by Signet, an imprint of Dutton Signet,
a member of Penguin Putnam Inc.

First Printing, April, 1998
10 9 8 7 6 5 4 3 2 1

For Mary Lynn . . . of course.

PROLOGUE

Buenos dias, Ran-jur, the little girl had said, smiling, her face slightly shying to one side as she padded barefoot past him along the dirt street. A strand of black hair swept forward and glistened across her face. She pushed it aside with the tip of a finger and walked on, an empty brown water gourd swinging on its leather loop in her hand. The rain season had come and gone with no rain falling and none to speak of the season past. About her the land and sky stood stark and unyielding, as dry as the heart of a broken stone.

The frayed edge of her thin serape dragged along in the dirt behind her, stirring a low rise in the burning dust. When the ranger did not answer but only looked up from his thoughts and tipped the brim of his tall gray sombrero, she slowed but did not stop; and turning quarter-wise she looked back at him as she moved on toward the well.

A gaunt red chicken cocked up from its pickings in the dirt and scolded her, and fled from her path in a flurry of dust and batting wings. A single dry feather stood in the heat, then lighted back and forth to the ground. She walked on, with the chicken watching from beneath a spent and tilted wagon, where so long

it had sat broken that a single clump of pale dry grass
had weaved upward through its bleached spokes.

Like all things abandoned in that bare fiery basin,
dust had lapped in and crept up the wagon's brittle
spokes until the wagon seemed to have grown unnur-
tured from the barren earth itself. The rib caging of
some small creature lay glistening white near the
wagon, half sunken where some predator of the night
had left it.

On her way back, with the gourd full of water resting heavy down her side, she smiled again, cupping
her free hand near her cheek to hide the gap left there
by a missing front tooth.

"*Hola,*" he said, this time as she passed. With a
gloved finger he pushed up the brim of his sombrero.
And this time he returned her smile and added as she
shied her face, "Aw, don't you fret about that tooth.
It'll grow back twice as pretty." Friendly now, yet his
eyes and his voice seemed lost and distant in a way
she'd never seen before, and she cupped her hand
closer and did not look back again until she stood before the open door to the adobe. Then she stole a
guarded glance back to where he sat in the wooden
chair beneath the shade of the ragged canvas overhang. A hot breeze licked at the canvas.

He sat looking back down at the ground now, his
sombrero tilted forward. Bowed in prayer, she
thought, or—if her young mind could fashion such a
thought—perhaps succumbed to something dark inside himself.

Midmorning heat wavered atop the billowing canvas and up the sides of the crumbling adobe walls behind him. His horse stood in the shade near him and
lifted its nose west toward things unseen. The shade

about them stood out in its darkness against the white hot glare of sun, the two of them appearing to be drawn into a black hole and swallowed up on the hard flat belly of the land.

Beyond the crumbling adobe stood the well some twenty yards off. Beyond the well stood no artifice of humankind's manifestation but for a small frail corral patched and strung with scraps of board, dried mesquite, and knotted wire with strands of mane and fur entwined in it. Beyond that, nothing, except a low drawing breath of wind over sand and a narrow trail snaking off across the desert floor. Dry stands of pale gramma grass and mesquite brush stretched outward to the far end of vision.

He looked small and brittle and ancient to her against the long backdrop of earth and sun, him with his tall sombrero pulled low across his brow and his broad duster collar raised against his cheeks. Her mother had told her that he had many things on his mind today . . . and *yes* it was so, she thought.

She squinted in the sun's glare, concerned for this man who always before would bring her rock candy when he brought flour and tins of beans and corn to her and her mother. She had been asleep when he came to the door last night and had only heard his voice and her mother's voice from some faraway place. In a second the door had creaked shut again and the voices had ceased, yet she knew that had she been up, he would have swept off his dusty sombrero in a grand gesture and bent down to her to say something in his broken Spanish just to make her laugh. She knew he liked hearing her laughter.

She was allowed to take candy from *this* man, and from *this* man only, because her mother had said that

in *this* man there was no meanness, no harm to come—
no *evil* to be read or felt. Not in *this* man. Yet today
there was a darkness about him she'd never seen before. Seeing it frightened her. She was not frightened *of*
him, but rather *for* him; and for reasons she did not understand, she crossed herself and whispered the name
of the Virgin Mother under her breath as she swung
open the sun-bleached door to the adobe and stepped
through it out of the heat. Today she saw no laughter
in him.

Beneath the dusty canvas overhang he stirred restless in the rickety wooden chair until at length he
stood up from it, propped a dusty boot up on it, and
adjusted his belt and holster and the brim of his pearl
gray sombrero. He stared off, out to where the burnt
land turned into a long narrow haze and bled blue-
silver upward into the sky. Beside him, the big dun
horse jerked its sweat-darkened head and blew and
grumbled and looked down, scraping a hoof on the
hard dirt.

Horses knew man better than man knew horses, he
always thought. He whispered something to it under
his breath and watched its sharp eyes bore back into
his. A wisp of damp mane raised on the wind, and the
horse nickered low and breathed deep, and held his
gaze until he turned and looked away.

His Christian name was Sam Burrack, but to be honest about it, he'd almost forgotten it over the years. If
paperwork was forced on him, he simply initialed it in
a loose scrawl, "SB.RNGR." He had short tolerance for
paperwork and had managed to reduce *his* to a single
list he carried in his breast pocket at all times. His
records were easy to keep and simple to understand.
Should a man's name appear on his list it meant that

man was *wrong*. Should a man's name become crossed off his list, it meant that man was *dead*.

After a time he'd even dropped the "SB.," and for years had only scrawled "RNGR." As far back as he could now remember everybody called him *the ranger*, and nothing more. Even other rangers called him *the ranger*, as if unlike themselves, who had taken on the title along with their oaths, their badges, and all the more formidable trappings of the job, *he* had somehow been born with the title instead of a name—the job having taken the man as surely as the man had taken the job.

And the job had swallowed him.

The job . . .

He straightened and raised his boot from the chair, and stood in the dirt beside it, still staring off, yet no longer seeing the land or the sky, but seeing instead the picture of the young woman's cold dead face where she'd lain in the dirt in the black puddle of blood, and where the dust had blown in across her naked body and her hollow open eyes as if dust and dust alone had come at the sound of her dying plea.

Though it had been over a month, the picture remained, as clear in memory as it had been in flesh. Beside the dead woman he saw as clearly the body of the Indian boy, half of his head gone and flies swarming there. What he'd seen he could not abide, and at the dark picture of it he winced and looked away and still could not shed himself of it.

The picture clung deep in the center of his being and all other thoughts that came and went were only thin clouds passing across some terrible mountain. Behind the passing of the clouds the terrible mountain remained. Nothing moved it. A tendon stiffened in his neck and he swallowed against it and ran a gloved hand along the dun's damp mane.

When he spotted the lone rider come up out of the distant haze, he picked up the reins to the dun horse; yet it seemed a full hour would pass before the rider swung the big bay off the dirt street and beneath the overhang. The bay stood wet and frothed and slung its head, the heat of it filling the space around them. "What did he say, Captain?" The ranger asked as the captain's boot touched the dirt.

The young captain turned to him, sweeping off his hat and slapping dust from his trousers. "You sure don't waste no time, do you?"

"Got none to waste," the ranger said. "Was it Red Hollis or not?"

The captain stalled for a second, wiped a hand across his sweat-streaked jaw, then let out a breath and said, "Yes, it was Montana Red Hollis, just like you said. Him and three friends of his. But they're long gone north. Judge said forget them for now. We can't spare a man. And he said tell you if you expect to get any expense reimbursement from now on, you best start holding receipts."

"What's the others' names?" The ranger stepped in and ran his gloved hand down along the bay's neck. The horse bobbed its wet head up and down and sniffed against him.

The captain cocked his head to one side. "You're not listening to me, are you?"

"Sure I am." The ranger spoke without turning to him. "Judge said I better keep receipts. So I will." He rubbed the horse under its chin, and asked, "Now. You gonna tell me their names?"

"Well . . ." The captain pushed his hair to the side

and sat his hat back on his head. "It's a couple of drifters named Hurley Yates, and Donald Kurtz. Real bad eggs. But it doesn't matter to you. Judge said we got more trash pouring up out of Kansas than we can shove back with both hands. He said tell you—"

"You said there's *three* of them." The ranger cut him off, turning to him, his eyes fixed on him.

"What? Oh . . . there is. Third one's a young cowboy named Bennie Burdett. Judge figures he's just a cowhand got into bad company and got pulled into it."

"Just pulled into it, huh?" The ranger nodded and glanced down. A hot wind swung through, lapping the canvas overhang up and down in its frame. Dust swirled.

"Now listen to me *good*," the young captain said. He raised a dusty gloved finger for emphasis. "The judge is just as torn up about this as you are—we *all* are! But this isn't the time. We've got too many miles and too few men to cover them." He stopped. Seeing how the ranger stared at his pointing finger, he lowered it and rubbed his hand on his trouser leg. "And— The thing is, we've got jurisdiction problems. The United States federal government's saying we can't go crossing lines unless we've got something in writing from—"

"In writing?" The ranger pitched an arm up and let it drop. "Well, *there* we are. Now if Red Hollis and his boys'll put it *in writing* every time they get ready to go on a killing spree, we'll have ourselves a *dandy* thing here."

"I knew you'd act this way," the captain said. "But you can't go and that's that."

"*Can't* go?"

"You know what I mean." The captain gazed off toward the adobe where the little girl had come forth at the sound of their voices and stood watching from the open door. A silence passed beneath a hot gust of wind until the captain said in a lowered voice, nodding toward the child, "That little girl— Isn't she . . . ?"

"Yep, she is."

"My, my." The captain rubbed his chin. "Does she know who you are?"

"No. Not altogether." He'd stepped back along the side of his dun horse, flipped open his saddlebags, and he took out a dusty bottle of rye. "I come through here when I can. Try to help out some." He uncorked the bottle and handed it to the captain.

The captain took it without taking his eyes from the little girl. He threw back a shot, let out a whiskey hiss, and handed the bottle back. "Is this why you wanted me to meet you here? Thinking this would move me some way?"

"No. But here's where we are." The ranger corked the bottle and bounced it gently in his palm. "Your daddy was a good man. I know what he'd be telling me about Red Hollis right about now."

The captain only nodded slightly. "It's different now. There's just so many *crazies* out there . . . more every day it seems. I think the world's lost its mind or something. You ever wonder what it's all worth?" He still watched the little girl until her mother appeared at her side and looked over at them and drew the child back.

"Nope. I just cross them off my list and go on to the next. It's better that way."

The captain rubbed his eyes and turned them away from the closed door. "Think her mother will ever tell her?"

The ranger dropped the bottle back in his saddlebags and closed the flap. "What good would come of it? She never knew her father, or what he was. At least you got to know yours. That's worth something to you, ain't it?"

The captain pushed his hat brim up an inch. "So, you're just some kindly old gentleman who comes by now and then?"

"They've still got to eat. I killed him straight up for what *he* done. They weren't no part of it."

"Was he worse than Montana Red Hollis?" The captain turned his eyes to him.

The ranger shrugged. "He was just one more killer. They're all about the same in the end. His luck was *up* the day he killed your daddy. It was *down* the day I caught up to him."

"But still . . . Montana Red Hollis?" He glanced down at the big pistol on the ranger's hip, then back up to his eyes. "I don't like you going after him alone."

"Don't make him bigger than he is," the ranger said. "It's just a manhunt, no more no less."

"It's never *just* a manhunt when you go out there." The captain nodded out into the distance. "This is not a one-man job."

"It'll come down to one man though. It always does." He smiled a little.

But the captain didn't smile. "Montana Red Hollis is one of those fast-gun handlers you hear about lately. He draws and fires from atop his holster. How quick are *you* on the draw?"

"I don't know. I always draw before I get there. It's just one less thing to do." He smiled again. "But I'll work on it, if it makes you feel better."

The captain ignored his smile again. "Don't go in shooting first and asking questions later, all right? It would look good on you if you brought somebody in *alive* for a change."

"I always give them a choice," the ranger said.

"But not when you get to Montana Red," the captain said. "You won't give him any, will you?"

The picture of the dead woman and the Indian boy streaked across the ranger's mind. "What do you think?"

"You better not."

Another silence passed as the young captain glanced away, back at the closed door of the adobe. Then he shook his head and looked back to the ranger. "I don't understand you sometimes."

"Neither do I, sometimes." The ranger let go a breath, stepped over, and raised a boot into the stirrups.

"Well . . . I'll cover for you best I can with the judge," the captain said as the ranger turned his horse and stepped it out of the shade.

"I know it." The ranger raised a gloved hand and adjusted his sombrero down on his head.

"We didn't meet here today," the captain said. "Never met, never talked. I haven't seen you since *February*. But you start keeping some receipts, you hear me?"

"I hear you."

The captain murmured something under his breath and watched the ranger's horse right itself toward the distant swirl of heat and dust, and where above it a buzzard swung low and circled as if in waiting. He smiled a thin smile to himself and shook his head as he saw the ranger stop the horse in the dirt street outside the adobe and raise a small bag toward it in his gloved hand. "You beat all," the captain whispered under his breath.

"Did you think I forget you, little princess?" the ranger said, speaking down to the child in his broken Spanish when she ran out to him and reached up and took the bag.

She replied in Spanish that *no*, of course she had not thought that. Her mother told her that she had seen him like this before and that he had much on his mind regarding his job.

His job . . . He smiled and leaned from his saddle and placed a gloved hand on her cheek. "When I come back through, I expect I'll see a brand-new tooth more shiny and pretty than any I ever saw."

"*Sí*," she said; and stepping back a step, she went on to say how her mother had told her that these teeth she shed as a child would all come back like before, only stronger and better, and the new ones would last her a lifetime. "*Gracias*," she then added, holding the bag of rock candy. In her dark eyes he saw his reflection, small and distant, and he watched his hand draw away from her cheek.

She blinked and visored her eyes with her hand, and his reflection disappeared, gone and away into the breadth and depth of all shadow and light that wrapped itself around him. Behind him at a glance he saw the young captain step up into the stirrups and move his horse out of the black slice of shade and onto the dirt street toward the well. The girl had stepped back farther and made room for the ranger to heel his horse forward.

The ranger raised his faded bandanna up across the bridge of his nose and adjusted it with a gloved hand. At the door of the adobe he saw the child's mother stare at him through caged eyes. He stared back at her across the bandanna until beneath him the dun horse rose high-hoofed and restless, grumbling, stepping side-wise and swishing its damp tail. Then the woman raised her hand slightly and nodded; and he gave the horse reins and moved off.

Red Hollis, he said to himself, catching a flash of the two bodies in the dirt and the flies and the dried black blood; and in his mind, along with the scene came the stench of it, as real as the wind and the heat around him. *Montana Red Hollis* . . . His inner voice spoke the name, yet even in silence the sound of it seemed to echo out across the badlands and beckon back to him, taunting him like the cry of some crazed beast . . . calling him to come and give chase to it, to hunt it down in its lair and there destroy it.

PART 1

———————

Wild Cards

CHAPTER 1

He was a good gambler if nothing else, he thought. He knew when a streak had run its course and was about to change, one way or the other. For the past six weeks his luck had held, running good and strong at the tables and even better with the ladies. But now . . .

Through the open window he kept an eye on the lone rider coming in down there on the far end of the wide rutted street, the big sweat-streaked dun horse jutting its head high to one side in spite of the white froth swinging from its muzzle and its wet mane clinging down its neck. He'd watched the rider appear up out of the desert at a great distance, and he'd sipped on the bottle of whiskey and watched, watched through the shimmer of heat and dust, and through the dirty lace curtains as they licked back and forth in the hot wind.

He'd sipped rye whiskey until the rider drew in deeper from the edge of town, then he'd taken one last long swig, corked the bottle, pitched it on the bed, and began stuffing his belongings into a faded purple carpetbag. His name was Joseph Sharpe, but the players and whores called him "Gentleman Joe." He could outbluff the devil, betting hell against Cincinnati if he had to—but not today. Today it was time to fold and fade.

Gentleman Joe had become a master at the art of leaving a town. He could quit a place at the drop of a hat and disappear like smoke, leaving neither a trace nor a whisper.

He'd killed a whore up in Creed four years back. Her name was Peg-Leg Molly, a name he'd never forget. How could he? She was the only person he'd ever killed, the only person he'd ever *shot* for that matter. He was drunk at the time, and she'd robbed him in his sleep. She'd taken his watch, his stickpin and ring, and was about to cut his throat for good measure. But that's when his luck kicked in.

A fly had lit on his nose, waking him just in time to catch a glimpse of a straight razor near his cheek. Rolling away off the lilac-scented bed and onto the hard wooden floor, he'd gotten both feet beneath him when Peg-Leg Molly came screaming at him like a wildcat. His hand found the little derringer inside his vest and he jerked it out and shot her down—put just one tiny hole right above the yellow plume trim on her bustline.

Damn . . . He'd thought about it ever since, time to time, especially when he saw the glint of a badge.

He always saw the way she'd just backed across the room, sighed and sat down in a chair. *You . . . shot me*— The razor fell from her hand and in a minute she was dead. No struggle. Just a small hole like that and she'd sat down and died. Hardly any blood at all, only a thin red trickle down her bright yellow dress.

Of course he didn't stick around to explain. No sir! No sooner had her eyes glazed over, than he'd left without stopping long enough to even pick all his money up off the floor. He'd managed to snatch up his watch and stickpin and go. And he'd been running ever since.

You'd think that four years of running and hiding would be enough, that maybe it was all forgotten, that no lawman would even remember it anymore, and maybe they didn't. Maybe most of them didn't. But that one down there now—riding in on a sweat-streaked dun with the tied-down .45 stretching nearly to his knee—that one would remember. That one never forgot anything.

Damn! When he latched the single leather strap on the carpetbag, he ran a hand across his wet forehead and stepped back to the window. It was boiling hot in the room facing the street. The cooler rooms were all along the back of the building, out of the sun. But he'd asked for this one just to keep an eye on the town's comings and goings. Now he was glad he had.

He jerked the watch from his vest pocket, checked the time, and put it away. In twenty minutes the stage would roll in from Wakely, then head over to Grafton; but he wasn't about to wait that long.

He held one curtain still and looked down through it, shadowed by the darkness of the room against the sun's glare. Now the rider turned his horse to the hitch rail across the street and just sat there for a second. Peculiar-looking from this angle up here—a riding duster hanging from beneath a wide round sombrero, one side of the duster pulled back and hooked behind his long holster. A glint of sunlight shone off the butt of the big pistol. Two gloved hands stuck out from beneath the sombrero brim, holding the reins.

He saw the gray sombrero turn, taking in the street; and although the sombrero made no attempt to tilt up toward him, he stepped back from the window just the same. Still watching, he saw the rider swing down from the saddle and stand for a moment, watching the boys from the Flying Cross shove each other back and forth in the street out front of the saloon. They were drunk now and going at it. Playing rough, getting rougher.

So that's him . . . The thought crossed Gentleman Joe's mind, that if he were a braver man, a gunman, he could get one good clear shot off from up here and end it. He could do that. Sure he could. It had only taken one tiny bullet hole to kill Peg-Leg Molly.

He slipped the nickel-plated .38 from his pocket and eased it past the curtain into the sunlight. A sudden flash of sunlight streaked off the shiny pistol barrel. It startled him. He jerked the gun back inside the window and saw his hand tremble. Who was he kidding? He couldn't do it. He didn't have it in him.

He was no gunman. He was a gambler, nothing more. What if he missed? What if he only wounded him? *No* . . . He shook his head. *Bad odds.* He dare not think it. Not about this man. Better to run, get out now through the back, grab a horse and go. Yet he only stood there watching like a man charmed by a snake.

On the street, the ranger stretched, pressing a hand to the small of his back. He watched the Flying Cross boys from twenty yards away; and when he'd spun his reins around the hitch rail, he stood beside the big dun, watching them even closer as he took off his gloves and stuck them in his duster pocket. The Flying Cross boys were busy, cussing, spitting, threatening anybody foolish enough to walk their side of the street. They hadn't noticed the lone rider come in, didn't see him untie the leather straps and let down the rolled-up canvas atop his saddlebags.

One of them threw a whiskey bottle high in the air, let out a long squall and exploded it with a blast from his pistol. "Damn'er Hurley, let's shoot sumpin! I ain't shot nothing all day!" He let out another whoop and fired two rounds straight up. Townsfolk scurried. The ranger caught a glimpse of two women hiking up their dresses and slipping into a doorway. A parasol dropped to the boardwalk and rolled off into the dirt. Faces peeked through windows, then dropped down. Signs on doors turned from open to closed with the flick of a nervous wrist.

"The hell ya'll looking at? Hunh?" From amid the Flying Cross boys, the tall gunman, Donald Kurtz, stepped into the middle of the street, waving his pistol. He spread his feet, pulled off a shot, and blew a hole through the barbershop window. Then he hooted and laughed and looked all around, spinning his pistol back into his holster, his big teeth shining beneath a mustache streaked with beer foam.

But then his laughter fell away and his grin faded as he caught sight of the tall gray sombrero and the riding duster stooping down in the middle of the street. He saw the man was doing something there, setting something up? Some kind of equipment? What?

"Look at this, boys," he said in a low tone, spreading a curious smile. The stranger in the duster did not look up from whatever he was doing. He kneeled there—*a Mexican, maybe? Now wouldn't that be some fun*—his face hidden beneath the gray sombrero, out there busy, on one knee, clicking something together, snapping something in place. What was all this?

The cowboys stood silent for a moment, just watching. Then Kurtz called out: *"Como estes—"* *Aw hell with it.* "Hey, you there, greaser! The hell ya think you're doing? Hunh?" He took a step closer when he got no response. "You're in a bad spot there, in case you don't know it." He glanced at the others, grinned, then added, "You're squatting right where I'm getting ready to empty this pistol. *Comprende*?" He patted his hand on his pistol butt and had started to lift it from the holster when the duster stood straight up and stepped to the side. *Huh-uh. No Mexican standing there . . .*

Kurtz's hand tensed but stopped; his head cocked to one side. In the middle of the dusty street stood a tripod, four feet high.

"The hell's that?" Kurtz took a step back, opening and closing his hand, his palm rubbing the butt edge of his pistol. One of the others laughed behind him.

"I know. He's a photo-grafter," said one.

"Gonna take a likeness of us for pos-terity," said another.

Kurtz grinned again, wiped a hand across his mustache, and said in a mock tone, "Naw, that's too short for a bunch of long-legged ole boys like us. Maybe he wants a likeness of our boots. Is that it? You taking a likeness of our boots?"

"Maybe he takes tin plates of little-bitsy fellers," one said with a laugh.

Then Kurtz called out to the stranger in the duster, "Is that it? You looking for some little-bitsy fellers? Gonna take their . . ." His voice trailed down, and he stood staring, seeing the tip of a long holster tied down right about knee level. A ranger's badge shone on the stranger's chest. A breeze raised the brim of the sombrero an inch and held it there.

The ranger had just pulled off his duster. He hung it on the tripod, took a good solid breath and started walking toward them, calm and steady, drawing the long pistol and letting it hang in his right hand. "No," he said; and he kept walking closer as he slipped his left hand inside his shirt and took out a wrinkled piece of paper.

"I'm here to take in four men." He held the paper up, tapped it against the breeze, and without glancing at it, he said, "Hurley Yates, Donald Kurtz, Bennie Burdett, and Red Hollis . . . dead or alive." Just like that, *dead or alive*, the *alive* part sounding more like an afterthought, something he'd shrugged off more or less and hadn't really planned on. "Any of you cowboys are free to leave. But you better do it now before we commence."

He waved the paper slightly, still coming closer, a determined bearing about him. He was no taller than average, but swinging a lot of iron in that right hand, that right shoulder stooped a bit low. "Are you Donald Kurtz?" the ranger called out.

"Who's asking?" Kurtz felt a nerve twitch in his jaw. Now he *knew* who was walking toward him. The ranger kept coming. "Whooa now! Stop right there!" Kurtz's hand tightened on his pistol butt; his eyes locked on the big pistol swinging back and forth in the ranger's hand, the tip of the barrel brushing past his knee, coming closer.

The ranger didn't so much as slow down. He kept coming, steady, unwavering. "I mean it!" Kurtz shouted, loud. But he took a step back. Behind him, four of the Flying Cross boys spread out. One man slipped around the corner of the saloon and ran, his boots pounding through the alley toward the livery barn.

"Are you Donald Kurtz?" Now the ranger's eyes bored into his as he came closer, ten yards, then nine, eight, seven.

"That's right, I am." He took another step back, and stopped. Nobody in their right mind came this close to a man. It had Kurtz shaken. "And now I know who *you* are, Ranger! But you ain't taking me *no damn place*, not alive—"

"Fair enough." The next thing Kurtz saw clearly was the big pistol explode on the upswing from ten feet away, then he caught a glimpse of his left boot spinning through the air above him as he hit the ground. The very *last* thing he saw was the sky tilting out of shape, churning red, and the ranger walking past him, sweeping his free hand down, picking up Kurtz's pistol as he went. And Kurtz's world went black and silent there in the dirt, even as the sound of gunfire exploded above him.

Like four solid steady beats of a large drum, the big pistol bucked in the ranger's hand, from one man to the next, as he walked forward in the dirt street. He felt a bullet burn through the sleeve of his shirt across his forearm, but he didn't flinch. By the time the last man started to fall, he'd walked so close to him, he reached out, shoved the man's gun to the side and grabbed it from his hand just as it went off. Fire streaked past his side, then he pitched the smoking gun away.

The last man dropped straight down beneath a drifting gray haze, rocking back and forth on his knees, holding his stomach. "Oh Lord," he gasped. He looked up at the big pistol pointing down at him. "You're him, ain't ya? Kurtz is right. You're that ranger, ain't ya?"

"Kurtz is dead. Where's Bennie Burdett, Hurley Yates, and Red Hollis?" He cocked the big pistol and held it close to the wounded man's face. "You just as well tell me before ya die. Might make it better for you once you get where you're going."

"Yates lit out. Bennie's . . . at the . . . Flying Cross. Don't know . . . where Montana Red's at." He rocked forward, then caught himself. "I hope you find him though." He struggled for another breath. "So's . . . he can kill ya. Same as you kilt us."

"We'll see." The ranger pulled bullets from his belt and replaced the five he'd spent. He stepped back, looking around at his handiwork in the dirt street, a master craftsman inspecting a finished project. He swallowed the dryness in his throat. Turning his head slightly, he slid a gaze up through the hovering drift of powder smoke, to the window where one curtain had been hanging straight and still as he rode into town, the window from which the flash of metal had come—the flash he'd seen dance across the toe of his boot as he'd stood there beside his horse.

One curtain had hung still and straight while the other fluttered in the breeze. How blind would you have to be to miss that? Now both curtains licked back and forth. Whoever'd been there was gone.

He shoved the big pistol down in his holster and looked out past the edge of town at the wake of dust left by Hurley Yates. And that *was* Hurley Yates, the one who'd ducked out around the corner before the shooting started. No sign of Red Hollis though. He might have to thin out half the outlaws in the territory before he got to that one. . . .

He turned and walked back to his horse, slid the big .58 caliber Swedish rifle from its boot, and walked back to the middle of the street, running a hand along the barrel. Townsfolk ventured out now, walking carefully, cautiously there among the dead. One of the two women slipped from the doorway and hurried out to the parasol in the dirt. She snatched it up, shook it, and hurried away with it under her arm. The wounded man still rocked back and forth in the street, but now his words were slurred when he spoke.

"Sheep-licking bunch of trash," he said. A red string of saliva swung from his lips.

When the ranger had put his duster back on, he snapped the rifle in place on the short tripod, kneeled down behind it, adjusted the sights, and stared off at the stream of dust in the distance. This was not the way he wanted it, not a back-shot. But he'd figured coming in—throwing down on this many at once—somebody was bound to make a run for it. So he'd prepared himself for it.

He took a short porcupine quill from his duster, took off his sombrero, pinned up the front of the brim and put it back on. He relaxed for a second and glanced up at the window with the billowing lace curtains. Who in the world would stick a shiny gun out in the sunlight that way? Nobody he could think of. Nobody who knew what they were doing. Not Red Hollis . . .

Then he glanced around the street at the anxious faces watching him, and at the dying man, the man not rocking now, but down on his side, scrapping his boots back and forth in the dirt, struggling for purchase on the earth, finding none. Dark blood puddled about him. His boots were soaked with urine. He babbled now, low and mindless, cursing the dark shadows moving about him in the street. His hand scratched in the dirt toward the pistol three feet away.

"When ya gonna shoot him?" said a voice beside the ranger.

The ranger turned and looked into the wide-eyed face of an old townsman leaning near him, squatting with his palms on his knees.

"When I'm good and ready," the ranger said.

The townsman nodded toward the rise of dust far away, then back to the ranger. "Well, it's for sure he ain't getting no closer. That's a hard shot, even for a big rifle like that—the dust and all."

The ranger glared at him and the man backed off a step, then leaned back down on his palms. "Reckon you'd just be wasting all them big bullets, hunh? No sense in that."

The ranger sat studying the stream of dust until a dark speck rose up out of the narrow tip of it, ascending up above the thick brown cloud, climbing the rising land toward the foothills at the end of vision.

Then he leaned forward into the butt of the rifle, aimed it, locked it on the tiny dark speck, followed it as it climbed higher, then eased his finger back against the trigger until the slam of the butt stock jarred him to his bones. The sound of the shot cracked along the front of the buildings, jarring them as well, and echoed off through the swirling heat.

For a second even the wind seemed to stop and watch, holding its breath as the tiny dark speck climbed higher. Another second passed, then the townsman clucked his tongue in his cheek. "Too bad . . ." But in another second he squinted and turned his head to one side, not believing his eyes as the tiny speck seemed to split in half, and the top half sailed off to the side and fell as the bottom half climbed higher into the foothills. "Well, help, my time . . ."

The ranger leaned forward, pulled down the sights on the rifle, and stood up dusting his knees. He stared off at the distance as he untied his faded bandanna from around his neck and pressed it against the graze across his forearm. "I'll pay you a dollar to take out a wagon and haul him back here," he said without looking at the old man beside him.

"What if he ain't dead?"

The ranger just stared at him.

"All right. I'll do it then." He nodded toward the bodies in the street. The last man lay dead now, face-down in the dirt, dust settling on his back, his fingers only inches from the butt of the pistol. "How much to haul them out of here and tidy the street up some?"

The ranger unsnapped the rifle, picked up the tripod, and kicked it shut. "It ain't my street," he said, and he walked away to the hotel with his rifle and tripod over his shoulder.

When he stopped at the desk, the clerk came running in behind him from the street and swung around the counter, smoothing back his hair. "Whooie! Now that was something, I'm telling ya. I never seen such carrying on in my life."

The ranger swung the rifle and tripod down onto the counter, reached down and turned the register around. He ran a finger down the list of names. "What's the number of the room up there on the right end, facing the street?"

"Now see here!" The clerk tried to turn the register back around but the ranger grabbed his hand, picked it up, moved it aside and laid it down on the counter.

"The number. If you please."

"It's number seven," the clerk said; and although his hand had not been squeezed hard, he looked down at it and rubbed it as the ranger ran his finger down the register page.

Mr. J. Jones, huh? Figures. He turned and walked to the stairs, leaving the big rifle on the counter. "Watch that for me," he said. And he walked up the creaking stairs without bothering to quieten his steps. He knew the room would be empty, knew it had been since about the time the shooting started. Whoever Mr. J. Jones was, he was at that very moment putting distance between himself and this place.

Inside the room he looked at the bottle of whiskey on the bed, saw where Mr. J. Jones in his haste had taken one last drink and pitched it there, leaving a wet stain where whiskey had run down the side of the bottle. He picked it up, pulled the cork, and sniffed the bottle as he sloshed it around. He threw back a drink. When he'd corked it and pitched it back on the bed, he looked around the room, taking his time.

All that remained of J. Jones were two aces and a king on an oak dresser; and he picked them up and saw where the corner of each card bore the slightest thumbnail scar. *Gambler . . . that figures too. The shiny gun.*

He walked over and looked out the window toward the west, the way he'd rode in, the way J. Jones had watched from this very spot through the lace curtains. From here, Jones could have picked him off *too* easy with a rifle—not much harder with a pistol, if he was any shot at all and had no qualms about it.

Whoever Jones was, he was no killer, that was plain enough. That being the case, he wondered what reason the man could've had for running. Everybody in the territory knew that he had no truck with gamblers, even those who marked their cards.

He took the wrinkled paper and a pencil stub from inside his shirt, unfolded the paper, and ran his eyes down the list of names. At the top of the list was the name Montana Red Hollis, beneath it Hurley Yates, then Donald Kurtz, then Bennie Burdett. Beside each of the top four names he'd written the words "Killers, rapists." Now he circled Red Hollis and Bennie Burdett's name, and marked the other two off the list.

The list ran long with other names, some marked out, others now faded and barely legible—the ones down there near the bottom. On the very bottom of the list, he could no longer make out anything at all. Some of those names he knew by memory, others he just considered pardoned. Once the bottom of the paper turned worn and ragged and crumbled apart in his hand, unless that person was a hardened killer, he figured they'd served their time . . . hiding out in the badlands.

It was dark when the gambler settled down and stopped looking back over his shoulder. The horse was winded and blowing froth as he led it up into the shelter of rock. He himself was breathing hard; and he dropped down on a flat rock with the reins hanging from his hand. Something dark and shiny slipped from under the rock and away into the darkness.

His hands trembled. He wiped dust from his face on his coat sleeve and thought of the bottle of whiskey he'd left back in the hotel room—needing it now. He thought of the breakfast he'd had that morning, eggs, pork, hot coffee, rich and strong and poured full of fresh cream. *Damn.* He hadn't eaten since. Nothing else had touched his empty stomach all day but the bite and burn of rye whiskey. Now he missed it, the food, the whiskey, even the bed, which wasn't the best he'd ever slept in, smelling as it did of old urine and strong lye soap.

Maybe he should've stayed, laid low and taken his chances. There was no reason to think the ranger was looking for him, not after what he had seen going on in the street. Then again, his name was somewhere on the ranger's list. Who could say; maybe he'd come to clear that list of old business. If that was the case, what chance would he have had against such a man. He saw part of what happened to the Flying Cross boys before he hightailed it out of there. He could've been next.

Montana Red Hollis. Wasn't that one of the names he'd heard, lurking up there behind the curtains, afraid to drop the hammer on the man. *Hollis, Hurley, Kurtz, Burdett.* If only they'd killed the ranger, that would've solved his problem. But now Kurtz and Hurley were dead. He'd seen Kurtz fall without getting off a shot, and he'd watched from a mile away and seen Hurley Yates spill from his horse like a bag of bones. Was there any way in the world to get away from this ranger?

And where in God's name did he find a rifle that could make a shot like that? It almost didn't seem fair, riding off, thinking you'd made a getaway, then all of a sudden your heart's blown out of your chest. Didn't seem right somehow.

He'd taken a chance and rode over to Hurley's body lying there in the sand, lifted his shooting gear, a canteen of water, and a long boot knife. Never in his life had he seen such a hole in a human being. He tried not to look at it, but he couldn't help himself. Right there where the man's heart should've been was a hole you could've looked straight through and saw the ground, had it not been for the blood and gore. . . .

He shivered, stood up and pulled Hurley's pistol from the holster draped across the saddlehorn. He turned the .44 in his hand, a stripped-down Colt with a shaved front sight. At least he now had something better than the short-barreled .38, if he needed it. At least, if it came down to it now, he could put up a fight if the ranger got him cornered.

Who was he kidding? If it ever came down to it— him and the ranger faced off in a life-or-death battle— he could just as well pitch this pistol in the dirt for all the good it would do him.

How do you stop a man like him? It was as if he wasn't even human, walking in like that, that close! Killing Kurtz before he even got a shot off. But it would have been different if the ranger ever caught up to Montana Red Hollis. Hollis was not from the same cut as Kurtz and Hurley. It would've gone different if Hollis had been there today. You bet. In spite of what he'd seen today, if it came down to the ranger and Montana Red, as a gambler he'd have to go with Red. That's what the smart money would do.

He might not be a gunman but he sure knew how to figure odds, and Red Hollis . . . well, nobody would take the ranger against Red Hollis, no matter how long the odds.

He spun the dead man's pistol on his finger, almost dropped it, but caught it, and looked at it again. There, alone in the darkness, he felt embarrassed for a second, as if someone might have seen him fumble the big .44.

He glanced around and slipped the pistol back into

the holster. Who the hell was he to even speak the names of men such as these. He'd been spooked by the flash of sunlight off the barrel of his pistol. What would he have done had he pulled the trigger? He pictured the pistol going off in his hand, missing the ranger by a mile and kicking up dust in the street, the ranger turning, looking up at him with hollow eyes, the big pistol raising. *Damn* . . .

He shivered and shook his head, clearing it; and he sat on the flat rock and folded his arms against the chill of the desert night until he fell into a restless sleep, missing the hot room on Front Street and the smell of the musty bed.

CHAPTER 2

The bar was not lined with drinkers as it should've been on a night such as this. All the tables stood empty save for two: the one where a young whore called "Little Honey" dealt herself hand after hand of poker, then played against the five blind cards she had laid out across from her; and the table back in the shadows against the far wall, where the ranger stared into a half-empty bottle of rye.

The bartender chewed his warm cigar and swatted flies with a bar rag. You'd think after all that had happened today in the street the place would be packed, alive and kicking, and buzzing with voices. But few ventured in because of *him*—that blasted old ranger—being there. Those who did stop in were quiet and subdued. They only drank one or two, and they only mentioned the weather as they shot a cautious glance toward the rear table. Then they moved on.

Damn ranger. The bartender slung the rag over his shoulder and crossed his arms on the empty bar. By now the word had gotten out to the Flying Cross. Any second the whole crew might step through the door. If they did, he'd already made up his mind to crawl along the floor behind the bar and skin out through the back window.

When Little Honey raised her face and rubbed the back of her neck, she saw the ranger staring at her and gave him her most seductive smile. She could not read the expression in his eyes when he nodded, beckoning her over to him, but she knew that behind every nod there was another dollar to be made, for any woman who knew her business. She knew hers.

She stood up just slow enough to let the slit in her dress fall away from her bare leg, then she walked over slowly—no hurry here—letting him get a good look at her wares, wanting to look just a little bored, a professional look. She watched his eyes for any sign of what he was looking for, any clue as to how she should play it. Yet his eyes said nothing to her.

He raised a boot beneath the table and pushed out a chair for her. "Oh . . . a gentleman." She touched a hand to her breast, raised her brows slightly, and sat down. This might not turn out to be the easiest dollar she ever squeezed off, but on a slow night what could she do. . . .

"Buy you a drink?" He leveled his gaze into her eyes, and before she could answer, slid the empty glass across the table with his fingertips, filled it, and kept his hand around the bottle when he sat it down.

She shrugged and said, "Sure," and touched the tip of her tongue to her lips. "Will you be joining me?" She raised the glass slightly.

He raised the bottle, tapped it against her glass, and waited until she took a sip. Then he threw back a drink and watched her eyes for a second. "I'm looking for a man," he said. His expression was the same, indiscernible, almost grim.

This one could take a while, she thought. She relaxed, shifted sideways, crossed her legs, and draped an arm over the chair back. "Well, then, aren't we *all* . . ." She waited a second, then a quiet laugh spilled from her lips. But he didn't so much as raise a brow.

"He's a gambler. Left town today, but he's been playing here. Drinks single-cut rye. Been winning pretty good, I figure." He watched her eyes to see if she'd lie—if so, how much. "He was staying over at the hotel. Corner room facing the street. Goes by the name *Jones*. Know him?"

She studied his eyes, deep-set and gun metal gray, piercing, too sharp and deep to look into for long, she thought. Eyes that could cut flesh and chill bone. "I know him," she said, and she glanced away, then back to him, only this time not directly. This man was at work, nothing more. There was no room for play here. "Of course, if I had a dollar for every *Jones,* or *Smith* I've known in the past year, I wouldn't be charging a dollar for *telling* somebody about them." There it was; she was working here too. Let him know it right off.

She threw back the drink and slid the empty glass to the middle of the table. She stared at him, until this time he glanced away, long enough to slip a dollar from his vest pocket and lay it beside the empty glass. "Yeah, him," she said, all business now, sliding the dollar over to herself as she poured herself another drink. "The young guy, twenty-four, twenty-five— stud player. I know him. Why? What's he done?"

"For a dollar, you tell me."

Again, the cutting eyes. She felt them on her even as she glanced down at her drink. She ran a finger around the edge of the glass. "Nothing that *I* know of." She shrugged. "Not a bad guy, really. Plays straight, far as I can tell. I think he had some trouble in Colorado. He mentioned it one night, drunk. He might've done something there." She ventured a gaze into those eyes. "Is that why you're looking for him?" She couldn't hold the gaze, but focused instead on the scar that curled across his cheek toward the corner of his mouth. That one had hurt, had gone to the bone. An old scar, she figured.

"Maybe," he said, thinking back, running his mind down the list of names inside his shirt, somewhere down low, where the writing was faded from sweat, heat, and time. Somewhere there . . . a name.

"But, you're a ranger . . . that was in Colorado. You wouldn't be looking for *him* would you?"

"Where's he from back there?" He nodded east toward the bar, but she knew what he meant.

"He mentioned Ohio. But who knows? Whatever he did in Colorado, I don't think he'll be doing it again . . . if that means anything to you."

He shook his head back and forth slowly. "What kind of horse does he ride? What kind of gun does he carry?"

She shook her head. "No horse. He came in by stage. Probably left the same way. Carries a shiny little pistol. I can't see him using it though." She smiled, rolled her eyes slightly. "He's kind of a dandy."

"Yeah?"

"Not a lot . . . but kinda. I don't think he likes it out here much."

Kind of a dandy . . . He thought about it a second, placing faces to traits. Nothing came. "How is he with women?"

She fixed a gaze on him now, cutting eyes or no. "*Details* cost another dollar."

He almost smiled. Almost, but not quite. "That ain't

what I mean. I mean how does he treat them? Smack them around? Squeeze them for money . . . what?"

"No. He's on the square—was with me anyway. I might even miss him, some." She looped a ringlet of hair around her finger, smiled and let it go. "He spent it when he had it . . . and he usually had it. Yep, I'll miss him."

Big spender . . . kind of a dandy . . . Ohio. He stared at her, not seeing her, but shuffling faces, names, places in his mind.

Colorado. Creed? The bank robbery? No, not this guy, not *J. Jones.* What about shooting the whore, Molly Frome? He could see that, maybe. Peg-Leg Molly Frome. Not Peg-Leg because she was missing a limb, but Peg-Leg owing to the way she kept one leg flat and straight down the bed, not giving it all up, not to most of them anyway. Who was it that shot her? Joe something. Joe Sharpe? He'd go with that for the time being. . . .

"Do me a favor?" He reached over and filled her glass.

She folded her arms. "Watch your language." But then she unfolded them when he reached in his vest and brought up another dollar.

"If he shows up here again, tell him not to try something stupid on me, or I'll have to kill him. Tell him I ain't looking for him for what happened with Peg-Leg Molly, if that's what he's worried about." He laid the dollar on the table, watched her slide it away, and wondered what she would think if he asked her for a receipt. "What do they call you?" He leaned back a little and she thought she saw his eyes soften . . . not much, but some.

"Little Honey." There was the slightest suggestion in

her eyes now. Not all business, he thought. But then, how could you tell with a good whore.

"Little Honey, huh? Figures," he said. He reached beneath the table, slipped the big holster off his lap and back down along his leg, whipped the rawhide string around his leg and tied the holster down.

She cocked her head. "What do you mean, it *figures*. What's that supposed—"

"I mean, your voice," he said, standing, adjusting his hat. "Little Honey suits you. You've got a real pretty voice, smooth like honey."

"Oh . . . well, thanks." She looked surprised; he'd almost smiled again, there for a second. "You're leaving, so soon? Aren't you concerned that the Flying Cross boys could be out there waiting for you?"

"They ain't coming," he said. Then he turned and walked across the floor, out through the bat wing doors, leaving a good six or seven shots in the bottle of rye.

"Whooie!" She smiled and fanned herself with her hand on the way back to her table, carrying the bottle of rye. "I felt like I was outstaring a rattlesnake. Is he as bad as they all say he is?"

The bartender grunted, then took the cigar from his mouth and said, "He's worse! If you've got any sense you'll stay wide and away from that crazy old ranger."

"Oh . . . I don't know. I like 'em crazy now and then, just to break the monotony."

"*Ha*. You like 'em any way you get 'em, long as they ain't polecat ripe and molded over—"

"Shut up, Earl. The hell do you know about anything?" She cut him off, giggled, sat down, and crossed her legs toward him, letting the slit in her dress fall open above her knee, giving him a look, feel-

ing warm and wiggly up there under the dress. Warm
from the whiskey, restless and wiggly from the slow
turn of the night. "So, Earl, tell the truth, do you *miss*
it a lot . . . now that Tessy's gone back to Omaha?" She
giggled again, ran a finger along her bare leg. "I know
I sure do."

In minutes they began straggling in, one, two, and
three at a time, until soon the place was blanketed by
a heavy drift of smoke and the rise and roar of idle
chatter. "I never seen anything like it!" a voice said.
"What all did he have to say, Earl?"

The bartender had thrown the rag on the floor behind the bar and kicked it away. He grinned to himself
in the mirror. It was the ranger being there that had
kept them away. Now it was the ranger's *having* been
there that would pack them in. The bartender hiked up
his shirtsleeves above his garters. "Boys, he's something all right. But wait till them Flying Cross
cowhands get a hold of him." *Damned old ranger . . .*

He made his camp a mile out in the darkness and picketed his horse to graze in a sparse stretch of gramma
grass. He'd built his low fire a foot deep in the ground
and worked a mound of sand up around it. From a distance his camp would go unnoticed; up close, he had
the hearing of a predator, tuned to every rustle of dry
brush or bat of wing in the night, there on the desert
floor. Above him stars spilled like diamonds and silver
dust in a wide trail curved to the dome of the universe.
A night creature swung down, then away across the
black velvet sky.

He sipped a steaming cup of Duttwieler's tea, listening to the faint sound of hooves that had stopped
just now, no more than ten yards out. A silence lin-

gered before giving way to the soft drop of footsteps on the cooling sand. But no concern showed in his eyes as he kept attending to the big pistol broken apart on the blanket before him. Inside the loose button on his shirt lay a short-barreled .44.

"Hello the camp," said a voice just beyond the grainy circle of firelight. Still he did not look up from holding the freed cylinder between both hands, rolling it up and down, looking through it into the low flames. Firelight spiraled back on polished hand turned steel.

"Tea's hot," he said; and he laid the cylinder down, raised his left knee, and rested his forearm across it. He picked up a stick with his right hand and stirred the embers, his hand close to the front of his shirt. "Come get ya some, Tackett."

"How'd you know it was me, and not the Flying Cross boys?" The voice asked from the darkness, and when the ranger didn't answer, the voice added, "You left a hell of a mess back there, you know." Now the voice came from beneath a wide hat brim as the man stepped closer, leading a sorrel gelding. He stopped across the fire.

"Evening, Sheriff," the ranger said, barely glancing up from the fire.

The man grunted, touching a finger to his hat brim. "Evening hell. What was you trying to do to me? Make me look bad?" He squatted down, touched his fingertips to the tin pot, then drew them back and rubbed them together. "Your tea don't smell no worse than it ever did." He stood and raised the flap on his saddlebags, took out a tin cup, and wiped his finger around in it. "You had no call to make a move in my town without me."

"Shoulda been there," the ranger said, just flatly, no

implication on his part. "I looked around for you first. Didn't see ya nowheres. How's the Widow Morris?"

Sheriff Tackett squatted again and reached for the pot, then hesitated and raised his eyes to the ranger. "How'd you hear about me and the widow woman?"

The ranger laid the stick down and picked up the barrel of the big pistol. He looked through it, blew through it, and laid it back down on the blanket. Tackett's eyes followed his hand. "Heard it on the wind I reckon," the ranger said. "Ain't none of my business, Sheriff. Just keeping up on the gossip."

"Well, what of it?" Tackett poured tea and pushed up his hat brim. "She's a lonely widow woman. I never took much to playing with whores. She does my shirts for me, you know. I've got four now." He raised four fingers, then smiled. "Every one of em's crisp as a new dollar. Hell, I might marry her, if she'll have me. You oughta get a woman yourself, let her ease your mind some, instead of you coming in all stoked up and killing off the day drinkers." He cocked his head, squinting. "What'd them boys do anyhow?"

"They were running with the wrong crowd. Kurtz, Yates, Burdett, and Red Hollis."

"So that's who you was after. I oughta known Montana Red's name would come up."

"Yep. It's come up a lot lately. The four of 'em raped and killed a white girl and an Indian kid down in my territory. The Indian kid was the son of a chief."

"Hold it. You're saying—?"

"That's right, the chief's *son*. The white girl was a school teacher come down from Chicago, teaching the Indian kid to read." He stopped and shook his head. "Red Hollis will do anything, you know that. I figure the others were just afraid to stop him . . . so they went along with it."

"My God." Tackett let out a breath. A silence passed. "Yates and Kurtz ain't no good either though. Red never made them do nothing they didn't *want* to do."

"Well . . . they won't do it again," the ranger said.

"Still, you coulda come to me before you killed 'em. It woulda looked better. You got no jurisdiction around here."

"You was busy getting your shirts done." The ranger smiled a little, sipped off his tea, and set the cup down. "I thought I'd catch up to Red Hollis here if I got in quick enough. He don't stick anywhere very long. I shoulda killed him a long time ago."

"Montana Red *was* here, gambling and drinking with the cowhands. But he left five days back. He lays down higher up, up around them ridge towns. Thought you'd know that?"

"I do, but there's no telling where he's at up there. Figured I'd catch him down here. Hoped it anyway."

"Dang it. What do you suppose got into them Flying Cross boys? It ain't like them, backing the likes of that bunch. Donahue's gonna throw a fit. You killed off a third of his line crew."

"They were whiskey drunk. Just feeling rowdy, I reckon. They might not'a known what Hollis and his friends did. They was just sticking up for 'em because they was drinking together. You know how cowboys are—men who drink together, die together, I reckon, the way they saw it. A man like Hollis has a way of making everybody around as bad as he is. Burdett's holed up out at the Flying Cross. I'll get him come morning."

"You can't go out there. Not as riled up as Donahue's gonna be. I'm surprised he and his boys ain't rode in already. You just don't know him like I do."

"Yeah? Well—" The ranger blew a fleck of dust off the pistol butt. "Your Mr. Donahue'll just have to blow wind, far as I care. I tried to let his boys go, but they all chose to throw down on me."

"He ain't *my* Mr. Donahue," Tackett said. "I'm my own man here."

The ranger lifted his eyes from the pistol for a second. "Oh? Wanta ride out there with me? Maybe you can explain it all to him . . . keep me from having to kill him."

"Naw, sir, hell no. You can't explain nothing to Donahue, and I ain't having him down my back for the next year over this."

"Your own man, huh?" The ranger looked back at the pistol and turned it in his hand.

"I *am* my own man, but Donahue's powerful enough to make or break a lawman in these parts. I ain't a danged fool."

"Since when is one man more powerful than the law?" The ranger narrowed his gaze.

Tackett wiped a hand back and forth across his forehead. "Well, Donahue's been good to me, far as that goes. Now I'd of helped ya today, if I knew what Kurtz and them done. But you can't expect me to go out there tomorrow and take a chance on ruining what I got going here, can ya?"

"I suppose not." The ranger shrugged. "It don't matter. Red Hollis has been let go too long. If I'd killed him sooner, none of this other would've happened. I'll just drop by the Flying Cross, take down Bennie Burdett, and ride on. If I don't keep after Red Hollis, he'll soon kill again. He's acquired a strong thirst for it."

"I don't begrudge you hunting Red Hollis. You orta get yourself up a posse first. Nobody'd blame ya."

"Hear what happened to that five-man posse tracked him over on Wind River?"

"I heard. But you still orta get one up. Things ain't like they once was. You need somebody to cover ya—"

"You offering?"

"No sir. Not me. I got no stomach for manhunting anymore." He shook his head. "Time was when I would've . . . but I *can't* do it."

"Know anybody who *can?*"

Tackett felt his face redden; he rubbed it. "No, but surely—"

"So there's your posse," said the ranger. Another silence passed as he reached out, picked up the bandanna from the blanket, and started wiping the barrel of the big pistol. He snapped it in place and picked up the cylinder. "Hollis still wears them crossèd pistols on his belly, I reckon?"

"Yeah. Best I know, he does—slicker than lightning with 'em too." Tackett sucked a tooth and nodded. "You know, you ain't the only lawman in the world. Somebody'll take him down sooner or later, if you don't."

"Meanwhile, he keeps on killing. I saw the bodies. Looked more like an animal had a hold of them." His throat tightened; he swallowed. "I haven't been able to see much else since. Won't till I set it right. I believe he might tasted their blood."

"Aw now," Tackett said. "How you know that?"

When the ranger only stared at him, Tackett added, "Still and all, it don't have to be you that stops him. There's others, *younger* ones than you. Let them go after him. You orta had enough of this kinda killing by now." The sheriff looked down and rubbed his palms on his knees. After a second he said, "Dang it. I'm *asking* you to stay away from the Flying Cross."

The ranger ignored him and said, "She washes your shirts, huh?"

He nodded, still gazing down. "Yep. And I ain't a damn bit ashamed of it. It's took some getting used to though."

"I bet it has. She cook for ya?" He connected the cylinder and spun it.

"Some. I'm still partial to my own cooking. Always said a man orta stay shy of a *widow's* cooking . . . depending on what killed her husband, of course."

"That's wise thinking." The ranger nodded, held the pistol close to his ear, and clicked it, hearing the smoothness of it, hearing the soft perfect turn and drop with each touch of his thumb.

"You owe ole Greely a dollar for toting Hurley Yates's body in. I said I'd get it for him, if you will. Figured you didn't want him prowling around out here looking for ya in the dark, stepping on a rattlesnake or something."

"Sure, thanks." He reached in his vest and pulled one up and flipped it across the low glow of fire. "I'm supposed to ask for a receipt."

"Really? Umm-um. What'll they come up with next?" He squinted, put the coin away, and shook his head. "Oh. Greely said for me to tell ya, '*Good shooting.*' Said you stopped his clock with one shot. Somebody already took Hurley's shooting gear and made off with it before Greely got there. Can you believe that? Damned *comadreja* probably. Can't leave nothing laying loose on account of 'em anymore." Tackett sipped off his tea and slung his cup toward the ground. "I'm gone a day, come back, got a string of dead cowboys, a horse theft . . ." He shook his head and wiped his finger around in his cup. "It's worse out here every year."

"Don't see how you manage." The ranger looked up, almost smiling again, dim firelight highlighting the scar across his cheek. *Hurley's shooting gear . . . a horse stolen . . . J. Jones?* He picked up the bullets one at a time, and loaded the big pistol.

Tackett chuckled, then said, "What the heck, don't I deserve a good job after Clinton County, Hayes . . . Rileyville? Dang right I do, and you know it. I put my time in. You seen what all I done back then. I ain't fairhaired."

"I know it."

"I *know* you know it. So what if I ride a little shy of a man like Donahue? Can you blame me?"

"No, I don't blame you. Do what feels right to you, I reckon."

Tackett sucked a tooth. "I still wish you wouldn't ride over there."

"I'm going," the ranger said. "And that's all to be said about it."

"All right then, be hardheaded. I ain't about to mention it again." A silence passed, then he chuckled again. "Remember that night you and Edsen and me threw down on them cattle hawkers outside of—"

"What do you know about Little Honey?" The ranger cut him off. *So that's how it is now.* Tackett stared at him. *No good ole days here. Not with him. It was always a day's work. Still was.* "She's a good girl, for a whore," Tackett said. "Why, what'd she do?"

"You tell me?" He reached and poured the last of the tea into his cup.

Tackett grinned. *Fishing, huh? Squeezing informa-*

tion, as if he wouldn't see it. As if he'd been so long out of touch, he wouldn't know when another lawman was grilling him down. Some nerve . . . "I just told ya. She's all right as whores go. Been here a year, ain't cut nobody, ain't clapped nobody out, or cheated 'em much as far as I know. Deals no dirt. Why?"

"Can ya believe what she tells ya?"

"Probably—if the money's right. I told ya I don't play around with whores much. You—*of all people*—know what they'll do to your head, if ya let 'em."

"I reckon." He sipped the tea. "Ever heard of a gambler named Joe Sharpe? Goes by *Gentleman* Joe. The one they say kilt Peg-Leg Molly over in Creed?"

"Sounds familiar, can't say though. Why?" Tackett cocked his head slightly.

"Had him on my list a year or more. Never caught him."

"Well, I don't figure you *tried* very hard."

"Maybe. I heard it mighta been a clean shooting. She was bad about razoring a man. I tried telling her it'd get her killed someday."

"Lot of folks tried telling her. Sooner or later, it was gonna happen. Blackhearted, throat-cutting whore . . ."

"Yep. But ya say this Little Honey keeps her nose clean, huh?"

Tackett cocked his head again. "What are you wanting to hear? I told ya—" He stopped, then a smile crept across his lips. "Aw, I get it. I see now. You got yourself a little interest there?"

"No, I don't. I just want to know, is all." The ranger glanced away, then back. "What kinda horse got stolen today?"

"Huh?"

"You said while you was gone a horse got stolen—"

"Aw-yeah. Just a stable plug, belonged to the undertaker. A spindly-legged paint horse. Won't get far, I don't reckon. You sure ask a lot of questions for one cup of Duttwieler's."

"Been a while since I seen ya. Thought we'd catch up some."

"Yeah, sure you did." He stood up, grinned, and picked at the seat of his pants. "What's it all got to do with Montana Red Hollis? Or, are you just cleaning up your list?"

"She's got a nice voice, Little Honey."

"She won't wash your shirts." Tackett nodded toward the big iron. "But I reckon it'd be warmer than sleeping with that cold steel pistol."

"What're you getting at?" The ranger looked up at him, almost smiled again.

Tackett shook his head. "Nothing. Don't mind me." He stepped around and put his cup in his saddlebags, tugged his vest, and stepped up in his stirrups. "I just rode out to pay my respects. Wish you'd stay the hell away from Donahue. There's over a dozen armed men out there." He cocked a half smile. "Not that it matters to me. But it's good seeing you anyway."

He looked down at the low fire, over at the ranger's drawn face hidden partly by the slope of the battered gray sombrero. A fire, a horse, and a clean gun . . . all this man had. All he'd ever had. But not him—not anymore. To hell with 'em all, the rapists, the killers, the buggers, muggers, and thieves . . . whores and razors, lunatics with six-shooters, tasting people's blood. If a man wanted to ride out and face a dozen gunmen . . . well, let him.

He smoothed a hand along his clean shirt collar. "Do

you really believe there's man alive can take down Montana Red?"

The ranger let out a breath. "No. None except me. I'll let ya know more once I've killed him."

"Still smug and cocky as ever, huh?" He chuckled and shook his head. "Reckon there's no point in me mentioning again that you're out of your jurisdiction."

"Nope. I'll stay in my jurisdiction once these hard cases start staying in theirs . . . not before."

"I swear. To be a lawman, you sure never paid much attention to the law."

"When you're sheriffing in town, you play by the rules. Out there it'll only get ya killed. Where I go, the only law is what ya make right between yourself and God. The rest ain't worth a spit in a river."

A silence passed. "Then you take care with Montana Red now, ya hear. Keep him upwind." His voice turned low, serious. "If he shoots ya, try to die quick. Know what I'm saying?"

"Good to see you too, Tackett," said the ranger.

"Maybe I've helped, some?" He hesitated a second, waiting, but saw nothing obliging in the ranger's eyes. Then he tugged his hat down, grumbled, and turned the gelding. "All right then, dang it. I'll be back here come early morning . . . show you the way out there."

"You don't have to go," the ranger said.

"I know it. But if you get yourself lost and starve to death, I'll feel guilty for a month."

The ranger smiled, nodded slightly. "I knew you'd go."

"Yeah? Well, I ain't wanting to."

"Neither am I." A second passed as Tackett's horse stepped away. "Bring a shotgun," the ranger called out in a quiet tone.

"Ha— That goes without saying." Tackett raised a hand without looking back.

The ranger watched him until he faded out of the thin circle of grainy light. He thought for a second of the gambler, J. Jones, almost certain now that it was Gentleman Joe Sharpe; and he pictured him atop a spindly-legged paint horse—an undertaker's horse— kicking up sand with Hurley Yates's shooting gear hung around his waist, sucking hot air through parched lips . . . scared, looking back. He hoped he wasn't riding the same trail as Red Hollis—hoped to God he wouldn't run into him out there. The ranger rubbed his face and touched his fingertips lightly to the scar on his cheek. He didn't want to kill that gambler.

CHAPTER 3

"You don't have to go," she'd told Sheriff Tackett that evening while he'd wiped his horse down with a handful of straw, grained it, and led it to a stall in the rear of her barn. He'd looked back at where the Widow Morris stood holding up a lantern with one hand and with her other hand slightly hiking the hem of her black dress up off the dirt. She'd gone on to say, "So what if Donahue's cowhands get a little rowdy now and then. They're just hardworking boys letting off steam."

Then she'd just stood there in the circling glow of light, and watched as he walked past her and on to the house, where a plate of warm supper sat waiting for him. "You don't understand," he'd said.

Didn't understand? Hiking her hemline a little higher, she'd followed and caught up to him; and after supper as he sat cleaning and checking the ten-gauge shotgun across his lap, she'd gone on and on, reminding him that it had been Maxwell Donahue who had first recommended him for the sheriff job, or was he forgetting that? "So tell me, *why on earth*, you would even think about going out there and upsetting the man? Have you lost your senses?"

"You wouldn't understand," he'd said again, looking up at her as he clicked the shotgun shut.

He couldn't answer, because to answer would mean he'd have to tell her what Montana Red Hollis and his pals had done. She didn't need to hear something like that. He'd have to explain to her that the Flying Cross boys hadn't really done anything *wrong* except to stand up for the wrong kind of men. But that in itself was wrong enough—wrong enough for the ranger to burn them down.

Tackett had thought it over and he couldn't fault the ranger for it. Besides, for Tackett it was a matter of principle. This was his town as long as he wore a badge, and the fact that the Flying Cross boys would do something so foolish in the streets of *his town* was because he'd allowed them to go too long unchecked. He'd grown slack in his duty, and they had lost all respect for him and what he stood for.

"Then it's just pride, isn't it?" She'd stepped back with one hand on her hip. "Just foolish, stubborn, *pride*."

"Yeah," he'd told her. "Let's just call it *that* and say no more about it." And she'd kept her distance from him the rest of the night. She'd never seen him like this before. It had something to do with him riding out and talking with that ranger. She'd bet on it. It all had to do with their sacred *law* . . . with law and lawmen and the dark stuff that bound them together.

The next morning he'd rode away wearing the same shirt he'd worn the night before because she'd hidden his other three from him. She stood in the doorway watching him until he rode out of sight. Then she turned, twisted the apron from around her waist, and tossed it across the room. *Blasted ranger* . . .

When Tackett got to the ranger's camp, the ranger was suited and geared and waiting for him. He stood with his gray sombrero cocked to one side and his reins in his gloved hand, wiping away the ashes of last night's fire with the edge of his boot. "Got a good night's sleep, did ya?" the ranger asked, stepping up into his saddle.

"You know I did," Tackett said in a wry tone, raising the corner of his duster collar and adjusting his hat brim down level across his brow. "Let's get to it."

The ranger looked him up and down, then looked away.

They turned their horses and rode west in silence across the flatland until the ranger turned to him and said, "She gave you a hard time, didn't she?"

Tackett looked at him with a flat expression and jiggled the shotgun across his lap. "I'm here, ain't I."

At midmorning as the sun beat down on them, they stopped where the flatland dropped away, and they sat their horses, looking down into a broad valley basin where an endless milling herd of cattle stood half sunken in a brown haze of dust. "Much wind as there are lately, seems it'd blow a rain in from somewhere," Tackett said, gazing up and around. "Don't you suppose?"

"I don't know. I only attend to the weather around me," the ranger replied, crossing his wrists on his saddle horn. "I've got no time for what's not here."

Tackett slumped a bit and leveled a beaten gaze on him. "Just making a little conversation is all. You remember *conversation* don't ya?"

"I remember it." The ranger smiled a thin smile, slipped his big pistol up, turned it in his hand, and let it back down in his holster.

Tackett watched him, then said, "When we get over there, let me try talking to Donahue first, all right? If you say anything at all, try to keep it respectful? Don't go flying off the handle and making things worse."

"I never do. I'll yes-sir and no-sir him if that's what you're asking. All I want is Bennie Burdett. Anybody else dies, it's their own fault." The ranger pulled his faded bandanna up across his nose and heeled his horse down over the edge of the flatland.

"Dang it," Tackett said under his breath.

An hour later they came slowly out of the dust and rode another two miles before coming to a row of sun-bleached shacks strung out behind a scrub timber fence. They rode through a break in the fence and saw burnt faces look up at them from the ground where a half-dozen cowhands sat taking their noon meal, sprawled around a dust-covered chuck wagon. "It's him," a voice said from their midst.

Tackett spread one hand toward them as the men rose to their feet in a clinking of tin plates and spoons. "Easy now, boys," he said. "We're here to see Mr. Don-ahue. Go on back to your eatings."

But they didn't. Instead, they brushed dust from their trouser seats and moved forward, adjusting their holster belts, turning their gaze from Tackett to the ranger. The ranger pulled his bandanna down from his face, peeled the glove from his gun hand, and stared at them with his hand resting on the butt of the big pis-tol. Beyond the cowhands and the chuck wagon, on the porch of a larger shack with a tin gable roof, a Chi-nese man wearing an apron ran inside. In a second a large man stepped out and down off the porch, yank-ing a cloth napkin from his shirt collar as he moved across the dirt yard.

"You're the one kilt our buddies!" A young cow-hand stepped forward ahead of the others, glaring up at the ranger. Half crouching, he wrapped a dirty hand around the butt of his pistol, ready to bring it up. "Don't try denying it," he shouted. "You kilt 'em, didn't ya!"

"Hold on, boys—" Tackett tried to speak but the ranger cut him off.

"Yep . . . I killed them *deader* than hell." Then he just stared down at the man, raised his big pistol from its holster slow and easy, and had it cocked and hanging in his hand. "You too, *boy*, if you raise that smoker another inch." Just like that he'd taken an edge, before the cowboys realized what he'd done.

Jesus! Tackett shot the ranger a stunned glance, swallowed hard, then raised the shotgun as the rest of the cowhands spread slightly apart, ready to snatch their pistols and start shooting. "Now listen, boys! He ain't fooling. What he *means* is, your pals were in the wrong. They sided with Kurtz and Yates against the law, and it got 'em killed. Don't be stupid here!"

"Shut up, Tackett," another voice called out. "You ain't nothing but a mouth."

A mouth? Tackett's face burned red beneath a sheet of dust and sweat. *A mouth! Well by God . . .* His thumb went across the hammer of the shotgun, cocking it back as he swung down off his horse. "Who said that? Huh? Step forward! Think you can talk that way to the law?" He moved forward a step; the cowhands stood firm.

"All right, Tackett, that's enough," the large man said, stepping in now, wiping his hands on the cloth napkin and flinging it away. Grease shined in his beard stubble. "You boys stand down too," he added over his shoulder to the others. Then he stood glaring at the ranger, with his big fists clenched at his sides.

"Mr. Donahue," Tackett said, his shotgun still leveled on the cowhands. "I brought this man here to talk. Told him I'd try to explain what happened yesterday. Said you're a reasonable man, and that maybe you'd see—"

"Came to talk, eh?" Donahue spoke to the ranger, ignoring Tackett. "After shooting some of my top hands? Now you think we've got something to talk about? You've got some gall, mister."

The ranger said in a quiet tone, "We don't *have* to talk about a thing. Your top hands shouldn't been drinking with murderers and rapists. I came here for Bennie Burdett. Give him up or you'll die with him. Where is he?"

Donahue flinched. Nobody talked to him this way. He stepped back, turning his gaze to Tackett. *Jesus!* Tackett stared, struck speechless by the ranger. Then he swallowed and turned his eyes to Donahue.

"You call that talking?" Donahue sneered. "Threatening a man on his own land?" His hand went to the pistol shoved down in his waist, but stopped there, seeing the ranger's big pistol rise an inch from his side. "You forgetting who you are, Tackett? Who you work for?"

"No, *sir! Mr.* Donahue!" Tackett's eyes flashed red. The cowboys had humiliated him, calling him nothing but a mouth. Now Donahue had talked down to him like he was a houseboy. His hands tensed as he spun to him with the shotgun leveled. "This ain't how I intended it to go here. But I'm backing this man's play. We're the law, and *by God* you *give* him Burdett, or I'll drop a hammer on ya myself right here and now!"

Donahue flinched. He'd never heard Tackett talk this way. Now he felt the tension and the heat—the cowhands behind him and the two lawmen before him. He glanced from Tackett to the ranger, and raised his gun hand slowly to settle his cowhands. "All right, everybody hold on. Burdett told me what they did to the woman and the Indian boy. Said he had nothing to do with it, neither the raping nor the killing. He was just there. He came from good folks and he's real remorseful about it."

"Remorseful. Where's he at?" The ranger asked in a firm tone, secured the cocked hammer with his thumb, and stepped down from his saddle without taking his eyes off Donahue.

"You ain't killing him here," Donahue said. His eyes flashed on the big pistol. Sweat beaded on his brow. This was making him look small in front of his men and the ranger knew it.

"Where's he at?" The ranger stepped closer, giving him no room, the big pistol still hanging cocked in his hand, his thumb coming off the hammer. The cowboys watched, tense, waiting. A hot wind swept past, nipping at loose clothes and raising dust.

"I said you ain't killing him here—not in front of us. He was a good man till he hooked up with Montana Red and that bunch."

The ranger stared into his eyes for a second. He'd pushed him hard, but now he had what he wanted. He could give an inch. He took a deep breath and let it out. "He's real remorseful, huh?"

"Yes, and that's a fact," Donahue said. "I don't hold with what he did. But I can't let ya kill him like a dog."

"I won't," the ranger said, looking around at the others, raising his voice for them to hear. "If Burdett's truly remorseful, I won't kill him. You've got my word.

I'll just talk to him." He looked back at Donahue. "Where is he?"

Just talk to him? Tackett's eyes flashed back and forth between them. What was this?

Donahue nodded toward one of the sun-bleached shacks. "He's been in the storeroom all morning, half out of his head." His voice lowered just between the two of them. "These boys are all friends of his."

"I know," the ranger said. He took a pencil stub and the wrinkled list from inside his duster, drew a line through Bennie Burdett's name, and walked to the shack with the list in one hand, pistol in his other, his duster tails stirring sideways in the hot wind.

"Stay back," said a trembling voice from inside the shack. "I know who you are . . . you're that devil! Get away from me!"

The ranger glanced around at the others, watching from twenty yards away, then stepped to the side of the door, with the list still in his hand, but his big pistol back in its holster. "I'm coming in, Bennie," he said.

"I'll kill you! I'm warning ya."

"No, you won't. Just settle down." He reached a hand over and slung the door open. After a second when no gunshot came through the doorway, the ranger stepped over into it with his hands spread, and gazed into the darkness. "Where are you, Bennie? I'm coming in. Can't see a thing."

"Stay right there," the frightened voice said in the darkness.

The ranger's eyes followed the sound of the voice to a stack of wooden kegs, and made out the dark shadow looming there with the pistol hanging in its hand. "I never kilt 'em," Bennie Burdett said. "I swear to God I never. I just watched Red do it, is all."

"I know it, Bennie," the ranger said. "Figured it was all Red's doings. His and Kurtz. You and Yates just watched, huh?"

"I never even wanted to do that. It was the most awful thing I ever saw." His voice cracked and trembled. "Red's like an animal! He—He—"

"I know." The ranger stepped closer, seeing his red-rimmed eyes in the darkness, smelling his sweat from ten feet away. "You couldn't stop Red Hollis could you? I mean, him and Kurtz raped them and killed them and you and Yates couldn't do nothing but watch it happen, right?"

"Red—he made us watch, and—and—" He stopped short.

"Go on, Bennie, what else?"

"He made us . . . laugh about it." He sobbed and ran a hand across his eyes. "Oh, God . . . he made us *laugh* like it was the funniest thing ever. Their blood was all over his face!"

"Whew." The ranger shook his head, gazed around the dark shack, and looked back at him. "Just think, Bennie, the last thing that poor woman and kid ever saw was you and Yates laughing at them. Laughing while Kurtz and Red did those terrible things."

"Lord I can't stand it no more. I've gone crazy ever since, seeing their faces, hearing 'em scream and beg." He raised both hands to his temples, kneading them, one with his free hand the other with the hard butt of the pistol. "I can't make it go away!"

The ranger eyed the pistol in Bennie's hand as Bennie squeezed his head as if to force the ugly picture from it. "Well, that's why I'm here, Bennie . . . to make it go away."

"You—you came to hang me, didn't ya?"

The ranger let out a breath and raised the wrinkled list in his hand. "No. I came to kill you, Bennie. See? I've already marked your name off my list."

"Without a trial or nothing?" He lowered his hands, the pistol hanging at his side.

"Be honest, Bennie. Do you really *deserve* a trial? Do you even *want* one? All them boys out there, friends of yours, hearing what you had a hand in—"

"But I never done none those awful things."

"It don't matter. You were there. You didn't stop it. Do you want to face all those people in a courtroom, maybe after you think about it some, it turns out you did more than you're saying?"

"Wha—what do you mean?" He sniffed and rubbed his face.

"I mean, if Red had you scared enough to make you *laugh* while he did those terrible things, he might've had you scared enough to make you do more. Huh? See what I mean? Did he?"

"He—he might've. I mean . . . it all got real confusing to me. He told me if I didn't hold them down for him and Kurtz, he'd kill me too."

"There you are," the ranger said in a resolved tone. "You don't want to repeat all that in front of people, do you?"

"No. No I don't. I reckon I'd druther die in a fair fight with you than go through it."

"It wouldn't be a fair fight, Bennie, to be honest with you. I'd kill you so quick it probably wouldn't even hurt."

"Yeah?" Bennie sniffed and ran his hand with the gun in it under his nose. "That wouldn't be so bad then, would it?"

"It'd beat hanging I reckon. But still, all them boys

out there would go the rest of their life thinking you did those things along with Kurtz and Red Hollis." He shook his head. "Naw . . . you don't want that either, do you? Really?"

Bennie sweated. "Damn Montana Red! Damn him to hell! He got me to do all that. I *never* would've done it!"

"It's what Red Hollis does, Bennie. It's what he's good at." He paused for a second, then added, "I promise you I'll set it right . . . if you will."

"Hunh?" Bennie raised his sweaty brow.

"Like I said, all them boys knowing you had a hand in it. You don't want that."

"No, I don't. But what else can I do?"

"Make things right," the ranger said; and he just stared at him in the darkness, shook his head slowly, nodded at the pistol in the young cowboy's hand, and in a soft tone added, "Go on now, Bennie, cock that hammer."

When he walked back across the dirt yard the hot wind had stilled and Donahue and his cowhands turned and stood glaring at him. Tackett stood with the shotgun still leveled. "Well," Donahue said, "what's come of it?" He and the others glanced past the ranger toward the shack.

"He said tell you boys good-bye for him," the ranger said, walking through them to Tackett, stooping to pick up his reins.

"Said what?" Donahue swung around facing him. The cowhands glared, their hands still on their pistols, but not as tense as before.

The ranger straightened up with his reins in his hands and put his list back inside his duster. "He said for me to tell all you boys"—his words were cut short beneath a single pistol shot from inside the shack— "he's sorry for all he done."

"Lord have mercy," one of the cowhands said. "Bennie done himself over," said another.

They looked at one another, stunned, then ran all together toward the shack. The ranger looked at Donahue, who stood glaring at him with his fists clenched. "You had no right telling him to do something like that! You saw the shape he was in! He was worth saving!"

The ranger pushed up the brim of his sombrero. "I just told him where he stood. He *saved* himself."

"Get off my land! Both of you!" Donahue bellowed; his face swelled red.

The ranger had already swung up on his saddle while he spoke, but Tackett still stood there, and Donahue turned his rage to him. "You might as well pack your grip and leave this territory! I'll run you out of office next election. I swear it!" As he spoke, he raised a finger and poked it close to Tackett's chest. Tackett knocked it away with the barrel of the shotgun.

"You ever stick a finger out at me again, I'll take it off to a stub." He jerked the shotgun back, feigning a butt swipe at Donahue's face. The big man cowered back a step. Tackett swung up on his saddle, then looked down at him. "As long as I *am* still the sheriff, don't you ever make me have to come out here and do something like this again."

They turned their horses and rode away without looking back. "That wasn't so hard, was it?" The ranger asked as they swung wide of the herd this time and on toward the rise up out of the basin.

"You nearly gave me heart failure," Tackett said,

"talking that way to Donahue. Thought you was gonna show some respect, let me do the talking?"

"I saw you was about to lose your temper." The ranger grinned. "Figured I better do something before you got mad and hurt somebody."

Tackett chuckled and adjusted the shotgun on his lap. "You ain't changed none. No sir! None at all."

"Neither have you, much," the ranger said. "You just needed some airing out . . . something to get your blood pumping a little. Tell the truth. Don't you feel better now, standing up for the law against that bunch?"

"Humph. It probably cost me my job, come election time."

"Naw. Donahue's no fool. I saw that much about him. He knows a good lawman when he sees one. He'll tell his boys to walk a little easier in your town from now on. That'll keep them away from bad company, keep them from getting killed."

"Maybe you're right," Tackett said. He grinned. "But job or no job, I ain't felt this good in years. Can't wait till we catch up to Montana Red."

The ranger just looked at him.

All the way back to the main trail, Tackett talked about how all he had to do was pick up a few belongings in town—a couple of his new shirts—talk to the Widow Morris and let her know that he might be gone for quite a while. He'd have to say good-bye to a couple of friends, maybe appoint one as acting sheriff. He went on to say, "I figure with the two of us, our best chance is to split up once we find his hideout . . . one come in from behind, one from the front, close him in and starve him out. What do you think?"

They'd just reached a crossroads at the main trail,

where to their left the trail reached out and was swallowed up by the swirling heat of the badlands. And even as Tackett spoke, the ranger reined his horse down, sat with his wrists crossed on his saddle horn, and said bluntly, "Go on home, Tackett."

"What?" Tackett turned his horse in a tight circle, then stopped it and stared at him. "What about Montana Red? You're gonna need some more help—"

"Thanks for your help so far. But I'll take it from here."

"Now just one danged minute," Tackett said, pushing his hat brim up. "We're both lawmen. We both know how to handle this work. We just proved that. I mighta let myself get a little rusty, but I'm back where I oughta be now. You can't ride in, get me all fired up like this, then cut me loose. I swear, I'm back, sharp as ever!"

"No, you're not," the ranger said. "You've settled in and put all this behind you. You found something better for yourself, remember? If you come back to this now, it'll soon eat you up and kill you. Go on back and take care of that town. That's where you belong from here on."

Tackett's face flashed red as he stared at the ranger. "You saying I can't handle it?"

Their eyes locked on one another as a tense silence passed. Then the ranger said, with no regard for the sting in his words, "That's right, you can't handle it. Now go on home."

Beyond the ranger lay the angry swirl of badlands, and in the harshness of the sun's glare Tackett could hardly distinguish the man and his horse from the stark backdrop of the land behind him.

"Danged right then, I will." Tackett sliced his words

through clenched jaws. "I was a fool to come out here with ya. They all say you're crazy—and they're right." He sawed his reins, causing his horse to step back and forth on nervous hoofs. "You've always been alone and if there's anything to justice you'll die alone."

"Go on home, Tackett," the ranger said in a quiet tone, "while we're still friends."

"Friends? You never *had* one and never will. I'd tell ya to never come through my town again, but I reckon when you catch up to Montana Red it won't matter none—he's gonna *kill you!*"

"So long, Tackett." The ranger's eyes had turned distant, caged, and empty. A hot breeze licked at his dusty bandanna gathered close about his stubbled chin.

"Dang it!" Tackett swung his horse hard away, slinging the shotgun up and slapping the barrel to its rump. The ranger let out a breath and watched him ride off in a flurry of dust. And he sat still until at thirty yards Tackett slid his horse down, swung around, and stopped, and waved the shotgun back and forth above his head. "Dang your arse. You be careful out there," Tackett called back to him. The ranger smiled slightly, raised a gloved hand, and turned his horse onto the badlands trail.

CHAPTER 4

Montana Red Hollis was a straight-up killer and he liked for everybody to know it—liked to be thought of as vicious and wild and unpredictable. A small ball of fire lay inside his head, somewhere above his eyes, he thought. He liked keeping that ball of fire spinning at all times. By his own admission he was a maniac who'd rather kill than drink whiskey if he had to make a choice; but he found it most to his liking when he could do both at once. Like today . . .

He threw back a mouthful of rye and blew it in the bartender's face. Before the bartender could raise a hand, Red reached across the bar, snatched him by the shirt with his left hand, and stabbed the big knife into the bar top with his right. The man spluttered, batting his eyes, his hair hanging down his face, dripping brown whiskey.

Red jerked him down close to the big knife, letting him get a good look at it there, see it while it still quivered. Sunlight from the window glistened on the cutting edge. "Don't lie to me! Every time you lie to me, I'll cleave off one of your fingers." He banged his head on the bar. "You want that? Do ya?" He almost smiled—*loved* batting people around this way.

"Please! I swear to God, Red!"

"Don't get *religious* on me, either. You let my name out, didn't ya?" He held the bartender's face down with one hand, threw back a shot of rye, ran the back of his hand across his mouth, and said to the man beside him, "Bert, keep an eye out for that boy of his once he goes to screaming. The kid's a shotgunning little turd."

"Red, he ain't here. I ain't lying!"

"All right then. Tell me who all you told." He threw back another drink; rye trickled down, spreading and shining in his rusty beard.

"Nobody, Red! Just Hurley's brother, Dick! Just him! Just him and his partner! I thought you'd want 'em to know where you was!"

"*Lying!* Ain't ya?" He jerked the knife up from the bar, let go of the bartender's shirt, and grabbed his hand before he could get away.

"No! I ain't! I swear I ain't!"

Red slammed his hand down on the bar and raised the knife high.

"Better lop one off, just in case you are. Don't want you thinking ya got by with it."

"No, please!" He slumped down, his free hand covering his eyes, ready for the sound of the big knife sinking into the wood.

But Red Hollis laughed, pulled him up, and shoved him backward against the bottles lining the wall. Bottles toppled and broke on the floor. "Damn fool. What do I want with your dirty fingers? No telling *where* they been."

He slipped the knife in the sheath on his belt, pulled one of his crossed .44s, and shot him once in the chest, the bullet going through, cracking the mirror behind him in a bloody spray. "Drinks are on the house!" He turned with the pistol smoking, laughing at his little joke, wishing somebody besides Bert was there to hear it.

He glanced around the empty saloon, chairs knocked over, a cigar curling smoke from an ashtray, poker chips strewn across the floor. *Aw, well, can't have everything.* He threw back another drink and glared at Bert, there by the window. "We just wells ta go, hadn't we?" He walked across the plank floor, big spurs ringing like silver dollars, the bottle of rye hanging from his hand.

Almost to the door, he heard heavy footsteps running from the stockroom. Behind the footsteps a woman's voice screamed something in Spanish. Red crouched and spun, swinging a .44 up, careful not to spill the rye. As the curly-headed kid rounded the corner of the bar, Red Hollis dropped him with one shot. Then he aimed at the squat little Mexican woman, who ran screaming for the shotgun no sooner than it hit the floor.

"Gonna shoot anybody today, Bert?" He yelled over his shoulder; but before Bert could make a move, the woman snatched up the shotgun and swung it up. "Yeeesss, ma'ammm!" Red fanned three shots, laughing, watching her large belly tremble as the shotgun flew away. She hit the wall and crumbled, her long skirt tossed up over her face. Red straightened up, looked at her, and cocked his head. "They don't none of 'em wear bloomers, do they?" He spun the .44 backward, slipping it in his holster.

"There's a sheriff out there, Red. Here he comes."

"So? It was a fair fight—three agin one. I don't know about you, but I'm getting hungry."

Outside, they walked to the hitch rail, seeing faces

duck back into doorways; and Red saw the old sheriff walking up the middle of the street with a rifle pointed at him. "Hold it now, old man," Red called out, raising his left hand with the bottle in it. "You don't wanta go in there, it's a damn mess. They got ta shooting each other and couldn't stop."

"You beat all, Red." Bert chuckled in a low tone.

The old sheriff stopped twenty feet away; Red could see his knees shaking through his pants leg. "Go on away, old man. I know where ya live—I'll thump your old head and burn your house down, ya hear?"

"You can't keep coming here doing this," the old man called out, backing away. He let down the rifle and edged toward a stack of nail kegs at the corner of an alley. "You gotta quit it. It just ain't right."

"Hell, I know it. I'm trying to quit. It just takes a little time." He stepped over and unspun his reins. "You go on about your business now. This town can't afford ta lose ya. Injuns would carry this place off in a week."

"Red?" The old sheriff called out as the two outlaws stepped up into their saddles. "I got to ask you not to come back here. You hear me?"

"Of course I hear ya, ole pal." Red grinned. "I ain't deaf, ya know." Then he turned his smile to his partner, leaning toward him a little as they swung their horses into the street. "If he wasn't so funny, I'da shot his nose off long ago."

On their way out of town, he saw a young Negro girl peep around from behind a water trough, and he reined his big bay up in the street. "Now look at that little sweetheart," he said. "Wouldn't that go good with grits and gravy? Come on out here, sugar. Let me see ya better." He shot Bert a glance. "Reckon they don't wear bloomers either?"

"I don't know. Want me to go see?" Bert sidestepped his horse in the street.

"Yeah, and bring her out here to me." Red drew his reins so tight, his bay back-stepped and almost lowered on its haunches.

"What for?" Bert asked.

"*What for?* Damn what for! Bring her out here, you idiot. I'm taking her with us."

But the girl heard them and slunk from behind the trough, up onto the boardwalk, toward the corner of the alley, her thin arms spread along the front of a building.

"You mean it?" Bert looked at him and grinned.

"Hell yes I mean it! Go on and get her."

Bert turned back, but the girl was gone; she seemed to have disappeared without a sound. "Where is she?" He looked back and forth, swinging his horse with him.

"See, Bert? You don't do nothing like I tell you. You fool around too much. I bet I shoot *you* before it's over."

Run, Myra, child! Run! Ray Gilliam stood watching through the dirty window, squeezing the pick handle in his broad black hand. Then he let out a tense breath, wiping his brow as the two riders kicked their horses off along the dusty street. *Thank the Lord!* He couldn't leave that girl alone for a minute. Her out there like that, Montana Red Hollis on a drunk, killing crazy. What was ever gonna become of the girl?

He felt like scolding her, but he knew it would do no good; and when she slipped through the door still crouched low, he snatched her up and held her against his chest. "Myra, child! What's wrong with you? Don't you ever be on the streets when that man's around. I've told you, and *told* you!"

"It's a sin and a shame, when a child like her can't even play in the street," said Joy Decker behind him, leaning, peeping around him and out the window. He let his daughter down but kept a hand on her shoulders, and slipped the ax handle back into the barrel with the others.

"Yes, ma'am, it truly is." He pulled his cap from his hip pocket. "Can she stay here with you, while I go over there?" He nodded toward the saloon. "See if I can help out some way?"

"Well of course she can . . . certainly. Here, take this with you," Joy Decker said. He saw her pull the small pistol from under the counter and wipe a hand over it. She held it out. "My husband always kept it here. Said you never know when you might need it."

"No, thank ya just the same, ma'am," Ray Gilliam said. He raised a hand slightly as if to push the gun back to her. "They've left for now, ma'am. I'll just go on over . . ." He looked at Myra. "Stay right here with Mrs. Decker, nowhere else. You hear me, child?"

Myra nodded and stepped over near Joy Decker's side. Joy put her arm around the girl's waist and hugged her. "Don't worry, sweetheart. Your papa will be right back."

He hurried across the dusty street and up on the boardwalk just as the old sheriff came creeping out of the alley. Jake the blacksmith had already gone inside, and he came out now, stopping at the door, leaning there shaking his head. "Everybody stay back. Don't go in there just yet. Nothing you can do—nothing anybody can do now."

Ray Gilliam peeped past him, inside, across to the

bloody cracked mirror. His dark eyes moved down across the floor, over the bodies of the woman and the boy, the boy, who only two weeks before had helped him scratch in the rocky dirt on one of the played-out silver claims. He winced and turned away.

"There ya are, Sheriff Turner," Jake the Blacksmith said, looking past Ray Gilliam. "How long you gonna allow this kind of madness to go on?"

Ray Gilliam turned and saw the old sheriff walking over to them, slump-shouldered, the rifle hanging useless from his weathered hand. "What could I do, Jake? Get myself killed? What would that get us, huh?"

"Something's gotta be done." The blacksmith's jaw tightened. "We can't go on like this. The town is dying because of that monster!"

"I can't handle Montana Red Hollis," said the sheriff. "There's no denying it. Y'all can have the badge back, if ya want it." He raised a trembling hand to the tin star on his chest, unpinned it, and held it toward Jake the Blacksmith. Jake refused to take it.

The rest of the townsfolk came out—what few were left—moving closer, some looking back, off up the street toward the wake of dust drifting away on the breeze. "Don't push that piece of tin off on me," the blacksmith said, stepping back. "You're the one responsible. I'm no lawman—never wanted to be. There's not a bully or a hothead in the world I've ever backed down for." He gestured his thick hand off in the direction of the rising sheet of dust. "But that man's not human I tell ya."

"Somebody's got to take a hold here, Jake," the old sheriff said, still holding the badge out. "Somebody, *please*." His eyes swept the small gathering, each man stepping back from the badge as they would a venomous snake. Ray Gilliam did not step back, but then the old sheriff's eyes only slipped across him and back to the blacksmith.

"Not me though." Jake lowered his hand and wiped it across his broad forehead. "I'm— Well, to be honest, I'm moving on like the rest. Found me a new business south of Wakely. It's something I've been planning for a while now."

"What?" asked a voice from the townsfolk. "You're not quitting us too, are you, Jake?" The others moved closer around him until he turned and walked away shaking his head, his broad shoulders slumped and seeming to carry across them some terrible burden.

"We gotta do something," said Ray Gilliam, low, to himself, beneath the murmur of the crowd. He had his daughter, Myra, to think about—fifteen years old, starting to look like a woman, but with a child's mind. What could he have done to save her? He owned a pistol, but it hadn't been handled or fired in years. What could he have done? Take a pick handle to Montana Red Hollis and Bert Clemens? Watch them ride off with his daughter?

He would have *died*, that's what he would have done. Nothing more, nothing that could've saved her. Just died there in the street. He let go of a tight breath. *Don't think about it. It's over for now. . . .*

But what about the next time? Maybe it was time he and Myra left here as well. She needed to be somewhere around other children like herself, somewhere where people knew how to teach her things. He'd heard of special schools for children like Myra—but none out here. This country was harsh and dangerous at best. It was no place for someone like his Myra. He ran a nervous hand across his forehead. She'd been at risk here throughout her life. And now Montana Red Hollis had seen her. Red had seen her, and he'd be coming back.

For years now, Montana Red Hollis had come to the conclusion that people didn't like him. He knew they talked ill of him behind his back, and that they had all his life. He just seldom caught them at it. Maybe it was just as well folks didn't like him because he didn't much give a damn for them either. He stood at the edge of the cliff below his cabin at Rocky Roost and gazed out across miles of high jutted rock reaching toward the sky.

He tapped his thumb from the tip of one finger to the next, taking a little tally there of how many people he'd killed over the years. He'd run his thumb over his fingertips so many times, back and forth, now he'd lost count. Must've been eleven though, plus the three yesterday, that made it . . . fourteen? Yep, fourteen. And this was just counting the innocent people. This didn't include the gunmen and lawmen he'd killed over the years. He'd been in a couple of dozen straight-up gunfights and won every one of them.

The killings that meant the most to him were the lawmen—those men with their shiny badges and their *so*-righteous attitudes. You couldn't help but love killing somebody like that. *Burn 'em down and watch 'em fall* . . . He counted them different from the others he'd killed here or there.

He looked back over his shoulder and saw Bert up there on the porch, skinning down a long fat bull rattlesnake he'd shot earlier on their way in. Bert couldn't cook worth a damn. But that was okay. Once he got the snake worked down good, and the fire started, Red figured he'd go up and cook it to suit himself.

Bert Clemens was an idiot, slow-witted and slow to act, an inbreed of some sort, Red always figured, if the truth was known. And if there was any point at all in Bert Clemens's being alive, Red failed to see it. He'd proved himself a fool yesterday, letting that little brown girl get away the way he did. There was no excuse for it, and that'd pretty much cinched it for Red. That and the fact that Bert never seemed to see the humor in anything Red Hollis had to say.

Red liked to see people laugh at his jokes, but he couldn't tell anymore if they were laughing because what he said was truly funny, or if they only did so thinking maybe he'd shoot a hole in them if they didn't. He couldn't always tell.

Most times lately when people laughed at his little jokes and sayings, they seemed nervous, like their hearts weren't really in it. But now and then he'd come across somebody who seemed to genuinely appreciate his rare and gifted sense of humor. Like the young gambler two weeks back in the town along the trail toward the badlands, back where he'd left Hurley and Kurtz. Now that ole boy knew what was funny.

He'd lost seventeen dollars to the laughing gambler, and didn't mind it at all. Ordinarily he might've shot a man—accuse him of cheating, pop a cap on him and take his money back. Who would've said anything? But the way that boy raked in a pot, threw that head back cackling like a crazy man at anything Red had to say, hell, it was money well spent, far as he cared. See . . . why couldn't Bert be more like that?

Yesterday, when he said what he said about drinks being on the house after he shot the bartender? *By God that was funny!* Then the thing about the Mexican woman not wearing bloomers? *Damn right it was funny* . . . But Bert Clemens never cracked a smile. He kinda laughed at something Red said to the old sheriff out in the street, but Red hadn't meant that to be funny at all.

But the thing about the Mexican woman? Personally, he *loved* that! He could see himself setting around up at one of the line camps this winter—maybe at the Flying Cross—all snowed in, drinking with a couple of them cowboys. Wait till the time was just right—maybe after a meal of beef and beans. And he could see himself raise a boot up, drop it on the table, all leaned back, comfortable, maybe trimming his thumbnail with his boot knife, and he'd just slip that story right in there.

He'd bring it up like he'd just thought of it, say, *That's like the time last summer, me and an ole boy named Bert Clemens went into a saloon* . . . Bet they'd get a kick out of that.

He grinned to himself and started all over counting on his fingers. From the time he turned twenty till he turned twenty-eight, he'd only killed five or six people. These were people he'd met along the road somewhere, or else slipped up on them late at night and caught them wrapped up in their blankets. Didn't even own a gun there for a while. He'd kill them with a rock, choke them with his hands. Didn't matter to him.

Back then he'd spent a lot of time around the mining camps and community sleeping quarters, and he'd kill a person in their sleep sometimes just for the thrill of it. He'd kill one here, then one there, traveling, wandering about. Hell, people probably never stopped to think it was the same person doing it. He could honestly say that aside from seeing people laugh at his jokes and stories, killing people and getting drunk were about the only things he enjoyed doing.

Of course, once he started carrying a gun, getting good with it, letting word get around about how fast he was, that's when he took to killing lawmen any chance he could. Thinking about it, he raised the .44 from his holster and twirled it, cocking and uncocking it. He spun around once and cocked it at Bert Clemens twenty yards up, too busy with skinning the snake to even see him do it. "Bam," he said, pulling the trigger, but catching the hammer with his thumb just before it struck the bullet.

He liked the look that came over a lawman's face about the time that bullet popped out of his back. Liked to see their eyes go off to a strange place, trying to figure it all out in a hurry there at the end, there when it came to them that maybe they should have written home more often, maybe treated their mama a little better when they were a child. Stuff like that. "*So there*," he always felt like saying. "How'd ya like that?"

He loved that last second, when their confidence came undone and fear shone in their eyes, and everything about them that was all tense and tight and determined just a second before now melted inside them like candle wax. And they'd drop to the ground and never rise again. He liked that. It was as much fun as hearing people laugh, maybe more. Lots of times they looked real surprised, sort of like when he was a kid running around goosing people at the county fair. *Whoooa!* Their eyes got real big, they'd stiffen up. Then they'd let go with a *you-got-me* look in their eyes. That's how it was when he killed a lawman.

Or, he loved wounding one, then torturing the hell out of him before he died. Catch him there all bent over holding his guts in, grab him by both ears, throw his head up and kick his teeth out. Damn! You just couldn't beat that. Some of them went out fighting, but it didn't do 'em much good all shot up that way. Most of them laid down and took it there at the end—died like a woman, all limp and frail.

That's the thing he didn't like much about women. They died too easy, before he got all he could out of 'em. Sure, he'd drag one up here now and then, have his way with them, slice 'em up some before he killed them; but they weren't as much fun as killing them ole lawmen. Sometimes his blood got to boiling just thinking about it.

He got worked up easy, seeing people laugh, cry, scream, bleed, and die. For two cents he'd ride back to that little dirt-stuck town, shoot a couple more folks, and snatch that little brown girl up on his way out. Hadn't been for Bert Clemens and his idiot ways she'd be here right now. Instead of only *thinking* about all this stuff, he could've been doing some of it. She was just a little ole thing, not much older than that Injun kid, but hell, it was something to do.

"Bert, get down here," he yelled back over his shoulder. Then he stared out across the sky, feeling his breath quicken. A hawk circled down and he watched it sail below him in the canyon and head back up. When it rose above him again, he jerked up the pistol and blew it away with one shot. Then he waved at it, watching it fall, leaving behind it a trail of blood and broken feathers.

"What'd you do that for?" Bert asked, scratching his head, walking up beside him, a butcher knife in his hand, pink snake blood staining his shirt.

"Shut up, Bert, and come over here. I wanta ask ya something." Red took him by the arm as they stepped sideways along the edge of the cliff. "Look down past the ridge there with all the scrub pine." He pointed, the two of them leaning. "Is that a rider? Looks like a rider to me. I been watching awhile."

"If it is, you sure tipped him off, shooting that pistol." Bert leaned, scanning out and down across the wide gap of open air.

Red reached down and took the knife from his hand as he stepped back. "So long, Bert," he said, raising his boot. And with one kick he sent the man screaming, out and down, arms batting the air like a bird learning to fly.

He grinned, watched Bert drop a hundred feet, strike the jagged side of the canyon wall, then bounce out and on down, until he splattered on rocks near the edge of the winding stream.

He shook his head and turned back to the cabin, already sorry he'd kicked ole Bert off the cliff. If he'd thought about it first, he could've nailed that idiot to a tree and had something to shoot at for a week or two, off somewhere in the woods, away from the cabin so the stink wouldn't get too bad. Thinking about it, he snatched out his pistol and spun it, holstered it, and snatched it again. *Boy, he was fast!*

He pointed the gun, flashed it from one imaginary target to another, picturing men out there reaching for their gun, but falling away like broken twigs as he made a shooting sound. The ball of fire spun inside his head. He chuckled and put his pistol away with one last twirl. Nobody in the world was faster or more deadly with a gun than him. He loved knowing that. It had gotten to a point that he didn't even have to practice anymore—gotten to where it seemed like all he had to do was just think about his pistol being out and cocked, and all of a sudden there it was.

"Ole Bert, ain't you something," he said aloud; and he chuckled again, thinking how funny that would be telling it to some of the boys this winter, maybe right after he got 'em good with that Mexican bloomers story. *There went ole Bert, them arms and legs flapping, and I yelled down at him, said, Bert, you shoulda started leaning a little closer to the ground.*

He had tears in his eyes by the time he reached the cabin; and he had to lean against the porch post, catching his breath for a few seconds before cutting down the snake meat and throwing it over his shoulder. For a moment he looked out past the edge of the ravine, wondering what might have gone through ole Bert's mind there at the last minute, sailing out like that and down, knowing there wasn't a thing in the world to hold on to, realizing that all he had left were the seconds flashing and coming toward him. At the end, nothing, nothing but the blackness on the hard rocks below and no escaping it.

He smiled. *Poor ole Bert . . .* At least he'd done a pretty fair job skinning the rattlesnake. He ran his hand down the cold wet snake meat, thinking about the little brown girl as he walked inside the cabin. For two cents he'd ride back to town and get that little thing right now and bring her back here.

But he was tired and hungry, and that was a full day's ride. She would have to keep till another time.

PART 2

———◆———

Higher Planes

CHAPTER 5

The gambler, Gentleman Joe Sharpe, took in a breath, pulled the stick back from the fire, blew on the sizzling meat, touched his tongue to it, and drew it back. It had to cool some. If anybody had bet him a week ago that he'd be sitting in the desert in the middle of the night eating cat meat on a stick he would've given them long odds against it. But he hadn't eaten in a day and a half and the big cat was the only thing he'd come across. It was only by the slimmest luck that he'd managed to shoot it.

He'd come upon the small rock basin of water just before dark, and after he watered the horse and himself, he'd led the horse to the top of a short cliff up above the basin, reined off on an edge of rock, and collapsed for over an hour in the shadow of a short overhang without even checking it first for lizard or snake. When the low nickering of the horse woke him, he saw it shying back, drawing taut against its reins, and he crawled over to the edge of the cliff and peeped down at the water basin.

There he'd seen it in the late evening light, a streak of tan behind a pair of shining eyes, blending into the night as night fell gray and looming. It had just turned its head up toward the sound of the horse. Brown water ran in long strings from its muzzle as it stood slightly crouched and silent as stone.

He froze. The cat took a slow turn toward him. Its long tail whipped once like a snake, then stopped. Was it coming up here? Oh, God! He forced his hand to move; reached down and pulled up Hurley Yates's big pistol from his waist, his hand shaking so bad he nearly dropped it. He cocked the pistol, heard the metal on metal sound as loud as the creak of a freight car, he thought; and now the cat had seen him.

Aw-naw! Now what? And now the cat stiffened, swung partly sideways to him, sixty feet away down there, its one paw thrown up and its mouth thrown open in a deep rasping snarl. Gentleman Joe's mind raced, then stalled, almost went blank with fear, then raced again. What could he do with a cat? A man he might bluff, or cower away from, or run from if he had to. But from a creature of prey there was no escape. *Calm down, think! Do something!*

He threw the pistol out before him with both hands, tried to still himself, but saw the barrel shaking back and forth, too shaky to hit anything. *God almighty!* Yet when the flame shot out of the pistol barrel, the cat went straight up off the ground and seemed to hang in the air for a second, a twisting, snarling ball of fur.

Jesus! He'd hit it. Actually hit it!

He pulled off another shot and heard it ricochet off rock, far to the left of where the big cat hit the ground, still twisting, still screaming, the horse rearing against the reins, whinnying in reply from behind him. And Joe jumped up now, ready to bolt and run if the cat started up toward him; but he held his ground for a second, aimed again, and pulled the trigger over and

over until the gun only clicked. Empty now and useless.

Still the big cat slung its head and sprang forward,
toward the narrow path up to him and the horse. The
horse reared harder against the tied reins, bellowing,
thrashing.

That was it . . . all he had. He was gone. . . . Forgetting
the horse as the horse fought to free itself, he dropped
the gun and had just started to turn and run when he
saw the big cat falter, staggering like a drunk, its fluid-
like motion broken now and spending down. It
dropped to its belly. Joe Sharpe stopped and held his
breath. The cat dragged itself forward two feet and
stopped there, leaving a smear of blood behind. Then
the big tan head lolled up, back and forth, and fell back
to the ground and laid there, as if all life source inside
it had melted into the warm earth.

Joe Sharpe stood breathless there for a long time, listening to the cat's labored breathing until it grew too
faint to hear. Then he leaned down, took up the pistol,
jerked bullets out of his holster belt, dropping two or
three from his trembling fingers, until he'd finally
managed to reload it.

He waited a few more minutes. By now darkness
had set in, and he moved cautiously, worked his way
down the narrow path, halting every few feet and listening for any sound from the still tan body. He
stopped again, fifteen feet away with the pistol cocked
and pointed; and he had to force himself forward the
last couple of yards until he stood looking down at the
limp, lifeless creature at his feet. *All right, it's dead, now
what?* He reached out with his boot toe, raised the cat's
paw, and let it fall. Then he'd let out a breath and
slumped with the pistol hanging loose in his hand. . . .

Now he blew once more on the meat, touched his tongue to it, then took a bite, having to chew and grind to get off just a tiny piece, finally having to pull it off the stick once it had cooled and hold it with his dirty hand. That was all right though, it was food, and he had killed it.

He managed to wrench and tear and rip off a larger piece. It was tough and strong and had a musky smell to it. Worst of all it was *cat meat*. But it was cat meat at a time when there were no beef or elk or anything else around; and cat meat or not, it beat the hell out of going hungry.

When he'd eaten enough to feel his strength returning, he dragged the cat's body a few yards off and behind a rock, not wanting to look at it, not wanting to be near it, and he rinsed the musky-smelling grease off his hands in the small basin of brown water, dried them on his dusty trousers, and went back up above the cliff to spend the night.

His sleep was restless throughout the night, filled with the muffled sound of pistol fire and screaming cats, his stomach queasy and churning. Before dawn he staggered up from the ground, filled the canteen with dirty brown water, watered the horse and grazed it for nearly an hour on the tufts of gramma grass above the cliff. Then he rode on—rode another day and spent another night.

Once again he ran low on water, and once again his stomach ached from hunger. He left behind him once more an impression in the dirt where he'd slept, knowing the wind and dust would soon fill it. By the time the sun had climbed high in the east he'd circled down to a stretch of rolling flatland—flat but ever leaning upward—and found a trail heading north, up into the distant line of high ridges that he knew opened up and spilled out onto the badlands.

By noon the paint horse had come up lame. He led it on, the distant ridge line appearing no closer than when he'd started out that morning. He'd taken two white handkerchiefs from his carpetbag and made them into a head scarf to provide at least some protection from the blazing sun. When he stopped and took a sip from the canteen he saw a rider top a low rise slowly and come down toward him on a tired-looking roan, leading another horse along behind him.

His first thought was of the ranger, and a jolt of fear shot through him; but he reminded himself that the ranger would not be riding out of the north. Then he let out a breath, and though the rider had to see him, had to pass him here on the trail, he took the handkerchiefs from his head and waved them in the air.

When the rider made no offer of a response, he called out at twenty yards, "Mister, I am *more* than glad to see you!" He waited as the rider came closer without making a sound or raising a hand, or acknowledging him in any way. He cocked his head to the side, ready to turn and bolt away if need be, but bolt away to where?

The man sat there slumped a bit in his saddle with his right hand on the pistol butt at his hip. "Horse has gone lame on me," Joe Sharpe added; and he swallowed a dryness in his throat.

Still nothing from the rider, the man coming on straight and steady the way the ranger had done toward Kurtz and the Flying Cross boys.

Again fear stirred through him and he glanced around quickly at the bare open land. Nowhere to run, horse gone lame, no place to take cover. *Jesus* . . . Even if there was, then what? He watched the rider come closer, not even slowing down a step. Just the way the ranger had done the day he'd done his killing. "I'm not looking for any trouble here," he called out, hearing the pleading tone in his voice. "It's just that this horse . . ." His voice trailed.

As the horse the rider was leading swayed to the side, he caught a glimpse of a body lying across the saddle. Then he stiffened as he suddenly heard a strange sound, and saw a big buzzard rise up from the dead man's back and bat away into the air. *Holy Mother!* Then he saw the drawn wasted face on the rider. *Both of them, dead! The one in front still riding. Dead!* He saw the buzzard circle up high in a long lazy swing.

He turned slowly on the dusty trail as the rider passed, the rider's blank eyes staring ahead, his hand locked in death on his pistol butt. Joe saw the tin badge on the man's chest, saw the thick black stain that started beside the badge and reached down, all the way down his leg. Blood hung in thick black strings from the rider's boot sole.

Behind the rider the sound of flies filled the air, snarling and spinning, and the sound of them snapped Joe Sharpe to his senses. "Whooooa," he said, stepping in behind the first horse and taking hold of the reins tied to its tail. The first horse just stopped, spent and weak, the rider tilting forward and swaying there. The second horse staggered and also stopped as Joe pressed a hand on its wet neck.

He walked to the front horse, pulled the reins from the dead man's hand, pulled his stiff foot from the stirrup and hefted up on it until the man toppled over like a downed tree. Joe shuddered at the sound of the body landing with a heavy thud in the dirt. Still holding the reins, he walked around and looked down at the man, saw the paper that had fallen from his shirt pocket, and he bent down and picked it up.

He glanced up at the buzzard, saw it had been joined by another and circled with it higher up, the two of them lying adrift on an updraft of hot air, staring down at him, he figured, wondering how this newcomer played into their plans. He looked back at the dead man lying across the saddle. Well, now that he had a choice of horses, maybe some food from the dead man's saddlebags, he didn't play into their plans at all.

He unfolded the paper and saw it was a wanted poster, and before he even walked back to the body draped over the saddle he knew it was that man's likeness he held in his hand. And so it was, he saw, holding his breath, fanning aside the snarl of flies and getting a good look at the drawn blue face staring back at him through glazed eyes. A black swollen patch of skin on the corpse's neck bore two deep round puncture wounds. Snake bite. *Jesus*. A snake had killed him.

He moved back away, still holding his breath against the sour stench of death. Finally a piece of luck had come his way, luck with a buzzard picking its back. His mind started working, better than it had in days. Stench or not, this blue swollen body was just the kind of break he needed. He let out his held breath.

When he'd rested the horse and changed saddles from the undertaker's paint horse to that of the dead lawman's, Gentleman Joe dragged the blood-crusted saddle to the side, stuffed the badge and wanted poster inside his shirt, and left the lame horse standing the trail beside the stiff corpse.

He'd taken the dead man's low crowned hat and duster—no blood stains there—wiped the hat with his sweat-soaked handkerchief, and put it on. He rode off leading the horse with the wanted man's body across it, thinking of the five-hundred-dollar reward that was his once he got to a town somewhere up ahead.

In his carpetbag he had seventeen dollars, all that was left after a night of drinking and charming the whores when he should have been working the table. Well, how did he know he'd be leaving the next day? Had he stayed he would've turned the money into a nice fat roll that night, playing the aces at just the right time, just a little here and there, enough to keep taking the big pots, but not enough to raise suspicion.

He uncapped the dead lawman's canteen and threw back a shot of water. He'd stop later, up ahead when the sun lowered, and he'd go through the saddlebags for something to eat, jerked meat maybe, maybe even some coffee. This whole nightmare might turn out better than he'd dared to hope. He could cash in the reward money and get completely out of here, out and away from this part of the country. Hell, he shoulda done it sooner anyway. This was no place for him, no fit place for anybody with any sense at all, he thought.

He looked up at the buzzards—four of them now, but staying up there high and just watching—and he smiled to himself, slapped a fly from his face, and rode on. Luck had dealt him back into the game.

That night he slept with the duster thrown over him, his belly warm inside from the coffee in the lawman's saddlebags. He'd chewed a piece of hardtack and gone to sleep with the horses picketed to a low scrub piñon. Now that they headed up into the scraggly foot hills, he'd find water easy enough, and shade now, now that the land had started to change, started to give something of itself toward keeping man and animal alive. This would all work out. He knew it would.

He'd seen more and more hoofprints as he'd climbed the trail upward, somewhere up there a town, whiskey, food, reward money. Hot wind pushed in against him. He held the dead lawman's hat down on his head and let the horse move quarter-wise into it, its mane whipping and its head cocked back to one side. Things could still be better, he thought. But then again, they could be a whole lot worse. In the morning before he left, he'd have to take a pistol and shoot a hole in the corpse to hide the snake bite. But he could do that, couldn't he?

A hundred miles behind Gentleman Joe Sharpe at the edge of the desert, the ranger leaned against the wall inside the adobe church, his right hand resting on the big pistol, his gray sombrero hanging from his hand. He glanced out the window through the blazing sunlight at the two horses at the hitch rail across the street, then back to the old priest who sat behind the wooden table before him.

"Well," the ranger said. "I reckon if God really meant for his laws to be followed, he'd do a little more enforcing and a little less talking about it."

The old priest rose slowly behind the wooden table, raised a finger, and smiled. "Ah, you have given it more thought, at least." He smiled. "Each time I see you, your hands are a little more bloody, and each time, I see that you are more angry with God *and* man than the time before." He tapped his finger against his temple. "But at least you are giving it more thought. This is good."

"I ain't mad at nobody. There's just things don't set right, whether it's God's doings or man's." The ranger stared at him for a second. But instead of seeing the gentle smile of the old priest, he saw instead the faces of the dead woman and the Indian boy. Then he slid his gaze from the priest, back out the window, and saw the horses there, their manes lifted by a hot lick of breeze. Thought about it? Most of his life he'd thought about it. What good had it done?

But he wouldn't tell this old man. Instead he only nodded and said in a resolved tone, "So, if you'll just bless me, Father, and I'll be on my way."

"Ah, my son . . ." The priest sighed, stepped from around the table and over near him. He folded his hands and let the long sleeves drop over them. "You come here, not of the faith, not willing to confess your sins, not willing to bend down on your knees and humble yourself before God. Yet, always you ask God's blessing from me. Why is this?"

"All I ever seen *humble* get a man out here is a face full of dirt. You don't *want* to hear my sins. My knees don't bend easy, Father. Besides, it's not God's blessing I ask for, just *yours*."

"My blessing is worth nothing if it is not from God. I do not judge you, and I do not judge others. I see what passes on the road before me, and I do not judge." He glanced out the window himself, then back at the ranger. "All are welcome here in this house of God. Both the hunter and the hunted. Even if the madman, Montana Red, came here, he would be treated no differently than you."

"That's a *real* comforting thing to know, Father." The

ranger almost smiled at the irony of it. "But *you'll* have to answer to God for that—if there's a God—and if he really cares about answers."

"See?" Again the priest raised a finger. "You asked to be blessed by God when you are not even sure *God* exists."

"Then what does it hurt?" He glanced again through the window, then back to the old priest, and added, "Go on and bless me, padre, get me out of here."

The old priest almost smiled himself. "Then why must you have it, if you do not believe? What meaning does it have for you? What does it bring to you?"

"Let's just call it luck. Sort of like carrying a rabbit's foot or a buckeye." The ranger smiled.

The priest grimaced, shaking his head, and made a quick cross with his fingers. "Then you have *my* blessing for who you are as a human, but not for what you are as a man."

"Well, I reckon that's better than nothing. That wasn't so hard, now was it?" The ranger seemed to relax for a second, and before the priest could answer, he glanced again through the window and said, "Tell me— The man who rides that white Spanish barb with the black ring around its eye, has he been around here very long?"

"Why? Why do you ask me this?"

"Because if it's Bent Jackson, he burnt up a Cherokee family down in the nations a year back." He started to pull out the list from his shirt but the old priest laid a hand on his arm, stopping him.

"Do not tell me these things. I must close my ears to such talk as this. I know what you do, and I cannot help you. I cannot tell you anything that contributes to the cruelty man does to man—"

"So, you wouldn't even tell me if Red Hollis has been through here lately?" The ranger watched the old priest's eyes.

"That one—" The priest shook his finger slightly. "That one I would tell you about, may God forgive me." He rolled his eyes upward, then down to the ranger. "But no, he has not ridden through here. I pray he never does."

"Then maybe that's one prayer *I* can answer for *you.* I'm going on up after him."

"Please, do not tell me about it. But try to go with God all the same, my son."

"God's welcome along, if he's got the stomach for it." He heard a laugh from the boardwalk across the dirt street and he looked out at the two men stepping down to the hitch rail, one of them tall and bowed and limping. *Yep, ole Bent Jackson . . .* "Father," he said, looking at the old priest as he slipped his sombrero back on his head. "It's been good talking with you, but I got to go now. There's one of the men on my list."

"I know. Now you go to kill him. You only came in here to wait for him out of the sun."

"That's not altogether true, holy man. But it's still nice seeing you—" He glanced around the small church, at candle flames dancing on the bare altar beneath the cracked and splintered cross with its carving of Jesus nicked and scarred by the passing of time. "Always nice to visit this peaceful place." Then he turned and stepped out in the dirt.

"Bent Jackson," he called out as he walked toward the two men, steady and straight, taking off his right glove. And he stopped in the middle of the empty street with the sun at his back, took out the paper from inside his shirt, and held it up.

"Yeah, what of it?" The two men stared at him, there beside the horses, reins already in the other man's hand. The white horse's flesh quivered; his hoof scraped the dirt. Jackson took a slow step sideways toward the middle of the street.

"I gotta take you in, Bent, dead or alive. How you wanta do it?" He raised the big pistol from his holster and let it hang at his side.

"You best think about it, Ranger," said Jackson, and he flipped back his ragged duster.

"I have." He looked at the man by the horses. "You a friend of his?" The man nodded slowly. The ranger's gaze narrowed down on him. "How good a friend?"

The man dropped his reins, raised his hands cautiously, and stepped away, back onto the boardwalk, then disappeared into the open door.

Jackson chuckled. "What the hell's this about? I ain't done nothing—not lately anyway, not in your jurisdiction."

"But you might've rode through my jurisdiction on your way here."

"Well, that's the stupidest thing I ever heard of. What are you charging me with?"

"Officially? I don't know." The ranger shrugged. "Let's just call it burning up a man and his family without their permission. How's that suit you?"

"You're crazy. I never heard of such a damn charge!"

"You burnt them up didn't ya?" The ranger tapped the list against the air, shoulder level.

"Hell, I mighta, it's been over a year—"

"Didn't ask them if ya could first, did ya?"

"I don't ask nobody a *damn* thing."

"So, there you are, Bent." The ranger started walking, steady and straight, his right shoulder drooped a bit, and the big pistol swinging back and forth past his knee.

"Come on then, *Ranger!*"

The old priest made the sign of a cross as he turned from the window. He walked to the altar and kneeled and crossed himself, hearing the explosion from the street and the sound of a frightened horse calling out through the stillness that followed.

CHAPTER 6

"Running with the wrong crowd has killed more men than any disease I know of," the ranger had said to the man who'd been riding with Bent Jackson. The man's name was Frank Bacon, and the ranger told him that it was only by the slimmest benefit of a doubt that he hadn't killed him in the street beside his friend.

"I—I hardly knew him," Bacon told him. "I only rode with him this far because he said he knew this territory. If I'd known he had a hand in doing like you said he did, believe me, I'd've never thrown in with him."

The ranger looked him up and down standing there over Bent Jackson's body. Although he wasn't completely taken in by the man's line of talk or the general appearance of him, he just nodded as he reloaded his big pistol and said, "Since you hardly knew him, I don't suppose you'd mind at all if I took this white horse of his along with me?"

"Well no, of course not," the man had told him, and he went on to ask, wasn't it a custom in these parts that a man's horse went to the undertaker to pay for a decent burial? "Since I hardly knew him, I'm not gonna pay anything for burying him. Can you blame me?"

"Nope. I'll see he's buried," the ranger had said.

"Best thing you can do is cut out of here, and keep your nose clean from now on."

"You mean it?" Frank Bacon hesitated for a second, recalling how deadly the ranger was with his pistol.

"I wouldn't have said it if I didn't mean it." The ranger stared at him. Before he'd finished reloading the pistol, all that remained of Frank Bacon was a thin wake of dust settling behind a quick beat of hooves.

The ranger smiled to himself and took out his list and marked off the name *Bent Jackson* with the stroke of his pencil stub. When he'd taken on enough supplies to carry him across the badlands, the ranger picked up a bottle of rye at the rundown adobe cantina and loaded everything onto the white bard that had belonged to Bent Jackson.

"So, you have completed what you came here to do," the old priest said, padding up to him in his sandal feet and long tattered robe while the ranger led both horses away from the hitch rail. "Now you simply ride on as if it did not happen?"

"If you're asking how sorry I am for killing him, I'm *not*. No more than he was for killing that family who'd done him no earthly wrong." He walked on, staring straight ahead. "But killing *him* ain't why I came here, padre. He just happened to be on the list. I told you who I'm after."

"But he *is* why you came here, as it turns out," the old priest said, reaching out and placing a hand on the ranger's arm, stopping him in the dirt street. "This is what you do not see of yourself. Where you go, death follows, because you have made yourself a part of death. For this I must pray for your soul."

The ranger looked down at the priest's hand on his arm and when the priest drew it away the ranger smiled at him. "Is praying for me the same as giving me your blessing? Because if it is, that's all I asked you for in the first place."

"No, it is not the same." The old priest huffed and stepped back a step. "Why must you twist words that are only meant to help your soul? This in itself shows that you do not like facing what you are."

"We'll talk some more when I come back through," the ranger said, pulling the horses forward. "Maybe I'll have Red Hollis laying across a saddle by then. We'll drink to it."

"Drink to the killing of another human being." The old priest crossed himself and shook his head as the ranger moved away. Then he added, "The *comadreja* are out in great numbers. Be careful of them, my son." He swung a hand toward the badlands and the wide sleeve of his robe spilled down his arm. "If they come upon you, they will do to you what you do to others."

"They don't want no part of me," the ranger said without looking back. "If they do, I'll dance with them."

But when he'd left the town and that night made camp up in the rocks where the town stood behind him as only a black dot on the dark horizon, he thought of the old priest's warning. There were signs everywhere of the *comadrejas*, and these were bold signs of man and horse made by many riders who had given little regard to hiding themselves. For the next two days he saw the signs and on the third day saw the riders themselves.

The *comadrejas* came upon him suddenly, up in the high ridges where it was easy to lie in wait for a lone rider; and though he'd given them heavy fire from his pistol, by the end of the day's chase he stood over their handiwork with the echo of his pistol ringing in his ears. A spire of gray smoke rose above the barrel of his pistol and drifted away as if following the echo across the jagged ridge lines on the far side of the flatlands.

He holstered the big pistol and kneeled down beside the big dun horse as its last nerves twitched, quivered, then went slack, all essence and energy of the animal gone in one last gout of blood.

"Sorry, old friend," he whispered; and for a moment resting a hand on its neck, he watched a schiff of breeze lick at the dead horse's mane. "I'll make 'em account for you."

Beneath the horse's withers, the shaft of the arrow had gone deep, yet he'd had no choice but to push the animal on as more arrows whistled past him. He'd taken an arrow himself, and had ridden on, pushing hard, until he managed to get the big rifle up and fire back at them. One of them went down in a spray of dust. The others pulled back, but still they'd dogged him; and he'd ridden the dun right into the ground, gaining yard by precious yard with his rifle fire until the dun spent itself and tumbled forward with him. He hated killing a good horse. . . .

Now, he broke off the shaft of the arrow sticking from his leg and pitched it away. He stood up, shouldered his saddle, picked up the bridle and reins, and limped over to where the white barb with the black circled eye stood tied to a low scrub piñon.

"You just got promoted," he said. Then he dropped his supplies from the white horse's back and swung his saddle up on it. The horse snorted and scraped a hoof in the hot sand. Sweat had turned dust into long streaks of mud down the horse's sides. Heat from the animal pulsed against him as he stood close to it. "So here's the deal—" He yanked the cinch taut, feeling pain sear the length of his leg, then dropped the stirrup. "You get us to the water hole up ahead, and I'll keep 'em off your rump while you do it. Are you up to it?"

The horse flared its nostrils and shook out its wet mane. He ran a gloved hand down its neck. "I thought so, you black-eyed devil. If you'd work for Bent Jackson, I figure you'd work for about anybody."

He picked up the big rifle leaning against the scrub piñon and struggled up into the saddle, using his hand to raise his right leg over the horse's back. Behind him, four hundred yards, he saw the cloud of dust lift up and drift away in a wide sheet. "All right then"—he batted his boot heels to the horse, again feeling the pain slice down his leg—"let's get to it."

The white barb stretched out across the sand flats toward the rise of foothills seven miles ahead. The ranger worked the pace of the animal, checking it down to a walk every few minutes, letting it gather its wind, then booting it again with an eye on the closing rise of dust. In the last mile the horse caught the scent of water and pressed harder. Now he let it have its lead; and he wondered as he rode, if the gambler, Joe Sharpe, had run into the same band of *comadrejas* when he came this way.

If so, the ranger had seen no sign of it. He'd found the body of a man along the trail that morning. It had been worked over pretty hard by night scavengers but there was enough left for him to tell that it wasn't Joe Sharpe's. Since then, he'd come upon the camp where the gambler had spent the night—he could tell it was Sharpe by the way the man banked his fire. Maybe the gambler's luck was holding. He could've made it up into one of the towns along the edge of the badlands. *Who knows . . .*

Right now he had his hands full. The *comadrejas* had hit him no sooner than he left the campsite. They'd been on him most of the day until he dropped down to the long stretch of sandy flatland. Now it would be a different story. He figured them low on ammunition— only twice had they fired on him with pistols, and that was only after he'd drawn them down out of the gullies and ridges. Up there, they'd managed to stay close to him and hold cover, using their poison arrows on him. With each drop of the barb's hooves, he knew he would turn the tables on them.

All he needed now was to make it to the water hole. He would wait for them there, draw them in, let them think they were ready to make their kill. Then, once they got all set to siege him and wait him out, he'd make his move. Beneath him, the white barb pounded on steady and fast until he reined the horse down the last mile to let the *comadrejas* get closer. He didn't want them to lose him now.

When he reached the water hole, he dropped the saddle and cooled the horse out, walking him back and forth, watering him a little at a time by dipping his sombrero and letting the horse draw from it. The dust behind them had dropped and faded two hundred yards out at the crest of a small rise; and he laid the saddle up on a rock, adjusted it good and steady, and leaned the rifle against it.

He walked the white barb over to the edge of the water, hitched the reins to a dead fall of bleached cottonwood, and after sticking his head into the water himself, he swallowed a mouthful, slung back his wet hair, and left the horse there, twenty feet away, to catch its full water.

And he waited. . . .

A half hour passed. They were resting below the rise now, seven of them, making their plans. Once they'd cooled out their horses, they would spread along the rise, maybe test out his rifle fire, then wait for darkness. They would come in closer tonight, draw his fire, find him by the flash of his muzzle, and pelt him with arrows. Whatever ammunition they had they'd hold on to as long as they could. This would be their plan, he knew.

Once they'd killed him, they could water their horses down and go on their way. The next water hole lay a good twenty miles off, at the bottom of a thin stretch of ridgeline leading up to the foothills. They had to have *this* water, and it had never entered their minds that one man could keep them from it. In a way, stopping here would only seal his doom. That's what they would think . . . at least he hoped they'd think it.

A few more minutes passed and he took out the quill and pinned up the front of his sombrero. He took off his gloves, wiped the back of one along the rifle barrel, put them aside, and steadied the rifle across the raised saddle. By now, the sun had turned into a large red ball with arms of fire spread wide, embracing the horizon.

He trained his sight on the line where the crest of the rise met the distant sky behind it, and squeezed off a shot just to let them know he was alive and ready. He waited another full minute, scanning the rise before pushing himself to his feet and walking over to the horse with his saddle on his shoulder.

"Hope you're good and rested," he said, "it's time to

get back to work." He swung the saddle up, made the cinch, and gazed out once more toward the crest of the low rise. *Seven of them, huh?* All of them half loco drunk by now, he supposed, on the bottle of rye whiskey they'd found in his abandoned supplies. "Lousy land pirates," he added under his breath. He could've used a drink himself right now.

The *comadrejas* lay south of him. For the first fifty yards he would ride on them slow and easy, covered by the low sun's brassy glare across the water hole behind him. From there, at a distance of about one hundred and fifty yards he'd catch them by surprise and do the one thing they'd never expect him to do. He'd charge them. Why not? The white barb horse was up to it: he was up to it. *Comadrejas* weren't all that smart anyway. . . .

Joy Decker had been the first to see Joe Sharpe coming up from the low pass, south of the livery station at the far end of the dirt street. She'd studied the stranger closely, and breathed a little easier seeing the glint of a badge on his chest when he stopped at the edge of town for a second before gigging his horse forward. Now other folks had also seen him, and they stepped out onto the boardwalk as she did, each of them looking toward the stranger leading the pack horse with the body thrown over it.

Stiff legs hung down one side of the packhorse and bobbed slightly with the sway of the tired horse's steps. Flies snarled in a glistening dark cloud as the man in front gigged his mount forward. *A lawman . . .* She touched a hand to her hair and let one corner of her day shawl slip below her shoulder.

Gentleman Joe felt their eyes on him and almost

stopped again, almost felt like turning his horse and getting out of there, as what appeared to be the whole town pressed toward him along the dusty street. But it had been a week since he'd come upon the dead men. The coffee and hardtack were gone. His horse and the pack horse had both fallen gaunt in the flanks. The harsh heat had dried him inside and out—scalded his bones and drained his marrow, he thought. He had to stop here, put himself whole, or face certain death in the badlands.

Behind him, the sound of the flies seemed to make the stench swell up even stronger; yet he'd somehow managed to overcome that god-awful smell and shut out of his mind that hateful endless buzzing. After all, this bloated half-baked corpse was his ticket out of this terrible land.

For a week he'd traveled, connected to this stiff bundle of soured flesh, feeling always through the rope in his hand the weight of stiff unyielding death so close behind him. He'd breathed the same sour air that encircled his bundle of death, and death trailed him in every rise and fall of the tired horse's hooves.

In the boil of sun and wavering heat he had imagined at times that this blue rotting corpse would follow him forever—his retribution, he'd thought, for *all* sins, past and future. He fanned a band of spinning flies away from his face and reined over to a hitch rail near a bleached-out sign that read: SHERIFF'S OFFICE. Across the bottom of the sign, three different names had been covered with whitewash, the whitewash baked away and faded now, and the names coming forth through it like dark omens.

"Are you—are you a lawman?" He stepped down from his horse, and at the sound of the voice, turned, looking into the gathering faces as they drew from the storefronts along the dusty street.

"Of course he's a lawman," said another voice. "Can't ya see his badge?"

He took a breath to calm himself, seeing in an instant what the glint of a badge could do for a man. But before answering, he weighed his words with care. Would being a lawman affect his receiving the reward money? He glanced back and forth at the eyes of the townsfolk, then reached up and unclipped the dead lawman's badge from his chest and dropped it into his pocket. "No," he said, "I left law work over a month ago. Just haven't had a chance to turn in my badge yet."

The old sheriff stepped forward, looking him up and down. "Never seen ya before, young man. What part of the territory did ya ride?"

"All over," Sharpe said. "My name's Joe Elliot." He glanced around, pulling out the folded wanted poster and spreading it out between his hands. "That's Felton McRoy's body back there. I'm claiming the reward on him, five hundred dollars if I'm not mistaken."

The townsfolk stepped along with him, the old sheriff close at hand, as he walked deeper into the sound of flies and the powerful stench. Then they gasped and pressed back a step as he fanned at the swirling ball of flies until it broke up and spun away in the air. Eyes grew wide at the sight of the blue rotting face. A woman gasped.

"He's kilt Fast Felton!" said a voice in the crowd.

"Deader'n hell!" said another. And for a second the whole town stood looking at him, some fifteen or more people, all of them with their mouths dropped open and their eyes in awe. He felt a weakness in his knees, and needed a drink to settle him. A silence passed. Not a sound on the street, except the snarl of the flies.

Then, after a second, "Well . . . my goodness! Where are our manners? If no one else is going to welcome Marshal Elliot, I surely am." Joy Decker stepped forward and extended her hand palm down, as if she'd just been asked to dance there in the dusty street. "You'll have to pardon us. We've so long waited for someone like you to come along, I daresay we wonder if you're *real*, Marshal Elliot." She tossed a glance across the others and back to him. "On behalf of those of us who—"

"Excuse me, ma'am. But it's not *Marshal* anymore," Joe Sharpe said, cutting her off, for some reason feeling a little crowded by the way she'd said the word, by the way the townsfolk stared at him. "It's just Mr. Elliot now." He smiled as he took her hand, and felt that extra ever-so slight squeeze before she turned loose. "Or, just Joe if you please." Her eyes lingered on his for that extra second, and he'd learned long ago what that extra second suggested.

"And I'm Sheriff Turner," said the old sheriff, smiling a tired smile. "I'm the law here, such as I am, for the time being anyway." He shook Joe Sharpe's hand, shrugging, then dropping his shoulders as if in a subtle act of submission. "I hope there's enough money in our Territory Fund to pay ya this reward. We've run short of funds lately."

"Now, now, Sheriff Turner. If there's not, I'm sure we can work the difference up among us," said a clerk, stepping close to him with his thick hand extended. "The main thing is, we've got ourselves a *real* lawman here at last."

Now the whole gathering pressed closer to him, *too*

close, he thought, and he stepped back feeling a rush of heat sweep through him. He nearly swayed, and he raised his hands slightly at his sides. The old sheriff took note of it and stepped between Sharpe and the townsfolk.

"All right now," Sheriff Turner said. "Let's all step back and give Marshal Elliot room to breathe here. Go on now—" He shooed them back with weathered hands. "Can't ya see the man's worn-out, riding God knows *how long* with this corpse stinking to high heaven."

"He's an answer to our prayers," called a voice from the crowd. Joe Sharpe cut a quick glance toward the sound of the voice, but the owner of the voice was lost somewhere in the faces surrounding him. "Here here!" Another voice called out, "Now we stand a fighting chance."

But a few feet back behind the crowd, Ray Gilliam stood watching, getting a good, close look at this man's eyes. They weren't the eyes of a lawman—not like any lawman he'd ever seen, and he'd seen his share. A lawman's eyes always searched a crowd as if deciding who in it was right and who was wrong. But not this man's. This man's eyes avoided the faces, as if at any second someone might step forward with some accusation against him.

And this man did not have the bearing of a man who made his living carrying a gun. This man struck him more as a rounder and a dude, a gambler maybe. Yet there was Felton McRoy's body, he couldn't deny that; and everybody knew that Felton McRoy was a stone-cold killer, one of the few gunmen—perhaps the *only* one—who'd ever stood his ground with Red Hollis and lived to tell about it. Now this man had killed him? *Killed Felton McRoy?* He couldn't help but question it.

Maybe he was being too leery of the man. Maybe he'd been without hope so long, he couldn't see it if it had truly arrived. Since the day he'd seen how Montana Red Hollis had looked at little Myra, terrible pictures came to his mind. Before he trusted his life, the life of the town, and more importantly *his daughter's* life to this man, he had to be sure of him.

Through Ray Gilliam's thoughts he heard the man tell the rest of the townsfolk, "But I'm no longer a marshal . . ." Then he heard Joy Decker say something, then the sheriff; and he watched the man, studying him, seeing how he handled himself, how he handled the pressing crowd. A rounder? A dude? A gambler? Maybe, he thought. The man dressed like a gambler come upon hard times. Why couldn't the rest of them see it? Or did they see it and not want to see it?

He looked the man over once more and came to a decision. Whatever doubts he had about this man, he'd keep them to himself for now. He wouldn't mention it to the townsfolk. For now this man would become the law if the town had any say in the matter; and whether he be lawman, mugger, bugger, or thief, when the time came, Ray Gilliam wouldn't care. When Montana Red Hollis came to take little Myra—and he knew that time would come—he would put this man's life between his daughter and the outlaw without a second thought. Meanwhile he'd stay close to this *Marshal* Joe Elliot and watch his every move. *Marshal, my arse* . . . He spit and ran a hand across his black furrowed brow.

CHAPTER 7

Fifty yards out, the ranger stopped the white barb and looked back over his shoulder at the water hole. In the sharpness of the evening sun's glare, the water hole became a dancing puddle of fiery brass that bit into his eyes. The image of it scorched itself into his vision and stayed with him after he turned away. He rubbed his eyes for a second until the red veil that covered them turned dark, then dissipated.

"That's how they're seeing you and me now," he said, patting the horse's sweaty neck as he scanned the crest. "Do some good here and it'll make up for all the *wrong* you did beneath Bent Jackson." He tightened his knees to the horse, chucked the reins taut, and felt the animal collect himself up and step sideways, high-hoofed, waiting for the boot heels to bat him forward. A pistol shot rang out; a puff of gray smoke rose and drifted.

"Get 'em, Black-eye!" He yanked the reins hard, high to the left, spinning the horse in place, raising a cover of dust around them, the horse snorting, nearly rearing. Its poll raised like a dog's hackles, its mane flurried as it spun. The horse's breath blew hot across his leg, slinging spittle on him; and as he straightened it, giving it his boot heels, he snatched the rifle out from across his lap.

They shot forward from within their rise of dust, and when he felt the white barb stretched out, bellied down in its wide open run, he spun the slack of the reins around the saddle horn and let the horse fly through the hot arid sand. His rifle bobbed in his hand to the beat of the horse's hooves, his arm cocked out to the side, using the big weapon for balance.

The pain in his leg gave way to the fury of the ride as he drew the big pistol, cocking it and leveling it at one of the figures who rose up to meet him along the crest of the rise. His big pistol bucked, and the figure blew backward as soon as it rose up. He saw the gun fly from its hand; and he recocked his big pistol as it came back down from the recoil, leveling instinctively on another of the ragged *comadrejas*. At fifty yards an arrow whistled past him, then another, and another.

The pistol bucked again. This time two of the men had mounted and charged up over the rise. The first one flew backward off his horse. The second one's horse veered, then crumbled and rolled in a spray of sand dust. A pistol shot kicked up a clump of ground near his horse's pounding hooves. By now he and the white barb were angled up, topping the rise, hearing beyond the crest the sound of horses, of men yelling in Spanish and broken English, and of pistol fire and arrows hissing in the air like deadly snakes.

A bullet sliced through his loose duster sleeve under his arm. Now the barb topped the rise and checked down its wide open gate, sliding quarter-wise as it slowed, then backpedaling down the long slope, kicking up a swirl of sand. He fired, side to side with the big pistol, cocking it at the end of each recoil and let-

ting the hammer fall. The men fell back on either side
of him, snatching at their reins, trying to mount as
their horses shied and tried to bolt from the explosion
of gunfire.

Then he was past them, had broken through their
line along the rise, and when the horse felt the lower,
more solid sand beneath its hooves, it lunged forward
back into its run. An arrow sliced across the horse's
rump and stuck low beneath the saddle cantle with a
hard thud. The ranger checked the horse down again
fifty yards from the *comadrejas* and spun it, looking
back at the men who had managed to settle their
horses enough to mount them. They'd bottomed out
beneath the rise and gigged their horses toward him.
The horses had stood the afternoon without water.
Now, he knew, they would spend themselves out on
the sand flats.

He batted his boots to the white barb's sides and
rode another hundred yards, hearing them yelling behind him. No gunfire though. They wouldn't waste
precious ammunition. They'd wait until they got close
enough to make it count. *Here's the part they ain't gonna
believe . . .*

He reined the white barb hard, sliding it down on its
rear haunches, turning it sharp in a rise of dust.

As the barb straightened, he slipped the pistol into
his holster and batted the horse forward, again giving
it its lead and settling himself into the pounding
rhythm of its hooves. When he felt the horse stretched
out beneath him, when the sway of the animal was
fully joined to the sway of the man, and when the two
of them no longer pounded across a rippling sand flat,
but rather slid as one across a ribbon of silk, he reached
down in his lap and brought the big rifle up into play.

There were only three of them now. They reined and slid and circled close together. Confused, he figured . . . wondering where it had all gone wrong on them. He was supposed to run *from* them! He was never supposed to break through them. Now that he had, he must be a fool to turn and charge them *again.* They looked at one another, spinning there atop their worn horses, this lone rider coming at them as if leading an army.

"De hell he is doin'?"

For a split second their eyes flashed across one another. Then one of them yelled, "Hyiii!" turning his horse. He used his pistol barrel, slapping it behind him against the tired horse's rump. The other two turned and followed, the three of them racing toward the water hole now, the madman bearing down on them with a big rifle. Behind them, a loud shot exploded and one of them sailed away with half his neck missing, his head slung to one side at a sharp angle. A shimmering coil of blood trailed behind him and whipped into a spraying circle as he struck the ground, rolling, leaving a wake of dust.

"Shoot him, damn it!" One of them yelled at the other, then kept riding hard without looking back.

"Shoot heem jourself!" The other yelled in reply, laying low on the tired horse, kicking it hard but losing ground to the big wild-looking white barb with the black-circled eye. The barb was watered, rested, and well grazed, pumping toward them, full energy, seeming to have joined into the sport of the chase. The one in the lead didn't look back when the big rifle fired again. But he heard the scream, heard the horse and rider go down; and he ducked his head, still whipping his horse with his pistol until he'd topped the crest of the rise and pounded on toward the water hole.

The ranger checked the barb down to an easy gait, circled west, putting the sun behind him, and rode up fifty yards from the water hole. He sat the horse still, watching the last of the *comadrejas* dip water up to his mouth with one hand while he held the pistol in the other and glanced toward him, searching for him in the harsh glare of evening sunlight. Beside the *comadreja*, the horse drew water with its cinch loosened until the man looked out toward the ranger one more time and snapped off two quick shots, his hand up, shielding his eyes. "Ged out of here, you sonoba beetch!"

The barb flinched, but the ranger settled it and smiled, looking back at the man who fanned the gun back and forth as if warning him away. The ranger took out a cigar from inside his duster, lit it, and watched the man mount up and gig the horse off past the water hole toward a distant stand of jagged rock three miles across the sand flats. Then he worked the cigar to one corner of his mouth and chucked the white barb forward at a walk.

He let the man drift forward a hundred yards, waited until he stepped down off the tired horse, and started leading it, glancing back with his pistol hanging in his right hand as he searched for him in the brassy swirl. Then the ranger stepped down himself, kneeled with a boot on the barb's reins, leveled the rifle out across his knee, and punched a hole in the *comadreja's* right shoulder, high up, just above the joint.

The man spun, dropping to his knees as his horse reared and pulled sideways. His pistol fell to the ground. But he held on to the reins and dragged himself up, hooking his left hand in a stirrup. In a moment he'd worked his way up the horse's side and managed to throw himself up into the saddle. He slumped, nearly falling, then righted himself and rode on, swaying, the tired horse swaying as well.

"Now *this* is the proper way to dog a man," the ranger said, speaking to the barb in a low voice and rubbing the horse's neck with his gloved hand.

He looked around at the wide basin skirted on all sides by the upturn of jagged rock, dotted with short clumps of pale green, and with taller, paler bundles of brush fighting to keep its life roots sunk in the burning sand. At last the sand would claim it, wrench it from its roots and send it spinning off forever in the wind.

He sighed, lifted his sombrero, ran a hand back across his damp hair, and watched the distant *comadreja* struggle toward the far side of the basin where black holes full of shadow stretched long across the floor. The pain pulsed in his leg and he winced from it. Seemed like it never got any easier, crossing these badlands.

A week had passed, and what a week it had been. Joe Sharpe stared out through the dusty window, watching the morning sun glisten in the distant branches of high swaying pine and spruce. He ran a finger across the windowpane and rubbed it against his thumb. He'd talk to them about cleaning this place up a little, he thought. He turned, looking around at the battered desk covered with dust, chewed scraps of paper, mouse droppings.

On a rusty wood stove sat a coffeepot too stained and grimy to use. After all, they couldn't expect a person to live in this squalor. He bet Sheriff Turner hadn't spent a day here in the past six months. But then, why should he? He had a shack out behind the mercantile store . . . he was temporary anyway.

He looked around again. Some curtains wouldn't be bad. Nothing fancy—just something to keep out the afternoon sun. He'd mention it. And while he was at it, maybe—*Wait a minute.* What was he thinking? He stopped and ran a hand across his chin. This was no place for him, not for long anyway. For a minute there he was getting caught up into something. He couldn't do that.

Sure it had been a week, no sign of trouble for him, no wild-eyed Montana Red Hollis riding down from the high ridges in the north, no pistol-wielding ranger riding in from the south. His luck was holding, but it could change any second out here. The ranger was out there somewhere, and sooner or later he'd come. Some warm morning while he wasn't expecting it, he'd look out this same window, and just like before, there'd be the sombrero, the big pistol. . . .

He shook the picture from his head, walked over to the fresh pot of coffee he'd brought over from Joy Decker's place and poured a cup. Just thinking about the ranger unsettled him a bit, and after a sip of coffee, he reached into the desk drawer, took out a bottle of rye, and tipped a shot into the cup. *Just a dab. Just to take the edge off . . .*

What these folks didn't know wouldn't hurt them. They'd been good to him—gone out of their *way* making him welcome here—but they hadn't been completely honest about why they wanted him to stay on here so bad. He'd been here nearly three days before Sheriff Turner just happened to mention in the course of conversation that, "Yeah ole Red Hollis keeps a place north of here, somewhere up in the ridges yonder." Then he'd watched Sharpe's eyes to see how he took it, and he'd added, "Suppose you know about ole Red, huh?"

Joe Sharpe took the metal flask from inside his coat pocket, filled it from the bottle of rye, and put it away. Who'd Turner think he was fooling? Wasn't the first time somebody tried to work a game on him.

Sharpe had kept his eyes calm and level, and said, "Every lawman knows about ole Montana Red." Calling him *"Ole"* Red, the way Turner just had, as if the term somehow pulled the fangs from a rattlesnake's mouth. "Played poker with him some weeks back. Won a few dollars off him. He's never impressed me much. Never had any trouble with him." Then he'd smiled, putting a little extra chin into it. "Won't have, so long as he keeps his nose clean . . ."

He chuckled thinking about it. Turner's eyes had widened, but then he'd caught himself, played it down, and said, "Well then. Folks'll be glad to hear that. We had a little trouble out of *ole* Red a while back . . ." *A little trouble? My God!* Joy Decker had told him what had happened over dinner, and she'd only told him then because word had gotten back to her that this young lawman, *Big* Joe Elliot, was not a man to take lightly.

Joy Decker. Now there was a hot one. Already fixing him meals, keeping him in coffee, *good cigars*, wanting to stick to him like flowered wallpaper if he'd let her. And maybe he should. . . . He sipped again and looked out through the window, catching a glimpse of the colored girl, Ray Gilliam's daughter, rolling a hoop along the boardwalk outside of Decker's Mercantile. A man could do a lot worse than Joy Decker. She'd been widowed over a year, ran a nice, clean business, probably kept a few dollars shoved back somewhere.

Yep, she was ready for the taking, he thought. Nothing had happened between them yet, but he knew it was there, knew she was ready anytime he made the move. *A fine-looking woman. A few years older, but . . .* He gazed out past the town toward the mountain line higher up, streaked in sunlight, but still capped in a silver morning mist. Where would a man like Hollis live up there? How long before he came down here again?

Old Sheriff Turner hadn't come out and asked the real question that was on his mind—was *Big Joe Elliot* as afraid of Red Hollis, as anybody else in their right mind would be? "No," he said, answering the question to himself, studying the mountains and the many miles that lay from here to there. He wasn't afraid of *Ole* Red, so long as he could see him coming from two miles off, grab the fastest horse in town, and run until he ran out of road.

Thinking that way, he caught a glimpse of all the townsfolk gathered around him, their trusting eyes on him, looking at him as though he were some holy figure come to save them from sudden perish. He felt a little twinge of guilt, picturing those same faces and imagining what they would think of him once they found out what he really was, just a two-bit gambler, a hustler, a man on the run, one step ahead of the law.

He threw back a longer sip of laced coffee to get it off his mind. *Forget it.* Someday they would know he was a fake. They were bound to. So why even think about it? A week earlier he'd thought his luck had ran out. But look at him. He'd somehow managed to land on his feet coming here. All he had to do was keep his chin up and play this hand that had been dealt him. He could do it.

He sat the empty cup on the windowsill and ran a hand down the breast of his new black linen suit coat, feeling the wallet there, the three hundred and eighty dollars in it—all the cash in the Territorial Fund, Sheriff Turner had told him. "But don't worry about the rest. We're getting it up amongst ourselves . . ."

Well, he *wouldn't* worry about, he thought. He'd brought in the wanted man, a dead outlaw with a price on his head. What good could it have done anybody for the five hundred dollars to lay out there until the coyotes picked the man's bones clean? He took the wallet from his pocket and stashed it under the edge of the desk for safekeeping, picked up his new long oval Stetson, put it on, and adjusted it. Smoothing both hands back along the firm, clean brim, he patted the flask of rye inside his coat and left the dusty sheriff's office with his new tan riding duster draped over his arm.

On his way along the boardwalk, eyes lifted toward him. Faces smiled. Merchants stopped sweeping the walk in front of their stores long enough to raise a hand and smile and tell him *Morning, Sheriff.* And he nodded and tapped a finger to his hat brim as he walked along.

The day he'd arrived the whole town seemed to be sinking in a sea of dust. Now, although dust still bellowed in as predictable as sunlight, with constant effort on the part of the townsfolk the town stood clean and bright. The people had been without hope, some of the few remaining merchants ready to pack up their inventory and move on, the way most of the others had.

The town existed on the trade of the Bradshaw silver mines some forty miles west, higher up in the mountains. At one time there had been mines as close as two miles out, but as the silver played out, the smaller mines closed, until the only holdings left were the string belonging to the Bradshaw Mining Company.

A few independent prospectors still searched the rock canyons, but knowing the threat of Red Hollis being so closeby, both they and the Bradshaw miners had been traveling thirty miles farther out of their way to pick up supplies and catch up on their gambling and drinking. Now that word was getting out about the new sheriff in town, the miners were drifting back, slowly but surely. Sharpe smiled, gazing ahead as he walked toward the ragged miners' tent thrown up in the alley beside the saloon.

"Howdy, Sheriff Elliot," said a bleary-eyed miner from inside the open fly of the tent.

Joe Sharpe only nodded as he passed. Then, pointing a finger back at an empty whiskey bottle in the dirt outside the tent, he said, "Don't leave a mess. We like to keep a clean town here."

"Sure thing, Sheriff." He heard the voice add as he stepped up on the boardwalk and to the saloon doors, "Clifford, that's your bottle out there . . . sheriff says pick it up. Now go on and do it."

Inside the saloon, the black man, Ray Gilliam, looked up from stacking a row of beer mugs. Joe Sharpe swung off his Stetson, walking over, and laid it on the bar top. "Morning, Ray. Looks like your business is starting to pick up," he said, nodding in the direction of the tent outside.

"Yes, Sheriff. Can I get you something?" Gilliam

spoke, avoiding Sharpe's eyes and not returning his smile.

"Nothing, thanks. It's a little too early for me." Sharpe watched him pick up a rag and wipe the bar top, looking busy, doing something to keep from seeming rude, but at the same time trying to ignore him, he thought. What was it with this man? Sharpe had been the one to suggest to the townsfolk that Gilliam run the bar until someone kin to the deceased owners came to claim it. Who knew when that might be. Meanwhile he'd given this man a chance to make something for himself. Gilliam knew it; you'd think he could be a little more appreciative. . . .

"So, how's things going for you?" Sharpe spoke, glancing around at the clean saloon, every wooden table polished, every chair in place leaning against the tables. He wanted this man's confidence, his respect for some reason; yet for some reason he sensed it wasn't there. From the first moment they'd met, he felt as if this man could see straight through him—knew he was a fraud, and any second might expose him. He'd thought that setting him up running the saloon would help. So far it didn't seem to. "Anything I can do to help you out?"

"You've been more than generous, Sheriff," Gilliam said, his tone of voice friendly but flat. He busied himself wiping a shot glass with the bar rag. A silence passed, then, rather than appear unfriendly, he added for the sake of conversation, "They asked when we're going to open the gaming table." He nodded toward the green-felt-topped table in the corner. "These boys like their gambling, faro, poker, or what have you." He shrugged and gazed away.

"Gambling, huh?" Sharpe smiled, also looking over

at the table. "Well now, we'll just have to get a game of stud poker going for them, as soon as we find ourselves a good honest dealer. Who knows, I might even deal a little myself . . . just to help out of course."

"Of course," Ray Gilliam said. Now as he spoke, his eyes came up and met Sharpe's for the first time. Sharpe caught the slight turn in his tone of voice, an accusation of some kind; and he almost drew away from the man's gaze. But he caught himself and held his eyes steady, the same way he'd done a thousand times when someone's eyes had questioned him— tried to call his bluff.

"That's right," he said. "I've played my share of poker." He held Gilliam's gaze. "You see any problem with that?"

Gilliam's gaze held firm, searching Sharpe's for any waver, any flinch of uncertainty. When none came, he turned his gaze down slightly and wiped the shot glass. "No, Sheriff, none at all. I'm just happy to run the place . . . get a chance to make something for myself."

"Good." Sharpe patted the bar with his left palm and swept up his hat with his right. "I want you to know that I'm behind you one hundred percent, Ray. I like to see a man do well for himself. Hope you feel the same way."

"I do." Ray Gilliam laid the shot glass aside. "This town has been good to me and my daughter. We've been here four years. My woman's buried here. I would never do anything to let these folks down." He paused for a second, bringing his dark eyes back to Sharpe's. "Nor would I stand back and watch somebody do something that might cause them harm."

There it was, he couldn't ignore it. The implication

was too strong for him to let it pass. Sharpe stood silent for a second, then said, "Maybe I will have a drink after all." He nodded at the long handle on the beer tap. "How about a mug of beer?"

"Sure thing." They watched each other as Gilliam drew a tall mug of beer and sat it in front of him. Sharpe stared down at the spill of white foam, lifted the mug, and drank from it. When he lowered the mug, he slid it back an inch with his fingertips and lifted his eyes back to Gilliam's. He said, "Ever since I came to town, you've watched me like I'm about to steal something, Gilliam. Now whatever's on your mind, spit it out and get it all said while there's just the two of us here." He leveled his shoulders back as he spoke, giving it his best gambler's stare—Gentleman Joe, calling the hand.

"All right then, I will." Ray Gilliam spread his big hands along the bar, took a breath and let it out. "I don't trust you, *Sheriff,* Big Joe Elliot—I haven't since I first laid eyes on you. I don't think you're really a lawman, and I don't think you killed that outlaw. I think you're building this town up for a big letdown, is what I think."

"You don't know what you're—"

Gilliam raised a hand, cutting him off. "I'm just a colored man, Sheriff, but you asked, so I'm telling you. I don't know who you really are . . . but you came at a time when this town was dying. Red Hollis and his bunch has just about killed it. You've got everybody all excited, feeling safe, feeling real good about things again—bringing back business. And that's good."

Gilliam paused, leaning forward against the back of the bar, studying Sharpe's eyes. "But what are you gonna do when that monster rides in here? Hunh? You

gonna try taking him down, like all them other lawmen did—get yourself killed? You ready to go that far,
playing your little game?"

"You're *way* out of line, Gilliam," Sharpe said, feeling the sting of his words, but playing it strong, not
about to let this man call his bluff. "You're forgetting
I'm the one who got you behind this bar, who put in
the good word for you—"

"That's right." He cut him off again. "And we both
know why. You couldn't stand the way I watched your
every move, always wondering what I was thinking
about you. For some reason you thought you needed
to win the *colored man* over, *Sheriff*." He spread a narrow smile.

"You're wrong. I thought you were the best man for
the job."

"Sure you did." Gilliam straightened up, spreading
his big hands. "But don't worry . . . you won me over.
I won't say anything, not unless I see you're about to
bring harm to these people. I'll sell the whiskey, wipe
the bar, laugh at the same ole jokes. And I'll keep my
head down and my mouth shut. It'll be our little se-
cret." He raised a thick black finger and lowered his
voice. "But the minute Montana Red Hollis comes riding in. If you think you're gonna disappear and leave
all these people at his mercy—you better think again,
Sheriff, Big Joe Elliot. You've made some *promises* here."

Suddenly the room grew small around him. He
needed to swallow the dryness in his throat. But he
dared not. Doing so would show weakness, betray his
bluff; and yet he dared not reach for his beer for fear
his hand would not be steady. He dared not speak
without first knowing the strength of his voice. He
only stared at Gilliam for a second, a firm, confident

stare before moving his gaze away. Slowly he turned and took a step toward the door. Then he swallowed the dryness, stopped, turn around halfway to the door, and looked back as if in afterthought.

"Think what you will," he said. "It just happens that I'm on my way right now . . . heading out to look for Red Hollis. If I find him and he offers any trouble, I'll bring him back, *facedown*, like I've done all the others."

As Joe Sharpe spoke he noticed Ray Gilliam's eyes widen slightly, gazing past him. Behind him he heard the ring of a spur and the scuff of a boot; and he saw the shadow fall past him onto the rough wooden floor. "Well now," a voice said behind him from the other side of the bat wing doors. The door hinges squeaked. "Should I be in fear for my life, coming here?" The voice was low and menacing and carried in it something dark and cold, as cold as the updraft from an open grave.

Joe Sharpe turned slowly in place and looked into the sun-hardened eyes of the outlaw . . . Montana Red Hollis.

PART 3

---•---

Stakes of the Game

CHAPTER 8

Well. There just went his luck, Joe Sharpe thought, standing in the middle of the floor, knowing there was no way in the world he could turn and run fast enough to keep from catching a bullet in his back. He sweated beneath his hat brim. He was dead and he knew it. His hands hung useless at his sides, filled with some heavy substance that would not move no matter how hard his mind commanded. But that didn't really matter because right then his mind was incapable of forming such commands.

All question of fate resolved itself and settled hard in his stomach. At last, here was what death looked like; death stepping in slow through a set of creaking bat wing doors, out of the glare of sunlight, staring at him from beneath a dust-streaked hat brim. Here came death—no way to stop it.

Montana Red Hollis stopped, less then six feet from him, with the thud of a dusty boot and a lingering ring of silver spur. The outlaw's eyes burned into him, his thumbs hooked above his thick studded belt, and he spoke in a quiet tone, gazing at Joe Sharpe's badge.

"Well, I be *kicked*," he said, "if it ain't another of these law-toters, come to sink a tooth in me." He smiled but it was not a smile of any human form. There was animal madness a-swirl in his eyes and his tight smile only emphasized it.

"Montana Red Hollis." Joe Sharpe heard himself say the name. His own voice sounded foreign to him. Never had he sensed a spot on earth as small and tight as the spot where he now stood. In the passing beat of a second, he knew that big pistol would flick up from its holster too quick for him to even see. It would belch forth a blast of fire, and whatever Joe Sharpe ever was or might've been would stop right here, on the rough plank floor, never to stir again.

"I most certainly am *Montana Red*," the outlaw said, and his right hand moved down from his belt and spread near the butt of his pistol. "If you're looking for me . . . you found me."

Sharpe's odds on living were long, and he knew it. Yet even then something stirred inside him. Somewhere deep in his gambler's soul, something spoke to his senses, saying that *this* before him was the game all gamblers reach for their whole life through. Here was the highest of stakes, the prime pot, the bet on which all other bets rested. The stand of a lifetime in a lifetime of chance. And with a hard single beat of his heart, he rose to it. He cleared his mind of all trivial thought to living and dying, and prepared to make his final play.

"That's right, Montana Red," Sharpe said. "You just saved me a ride. I'm the new sheriff here, *Joe Elliot*." He bored his eyes into Red's, a pair of duces forcing back a full house. He wondered if Red recognized him from the gaming tables a few weeks ago, but he dared not ask himself if this bluff was going to work. To question himself now would betray himself, would cause his eyes to show the doubt that trembled there, only one flinch beneath their clear surface.

"This town had hired me to straighten you out, once and for all. You've caused your last problem here." *Here goes* . . . Joe Sharpe drew back his coat with a steady hand and let the butt of his pistol stand free. "I'm here to kill you, Red . . . if I have to."

Montana Red Hollis only stared, the same tight smile beneath the same eyes full of madness, while the man's voice went on, saying that he hoped he wouldn't have to, but that the town would take no more of Red's killing sprees. . . .

Who was this man? This Sheriff Joe Elliot? He'd seen him before, somewhere recent, but without the badge. As Joe Sharpe spoke on—Red Hollis hearing his voice, not paying much attention to it—Red saw beyond him at the bar the bartender with his dark eyes looking real determined, one hand down out of sight. *A shotgun under there?* Sure there was, Red thought. He caught a glimpse of the holster and pistol on the sheriff's hip. *Hurley Yates's shooting rig? Ole Hurley's gun hanging there?*

Yep, it sure is; and now it came to him who this man was—the laughing gambler he'd played stud poker with three weeks back! Now what was this fool trying to do here? "So, lawman . . . you're gonna shoot me down? Right here? All over this clean floor?" His hand drew back up to his belt and hooked there. "Without giving me a chance to mend my ways, say my prayers, or nothing else?"

The outlaw's words staggered Joe Sharpe, Sharpe making a desperate play and not really thinking it might work. But his bluff had worked! Hadn't it? Gambler that he was, he felt the breath of luck caress his heated brow—*Yep, it had*—and he composed himself, and said like any man would who understood the turn of a card of the roll of dice, "Like I told you, Red. Killing ain't something I enjoy doing. But you've forced us to it here. If you can't abide our law you've got to stay away."

Red eased back a step, staring at Sharpe but seeing past him the black bartender's arm, tense, his shoulder stooped a bit. Red was no fool, and he was sure in no hurry. He could kill this gambler anytime. "I understand, Sheriff," he said, raising a hand in a cautious show of peace. "I only came here to see if there was any charge agin me . . . for involving myself in that shoot-out the other day."

Jesus . . . Joe Sharpe felt his heart fall back into place. He couldn't believe it—couldn't believe he'd pulled it off. He was alive and *still* in the game! Maybe he was tougher than he thought. "I heard about the shoot-out," he said. "Are you saying it wasn't your fault?" There was no way he could trust this man's words, but for now it didn't matter. For now, all he wanted was to let the pressure off a little, get past this point and at his first chance put himself astride a fast horse and kick this place into the distance. He let go a breath.

"That's the truth, Sheriff," Red said, raising his brow slightly, starting to take some sort of strange delight in his little ruse. "They got to fighting something awful— the bartender and his Mexican wife—next thing I know me and my partner was in the heat of it. I started shooting in fear for my life."

He managed a glimpse past the sheriff and back to the black bartender—*probably some kin to the little brown girl*—and saw the man's expression hadn't changed at all. The bartender just stared, his hand still under the bar. "That's the gospel truth, Sheriff. If there's a Bible handy, I'll put my palm on it."

Joe Sharpe took a step back, turning, and looked back to Ray Gilliam behind the bar. "That's what he told Sheriff Turner the day it happened," Gilliam said, his black brow standing beaded with sweat, his eyes fixed on Red Hollis as he spoke. "There's no *living* witness to say otherwise, unless it's his partner, Bert Clemens. I wouldn't count on him."

Red smiled a little, this time putting a little turn of his head into it. "No . . . ole Bert won't say much one way or the other. But if my word ain't good enough, I'm real disappointed in you people's lack of faith. I came here in goodwill." He spread his hands.

Gilliam felt his heart pounding in his chest, fighting the urge to raise the shotgun and put an end to this monster here and now. How fast *was* Montana Red Hollis? Gilliam felt his hand tighten on the shotgun beneath the bar. *Do it, man! Do it! Just one swing. One shot, and it'd all be over!* Could he swing it up, get a shot off? It would put his daughter out of harm's way. *Or would it?* What if he didn't kill Red? What if Montana Red killed him instead? Then what would become of his little girl? He swallowed hard. *Can't risk it . . .*

Red Hollis had seen the killing urge in the bartender's eyes. Now he'd just seen it pass; and he eased forward, stepping wide of the sheriff, *Sheriff Joe Elliot*—ha, and in a slow cautious manner said as he drifted to the bar, "So then . . . having cleared my *good name*, is anybody opposed to me having a couple of snorts, just to prove I'm sociable?"

Joe Sharpe watched him move to the bar. He'd won something here, hadn't he? Gentleman Joe taking a hand of some sort? Now here it came. Time to push it

just a little farther, see how it stuck. "Afraid not, Red,"
he called out in his best lawman tone. "Not today.
There's too much tension between you and this town.
You've got to go."

Red Hollis turned toward the bar, fire sweeping into
his eyes for just a second. Joe Sharpe saw it, and
added, "Let's let things settle here for a few days. If the
town sees you're serious about settling yourself
down . . . then you'll be welcome back. Fair enough?"
Jesus! He hoped so.

Red's eyes cooled. He forced another smile,
shrugged, looked back and forth between the two
men, and said, "Well, whatever you say, Sheriff Elliot.
But do you see any harm in me picking up some cabin
rye? It gets powerful lonely where I live."

Something in the outlaw's eyes told Sharpe not to
push it any farther. He glanced at Ray Gilliam. "Stand
him up a few bottles, Ray, for *the road*. After all, we
can't deny a man his whiskey, can we?"

Red chuckled and raised a finger. "Now see there. I
knew the second I laid eyes on you that you was an *all-
right* lawman." He spread a broad grin beneath his
rust-tangled beard—*you're one dead gambler!* "Given a
little time," he added, "I've faith we'll all get back on
friendly terms here."

While Red Hollis paid for his bottles of rye, Joe
Sharpe stood there, his eyes steady and fixed, and
somehow *willed* his face not to sweat; yet he felt the
long cold trickles run down his spine and pool at the
small of his back. Gentleman Joe, his cards on the
table, his arms spread on a field of green felt somewhere, the pot within his reach. In a second he'd circle
his arms around it and pull it in. God! He was good!

His chest stood wet against his shirt, clinging to it.

But he didn't so much as flinch when Red passed him again, tipping his dusty hat as he walked out in a fall of heavy boots and a ring of spurs. Only when Sharpe heard the click of the hooves fade off down the dirt street did he turn to Ray Gilliam and feel the room sway and tilt around him. He wanted to slump and shed himself of the tightness in his back, his legs, his mind. But he wouldn't. Not just yet. Not seeing Gilliam's eyes on him, no different from before.

He only stared at Gilliam, still standing rigid and silent until after a second Ray Gilliam eased and let go a tense breath and raised his hand from beneath the bar and ran it back over his wet brow. "Lord have mercy," Gilliam whispered.

"I seen it! Seen it with my own two eyes!" Turner's voice cried out from the doors. Joe Sharpe almost reeled at the sound of it. Turner stepped inside, his hands raised as if come upon by some religious reckoning. "Lord, Lord! He backed that killer down without batting an eye!" At the door heads leaned and peeped inside as Turner stood in the middle of the floor and raved. "Cold as a March morning and no fear in him! He did it!"

Along the end of the street, Red Hollis heard the commotion as a cheer went up from the saloon. He smiled to himself and raised the bottle to his lips. He'd looked all around for the little girl on his way out of town, but had seen no sign of her. That was all right. He had some things to hold his interest here for a while—let that gambler get himself all stoked up on the law. What did he care. He had nothing to do all summer but ride down here when he felt like it, kill that idiot, get the little girl, and go on about his business. Who could stop him?

*   *   *

Old Turner raved on. "The man killed—I'm saying *killed* Fast Felton McRoy . . . !" Joe Sharpe had held himself together as long as he could. He needed air. While the townsfolk pressed him, he offered them a tight smile, hooked his thumb in his belt, and drifted toward the door, feeling his stomach wanting to surge up and spill itself rid of the trembling fear. "And put Montana Red in his place the same as you'd slap a lapdog!" Another cheer went up. Someone whistled. At the door an arm swung around Joe Sharpe's shoulder before he could get outside.

"What say you, Big Joe? Did you straighten that killer out or what?" Joe nodded and tried to move free.

"Weren't just no ordinary killer! We're talking *Montana Red Hollis* here, for God's sake!"

Sharpe knew he had to say something. So he raised a hand, keeping his eyes as steady as they'd been on Red Hollis. "Let's not make him bigger than he is, folks. He's just one more hardcase in a world of many." He took a step back, needing to hurry, but moving slow and calm. "Just business as usual when you're wearing a badge."

They watched him as if in awe. He backed out the door with a tip of his hat, and moved along the boardwalk, taking his time. When he stepped down and around the corner into an alley, the sickness and fear in his belly made a powerful leap, and he broke into a run to the garbage heap behind the saloon.

Slinging his hat away, he bowed forward just in time and hung there as if against gravity until his insides ached and knotted and finally rolled back and settled into place. *Oh, God . . .* He reached back and found a handkerchief in his pocket and brought it up and wiped his face. He blinked and stared through a watery veil until he wiped his eyes, straightened, and collected himself. Had he been out of his mind? Of course he had!

"Jesus," he whispered aloud. And as he shook his head, he saw a hand extend toward him and looked up at Joy Decker standing there beside him. Aw naw! Not her! Not now! He looked away, sweeping the hat from her hand. Then he felt her hand on his arm.

"It's all right, Joseph," she said in a quiet tone. "Only a madman like Montana Red himself could face such danger and not be frightened by it."

He kept his gaze turned away. "I wasn't af-raid," he said, his voice cracking against the bitterness in his throat.

"Oh? Then I was wrong about you. I suppose you're not *human*? The way I imagined you to be? You're not interested in staying alive?" Her hand went up on his shoulder and rested there. And her voice droned on, but he only nodded as she spoke, not really hearing her, not wanting her here. *Jesus! This woman. Why? Why won't she just go away. Please!* "So, you see, *Sheriff*, courage is not facing something when there is *no* fear in you. *Courage* is when you stand your ground in spite of everything inside you telling you to run from it."

There he stood, he thought, his head bowed, nodding like some schoolboy, a woman staring into his ear because he couldn't face her. Some widow woman at that, a mercantile store owner on the far edge of nowhere telling him about courage, about staying alive? What was he doing here? Big Joe Elliot, a make-believe sheriff in a town full of fools. He lifted his eyes and gazed off across the stark scrub land to the barren stretch of hills beyond. What did she know about courage? About staying alive? What did any of them know, he thought. First chance he got, he was out of here.

"All right! There he is," Turner's vice called out from the corner of the alley. "There's our sheriff."

Joe Sharpe slumped for a second and shook his head. What next? The whole town back here? Everybody watching him, seeing him stand over his puddle of sickness in the dirt, back here by the garbage heap? He couldn't have that.

"What can I do for you, Turner?" he asked, stepping over toward Turner, wiping his handkerchief across his face.

"Didn't know where you went to," Turner said. "Some of us kinda wanted to buy you a drink."

"Not now, thanks," Joe Sharpe said.

Joy Decker stepped in beside Sharpe, looping her arm in his. "We were just talking, the sheriff and I," she said.

Sharpe glanced down at her, then back to old Turner. Again he felt crowded and he moved away from the two of them. "If you'll both excuse me," he said; and he placed his hat on his head and squared it and walked back along the alley toward the street.

"What'd you say to him, Miss Joy?" old Turner asked, scratching his head beneath his hat brim.

She stood watching as Joe Sharpe disappeared around the corner toward the livery barn. "Oh nothing really. Just about what happened and how proud we are to have him here."

Turner grinned, and the two of them walked along together. "Looks like we've got us a good one, eh? I mean once he gets his sheriffing legs beneath him?"

"Let's hope so," she said. "He's a brave young man, whether he knows it or not."

"Yes, he is. He's sure proved himself on that. Kind of a looker too, wouldn't you say, Miss Joy?" Turner smiled.

She blushed a bit, but didn't answer.

From behind the bar Ray Gilliam watched him walk past the bat wing doors. He still didn't know who this man was—this Joe Elliot, passing himself off as a lawman—but whatever his game was, he'd just shown Ray Gilliam that he was good at it. He'd stood firm—held his bluff with nothing but air and a gambler's eyes to back him up. You almost had to admire the man for that, standing there, facing that monster, not wavering an inch, playing it close and calm.

Maybe that was all this man needed to impress a few local townsfolk, Gilliam thought. But it wouldn't go very far with Montana Red Hollis. Red was up to something. Red could've snuffed Sheriff Joe Elliot like a candle, and Ray Gilliam knew it. He ran a damp shirtsleeve across his beaded forehead, picked up two mugs of beer, and slid them along the bar into waiting hands.

He gazed out into the sunlight a few minutes later when *Sheriff* Joe Elliot rode past from the livery stable on a big bay gelding. A two-bit gambler, he said to himself, shaking his head. It would take more than a gambler's cold stare to keep that madman away from his daughter for long.

When Joe Sharpe had taken the horse from the livery stable, his first impulse was to swing by the dusty office, pick up his few belongings, and disappear out into the badlands. After all, how long could he press his luck here? Montana Red would be back, and he didn't want to be here when that happened. He slowed the horse as he started past the dusty office, almost pulling over to the hitch rail.

But he lifted his hat brim and gazed out past the edge of town at the angry swirl of sunlight beating down out there on the badlands. A rat in a trap, he thought; and he looked back at the town with its shaded overhangs, its people, folks who'd made him welcome, folks who trusted him, who now thought him a hero.

Even though it was not really *him* they trusted, but rather the man he'd made himself out to be, it felt good somehow, peaceful and whole, to be looked at that way. The conversation with Ray Gilliam had shaken him, but it had also made him realize there was more at work here than just him taking these folks for all he could, then slipping out of town. Gilliam had been right. He had promises to keep here. Why shouldn't he keep them? Why couldn't he stick here, take his chances, build himself some kind of life, and—

Hold it . . . ! There he went again. Was he crazy? Montana Red had just came a hair's breadth of burning him down! What was going on in his mind? He cursed himself under his breath and spun the horse around in the street. Faces looked out at him, some smiling their *blind faith* smiles, others looking curiously at him, maybe seeing his state of uncertainty.

Now Joy Decker came stepping off the boardwalk and headed toward him. She raised a hand, smiling; but he ducked his head slightly, pretending not to see her. Damn it! He had to get away for a while, somewhere he could breathe, up somewhere in the higher passes where he could think without being disturbed.

"Sheriff?" Joy Decker called out to him, but he didn't

look around. What did this woman expect of him? "Oh, Joseph . . ."

Still he ignored her; and without looking back, he batted his boot heels to the big bay gelding and rode out of town at a fast clip. Joy Decker stood watching through a wake of dust until at the distant narrow end of it she saw the dark speck of man and horse disappear upward into the high mountain pass.

CHAPTER 9

It was nearly dark when the ranger stepped down from the white barb and led it up into the maze of crevices among the jagged rocks. He'd stopped and picked up the pistol the *comadreja* had dropped back where he'd shot him. He'd checked the wide spot of blood in the sand and finished his cigar before following the hoofprints and blood spots on toward the stand of rock. Now he pushed on, limping, feeling something going on inside the wound, needing it tended.

By the time darkness set in, he'd reached a high ridge above a narrow basin. Down in the basin a firelight flickered and glowed against the smooth surface of a tall boulder standing twenty feet high. He sat and watched the firelight for a moment, then tied the white barb's reins around a rock spur and headed down on foot, moving as silent as a cat, using the rifle as a crutch.

He stopped again at the sound of hushed voices coming from the direction of the fire, and huddled in the dark shadows out of the rising light of a three-quarter moon.

"He is gone now I tell you," a weak voice said,

twenty yards ahead near the fire. "He is heet . . . as badly as I."

"Hold still," another voice said, this one sounding like a woman's voice. "If the blood does not stop, you will die soon."

The ranger heard a loud slap followed by the woman gasping. Then the other voice said, "Jou do as jou're told, and be silentia."

A third voice said, "Et does not matter how badly he is wounded. Ef he is alive, he weel come for jou. He weel come here because there is no place else to go."

Now there's good thinking . . . for a comadreja. The ranger's leg pulsed with pain. This one was smart. He'd have to keep a close eye on him.

"Did jou not wonder why he deedn't keel jou? It is so he could track jou heer. He knows dat jou had a place to go to, an he does not, you estupido basterd."

Yep, this one showed promise, he thought; and he moved forward, circling their firelight, ascending a bulge of rock that rose above their camp until he could see the three of them there in a narrow clearing of sand. A young woman pressed a rag against the gaping shoulder wound of the one he'd shot. He lay stretched out near the fire with his head on her lap and a hand wrapped around the neck of a goatskin water bag. He coughed, raised the water bag, and poured a stream into his mouth, then coughed again and sent a surge of water down his chin. "Lay still for me," she said, pressing him back against her lap.

"He es goin' to die, jou know," the other man said, sitting back at the edge of the glowing circle of fire-light.

"Shut jour mouth," the wounded one hissed. "Go

up there and keep a watch for the gringo peeg. Be careful he does not keel jou."

"Sheeet." He stood, dusted his hand across the seat of his ragged trousers, lifted a battered derby hat from the dirt, and put it on his head. "If he is wounded like you say, it weel be long time before he find us. I weel bring heem back to jou *screaming* like a peeg." He patted a long dagger sheathed on his side, slung a drooping leather lariat over his head, picked up a bow and a quiver of arrows, and walked off into the dark shadows along the base of the rock facing.

Not too smart after all . . . The ranger smiled slightly to himself, waiting a few seconds until he caught a glimpse of the man rounding the tall boulder facing and climbing above it. Then, with his rifle under his arm, the ranger gritted his teeth against the pain in his leg, crept off into the shadows of jagged rocks, and headed around the camp, up the opposite side of the facing.

He moved as silent as a snake for the next half hour, out and around, up the embankment of sandy soil until he lay twenty feet behind the edge of the large boulder. There he lay for another few minutes, watching, waiting for the *comadreja* to grow weary of scanning out through the dark shadows surrounding the camp, twenty feet below. When he saw the man's silhouette slump back and raise an arm up along the edge of his rock backrest, the ranger crawled forward on his belly inch by inch.

The *comadreja* never got the chance to reach for the big dagger on his side; instead his hands clutched instinctively at the leather lariat as it snapped tight around his throat. "Even a *weasel* oughtn't stick its head in a noose." The ranger whispered in a hiss near his ear, drawing the lariat tighter, feeling the man jerk and twist. The neck swelled against the unyielding leather. He heard the leather creak as it held tight. The *comadreja*'s derby hat rolled from his head, and his thrashing feet kicked it, sent it over the edge of the boulder to the camp below.

The hat slid and skipped down the boulder facing, bounced off a short pile of rocks at the bottom, and landed upturned and wobbling, three feet from the low flames of the fire.

The woman saw it and gasped, jerking back from it as if it were some deadly living creature come down upon them. The wounded *comadreja* rolled up onto his knees, snatching up the big knife lying in the sand beside him. Their eyes searched the darkness above them in silence. After a moment, the woman started to speak, but the *comadreja* held a finger to his lips, and she backed up a step and gazed again into the darkness. A scraping sound descended slowly toward them.

"Coming down," a voice said from the darkness at the top of the boulder.

Now she could no longer remain silent. The sound came closer, just above the upper glow of the firelight. "Is it, Carlos?" Her voice was low, hushed, slicing each word.

"No, shut up!" His voice started out like the hiss of a coiled viper, then he let out a breath—a sigh of defeat—seeing the dead *comadreja*'s feet ease slowly into the firelight as the body slid down the facing inch by inch. "It is the gringo peeg."

"Oink . . . oink," the ranger said from the darkness above them; and with a slight jerk the dead *comadreja*'s body stopped descending, hanging there, the toes pointing to the sandy ground a few inches below them. The woman gasped again and threw her hand to her throat.

The wounded *comadreja* slumped and stared at the dangling body, almost unable to recognize it with its eyes bulged blood red, its purple tongue too large for its mouth. He could not recall Carlos's neck ever being this long. Never had he seen those broad shoulders droop so low. The body looked small now, small and misshapen.

Above him, the ranger bolted a round into the rifle chamber, slamming it shut a little harder than usual just to make sure it was heard. "Coming down," he said again.

"*Sí* . . . coming down," the wounded *comadreja* said, letting his knife fall from his hand. It landed with a soft plop, and he looked at it, shook his head, and lay back staring up at a deep sky where stars seemed to dance in place. *They should have let this man pass*, he thought. *I told jou so . . . but nooooo! Jou would not leesten to me!* He raged in his mind, calling out to the dead that lay cold in the night, miles behind in the moonlight on the flat stretch of sandy soil.

The ranger winced and clenched his teeth as the blade of the knife widened the cut in his leg. "You've got pretty hair," he said in a strained voice, watching her. She looked up at him with dark caged eyes and took note of the cocked pistol lying along his leg, pointed at her. Then she looked back down, laid the bloody knife aside, and burrowed her thumb and fingertip deep into the open wound.

The tendons stood taught in his neck and he heard himself make a clicking sound back inside his throat.

In a second the searing pain dulled. A cramp knotted up on his leg muscle and shot along under the skin and down to his knee like a snake racing beneath a blanket. Her finger probed deeper for a second, picking hard at something wedged in there; and when he felt her pull it out, he let go a deep breath and felt sweat run long and cold down his temples. The bib of his shirt clung wet and cold against his chest.

He looked across the fire where the wounded *comadreja* lay back against the boulder, watching him. Beside him hung the body, dead eyes staring into darkness at something too distant to discern. With much effort to keep his voice as strong and steady as normal, the ranger said, "Hadn't run into you weasels, I'da been sleeping in a bed somewhere in another day or two. Now I'm laid up for a week."

"So? Jou can't complain." The *comadreja* gestured a weak hand at his large shoulder wound stuffed with a dripping blood-soaked rag. "Look at me . . . I am dying here. Jou did thees to me."

"And I'm real broke up about it," the ranger said. He tightened his leg muscle as the woman dabbed at the wound with a bandanna she'd dipped into a pot of hot water. "Did you come across a lone traveler in the past couple days? A man riding a paint horse?"

The *comadreja* shook his head. "We seed tracks of a lone rider, but we no followed heem. Instead . . . we followed jou." He looked down and shook his head again, as if regretting the outcome in some great game of chance. Then he asked, "Are jou hunting dis man?"

"No. I'm just curious. I'm hunting Red Hollis . . . ever heard of him?" The ranger glanced down at the woman as she looked up from pressing the hot wet bandanna against his wound.

"Yes . . . I hear of Montana Red." The *comadreja* looked at him. "He is a *baaad* hombre, that one. When jou find heem, he weel keel jou. Then jou weel be with me and Carlos"—he nodded toward the corpse—"and all the others."

A trace of a smile moved across the ranger's lips. "I doubt it. We're riding different directions."

"No. We go da same place, de same way." He raised a weak finger. "Now I know who jou are. Jou are de one dey all whisper about. De ranger, eh?" He ran his finger along his cheek and smiled a weak smile.

The ranger almost touched a hand to the scar on his face; but he caught himself and looked away for a second. Once more the woman cast a glance up at him. "I'm the one," the ranger said, almost to himself.

When the woman had finished with him, he tied the *comadreja*'s hands behind his back with a strand of rawhide, took his belt from him, looped it around the woman's neck, and using his rifle as a crutch led her with him to where he'd left the white barb. "He will die soon," she said about the *comadreja* as they worked their way through the moonlit darkness.

"I expect you're right," he said, holding onto the belt with a turn of it wrapped around his hand.

"What will become of *me* now?"

He waited for a second, then said, "We need each other to get out of here alive. You're gonna help me until I get over this wound your boyfriends gave me."

"And what will you do with me, after you are well enough to travel?"

"That depends."

"On what?"

"On whether or not you try to stab me in my sleep."

"And if I *do not* try?"

"Then, we'll get along fine. But I'm gonna tie you up while I sleep, just in case."

"You cannot do that. What if you catch the poison and *die* in your sleep. *Then* what would become of me?"

"All the more reason for you to keep my wound good and clean." He smiled to himself.

They started back with the horse, and after a silence she asked him, "Are you really who he said you are?"

"Yep." He limped along with the belt in his hand, leading her while she led the white barb.

"Then—if you are him . . . you will kill me once you are ready to leave."

"What makes you think that?"

"It is what I have heard of you . . . that you keep a list of who should live and who should die. That you are a killer, no different than the killers you hunt."

"Don't believe everything you hear. The ones I kill know why I kill them. They spend half their lives trying to get on my list, whether they know it or not. If not my list, then somebody else's. They've all done things that can't be made right."

She didn't answer; and on the way back to the camp, she told him that she was only with the desert *co-madrejas* because they had stolen her from her family in Sonora a year ago. She said they had all had their way with her, and had beaten her many times. She said they hated her because she was Mexican, and the *comadrejas* hated all Mexicans, hated them as bad as they hated Apaches. She said she had prayed many times that someone would come free her from them because they were animals with no people, no land . . . and no souls.

She finished telling him all this and tried to slow

him down for a second, long enough to look in his eyes and see what he thought of the things she'd said. But he limped along, pulling her behind him with his hand holding no more or no *less* firm on the belt. "Well," he said over his shoulder to her, "you can't have everything, can ya."

And when they got back to the camp and checked on the wounded *comadreja*, they found him dead in a wide pool of blood beside the body hanging down the boulder facing. He'd managed to pull the rag out of his wound with his teeth and let his blood flow. A thick black jell of blood lay in strings from his shoulder to the bloody rag. The woman looked down at him with a hand thrown over her mouth. "They'll both be getting ripe by morning," the ranger said. "We'll have to drag 'em away from here at first light before the buzzards come."

He reached his hand up and swept her long hair back over her shoulder. "What are you doing?" She asked in a flat tone.

He smiled and said, "We might just as well start tonight, getting to know each other. Step out of your shoes."

So this is how it is with him . . . no different than the others. She hesitated, but for only a second, then held the back of one of her moccasins down with the toe of the other and slipped it off as his hand loosened the belt around her neck and slid it free.

"You do have real pretty hair." He stepped back, watching her slip off the other moccasin.

She let out a breath and lay a hand at the top button of her ragged dress. "Thank you," she said. "Now, what will you have me do?"

He bent, pulled the dead *comadreja*'s dagger up from

the well of his boot and handed it to her at arm's length. "I'll have you climb up there and cut this one loose." He nodded at the body hanging down the face of the boulder. Then he added, "Don't get lost up there. It's a long walk out of here. Awfully hard on bare feet."

He stood and watched her slip barefoot out of the circle of firelight. When she was gone and he could hear her struggling up the far edge of the boulder where wind and water and the footsteps of men hiding out had carved a narrow path around it, he limped over to the dead men's worn horses tied to a jut of rock. They huddled with their nostrils pulsing in and out toward him, watching him come to them from the glow of firelight where death lay on the ground and hung from the darkness above.

"Easy," he said, running a hand down a damp neck, feeling its skin tighten at his touch. Behind him near the low flames, the white barb made a soft sound like a person chuckling. He checked both horses over with his hand, looked inside their ears and their mouths and nostrils. When he found no outward signs of any disease that might be coursing in their veins, or any parasites that might cling to their intestines, he dropped their saddles and bridles by their hooves. With his fingers twined in the mane of the weaker-looking horse, he slapped a hand on the stronger one's rump, pushing it away. Then, as he turned to the one in his hand, he took his knife from the sheath behind his back and sank the blade deep in the horse's quivering flesh.

The horse jerked a step back, sawed its head up and down twice, and sank down on its front knees. "Easy," he said again, placing a hand between its ears on its poll as if blessing it off on a long journey. Warm blood gouted around the hilt of the knife and spilled, rising up and down with each faltering beat of the animal's heart. Then it stopped, and the horse turned over in the bloody sand.

A sound behind him caused him to turn, and when he did, he saw the body had been cut free from above and fallen forward on the ground. The lariat made a low hiss sliding down and gathering at the base of the boulder. She'd come back, he knew. There was food here, and a way out of the badlands if she helped him stay alive. Yet even as he knew she would come back and stay with him for her own sake, he stayed a ways from the base of the boulder just in case—lest a heavy rock fly down out of the darkness and crush his skull.

But no rocks fell; and when she came back, he nodded his approval to himself as she stepped close to him. "Good," he said. "Now I'll rest for a spell."

She nodded in return, gazing away into the darkness. What would happen next she did not know, yet she knew as all living things of pulse and substance knew at the end of night on the desert floor, she had lived another day.

For the next week or longer the fever came and went, falling on the ranger suddenly, much like the *comadrejas* whose poison had caused it. When it hit him, he would cramp and chill and his jaws would nearly lock from the force of it. His leg wound mended slowly; and when the fever racked and raged throughout him, he could feel something deep inside his leg, something crawling, wrapping itself around the bone and squeezing, almost crushing it at times, he felt.

But then the fever would slip away as quickly as it

came. He'd manage to get up and attend to himself, and drink warm broth the woman made from the horse meat, until after the third day when the remaining horse meat had given over to spoil, and flies blew it. The buzzards that squawked throughout the hours of daylight and dove down at the bodies of the men, where they'd dragged them by horse a hundred yards away, now circled closer and loomed above the camp.

At night, coyotes snapped and snarled at one another in the distance as they picked over the bones of the dead, drawing closer each night until the scraping of their paws whispered near over rock and sand. On the fourth day, they moved their camp down to the water hole, and the trek there left him spent and weak. He lay against the same rock he'd stood behind the day the *comadrejas* dogged him there; and he watched the horses blow themselves out and draw water while the woman filled the goatskin and set about making a place for a small campfire.

Once she'd done these things, she came over, kneeled beside him, and raised the flap of his torn trouser leg and the edge of the loose bandage around his wound.

"It looks much better," she said. "Maybe tomorrow?" She looked into his eyes and held her hand out palm up.

"Maybe," he said. He drew his other boot up, took the dagger from it, and laid it in her hand, his free hand resting on the butt of the long pistol on his hip. She took the knife and walked away, out as far as fifty yards at one point as she bent and hacked at mesquite bush and gathered up other bits of it already down on the ground.

As he watched her, he saw her seem to stiffen in a

crouch and drop her bundle of kindling. He rose up, pulling the rifle up with him and laying it over the rock. Now she ran forward and farther away from him, her long hair whipping behind her; and he craned his neck to see her when she slipped out of sight over the edge of the sand rise. He stood, ready to hurry over to the horse and ride out there. But before he made his move, he saw her appear again at the crest of the rise, and he eased back against the rock, seeing the long body of a sand lizard hanging from her raised hand.

That night, eating the bitter-tasting meat, they sat listening to the comings and goings of hoof and paw move closer in out of the night, then stop and slip away at the scent and sight of them by the low fire. Red fiery eyes blinked at them in the darkness, then slunk low to the ground, moving in a wide cautious circle around the water hole and rising back up and blinking at them again.

"Yes tomorrow, I think," he said. "I've lost nearly two weeks here."

She nodded, bending forward with her arms wrapped around her knees, her dark hair draping her forearms and glistening soft in the fire glow. "And where will you take me? Not to the law, I hope. Better that you kill me than take me to the law."

"You're with the law now. I ain't hurt ya none, have I?" She didn't answer, and he said after a silence passed, "No. You did like you should. You're free to go . . . first town we come to."

She nodded again and sat silent, staring at the flames. After a while she said, "This Montana Red Hollis you search for. I don't think you will kill him."

"Neither does a lot of folks," he said.

She shook her head. "What I mean is, you will not kill him and live. I think that you will kill each other."

"There's a thought." He gazed out through the darkness and saw a pair of red eyes cower down. It drifted over and joined another pair of eyes, and together they sank to ground level and stared back at him again.

"But, is this not what almost happened with the *comadrejas*? Did you not almost die, the same as them?"

"I'll never die like a *comadreja* . . . If there's any justice twix heaven and hell."

"Justice?" She looked up at the stars, her eyes following them as if searching in their endlessness for the justice he spoke of, yet, as if knowing in her search she sought a stranger whose name she'd heard throughout her life but whose face she would never see.

"Yes, justice," he said. His fingertips went to the scar on his cheek and followed along it, the way a lost traveler's finger might follow lines on a faded map. "There *is* justice to how a person lives . . . how a person dies. Maybe you've just been running with the wrong crowd too long, and don't want to see it."

"Perhaps." She shrugged and turned her eyes away from the stars, where no answer had come to her. "But I am not like they are. I did not steal and kill, the way they did."

"You ate the food they stole."

"That is true . . . I was hungry. But I did not lay in wait to spill blood. I did not kill with them."

"No." He let out a breath. His hand moved from the butt of his pistol to the wound beneath his torn trouser leg, gently kneading the tender mending flesh. "But you had a hand in mixing the poison."

They sat in silence; and something rose up from the darkness, ventured to the water hole, and lapped at the edge, then moved away with the night air bending its fur and its eyes shining. Then at length she said, "You do not judge me . . . you are not *God*."

"You're right," he said, smiling to himself in the glow of the low flames. He slipped the big pistol from its holster and laid it on his lap, to take it apart and clean it. "If I was, I reckon I'd never got stuck in these badlands."

CHAPTER 10

Red Hollis liked keeping things simple and didn't try to figure too many things out. He lived like a mountain cat, took what he wanted, when he wanted, and his life such as it was held few problems and very little wonder for him. He survived on the impulses of his spine and the ball of fire in his forehead. He liked it that way; and he grinned to himself standing on his front porch in the darkness and threw back a drink from his bottle of rye.

He listened, as he had been for the past ten minutes, to the soft drop of hooves on the trail leading up toward his cabin. If there was one thing that had always peaked his curiosity it was how a man could be alone on the highest peak of the most remote mountain in the territory, yet should that man possess whiskey in any substantial quantity, every no-account drunk, rake, and bummer from miles around were drawn to him as surely as flies were drawn to a bear's bottom.

He shook his head and capped the bottle. Whoever was coming had to be somebody he knew. Nobody else would be stupid enough to come slipping up on him this way. He'd been drinking for four days on the bottles of rye he'd gotten in town, just thinking about that little girl, how everybody there had her hidden from him, and how he might go about using that phony lawman-gambler to flush her out. He'd also given thought to what he might do to that gambler when the time was right.

It had been quite a while since he'd given much thought to planning anything beyond pulling his pistol and shooting somebody, playing along with the gambler was kind of interesting for a change. When the hooves drew closer, he stretched and yawned and turned and walked inside the dark cabin. Anyway, he'd find a way to get that little girl—the gambler too before it was over.

Inside his cabin, he listened in silence to the hushed voices as their leather saddles creaked and they tried to step down and keep their horses quiet. He heard a muffled giggle like some schoolkid come to pull a silly prank, and the sound of boots moved up onto the porch. Three of them, he counted to himself. He waited.

Once inside the door, the voice of the man in front snickered, then whispered in the darkness, "Red Hollis? You in there? Come out, come out, Montana Red, you got some company here." The voice snickered again, joined by two others as the three of them crept into the shack and across the creaking plank floor. "He's passed out somewhere in here. We'll just have to find him."

"I'm thinking this ain't a good idea, boys," whispered a nervous voice from the open door. "Maybe he ain't here. Either way, I don't think we oughta be sneaking in this way."

"Shut up, Yates," one of the others hissed. "Red loves a little joke, much as the next feller. He'll be glad to see us."

Now that would be ole Solomon Fish, Red Hollis thought, huddled back in the darkness, beneath a wooden table, out of the slice of moonlight that spilled through the open door. What was this? Red thought about it, reached back, and slipped the heavy knife from its sheath. A little, *Let's-tease-ole-Red-some?* A little, *Let's slip in, catch Red asleep, scare the living hell out of him, and spend the rest of the night getting his goat over it?*

Red grinned huddled down there in the darkness, and raised the big knife as a dirty boot stepped forward two feet from him. Well, boys, here's how that went! He reached out with the big knife and slammed it down hard with a solid thud, nailing the man's foot to the floor.

The man screamed loud and long, doing a one-foot shuffle, jerking his foot against the big knife blade, then screaming louder, the blade holding fast and slicing as he jerked at it.

"Jesus, God almighty!" Solomon Fish yelled, jumping forward, trying to grab him. "What's wrong with you?"

The man kept screaming until his scream was cut short beneath the blast of a shotgun that lit the whole shack and shook it on its pinnings. He fell, still screaming, yanking against the knife blade. Splinters from the hole blown through the roof showered down on him. "Lord! Red! It's Fish! Don't shoot! Pleeeese!"

Outside, Dick Yates's boots pounded down off the porch and across the darkness. "Who?" Red grinned in the darkness, rounded out the other barrel of the shotgun straight up, catching a glimpse of Solomon Fish cowering back in the golden burst of fire. The man still screamed on the floor.

"Solomon *Fissssh!* Damn it! Francis! Shut up!"

"Aw hell, Solomon," Red said, stepping into the slice of moonlight, speaking above the screaming man on the floor. "What brings ya this way?" He reached down with the shotgun barrel, poked it into the writhing, screaming man's ribs, and added, "Who's your vocal friend here . . . why was he sneaking in like that?"

"Damn'er, Red. It was a little joke is all. You know I'd never bring ya no harm, don't ya? Can we light a lamp here? See what the hell you've done to him?"

"Yeah," Red said, stepping over to a table and picking up an oil lantern. As the man's screams died down to a long tortured whine, Red lit the lantern and trimmed it high. "There we are. Now who's this?"

Solomon Fish leaned down and jerked the knife blade back and forth to free it up. The man screamed again as the blade came loose, and Solomon stepped back with both hands around the handle. "Damn, Red, you sunk her pretty good. This here's Frank Bacon. We all call him Francis, after"—he shrugged, pitching the knife to Red—"well, you know who I mean."

"Yeah, I know." Red wiped the knife across his trouser leg and sheathed it. "Here, Francis, let's get ya up from there." Together they helped the whining man to a wooden chair and worked his boot off his bleeding foot. "So, tell me, Fish. What brings ya up from old Mex this time of year?" He pitched the boot to the floor. A piece of bloody sock stuck up through the wide gash in the leather; two toes that looked like bloody mushrooms rolled out on the floor. "Your boot's ruint," Red Hollis said, chuckling a little.

The man screamed again.

Solomon Fish lifted his floppy hat and dropped it on the table. "I'm worn out on old Mex," he said. "I been longing to come back here for—" He stopped short, turned to Frank Bacon as he screamed and said, "Shut up, Francis. And clean up that mess. We're trying to talk here."

"He's—he's cut my toes off!" Bacon whined, gripping his hands around his ankle to stay the flow of blood.

"Yeah he did." Solomon Fish turned back to Red Hollis. "Been longing to come back to the territory. Ran into Yates . . . he told me what happened to his brother, Hurley. Then we ran into Francis here and he'd just had a run-in with that ranger. Said that ranger kilt ole Bent Jackson and stole his horse. I said, 'Well, let's just get over there and kill that ranger what's been shooting everybody.' And, here I am." He eyed Red's bottle of rye standing on the table and licked his dirty lips. "I just musta got homesick I reckon. Is that rye *single* or *double* cut?"

"What do you care?" Red nodded toward it. "You'll drink it if it's full of snake heads."

"Don't mind if I do, then." Solomon Fish wiped his grimy hand up and down his coat and picked the bottle up.

"Is everybody all right in there?" Yates leaned in through the open door and looked over at them.

"More or less." Red glanced down at Frank Bacon, chuckled under his breath, pulled the cork from another bottle of rye, and threw back a long drink.

"Come on in here," Solomon Fish said. "Get some salve or something . . . get an old rag you can cut into a bandage."

"What happened?" Yates stepped over cautiously, glancing up at the hole in the ceiling, then looking down at Frank Bacon's foot.

"Red cleaved his toes off. See what ya can do fer him. He's driving us nuts." Fish took the bottle and lifted back a shot.

"Look on the window ledge there," Red said to Yates; then he settled back in his chair. "How'd you know where I am, Fish? You ain't never been here."

Fish let out a whiskey hiss and sat the bottle down. "He told me." He wagged a thumb toward Dick Yates as Yates walked over and rummaged among some dust-covered jars on the window ledge.

"Did he now?" Red spread a thin smile and studied Yates's back. The glow of the lantern flickered in his eyes, and as if shaking a thought from his mind, he squeezed his eyes shut for a second, then said to Fish, "If you rode all this way to get me to help ya kill somebody, you wasted a trip. I got some things I'm meaning to do around here. My partner, Bert, is gone . . . left me short-handed here."

"Where'd he go?" Fish slid the bottle across the table to him.

Red Hollis picked it up and pointed it in the direction of the deep canyon before lifting it to his lips. "Out that way," he said.

They drank and talked; and as the level of rye whiskey sank lower in the bottles, Red Hollis felt his head starting to ring inside, the ball of fire spinning hot. He licked his lips, rubbed his palms on his trousers under the table, and pictured himself torturing that gambler back in town, while Solomon Fish rattled on and on making hardly any sense. Yates had helped Frank Bacon dress and bandage his foot, then helped him outside to the front yard and built a fire there for him.

Red watched the licking flames through the open

door and thought of the young girl, liking the fear he'd
seen in her eyes the day him and ole Bert had spotted
her there. He wished he'd brought her with him right
then—wished she was here right now instead of these
three stinky idiots.

"So, I rode on over to where that Mexican lived
at . . ." Solomon Fish talked on, spinning an account
of somebody who'd wronged him somehow either
real or imagined. But Red Hollis barely heard any of
it. He nodded now and then, and looked once into
Solomon Fish's eyes and smiled, just wondering for a
fleeting second what ole Fish would do if all of a
sudden he pulled up his pistol from beneath the table
and put a bullet through his eye.

"Said, 'Come on, get your arse out here, you stinking *greaser*.'" Solomon Fish shrugged. "He wouldn't
come out though. So I tied me a rope around his shack
and jerked it down around him with a team of turning
mules . . ."

Solomon Fish was an ugly man who liked talking
bold about all he'd done. But Red knew he'd whittle
his boldness down pretty quick. Inside Solomon Fish's
chest beat the heart of a coward, and all Red had to do
was push him some, get him knuckled down, and Fish
would fall in line and do whatever Red told him. Red
wondered if Fish ever stopped and realized how bad
he looked; then he once more felt the urge to raise the
pistol and shoot him—maybe tell him first: "You ugly
bucket of guts, you're too ugly to live." Then *bang!* Put
it on him and watch him drop. From all he'd heard
lately about that ranger and all the dust he'd been stirring up, these three idiots didn't stand a chance
against him.

Red Hollis scratched his chin, nodding, looking

around his shack, realizing what a mess shooting Solomon Fish through the face would make all over everything. Of course if he had himself a *woman* here, or even that little brown girl, he wouldn't have to clean up stuff like that.

Red thought things through and had come up with a little plan while the three men sucked down most of his whiskey. He sat alone at his table now, spinning his pistol in one hand and holding a bottle in his other. He gazed down at the rough wooden tabletop for a while, then stood up and walked outside, spinning his right pistol back into his holster. He looked down all around his front yard, shook his head, and took a deep breath.

"Wake up, Bacon, you toeless drunken rag." Red Hollis stepped over to Frank Bacon, who happened to be closest to him in the front yard where the three men had passed out just before sunup. Red kicked him once in the leg, but evidently not hard enough. Bacon only grunted and snorkeled and rolled over on his other side. Gray drool seeped from his lips. A blood-stained bandage covered his foot. *Damned stinking dog . . .*

Red stood over him with his hands resting on the crossed pistols on his belly. Solomon Fish came up from the ground and stood watching; and Red wondered how ole Fish would act if he'd lift that pistol and start shooting Frank Bacon where he lay—start at his bad foot and just shoot his way up.

"What's going on?" Yates asked in a bleary voice, then stood back when Fish raised a hand toward him.

"I *said*, get, your *stinking*, arse up!" Red kicked Bacon again, this time harder, this time straight in the ribs. Bacon let out a blast of breath, gasped and wheezed, thrashed around on the ground, finally swinging up onto his knees, his bandaged foot sticking out to one side. He stayed bowed over with his arms looped tight across his stomach. His face turned blue as he struggled to regain his wind.

"Lord, Red!" Solomon Fish stared wide-eyed. "Look at him! You've kilt him!" Bacon's lips turned purple; he fell over onto his side, making a strained sound in his throat.

"Aw, hell, he's all right." Red waved him away. "I hate a late sleeper. Is he always that way?"

"Well, naw, not I ever noticed. He's just having a hard time getting used to ya." Fish moved in with Yates and together they raised Bacon to his feet. Bacon wheezed, catching short spurts of breath. "What've you got agin him anyway, Red? He's one of us, you know." Fish dusted the front of Bacon's coat, reached down, picked up his hat, and sank it on his wobbling head. "You'll be all right, Francis boy, just *breathe*. That's right, there ya go."

Bacon spoke, squeezing out his words: "I . . . think . . . my . . . ribs broke."

"Shit. All night he belly-ached about his toes. Reckon now he'll carry on over his ribs all day." Red spit and walked toward the cabin. "There's hot coffee inside, if you want some before ya go."

Fish let go of Frank Bacon and caught up to Hollis. "Red, you're going with us ain't ya? Find that ranger? Shoot his eyes out?"

"Naw. There's no telling where he's at. I got things to do."

"But you said last night—"

"I was drunk." Red stepped up on the porch and Fish followed him inside. "Besides, you want me to help you kill that ranger, you got to do something for me first."

"What's that?" Fish sidestepped over to the cof-feepot while Red Hollis picked up his rifle from against the wall.

"I want yas all to ride down into town and bring me something."

"But we's all wanting to kill that ranger."

"Shit. Shut up about him. I want yas to bring me back a little girl I saw there." Red grinned. "I saw her there the other day, and kinda had my tooth set on her ever since."

Solomon Fish rubbed a dirty hand on his beard stubble. "Well, we could do that, I reckon. Then you'll go with us? Do what needs doing to that ranger?"

"Said I would, didn't I?"

"All right then, what's her name?"

"Name? Hell I don't know her name—I ain't writing her a letter. You'll know her when ya see her though. She's about this tall, brown as a little berry. Only little brown girl in that whole town. You'd be blind not to see her."

"Just tell her you want to see her, huh?"

Red glared at him. "No, you stupid *idiot*. She ain't gonna *want* to come. You'll have to snatch her up and bring her."

"Oh." Fish considered it for a second. "What about the law?"

"Ain't no law there," Red said, not wanting to mention the gambler. He wanted to see how Solomon Fish and these two idiots handled him. "I keep their law-men killed off. It's sort of a special place for me. They can't keep a real sheriff there for me putting a bullet in 'em. You won't have no trouble. Just act tough and tell 'em I sent ya. Shoot a couple of 'em if ya want to." Red spit on the floor and rubbed his hand across his mouth.

Fish grinned across dark stained teeth. "What're you gonna do, make her your bride, Red?"

"Ain't none of your business what I'm gonna do—hers either. You bring her up here is all."

"Do you mind if maybe the boys and me kinda play around with her, just a little bit, you know, get her all ready for ya—?"

"Lay a hand on her and I'll kill ya," Red snapped. His hand dropped to his pistol handle.

"Easy, Red!" Fish jumped back, spilling coffee down his chest. "Won't nobody touch her, I swear—except to snatch her up and bring her here to ya, all right?"

Red sliced out a breath. "All right." And then he let his gun hand drop from his pistol. "Now put down that coffee and get out of here. I'm sicka looking at yas. Tell that toeless, rib-broke idiot he better develop a sense of humor if he wants to hang around here."

"I'll tell 'im, Red, I sure will." Fish sat the cup down and backed to the door with his hands spread in a cautious show of peace. "We'll get right in there and back. Oughta get back here by sundown."

"You better. And you best bring back some whiskey if you know what's good for ya. Don't make me come looking for ya."

Red followed him out the door and stood watching from the front porch as the three scurried around, saddled their horses, and collected themselves. "Don't know if I can ride or not with these ribs," Frank Bacon said in a lowered voice as they stepped up in their saddles.

"Hush, you danged fool, don't let him hear you saying that." They swung onto their horses and batted them out toward the narrow trail. "We're gonna have to have a long talk about the way you're acting," Fish added.

"Me? I ain't done nothing."

Red Hollis watched them ride away, then he smiled to himself, running a hand up and down his bristly jaw. Yeah, this was the way to do it. See how that lawman-gambler handled these three. He'd give anything to see Dick Yates's face when he saw *Sheriff* Joe Elliot wearing his dead brother Hurley's shooting gear. Red chuckled.

Yeah, let ole Solomon Fish and these two idiots ride in there. Maybe if nobody saw Red with them, the little girl might show her face. Let them snatch her and bring her to him. Meanwhile, he might take himself a good bath, scrub himself down a little—hell, no reason not to be presentable when she got here.

He'd have that little girl whether she liked it or not; but once he cleaned himself up, maybe grease his hair down some. You never know, she might be real pleased with him. He pictured her there, just the two of them, him running his hands all over her, doing whatever he wanted to with her, her making little sounds when he pinched her good and hard. She *better* be pleased with him.

He reached down and drew the long knife from his boot well. And if she wasn't pleased with him, so what? He ran his thumb along the edge of the blade, testing the sharpness of it. There were a lot of things he could do with her.

CHAPTER 11

T he pistol with the shaved front sight came up
pretty quick, the hammer going back beneath his
thumb on the upswing. The barrel had cleared the
edge of the holster by less than an inch, then snapped
up, his hand holding the butt steady, almost against
his hip. His hand hardly flinched when the shot went
off; and Joe Sharpe watched the empty bean tin
bounce up in the air and back down on the rocks with
a clanking of metal. *Not bad. Not bad at all.*

He turned Hurley Yates's gun in his hand, looking at
it, feeling the sleek way the butt had come to fit his
hand, more comfortable with it every day, he thought.
He twirled it, then twirled it back. The weight and balance of it felt good to him now, not awkward and stiff
like it had back when he'd first handled the gun that
night on the desert floor.

He'd come to understand in these past few days
how a man might develop a habit of twirling and handling a gun. It was there, always, fingertip close, and
once it felt good in your hand, your hand seemed to
want to go to it, the way some men's hands went to a
good cigar. A habit. It could get to be, he thought. Had
he realized how quick good shooting would come to
him, he'd have started practicing a long time ago. He

was good with his hands, fast and smooth with them. What gambler wasn't?

Good gun handling worked on the same principle of repetition as working a one-hand cut with a deck of playing cards. All it took was practice—the will to make it work—to get better at it than the next man. He twirled the pistol back into the holster, let his hand fall relaxed for a second, then snatched it out again, cocking it, but this time not firing it. Now that was fast, wasn't it? He felt like it was, although he really had nothing to compare it to.

He glanced around at the wide stretch of rock land behind him, then off over the edge of the mecca to the wide valley below, as if to see if anyone had been watching. There wouldn't be of course, this far out, six miles from town and high above it. He'd no longer care if they were. He was their sheriff, Big Joe Elliot. Pistols were his stock-in-trade. They knew he came out here somewhere to practice. He holstered the pistol again and walked over to set the line of cans back up. The first couple of days he feared somebody might see him shoot, now he almost wished they would.

After his run-in with Montana Red, he'd gone off and thought about it. He didn't like it here in this hard barren land, but as long as he was here and until he got the chance to slip away, he wasn't about to get caught short again. He didn't deceive himself. There'd never be a day when he'd get good enough to take on a killer like Montana Red. There'd never be a time when he could face somebody like the ranger. But if he ever found himself on the spot like he'd been the other day, he sure liked thinking he wouldn't have to die without at least putting up *some* kind of fight.

Besides, he thought, setting the cans up and walking

back away from them, for him to get out of here he'd have to cross the badlands again. He wanted to better his odds at staying alive any way he could. It was only by the slimmest chance he'd made it the last time. Next time he'd be better prepared. He spun, crouching, snapping the pistol up and firing. But the shot fell short and kicked up a spray of shattered rock. All right, he still needed to work on it.

He sat down near the edge of the mecca and took out the flask of whiskey from inside his coat. When he'd had his sip, he capped the flask, laid it on the ground between his feet, and gazed out across the wide valley beneath him, where in the distance lay the roll of the earth in a veil of wavering heat. Since his facing Montana Red he'd spent three mornings in a row sitting there, sipping from the flask, getting his thoughts collected. The whiskey had helped.

He'd decided he couldn't go on, playing these people along, taking advantage of them, giving them a false sense of security. He was a gambler and nothing more. Any day the ranger would come drifting in through a rise of dust, or Red Hollis would ride on a wild killing spree. He wasn't about to be here when either of those two things happened. He was still waiting for the rest of his reward money, but ole Turner had said he'd get it today. Once he got it he was hightailing it out of here. He'd had to quit jumping back and forth, one minute thinking he could settle down here, and the next thinking he'd take the town for all it was worth.

Tonight he'd keep a horse outside the sheriff's office and slip away while the town slept. What could they really say? He'd done them no harm, yet. *Well* . . . He reached down and picked the flask up again. This time as he uncapped it and raised it, he saw the drift of dust rising up at the edge of the horizon, and he froze with the flask near his lips.

They came up out of the rise of dust, two riders at a trot. Then behind them as they straightened out on the flatland, a third rider, this one checking his horse down. He bowed over in the saddle like a wounded man, and Sharpe watched at a distance of a thousand yards as the two in front circled back and stopped beside him.

Red Hollis? Joe Sharpe felt a sickness ripple deep in his stomach. *Oh God no! Please, no* . . . He lowered the flask and scooted backward into the shade of a scrub piñon where his horse stood. Not now, he thought. Not when he'd just gotten clear on what to do. They were headed straight for town, and whether Red Hollis was one of them or not, it didn't matter. Whoever they were they weren't miners. Not these men, not coming from that direction.

When they rode closer, he saw their rifles, their pistols on their hips; and he saw a wild aura about them, their demeanor like that of predators as their heads turned from side to side, searching the land about them like prowling wolves. He swallowed a dryness in his throat. If only he'd brought his wallet with him, he wouldn't even go back to town for his other belongings. Just ride on from here and never look back. He watched until they'd crossed the flatland and dropped down out of sight; he kept his gaze fixed on their wake of dust until it drifted off sidelong on the wind.

Well, he'd have to go back for his money. No need to get spooked here. He had to fill some canteens with water—pick up some food. Making it once across the badlands without supplies had been a stroke of luck. Trying it again would be pure suicide. Maybe that's all these three men were doing, just stopping to pick up supplies—they sure weren't carrying any—maybe have themselves a couple of drinks before heading back.

All right, he'd wait and see. He was safe up here. He'd stick right here until they left, right here with his shiny flask of whiskey . . . all day if need be. He thought of the pistol hanging on his hip, of how good he'd become at handling it, and how confident it had made him feel only moments ago when he'd cocked it on the upswing and watched the tin can bounce in the air. But that was only a tin can, he thought, not somebody looking back at him from behind a gun of their own.

He stood up, dusted the seat of his trousers, took his riding duster from across the saddle and spread it on the ground and had started to sit back down when his horse stepped out of the shade and started to wander off to a clump of grass. "Whoa now." He stepped along beside it, caught up the reins, and stood with it until it had picked the clump of grass clean.

He had no reason to feel guilty here. This town had been here long before he ever showed up. What had they done then? He didn't owe them a thing. He pictured Joy Decker's face and the way she had of looking at him, as if he could do no wrong. Maybe he was getting worried about nothing. Maybe those three riders would swing wide and not even go to town. Maybe— Who was he kidding? He was scared; and even there alone atop the barren rock mecca, his fear shamed him.

* * *

The three riders sat their horses for a moment along the edge of the high trail, gazing down where the town sat stark and sunken in a low swirl of dust. At the far end of town two miners led a sorrel mule out toward the foothills far to the west. Halfway down the sunbeaten street a man stood sweeping the boardwalk, pushing a small bellowing roll of brown dust out into the larger body of dust that crept back toward him with the swipe of the broom.

"I wouldn't clerk a store for nothing in the world," Solomon Fish said. "It's the most dangerous job in the world." He spit and ran a hand across his mouth. "Had a brother lost his life clerking hardware in Arkansas," he added.

Yates sat staring at the town with a blank expression. He lifted his eyes to Fish. "How'd he do that?"

"Got drunk in a whorehouse and commenced slapping a whore around." He shrugged. "The owner shot him straight through the forehead."

"Oh," Yates said; and he turned his gaze back to the town. But Frank Bacon, who sat gazing down examining his bandaged foot, raised his eyes to Fish and asked, "How'd clerking in a store cause all that to happen?"

"You don't know much, do ya, Francis?" Fish glared at him, then said in an impatient tone, "If he hadn't been clerking there he wouldn't have been in that town in the first place. So he'd never've gone to that whorehouse, now would he?" Fish looked away, shaking his head. "I swear, Francis . . . I don't know what we're going to do with you."

Bacon rubbed dirt from his bleary eyes. "I still don't see how none of that has anything—"

"Leave it alone, Frank," Dick Yates said, cutting him off in a lowered voice.

Solomon Fish raised his pistol from his holster, spun it once on his finger, turned it side to side looking at it, and dropped it back down. "Reckon we might just as well get down there and do what we come to do. Keep your eyes peeled for that little colored girl."

"What's Red want that little girl for anyway?" Frank Bacon asked, lowering his bandaged foot and dusting his hands together.

Solomon Fish just stared at him, shook his head, spit, and turned away.

They turned their horses back to the trail and followed it downward single file along the switchbacks to the edge of town. From the edge of town they quickened their pace, three dust-covered creatures blown in off the wilds of the desert flats, dressed in bone-yard rags with guns strapped about them. They rode abreast along the rutted dirt street. The clop of their horses' hooves brought townsfolk out of doorways, where they stood and gazed with drawn faces.

Glancing back at them, seeing the fear and dread in their eyes, Fish said to the other two, "Looks like ole Red is right. He's got these folks whittled down to where he wants them. They look too scared to fart above a whisper."

They cut their horses to the hitch rail outside the saloon and when they'd unmounted and collected themselves, they stood for a second looking all around, slapping dust from themselves with their battered hats. Solomon Fish turned toward the faces back along the boardwalk. He grunted, then unbuttoned his trousers and relieved himself right there in the dirt.

Joy Decker gasped and pulled back inside her store.

The men of the town looked away, embarrassed, powerless even in their outrage; and ashamed to even cast their eyes on one another, they milled and moved back closer to their stores until by the time Solomon Fish finished spilling himself in the dirt the boardwalk stood empty.

Without a word Fish finished his business and stood there exposed a moment longer, staring along the abandoned street with his face tipped back, smiling a dirty smile. Then he hiked a leg, attended himself, fastened his trousers, and turned with Yates and Bacon and stepped up to the saloon. As they walked through the doors and stopped, an old miner turned from the bar with a fresh beer mug frothed over in his hand.

He'd smiled at first, thinking his two friends might've changed their minds and came back to join him. But when he saw the three men step out of the sunlight with their thumbs hooked near their pistols, his smile froze and he shied away to the far corner of the bar, the way a smaller animal will at the first scent of danger.

"The hell's that idiot grinning about?" Fish asked Yates, staring hard at the old miner. At that, the old miner sat the mug away, slipped from the bar to the far wall, and around the wall toward the front door. He ducked outside as they crossed the wooden floor— Frank Bacon limping on the bloodstained bandage, now covered brown with road dust and a loose tail of it dragging behind him.

Fish faced Ray Gilliam across the bar. "Did you just tell a joke, boy? And we missed it?" He struck a cold glare into Gilliam's eyes. "Maybe you'll tell it again, just for us." A sneer spread across his dirt-coated lips.

Ray Gilliam didn't answer but only stood watching

them with his left hand on the bar and his right hand beneath it near the stock of the shotgun. Sweat beaded his brow. "He was just leaving," he said. "What may I get you fellows?"

"Whoa," Yates said, flashing his sneer to the others. "Did you boys ever hear a muskrat talk that pretty?"

"He's a mannered gentleman." Fish shot Yates a glance, then said to Ray Gilliam, "You *may* draw us off some beers . . . and you *may* keep both hands up here where I can see them, 'less you wanta lose one." He raised his pistol from his dusty holster and laid it on the bar with a loud thump. Ray Gilliam moved away and took clean mugs from a stack and drew them full and stood them along in front of the men. Foam dripped and splattered.

They threw back a long swallow and stared at Ray Gilliam as he stood a bottle of rye before them. He picked up three shot glasses on his fingertips from the shelf behind the bar and when he'd spread them out, Solomon Fish sat his beer down, looked at his shot glass, and swatted it aside. He snatched the bottle up, pulled the cork with his yellow teeth and blew it past the bartender's face. "We won't be paying right off," he said. "You might wanta bill us in the mail."

An hour had passed when from her store across the street, Joy Decker heard the terrible racket from the saloon. Glass crashed amid the sound of men cursing. She looked out her front door and saw other townsfolk staring, but shying back. A chair flew through the doors of the saloon, then a shot rang out from inside followed by hoots and laughter. When Dick Yates came running out yelling, flashing his pistol over his head, old Turner and the few other townsmen drew back and melted away into doorways.

She bit her lip and saw the man running toward her store. When he ran up on the boardwalk outside, she ducked back from the door and watched him grab three pick handles from a wooden barrel and race back to the saloon. She knew what that meant, and she wasn't going to stand for it. Under the counter lay the small pistol. Grabbing it, she ran to the front door. Behind her, Myra Gilliam ran out of the stockroom. "No, child! You stay back there, stay hidden!"

"But my father!" She bolted for the door, but Joy Decker grabbed her arm and swung her back.

"No, you stay here. Mind your father. Don't come near them."

She threw open the door and ran toward the saloon, hiking her dress up with one hand and carrying the small pistol out before her.

"She'll get herself killed," a townsman cried out. "Where the blazes is Joe Elliot?"

"He ain't here," Old Turner shouted, moving past him with a shotgun held across his chest.

"Don't go in there, Turner. They'll kill ya!"

"Then they'll just have to," he said. "Ray Gilliam never harmed a soul in his life."

Inside the saloon doors, Joy Decker stopped with the pistol raised in her shaking hand. "I'm through fooling with you, boy," Solomon Fish said to Ray Gilliam, who stood panting with his back against the bar. On the floor lay the shotgun from under the bar, its shell lying spilled out beside it. Fish raised the cocked pistol in his hand.

"Shoot me then, but you'll never find out." Ray Gilliam glared at him, his shirt in shreds, hanging down his side. Blood ran from his nose and from a deep cut above his eyes. A heavy brass spittoon hung from his hand. Dick Yates stood four feet back, his breath heaving, a raised pick handle in his hands. Frank Bacon stood bowed over a table with blood dripping from his face.

"Go on, shoot him, Fish!" said Yates.

She saw the man's hand tense around the raised pistol, and Joy Decker yelled out, "Drop the gun!"

Their eyes swung toward her. "Back out of here, Miss Decker," Ray Gilliam. "Please! Leave!"

But she stood firm, her hand shaking a bit, but her expression determined. Solomon Fish chuckled low. "I'll be damned and dipped." His pistol eased around toward her. "Look here, Yates, I'm fixing to get shot at."

Yates turned facing her, his pick handle still raised. He grinned. "Yep, I believe you are, sure enough."

"Please, Miss Decker," Ray Gilliam said. "Go! Now!"

"Hush up, boy!" Fish swung the pistol back at Gilliam but kept his eyes on Joy Decker. "If the little lady wants to join us, I reckon she's welcome to." He took a slow step toward her. "And once I put this gun down, then what? You gonna take me somewheres and make me your prisoner? I've had worse offers." He laughed across stained broken teeth.

"I said put the gun down." Joy Decker sliced her words. Her hand settled and tightened on the small pistol. "We're going to hold you until our sheriff gets back. He'll do whatever he thinks best."

"Let her go," Ray Gilliam said to Solomon Fish as Fish took another slow step and widened his eyes on her.

Fish said, "Your new sheriff. Now who might *that* be?"

She tightened her jaw, steadying her pistol. "Big Joe Elliot, that's who . . . the man who killed *Fast Felton* less than three weeks ago. You'll wish you never ran into him. Now put it down!"

"Killed Fast Felton? My, my"—he shook his head—"I'm getting all tingly here." Fish took another step. "You might orta put a hand on me, see if I feel too warm."

"Stop it! Let her go!" Ray Gilliam shouted. "Hurting her won't change a thing."

"I bet it will," Fish said, moving slowly, ever slowly, closer toward Joy Decker. Yates dropped the pick handle and drew the pistol from his belt, cocking it, training it on Ray Gilliam, who'd started to take a step forward. "See, I don't believe this little lady wants to get blood all over that clean gingham dress . . . now do ya?" Fish's eyes riveted on hers.

"I'm warning you," she said; but Fish had moved within arm's reach.

"You ain't suppose to *warn* a person," he said, keeping his eyes on hers. With a swipe of his pistol across her jaw, he sent her spinning across the front wall. Her pistol fired off into the ceiling, and he lowered his pistol toward her, where she lay still as stone. Turning his face back to Ray Gilliam, he said, "Now where's Red's little girl? Or I'll blow this woman's head off."

Ray Gilliam's nostrils flared. Yates kept the pistol centered on him. "You think he's playing, boy, you just watch."

"I'll kill her," Fish said; and he stepped a few inches closer to her as she moaned on the dust-covered floor.

Frank Bacon had straightened up from across the

table and just started to say something across his swollen lips when a blast from old Turner's double barrel shotgun lifted him off his feet and sent him sailing up across the bar in a spray of blood.

"*Jesus R*—!" Solomon Fish flinched down, throwing his arm up as a shield. Gilliam and Yates had ducked down as well. Before Fish could straighten up, old Turner had jumped inside the door and jammed the shotgun down close to his face. Dick Yates saw a chance to make a break for it while Turner covered his partner. He took it, spinning away, leaping a table and crashing through a pile of wood beside a potbellied stove.

"Shoot him, Turner," Ray Gilliam yelled. "Don't let him get away!"

But Turner was too old and slow, and Yates crashed through another table and disappeared out the back door. Ray Gilliam snatched up the shotgun and a shell from the floor and took off after him.

Fish looked up at old Turner, his pistol still in his hand but pointing away. "Am I under arrest or what?"

"I'm not the sheriff anymore but—"

Before Turner could finish, Fish swung the pistol and shot him in the chest. Turner went backward, the shotgun belching a load of fire to the ceiling. "There, you meddling old fool. That'll teach ya."

Joy Decker moaned and tried to raise up, but Solomon Fish slammed a boot on the back of her neck and held her down. "You screwed everything up here," he said; and he held the pistol barrel down an inch from her head and had started to pull the trigger. But he flinched at the sound of Ray Gilliam's shotgun outside in the street, and jumped away from Joy Decker and over to the door.

Dick Yates came racing along the middle of the street and veered over toward the horses, leaving a wake of dust. A few yards back, Ray Gilliam slung the empty shotgun at him. The shotgun grazed off his shoulder and spun away. "Come on, Dick," Solomon Fish shouted, "we're done here." Running from the saloon to the horses, Fish snatched their reins loose.

Ray Gilliam staggered to a halt in the street as the two outlaws fell up across their horses and pounded away. His breath heaved. With his fists clenched he looked all around for a horse, something to chase them on. And he stood there, no gun, no horse, his face battered and bleeding. He cursed himself, seeing the few remaining townsfolk venture out from hiding now.

His daughter came running from Decker's mercantile, and she threw her arms around him there in the street. "It's all right, Myra. It's all over." He tried to soothe her, the two of them moving over toward the saloon where Joy Decker stood in the doorway with a hand on her bloody cheek. Myra pulled loose from her father's side and ran to her. Ray Gilliam hurried along behind her.

"He's—he's dead," Joy Decker said, nodding back to where Turner's body lay in a dark puddle. "That loathsome coward killed him."

Ray Gilliam winced, looking past her at Turner. "I expect they're going to kill us all before they're through," he said. "Maybe Jake the blacksmith was right in leaving."

She hugged Myra Gilliam against her to keep the child from seeing inside the saloon. "No. Too many of us have left already. We must stay. This would never have happened if Sheriff Elliot had been here."

Sheriff Elliot . . . Ray Gilliam just looked at her, then

to Turner's body, then past Turner and over behind the bar where a shattered mirror stood dripping long red strings of blood. Frank Bacon's body lay out of sight but his hat had been nailed to the mirror by buckshot pellets and hung there on a shard of glass. "They'll be back," he said under his breath. "This time they'll bring Montana Red with them." He shook his head slowly, looking down at her eyes, eyes full of hope in spite of the swollen purple gash across her delicate cheek.

"Then we'll fight them," she said, swaying slightly, she and Myra hugging each other as if each were holding up the other. "I know Joe Elliot," she added. "I know our sheriff. He's a good man."

He looked at her for a second longer, then looked away. He thought of the pistol lying wrapped and put away at home. How long had it been since he'd fired it? Would he still have the knack he once had, back before he'd settled down and made a life for his wife and child here? He considered it and swallowed a dry lump in his throat. What did it matter. He really had no choice.

"Sheriff or no sheriff," he said in a flat tone, "we're going to die if we stay here." And he raised an arm around the two of them and led them away toward Joy Decker's store while a few cautious heads ventured out from the shadowed doorways, then murmuring quietly, pulled back inside.

Solomon Fish and Dick Yates didn't slow down until they were well above the town and headed back toward the flatland leading toward Rocky Roost. When they did stop for a moment, Fish laughed and wheezed and hiked a gob of brown mud from his throat and spit it away. "I swear, Dick, you orta seen your face . . . laying down boot leather with that big Africano ready to whop your arse with a shotgun." He laughed and slapped a hand on his thigh. Dust billowed.

Dick Yates let off his reins, the horse blowing and standing straddle-legged in the dirt. "There weren't nothing funny about it. You shoulda gone on and kilt him, instead of playing around with that little woman."

Solomon Fish settled, coughed, and turned a more serious gaze on him. "It can't all be *work*, Dick. A man has to lend himself to a little fun now and again. Besides, you and Francis was suppose to whip that boy into shape, smacking him with pick handles, weren't ya?"

"That was that damn Frank Bacon's fault. He couldn't smack his pecker on a barn door." Dick Yates spit. "He got what was coming to him, I reckon. Red's gonna throw a fit. What're you gonna tell him about us not getting that little girl for him?"

Fish slumped his wrists on his saddle horn for a second, then let go a breath and said, "I'll just tell him the truth. Say they got a bad-arse new sheriff in town and he come upon so fast we never saw what hit us." He grinned. "Even Red'll have to understand that we ain't no match for the man what kilt Fast Felton, I reckon."

"I ain't lying to him," Yates said. "He'll kill us both once he finds out what really happened."

"He ain't gonna find out," Fish said, spitting and running a hand across his dirty lips. "He'll get all stoked up over what happened and ride in there shooting before anybody tells him different." He took up his reins and straightened in the saddle. "You just go along with me. I ain't never steered ya wrong, have I?"

"You better hope you're right," Yates said, collecting his horse up with the quick stab on his reins. "I come up here to avenge that old ranger for killing my brother . . . not to get Montana Red down my shirt."

PART 4

Gray Rain Falling

CHAPTER 12

They'd swung wide off the main trail leading up to the mining town, coming in from the east, up off the flatland now and into the shelter of rock and scrub piñon in case any remaining *comadrejas* had ventured this close to town. They'd moved quietly all morning, the ranger in front on the white barb with the black circle around its eye, leading the *comadrejas'* woman's horse at the end of a rope behind him.

The only sound above the soft clop of hoof on dirt was the stir of a warm wind among the boulders, and the protest of a bird now and then as it gave leave from its perch at their coming. "We will be there soon," she said in a flat tone. "What will then become of me?"

He smiled without looking back at her. "Still think I'm gonna kill ya, huh? Or stick ya in jail?" They moved along into a narrow rock canyon, and when she made no reply, he added, "Well, I reckon you'll believe me when we get there." He paused for another second, then said, "Far as I'm concerned, you kept your word. You took care of me . . . you did your best. That's all I require of a person. My plan is to get you some decent clothes, give you some traveling money, and put you on a stage. What you do with your life then is up to you." He glanced back at her where she followed along with her hands crossed on the ragged saddle horn on the dead *comadreja*'s horse. "Fair enough?"

"*Sí*—I mean, yes. If this is *truly* what you will do."

He shook his head and gazed forward. This woman had seen a lot in her time on the badlands. What had brought her here he did not know, nor would he ask. Perhaps it had been as she said—that the *comadrejas* had forced her to stay with them. He had no idea. Life had taught him long ago to take a person's words with a grain of salt, yet judge their actions on the weight of gold. She could've been telling the truth. There were those who ended up here not by their own choice or owing to any particular thing they'd done. There were some who just seemed fated to a lower state of circumstance. Perhaps this was her case.

There had been many chances for her to take the horses and leave him while he'd lain overcome by the fever. She must've thought of it more than once, he figured. But she hadn't done it. That made her better than most, in his book. She deserved a second chance; and thinking this, he glanced back at her once more, and added, "If I wasn't going to let you go, I wouldn't have said it."

She smiled to herself, a secretive smile, as he turned his gaze forward and up along the high ridge above them. She trusted him now, perhaps not completely, but more so than she had trusted anyone for as far back as she could remember. Once the poison was out of his system, when he no longer needed her, he could have killed her, or left her behind to fend for herself in this rocky inferno. Yet he didn't. It had been a few days since the fever had racked through him. Although he was still weak from it, he could have taken her during the night and done with her as he pleased—as most men had in her life—yet he hadn't.

Only the night before, as evening shadows fell long across flatland where they'd taken camp against a narrow stream of run-off water, she had tested him, teased him by dropping one shoulder of her dress as she bathed herself. He was watching, she knew; and she washed her hand slowly over her shoulder, easing the dress down until she felt the cool air on her naked breast. As she'd cupped water up in her hand and let it pour down her, she felt his eyes on her.

She had stopped bathing and looked over at him as if in surprise, her hand going over her naked breast, hiding it. With her eyes she'd given him the slightest suggestion. But after a second he'd taken a deep breath and said to her, "Prove it on somebody else." Then he'd turned and walked back to the circle of low flames, and sat down and gazed out across the flatland.

When she'd finished bathing, she dried herself and came to the fire. She'd ask him what he meant, *Prove it on someone else?* And he'd said that she only wanted to prove to herself what she already thought was the truth—that all men were out to take advantage of her. He'd said that he would not allow himself to be proof of it.

Then, in the falling darkness he'd gone on to say in his own words that people only choose to see the world they have created inside themselves, and in that world of their design they go about day by day doing whatever they must, to remind themselves that their acts and intentions were just, and that their opinions were always right about the people who lived within that world.

"Me, for instance," he'd added. "I created my own world a long time ago—a place where the law reigns high above every other thing."

"Law is only one more tool of man's making," she'd said. "I am only a poor woman, but I know that law is only a tricky set of rules made by the strong so they can rule over the weak. Law is unjust to all, except to those who make them."

"Not my law," he said. "My law is simple and just."

"Your law? Your world?" She shook her head. "Once again you speak as if you yourself are God."

"No I don't. But for all intent, God's given me both cause and benefit of enacting his law." He'd leaned near her, and she liked the way he spoke to her not in the way a man usually spoke to a woman, or in the way a *comadreja* spoke to a slave. Though his words were often less polished, he spoke to her in the way she remembered the padres speaking to her at the mission near her village.

"There are three levels of law in my world—" As he spoke, with the edge of his hand he divided the air before him three times, layer upon layer. "Way up here there's God's law. God is merciful, so these are common laws that all people know and live by, if there's any decency in them." He dropped his hand down slightly. "Then down about here, there's *man's* law . . . just in case somebody strays downward from *God's* law, loses sight of it, or decides he's just too ornery to live by it any longer."

He held her eyes in his until she nodded for him to continue. Holding his hand there, he reached out with his other hand and slapped himself on the wrist. "See? Man is vengeful, and when they step out of line, God reaches down by way of man's law and sorta slaps them people back in place . . . tells them they best pay attention."

He smiled and dropped his hand lower and held it there. "Of course, some of them don't listen even then. And they end up down here, on my *list*, and what you might call the lower end of *all* laws. They come into my world, into my law. God and man are no longer in the picture—they've washed their hands of it. It's up to me to set things right."

"Your list." She'd looked at his hand, held there rigid in the thin air of the dark desert night, then gazed into his caged eyes amid the flicker of the low flames. "And in this place where there is only your list and your law . . . where you alone become both God's mercy and man's vengeance—?" She paused. "In the end, who do *you* answer to?"

When she'd asked him this, he hadn't replied right away. Instead, he'd only leaned back against a rock and gazed down into the flames, the firelight flickering, casting a thin black shadow on the scar along his cheek. When he did speak again his voice had gone lower and it seemed to come less from him than from the endless dark around them. "No one. I've become only a hammer that cocks and falls . . . final redemption for man's greatest sin." He added in a whisper. "Both theirs, and my own . . ."

In that instant she had glimpsed a madness in him. Yet it did not disturb her. In *her* world she had grown accustomed to man's madness, and had, in the world she'd created within *herself*, come to determine that in some way all men were mad. But this man? She watched his back now as he led her horse along the canyon trail. This man would do as he said he would do. He would give her a new start, and she would take it. She trusted this man even in his madness, for his was a madness she'd come to understand.

Suddenly, she was jerked from her thoughts as the ranger pulled both horses to a halt against the side of the canyon. He stared upward at a distant rock ledge; and she sat silent for a moment before saying in a hushed tone, "What is it?"

"Shh." He held a hand back toward her, still studying the ridgeline. "Keep still. Somebody's up there." He'd seen something flash in the sunlight, and now waited to see if it came again. A rifle barrel? No. Too bright for a rifle barrel. A pistol? A shiny little pistol like the young gambler, Gentleman Joe Sharpe, carried? Maybe.

They sat as still as the stone surrounding them. After a moment he wondered if perhaps his eyes had tricked him in the sun's glare. Although the poison was out of his system, he was still weak, his reflexes still a bit slow, his eyes perhaps not yet as sharp as they should be. But then, even as he questioned himself, it came again. It was no more than a quick flash this time, but it was enough to pinpoint its location there at the edge of a jagged ridge.

"I saw it," she said behind him in a whisper.

"Yeah, me too." He nodded and motioned for her to step down from the horse in the shadow of the canyon wall. Whatever it was, it lay above them three hundred yards ahead, and he wouldn't risk passing below it down here in this narrow canyon. "Come on—" He spun his horse's reins around a jut of rock and did the same with the lead rope. "We're gonna have to get behind whoever's up there." He gazed around and up at a slice of broken boulder that led upward.

"Are you able to climb?" she asked, stepping over

beside him as he raised his big pistol from its holster and checked it.

"I'm able." He raised his eyes to hers. "You stay close by in case it's some of your old friends."

"I gave you my word," she said. "I am no longer a part of the *comadrejas*."

"That ain't what I mean." He holstered the pistol. "If they see you're with me now, they might not take kindly to it."

"Then give me a gun and I will do my part."

He considered it for a second, then said as he stepped forward against the crack in the boulder facing, "We'll see . . . once we get to the top."

For the next half hour they climbed until at last they'd moved over the edge and they lay quietly behind a rock. When the ranger had caught his breath, he eased up, peeped over the rock, and shook his head. Thirty yards away, sunlight glittered off the flask in Joe Sharpe's hand and danced in a silver streak. The ranger watched him for a few more seconds, then slid down beside the *comadrejas'* woman. "Is it them, the *comadrejas*?" she asked, seeing the ashen color of his face.

He leaned against the rock, pushing his hat brim up. "No, it's just one man. A fellow named Gentleman Joe Sharpe, if I ain't mistaken."

"You—you know this man?"

He checked the pistol in his hand, and let it lie across his lap. "We've never met . . . but in a manner of speaking, yes I do." He squinted and rubbed his eyes. "He's done himself some good it appears. Wearing a sheriff's badge, of all things."

"He is a lawman? Like yourself? Then we have reason to hide from him?" She started to stand up, but he caught her arm and stopped her.

"Wearing a badge ain't never made a man right. He could've picked it up anywhere."

"Then what will we do now?"

"We'll just wait here for a spell, see what he's up to. He's harmless most likely, unless he gets spooked. My guess is he's pulled some kind of shenanigan in that mining town. He wasn't dressed or mounted that well the last I heard of him." He squinted and rubbed his eyes, feeling the weakness come over him as it had for days. He shook it off.

"You are still ill," she said, looking at him. "Perhaps we should not wait here."

"I'm all right. Still get a little blind flash now and then. That was some pretty strong poison your friends shot in me."

She looked down at the ground, then back to him. "Yes, it is strong. And do not think it is finished with you just because the fever is gone. It can still kill you."

"Trying to cheer me up a little, huh?" He smiled a weak smile, his clothes more loose on him than before. His color was wrong and his eyes a bit sunken.

"I'm trying to make you see that we must get on into town, where you can rest and regain your strength."

He gestured a hand down himself. "I admit I ain't quite back to my fighting weight." He pushed himself up onto his knees, gazed around the rock toward Gentleman Joe Sharpe, then dropped back beside her, his breathing labored. "Afraid something'll happen now and you won't get that new dress? Want me to put something in writing just in case?"

"No. We have made it this far . . . I want to go on, and see you get well."

"I am getting well. It just has to catch up to me."

"This man." She nodded in Joe Sharpe's direction. "Is there trouble between you?"

"No, but he thinks there is."

"Then let him know, so we can go on."

"Can't do it. He's of a cowardly nature. I go surprising him, he's apt to bolt like a spring colt and break his neck . . . or else take to shooting at us and I'd have to kill him before I could tell him anything." He let out a deep breath and shook his head. "It's best we wait a spell. Besides, I'm curious as to what he's been up to. New clothes, new horse. There's no telling what he's told those folks back in the mining town."

"Then, can we at least climb back down to the horses and wait in the shade? He cannot leave without us knowing it."

"Yeah, we can do that, I reckon." He wiped a hand across his beaded brow. "But just let me sit here for a second. Need to catch my wind."

When he said that, she looked at him, knowing that he was not nearly as well as he wanted her to believe. "*Sí,*" she said quietly, and as they waited, she cursed the *comadrejas* for the low weasels that they were, and she cursed herself for ever being a part of such a world as theirs.

Joe Sharpe had finished off the flask of whiskey by the time the two riders crossed the flatland beneath him. Only two of them now, the one with the bandaged foot gone—but gone where? What had happened to him? Had he stayed in town? Had he gone off on his own? Sharpe wondered, watching as they streamed along at the head of a ribbon of dust. From his perch high above them the riders moved in silence, two small creatures weaving the thin brown trail past tall spiny cactus and through patches of cholla and pale green gramma grass until that ribbon of dust wrapped itself over the edge of the flatland and drifted away.

He rubbed his chin and gazed west where a thin darkness seeped upward on the horizon. Weather moving in . . . That's all he needed right now. Well, forget the third man wherever he was. Sharpe still had to go back to town long enough to get his things together and leave. He could slip in unnoticed maybe, not have to face the man with the bandaged foot, if the man was even there. With luck maybe he could get out ahead of the weather and outrun it to the badlands. He stood up, dusted his trousers, picked up his reins, and mounted the horse.

When he rode past the spot on the narrow trail where the ranger and the *comadreja* woman had moved their horses into the shelter of the sliced boulder, the woman watched him until he was out of sight, then she said to the ranger lying beside her, "Wake up. It is time we leave here. He is gone." She looked down at the ranger and when he did not move, she shook his shoulder gently. But he only struggled against her hand for a second and drifted back to sleep. Sweat stood on his brow—his system working against the poison, the poison making its last stand at trying to kill him. *Let him rest*. She ran a hand back along his wet brow, and sat with him for another half hour before trying to wake him again.

"We must go now," she said after the time had passed. Again she shook him by his shoulder.

This time he stirred slowly, and raised himself up, rubbing his eyes. He gazed around them looking confused. "How—how long have I been asleep?"

"Most of the afternoon." She helped him rise up and lean against a rock.

"That can't be," he said. He staggered and caught himself and rubbed his face.

"But it is so. I thought the man would never leave. Earlier I thought I heard gunshots from far away. But I am not sure."

"You did?" He collected himself. "Why didn't you wake me up then?"

"I tried but you would not wake up. We must get you food, and a place to rest if you plan on staying alive."

"Well—" He leveled his shoulders and slapped dust from himself with his sombrero. "I *do* plan on staying alive." He looked around once again with a determined expression. "I don't like *not* being warned when something's going on around me."

She saw that he was ashamed of his weak condition. "Then I was wrong and should have awakened you? For what reason? So you would hear the same faint gunfire, and wondered what it meant the same as I did?"

He didn't answer, but instead placed his gray sombrero on his head and adjusted it and nodded at the horses. "Let's saddle up and get on to where we're going."

"*Sí*," she said, lowering her eyes. "We have waited too long already."

But when the saddles were on the horses, they did not go on right away because she saw him falter to the side and had to catch him against her to keep him from falling. "You'll have to get us to that town," he said, his voice failing as she struggled with him and sat him back against the rock wall. "Take . . . off . . . my hat."

She took off his hat and fanned him with it. "Listen to me," he said. "If I'm not up to myself . . . don't tell anybody who I am."

"But why?" She laid his sombrero down and loosened his shirt at the collar.

"Just listen to me," he said, having a hard time breathing. "Hide my hat . . . somewhere." He reached a trembling hand down, loosened his gun belt, and brought his hand up to his badge. "Hide . . . these too."

She hurried, took off his badge, his holster, and gun, and wrapped the belt around the big pistol. As she stood, ready to pull him up and to his horse, she noticed a dimness sweep in about them and a cooling breeze that had not been there before. Above her and coming from the west, she saw a broad dark cloud seep upward on the horizon. *Of all times, now it must rain,* she thought, reaching down and taking him under his arms.

When she'd managed to get him up into his saddle, she shoved the holster belt with the big pistol in it down in his saddlebags and mounted her horse with the ranger's duster draped over her arm. She sidled her horse up against the ranger's and swung the duster around him as he sat slumped in his saddle. His hand caught the duster about him and held it closed at his throat. She reached out to place his sombrero on his head but he shoved her hand away. "Thought I told you to . . . hide my hat," he said.

"Not now," she said. "You must wear it until we get to town. There is a storm coming. Here." She reached out and shoved the sombrero down on his head. This time he didn't stop her. "Now give me your reins. I will lead you."

"I've never been . . . led in my life." His voice rasped. A low growl of thunder drifted in on the wind. On the far edge of the earth a streak of lightning licked down from the black cloud, twisted and curled and caught her eyes for a second.

Then she turned back to him and said, "Good. *I* have never *led* anyone in my life. Be still now, we must hurry."

Three miles ahead of them, Joe Sharpe heeled his horse into a quicker gait, seeing the storm moving in. Now it appeared even the weather would work against him. But storm or no storm, he wasn't sticking around any longer than he had to. His whiskey had worn off now, and he saw things clearly. Whatever indecision he'd felt before had resolved itself at the sight of the riders coming and going. No more thoughts about settling down here—no more curtains on the jail windows to block the noonday sun. It was time to make a run for it, plain and simple.

He kept the horse's pace strong and steady against the rising wind, yet even still by the time he rode down into the main street the storm was upon the town with a fury. Deep wagon ruts now ran with swift streams of muddy water. Heavy sheets of rain stood sideways on the wind, whipping silver gray, pelting the buildings with the sound of grapeshot. Above him the sky lay low and churning, the color of a dark nightmare.

His horse leaned and shouldered the storm quarterwise, making its way to the livery barn. Joe Sharpe shouldered with it, low in the saddle with his free hand crushing the crown of his new hat to his head and the wind-driven rain flattening the brim against his cheek. Thunder crashed behind jagged forks of lightning.

Once inside the shelter of the barn he forced the door closed and called out for the livery attendant. When no one came he called out again, then walked the horse along the center bay of the barn, past stalls where other horses peered out and craned their necks and nickered long against the pitch of thunder overhead. Lightning flickered through cracks in the walls. He called out again, taking off his wet hat and slinging water from it. Then he looked all around in the grainy light. "Is anybody here? Hello?"

A lamplight flared and settled from the far end of the barn, and Ray Gilliam's voice spoke in a low tone. "He's gone. Looks like you'll tend your own stock today, *Sheriff.*"

There was something unsettling in Ray Gilliam's voice and Joe Sharpe stood for a second before saying, "Ray? Ray Gilliam? Is that you? What are you doing here? Where's Ned?"

"Told you, he's gone, *Sheriff* Joe. He packed and left before the storm, in a one-horse buggy. Said he's going to join Jake the Blacksmith down in Wakely."

Sharpe read more in his tone than in his words, and he said to the glow of lamplight moving closer to him, "But, I thought he wanted to take up where the blacksmith left off here? He told Turner that he saw this as a chance to—"

"Turner's dead, *Sheriff,*" Ray Gilliam said in a flat tone, cutting him off. "Some of Montana Red's rats killed him while you where away *searching* for him." He stopped and raised the wick of the lantern until Joe Sharpe saw him clearly in the circling glow. He saw the look on Ray Gilliam's battered face and saw the long pistol slung low on his hip. And Ray added, "Don't suppose you ran into ole Red while you were out there?"

Joe Sharpe winced, seeing the swollen eyes and the puffed jaw with the cut across it, still oozing a thin trickle of blood. "My God! Ray. What did they do to you?"

Ray Gilliam stepped closer, showing his battered face as if it were an accusation. "What does it *look* like they did to me?" He searched Joe Sharpe's eyes, then added, "They did the same to Miss Decker—not quite as bad."

"Joy—I mean, Miss Decker? They hurt her too?" He wrapped his wet horse's reins around the pole of a stall. "Where is she?"

"She's better now. She's in bed. My daughter's with her. Turner killed one of them. Then one of them killed him." His swollen eyes bored into Joe Sharpe's. "Now what're you going to do about it, *Sheriff Elliot?*"

Sharpe fidgeted. "Well I—I'm going to see they pay for what they've done, of course. As soon as this blasted storm lets up, I'll— That is, once I find out exactly what happened here."

"You'll do what? Find a way to skip town? Leave us here at their mercy? Don't even think it, *Sheriff*. There's only a handful of us left here. But I'm staying . . . you're staying too." He moved closer to Joe Sharpe, too close—menacing.

Sharpe stepped back, raising a hand. "Now, Ray, you're upset right now and not thinking real straight. We're going to have to look at this from all sides—"

"He's coming for my daughter," Ray Gilliam said. His nostrils flared; he laid his hand on the butt of his pistol. "Do you hear what I'm saying?"

Sharpe felt his fear course through him. A sickness churned low in his belly. "Your daughter? Montana Red is coming *here* to take her? Take little Myra?"

"No!" Gilliam's voice turned harsh. "He just *thinks* he is. I'm armed now, and I'm not running from him. Neither are you. It's going to be you and me, Sheriff, just the two of us . . . and we're going to burn him and his boys down the minute they ride in. Any problem with that?" Thunder rolled in overhead and crashed like cannon fire.

CHAPTER 13

Myra Gilliam stood at the window above Joy Decker's store, looking out through the storm as the swirl of brown water raced in braids along the rain-slick street. From an alley beside the hotel she saw the woman come out against the wind with the man's arm looped across one shoulder and a saddlebag across the other. In a flash of lightning that hung wide for a lingering second, she saw the woman struggle up onto the boardwalk, her hair plastered to her face, the man's head hanging limp, water running off his face.

"Myra, dear? Will you fetch me a clean wet rag? This one is stained something terrible." Behind her, Joy Decker's voice caused her to turn from the window and walk over to the bed. She nodded and took the damp rag from the woman's outstretched hand; and without mentioning the man and woman who'd appeared from out of the storm, she went off with it to the linen closet.

On the street below, the *comadreja* woman made her way along the boardwalk with the ranger clinging to her side. Before leaving the alley she'd taken his sombrero and flattened it into a wet heap and stuffed it into one side of the saddlebags. At the hotel, she dropped the saddlebags and beat on the door with the heel of her hand. Thunder jarred the boardwalk beneath her, and she beat harder and longer until a voice called from inside, "All right, hold your horses." A bolt dropped inside the door.

She glanced around at the empty flooded street and drew the ranger closer against her. She couldn't remember the last time she'd been in a town. Being here frightened her.

When the door opened a few inches, a voice said, "Who in the world would be out in weather such as—"

"We need lodging," she said, the two of them spilling in through the door, pushing it farther open. The hotel clerk stepped back, catching his arms around the ranger as the woman's strength slackened. Her breath heaved in her chest. "Please help us." She staggered back, picked up the saddlebags, slung them inside, and closed the door behind her. She fell back against the door frame and caught herself.

"Well I should say so," the clerk said, turning and helping the ranger over to a divan and letting him down on it. The ranger looked up at him but didn't speak. A streak of lightning flashed in and out through the front windows.

The *comadreja* woman stepped in and said, "We must have a room. My *father* is very ill. He must have food, and rest."

The clerk took note of the bandaged wound on the ranger's leg and asked, "What happened to him? Snake bite?" As he asked, his eyes swept up and down her, taking note of her ragged clothing, her moccasins, her long hair hanging wet and tangled. She lowered her eyes from his and pushed her hair from her face with a wet hand.

"The *comadrejas* attacked us," she said. "My father fought them off, but not before one of their poison arrows hit him."

"I see." He looked back at the ranger. "He looks pretty much spent to me, but I'm no doctor."

"I must save him," she said, leaning in and running a hand back across the ranger's head. "This is the worst of it. With food and rest he will live."

The clerk looked doubtful and rubbed his pointed chin. "Well, we have plenty of empty rooms. This place is empty. As far as food, you're welcome to what's here, such as it is." He moved away and behind the counter, where he took up a key and came back with it. "But I'm afraid you won't find much. As of tonight this hotel is officially closed until further notice." He handed her the key and added, "I only run it for some folks back East. They left out of here last summer." He smiled, reaching down with her to lift the ranger. "I'm leaving in the morning. Feel free to help yourself to what you need, within reason of course." Above them thunder slammed hard in the sky and rolled away.

"Oh, you are leaving?" She looked at him as they stood with the ranger between them and moved to the stairs.

"Yes, ma'am. Most everybody else has already left. We've had a bad run here with an outlaw. It's drove away all the business. Of course the town was barely holding on anyway."

"I see."' On the way up the stairs, she asked him, "Then who do we pay for the room after you are gone?" The hotel groaned and seemed to lean slightly against a hard thrust of wind.

At the top of the stairs they turned and he nodded

toward the second door on their right, and he said as they struggled toward it, "You can pay it to the wind, far as I care."

"*Gracías*," she said; and when they'd gotten the ranger inside the room and over on the edge of the bed, the clerk looked at him closely and shook his head. "You might find you some leftover stew in the kitchen. There might even be the makings for a hot mustard poultice down there somewhere. If he's fevered, that'll sure burn it out of him."

"I must get him into a good hot bath first," she said. "Is there a tub here?"

"Sure, two doors down. But you'll have to heat the water yourself. I'm busy packing up and putting things to storage."

"Yes, I will take care of it," she said. "You have been most kind."

"Well, I *hope* I've helped *some*." He looked once more at the ranger, then shook his head again and left.

"That fellow . . . has me dead . . . and in the bone-yard," the ranger said in rasping voice. He coughed and shivered.

"Let us hope he is not right," the *comadreja* woman said, pressing him back onto the soft bed. "We must get your wet boots and clothes off of you."

"Is this that last surge you told me about?"

"*Sí*. The poison has done its worst, after this you will be rid of it, or—" She stopped speaking and turned away toward his feet as she began tugging at a wet boot.

"*Or* what? You can say it," he said, coughing a little. "*Or* I'll be dead?"

"Yes," she answered in a flat tone. "If you must hear me say it, you will be dead." The wet boot came off in her hands and she dropped it to the floor and reached for his other foot.

He raised slightly and took her by the forearm. "You had every opportunity . . . to leave me . . . out there today." His clouded eyes searched hers.

"*Sí.* I had the *opportunity.*" She took her forearm from his weak hand and tugged at his other boot. When it came free she dropped it and stepped back and looked down at him. "Now we take off your wet clothes."

He forced down a dry swallow. "All of them?"

"Of course, *all of them.*" She leaned, unbuttoning his dirty wet shirt. "If you wish for me to *act* embarrassed I will, but it will *only* be an act—to make you feel as a man thinks he must feel. Do not forget, I have been with the *comadrejas.* Nothing shames me. Living is all that matters."

He raised enough for her to pull his wet shirt from his arm and peel it from his back. "Why didn't you?" he asked as he collapsed back on the feather mattress.

"Why didn't I what?" She unbuttoned his trousers and stopped for second, looking down at him.

"Why didn't you . . . leave me out there today? I know you thought about it."

"At what place do we learn to trust one another?" she said. "At the place where you know my thoughts and fear them? Or at a place where you see my acts and believe them? You said you would set me free. And so you will. But it is I who must *free* myself from the life of a *comadreja* in order for it to be complete."

"You didn't learn that thinking . . . riding with . . . the desert weasels," he said; and he lay back on the bed and lifted himself and felt his wet trousers go down and off his feet.

"No. These things a person learns in spite of where they live or who they live with." She took a rolled quilt from across the foot of the bed and spread it over him. "Lie still now. I must go take the horses out of the storm."

She heated water on the wood stove in the kitchen of the empty hotel, bringing it up two kettles at a time and pouring it over the edge of the tub near his feet. Outside the storm raged and battered the building. While the ranger sat in the steaming tub, she returned to the kitchen, heated the leftover stew, and searched about until she found a string of dried red peppers and ground them in her hands and stirred them into the bubbling gravy.

She wiped sweat from her forehead and chewed on a cold, stale biscuit, then took the hot food up to him on a metal tray. On her way to the room she passed the clerk, who'd only glanced up at her from where he stood gathering paperwork from beneath the counter and stacking it into a wooden shipping crate. "How's he doing?" he asked, then glanced back down before she could answer, as if her answer could not be as important as the task before him.

When she'd sat the food beside the bed, she went to the room where the ranger bathed. He'd raised himself and stood from the tub, leaning against it with both hands. He shivered and turned his face at her with water dripping from him. He shook his head and said in a struggling voice, "Where in hell do they . . . find such a poison as this?"

"Where all poison is found," she said, picking up a towel and going to him with it. "Here, we will get you covered up now and get some medicine in you."

"Medicine?" He looked at her as she threw the towel around his shoulders and drew him against her side. She led him with his arm looped over her shoulder.

"*Sí*. Food *is* medicine," she said. "No medicine can heal a body that food has not nourished."

And helping him back to the room, she let him down to the bed and covered him to his chin with the quilt and fed him with a large wooden spoon until he at last turned his face away. "You've burnt my insides out," he said, his voice already sounding stronger than it had all day. He started to rise, but she pressed him back. "Let me up. I've got to have some water."

"You stay covered. I will bring you water."

She stood and left and while she was gone he succumbed to a lull of mind, a state of drifting that was not quite awake yet not fully sleeping. He fought it at first, but it overcame him, and it lasted throughout most of the night.

As the storm raged, he caught glimpses of her in the flashes of light that licked across the room and vanished. He'd heard her leave again for a time, then come back into the room with a towel wrapped around her. He drifted off again for a moment and returned to see her standing naked at the foot of the bed, outside the low circling glow of an oil lamp.

Staring at the dark shape of her, he watched her hair hang long to one side as she ran the towel down it. When lightning flared and lingered for a moment, she stood awash in the silver blue glow, and her shadowed eyes caught his until darkness settled back around them. "And now you have seen me naked as well," she said. Or at least he thought she'd said it. He wasn't sure. A fog drifted between him and his thoughts until he no longer knew what was real or what was imagined.

He saw her face close to his at one point in a lick of blue silver and could've sworn he felt her naked body sweep in against him beneath the quilt. He felt—or imagined—his hand brush down along her tight warm stomach until it stopped down there and could move no farther. And with her moist and warm against his hand, again he drifted.

In a distant dream he asked her as he'd asked her before, "Where do they get such poison?"

"From the earth," she'd answered through a heavy veil.

"You're wrong," he said. "There's no such poison comes out of the earth." Outside the lightning twisted and curled and flashed fire across the black heavens. Thunder pounded and rolled off and over itself like some powerful race of giants locked in terrible battle.

Her voice fell away from him, saying, "If goodness comes from the earth, does not evil come from it as well?" Her words formed a tangle of vivid green foliage whose vines turned like tentacles as she spoke, and within those vines purple blossoms unfolded, sharp and beautiful—the colors of poison, he thought as the foliage entwined him.

"Nooooo," he whispered long and fading, his voice not fully sounding like himself but rather like a darkened shade of himself come over from some foreign place. "Evil sprouts from the seed of man . . . from man and noplace else."

As that shade of himself spoke to her through the veil, he felt her hand on his brow and saw Montana Red rise up from amid a fiery brown dust, his eyes ablaze, the color of blood. "Man is a mountain of evil," the ranger heard himself whisper. "Evil courses his veins."

"*Sí,*" he heard her say, pressing her hand down on him. "And does *man* and mountain not come from the dust of the earth, as all living things do?"

When morning shadows seeped gray and damp across the window ledge, he raised up on his elbows and saw her standing, dressed now, looking out through the harsh downpour at the street below. Thunder grumbled in the distance, and he heard the rain falling straight and windless on the roof above them. "The storm passed, huh?" He asked, already knowing, and sank back into the bed, feeling whole and cool and at peace for the first time since the arrow had spilled its poison into him.

Without looking up from the street she said, "Only one has passed, but I think more will come. They are coming from Mexico, these black storms."

"Figures," he said, offering a thin smile toward the ceiling. "All I ever got out of Old Mex was a bad storm or a wrong cut of beef." He stretched and raised again. "Whatever you gave me last night sure turned the corner for me. What was it?"

"Only stew and peppers," she said, still watching the street below, her dark eyes piercing the grayness and studying something down there.

"Well, it gave me dreams like I've never seen in my life," he said. He squeezed a pillow up beneath his head and lay studying her form against the falling ray of grainy window light.

Her lips lifted in a trace of a smile. "I only gave you the medicine. The dreams were yours all along."

"Anyway. I feel well," he said. "I think we've beat it." A second passed and he added, "Was it my imagination or did we talk some, off and on through the night?" He thought of his hand and how he'd imagined it going down along her stomach and finding a place down there where she'd drawn it warm between her legs.

She didn't answer but only continued to gaze out the window as he stirred and rubbed his eyes. When he looked back at her, he said in a soft tone, "How old are you, if you don't mind saying."

Again she smiled, this time glancing at him, a quick knowing glance, then back to the street below. "In years you will consider me a child . . . but a child who is much *too old* for you."

"Just wondering," he said, blushing a bit. "I mean . . . last night, some things were said . . . I might have even done something untoward for all I know. It wouldn't be right if I did."

She turned now and looked at him, her dark hair clean and free of desert and glistening even in the pale gray light. "When a man is ill his stomach turns in circles. When he is well and whole, his stomach turns always to one direction." She smiled. "You *are* feeling better, I can see."

His face reddened, and he tried swinging up on the side of the bed, but couldn't right away. "Where's my big pistol?"

She stepped over and helped him up on his next try and sat him on the side of the bed. He took note of his nakedness and snatched a corner of the quilt over his lap. "Sit still," she said. "You will be weak for a while. Your pistol is in the saddlebags. I will get it for you."

"Well . . . thanks," he said, letting out a breath, embarrassed, as she slipped over to the saddlebags on the floor. He felt small and helpless, sitting there, naked beneath the quilt. He leaned forward with his palms on his knees and gazed at the floor, shaking his head. "I swear I've never been in such a shape. Whatever I mighta done, I apologize for it."

She shrugged, tossing his words away, and came back with the big holster and slipped the pistol from it. Bending down before him, she held it out on the palms of her hands, some offering in kind that might restore him from his awkwardness. "See, it is just like you left it." She smiled a guarded smile and leaned back from him. When he glanced at her, taking the pistol and then looking down at it as he turned it on his lap, she ran a hand back along his hair and smiled. "And I brought up your rifle. It is under the bed."

"Oh, that's good." He sat in silence, studying the pistol on his lap.

"You have been more ill than you knew," she said. "The poison of the *comadrejas* gets inside and works its way around a person's mind as well as their body. If it does not kill you quickly, it slowly drains from you the life source that makes you want to go on living. Soon you think you are fighting death when you are really only waiting for it to embrace you."

"Some poison," he said, "if it does all that."

"It is so," she said. "And last night if your hand found me, and found something that made life come forward in you if only for a second, then it is a part of the medicine you needed, in order to live."

He sighed, and shook his head and looked away from her. "Where'd you grow up, thinking things like that?"

She didn't answer, but instead stood up and picked up his damp duster from where she'd spread it across a wooden chair. She threw it about herself and rolled the long sleeves up above her wrists. "I will go find us some food in this town if there is anyone left who serves it. The clerk said most people have left because they are afraid of an outlaw. I think he meant the man you are hunting."

"Yep, that would be my guess. We're getting close to Red Hollis's stomping grounds. I can feel it in the air." He lifted the pistol and hefted it in his hand, the weight of it feeling different, heavier to him.

She saw how his hand went weak until he lowered the pistol back down on his lap. "I hate a town that packs and runs, lets themselves get scared off by some no-account like Hollis."

"But he *is* a dangerous killer, is he not?" She watched his eyes closely.

Instead of answering her he said, "Keep your eyes open for that fellow we saw yesterday. My guess is he's around here somewheres. I don't want him shooting at me if I can help it." He stopped and considered something for a second, then added, "Whatever you do, be sure and keep an eye out for Red Hollis."

"How will I know if I see him?"

"You'll know," he said.

"Then I will watch for him too." She nodded. "I will be your eyes and ears until you are able to go do what you must do."

He looked at her. "You've done more already than you had to. You're free to leave if you want."

"I know." Her dark eyes fixed on his, and she gathered the damp duster around herself and left the room.

As the sound of her footsteps faded down the stairs, he laid the big pistol aside, lowered himself down off the bed, kneeled there, steadying himself for a second, then reached out and pulled the canvas-wrapped rifle from beneath it.

CHAPTER 14

Joe Sharpe and Ray Gilliam stood in silence at the empty bar, Ray Gilliam cleaning the sawed-off shotgun, Joe Sharpe standing a few feet down from him, watching, the tension between the two men running high and tight. Sharpe ran it through his mind and decided that there wasn't a thing holding him here now except the intimidation this man held over him. He'd be breaking no law if he simply threw up his hands and said, *That's it, I'm leaving.*

Would this man try to stop him? How far would Gilliam go to keep him here? He'd run his bluff on Red Hollis. Was this any different? No it wasn't. He didn't owe this man, this town, or this *world* a thing. *Here goes* . . . He threw back a shot of whiskey, ready to say something; but just then the *comadreja* woman stepped inside out of the rain and Sharpe snapped his head around, startled at the sound of the creaking bat wing doors. But seeing the woman, he let out a breath and glanced at Ray Gilliam. Behind her in the distance a roll of thunder grumbled low, giving warning as another storm crept in.

"Take it easy," Gilliam said as he moved from the bar toward the woman standing there in the drooping rain-streaked riding duster. "Those rats weren't about to ride all night through storms just to get back here. Red thinks we're sitting ducks. He'll take his time."

Joe Sharpe stepped over to the woman with him, hoping he was right. Maybe he wouldn't say anything right now. Maybe he wouldn't say anything *at all*. Gilliam had been keeping a close eye on him, but once the weather broke that was it, Sharpe was leaving, shedding himself of this place before things got worse.

"What can we do for you, ma'am?" Gilliam asked as both of them tipped their hats slightly, Sharpe taking in the riding duster, much too large for her and full of brush marks. He eyed her closely as she spoke. And her eyes moved from one to the other, from the battered face of Ray Gilliam to the man with the badge, the same man she and the ranger had seen the day before. She moved a strand of wet hair from her cheek.

"My father and I have come here out of the storms. He is ill, and wounded, and needs food. I went to the place across the street but they are closed."

"Yes that's Gilda's Hash house," Ray Gilliam said. "But she's been gone over a month. I'm afraid you'll find little food around here unless you want to prepare it yourself. You must be the woman my daughter saw come in last evening. How's your father doing?"

She nodded. "He is better, but very weak. He must have rest, and food and water. We have spent many days in the badlands hiding from the *comadrejas*. They wounded him with one of their poison arrows." She raised her brow, taking note of Gilliam's swollen face, then nodded at the badge on Sharpe's chest. "Your town seems almost deserted, Sheriff. The hotel clerk said you have had much trouble with outlaws?"

"Yes we have," Sharpe said, feeling his face redden a bit. "We expect even more. Unless your father is armed and handy with a gun, you'll do well to take him away from here." He gestured a hand toward the rain outside and added, "Once it lets up of course."

Gilliam shot Sharpe a flat stare, wondering why he would say such a thing. But Sharpe waited for her reply, watching her eyes, and seemed relieved when she answered. "No, my father is a landowner from Sonora. He is a man of peace who would not raise a weapon against anyone . . . even the *comadreja* who wounded him." She turned her eyes to Ray Gilliam. "You said there is food if I will prepare it?"

"Yes, ma'am," Gilliam said. "Across the street at Decker's Mercantile." He leaned slightly and pointed through the bat wing doors. "And if there's anything we can do for you or your father, let us know."

"Yes, thank you," she said, turning.

But before she got to the doors, she turned as Sharpe said to her, "Maybe I should go see your father? See how he's doing?" He watched her eyes.

Something told her what he was doing, checking her out, worried about who her father might be. So she held his gaze and said in a level tone, "That would be most kind of you. But he is sleeping now and cannot be disturbed."

"Later then?" Sharpe narrowed his gaze. "Once he's rested some?"

Still she did not waver. Her eyes did not betray her words. "Of course. We would both be very much obliged."

Gilliam turned to him, trying to read his face as the woman left and Sharpe watched her cross the muddy street with the wet duster wrapped snug around her. "I saw the way you watched her. Want to tell me why you looked so concerned? Have you been expecting someone out of the badlands?"

Sharpe looked at him with his best gambler's gaze. Outside the rain fell heavy and straight down beneath a low gray sky. "I'm interested in all comings and goings here." He nodded through the rain toward the livery barn. "I'm going over and attend to the horses. Care to join me?"

Gilliam studied his eyes for a second, then shook his head, knowing that if Sharpe was going to make a move, he wouldn't do it now, not in this downpour. The man was no fool. As hard as the rain had fallen throughout the night and with no letup in sight, the gullies and washes that had stood dry all year would now be wide and rushing. "No. I'll wait here," he said. His dark eyes followed Sharpe as Sharpe stepped through the doors, hiking his collar and moving off along the boardwalk beneath the dripping overhang.

From inside Decker's Mercantile, the *comadreja* woman glanced over her shoulder, seeing Sharpe walking toward the hotel. She held her breath until he stepped down and crossed the muddy street toward the livery barn. "That's our new sheriff, Joe Elliot," Joy Decker said, seeing how the woman watched him.

"Yes, I met him a moment ago." She let out a breath and ran a hand across her wet head. She had stood just inside the door, telling Joy Decker about her father being ill when she'd caught sight of the sheriff. Now as he moved away from the hotel, she turned back to Joy Decker and continued. "My father will pay you for the food as soon as he is up and able to come here."

Joy Decker forced a stiff smile and felt the pain tighten in her cheek, thinking it odd that the young woman's father had not given her money in the first place. But she said, "Don't worry about that. Let's just take what you'll need for now. We can prepare it for him in my kitchen."

"The clerk told me I can use the hotel kitchen," the *comadreja* woman said, her dark eyes and flat expression looking tired, but steady and determined in her task. A very serious-looking young woman, Joy Decker thought, stepping over to her and placing a hand on her wet sleeve.

"Nonsense, my dear. My stove is still lit and ready, and you look dead on your feet." She drew the woman along across the wooden floor, the woman hesitating at first, glancing once more out the window toward the hotel. "You'll do your father little good if you let yourself get worn out and taken with something. You get off your feet for a moment. I'll fix a hot meal for both of you."

"Thank you. Yes, you are right," she said, giving in and following her. "I too am hungry." And together they walked back past the counter and through a curtain into Joy Decker's living quarters, where there stood a coffeepot with a curl of steam rising from its snout.

"Your new sheriff," the woman asked, "what kind of man is he?" She took closer note of the black bruise on Joy Decker's swollen jaw as they stepped into the kitchen; and there she saw the young colored girl who'd turned from laying a baking pan up on a wooden shelf as the two of them walked in.

"Oh, our Sheriff Elliot?" Joy Decker said. "Why he's an outstanding young man. We're very fortunate to have him here."

Joy Decker seated the *comadreja* woman at her wooden table without offering to take her duster because she could tell by the way the woman clung to it that she felt some sort of security, some comfort perhaps in having it around her. A strange young woman, Joy thought, studying the woman's dark face for a second before stepping over to the stove and filling a cup with steaming hot coffee.

The woman's dark eyes searched hers as she stood the cup of coffee before her. "*Gracias*," the woman whispered, wrapping both hands around the cup as if it had no handle. She raised it to her lips and sipped it with steam curling up her dark weathered face. Myra and Joy winced, watching her.

"Well, now then, Myra," Joy Decker said, offering once more a thin smile beneath her swollen cheek, "let's prepare something."

While they cooked food on the wood stove, the *co-madreja* woman ate a large piece of bread Joy Decker brought forth from a woven basket beneath a checkered cloth, and between bites she asked questions about their new sheriff. How long had he been there? Where had he come from? If this new sheriff was as good at his job as Joy Decker had said, why were people deserting the town?

Joy Decker answered her questions in turn, and as Myra stirred gravy in a small pot on the stove, Joy sat down and explained how Montana Red Hollis had terrorized the town, and how Sheriff Joe Elliot had set things right with the outlaw. Then she touched a hand to her tender swollen cheek and told her how three outlaws had come into town while the sheriff was away; but now that he was back, they better not return.

As they talked on, rain pounded the roof above them and turned more slanted as wind drew in from the west. And at the livery barn Joe Sharpe moved from stall to stall, feeling a little relieved when he'd seen no sign of the ranger's big dun horse. He'd moved with quiet care, as if even the ranger's *horse* might recognize him and come lunging out on him had it been there. But it wasn't; and he tipped his hat up slightly and looked at the damp saddles and tack thrown across an empty stall door to dry.

He had no idea what he was really looking for or what the ranger's saddle might look like if he saw it. Both of these had empty rifle boots hanging beside them, but this told him nothing. One saddle was shabby, with half the saddle tree standing bare and worn slick from use. He ran his hand across it, then looked at the saddle beside it, this one better kept, hand-tooled across the cantle.

When he ran a hand across this one, he noticed the deep gash in it. An arrow maybe? The woman had said they'd had trouble with *comadrejas*. Jesus! *Comadrejas*. If what she said was true, it was just one more thing to keep him pinned here. He'd seen tracks when he'd crossed the badlands, but he'd caught no sight of the *comadrejas*, *luckily*, he thought.

He lifted his eyes back into the darkened stalls at the two horses standing there. These horses were gaunt, wild-looking things, neither of them striking him as the kind of horse the ranger might ride. As he looked at them, the dirty white one with a black ring around its eye raised its head and snorted toward him and stomped a hoof on the dirt. The other horse drew near it, and the two of them huddled close and twitched their ears until Joe Sharpe turned and walked away. Before leaving, he pitched hay to all the horses and saw to it that rainwater ran in the long trough along the back wall of the stalls.

It made him feel a little better not seeing the ranger's big dun there, but nothing would settle him completely until he saw the wounded man's face. Perhaps she was telling the truth about her father being wounded, or perhaps she was only half telling the truth. What if it was the ranger up there? Who said the ranger couldn't have taken an arrow, and now lay there in the hotel weak and helpless and on the mend—unable to defend himself right now.

If it was the ranger, then what? Sharpe stepped back out in the rain and back toward the saloon, feeling tense. A dark thought passed across his mind. But he put the thought away and walked through the downpour while a low roll of thunder moved closer in the heavy dark sky.

But if it was the ranger, where'd this young woman fit in? Her dark eyes came across his mind, her standing there in the wet duster with the sleeves rolled up, black shiny hair, a tough look to her, Indian? Mexican, maybe. A *comadreja?* What else could he have run into out there? Sharpe stopped cold in the pouring rain, thinking about it.

Then he shook his head, let go of a tense breath, and walked on. *Easy here, getting too edgy* . . . Nothing said it *had* to be the ranger up there. After all, what would he be doing traveling with a *comadreja. A prisoner? Naw, no way* . . . If she was his prisoner, she'd be long gone before now. Thunder rumbled closer.

Above him, the ranger had moved on weak legs over to the window, using his big rifle as a crutch; and he stood back a step from the rain-streaked window, watching Gentleman Joe Sharpe move up out of the mud onto the boardwalk. He smiled to himself, re-membering how the gambler had flashed the shiny pistol out of a window no different from this one, ready to pop a cap on him if he'd only had the nerve.

Now the same man wore a badge, up here, in the high remote plains and rock lands, where a badge wasn't worth its price of tin unless a man stood firm and tough behind it. How tough are you, Gentleman Joe? the ranger asked himself, staring down long after Sharpe had gone out of sight. Tough enough to take down Red Hollis? He chuckled. *You better hope so, gambler*. He raised his eyes from the mud street and gazed off above the town, to the west, where a streak of or-ange lightning glowed and faded back into the boiling gray sky. Thunder cracked somewhere in the distance and rumbled overhead.

The *comadreja* woman brought back warm biscuits and beef and gravy in a crock jar with a lid clamped on it. She took the food from a basket and laid it out for the ranger on the lamp stand beside the bed. While the ranger ate she shook out the wet duster, hung it on the door peg, and sat down beside him on the bed with her legs folded beneath her. She studied his tired drawn face and told him all she'd learned from Joy Decker, and said that now it was time for him to let this lawman, Joe Elliot, know why he was here and that there was no bad blood between them.

"He's no real lawman," the ranger said when she'd finished talking. He offered a weak smile above a raised spoonful of hot gravy.

"How can you *say* he is not a real lawman? You do not know his mind, his heart. He wears a badge. They have made him sheriff. This woman tells me he faced the outlaw you are hunting and made him leave town."

"Not if Red hadn't wanted to leave anyway," he said. "It *is* surprising that Red Hollis didn't kill him, I'll give him that." He blew on the spoonful of gravy and sipped it. "But that's all I give him. He might have them fooled, but I know what he is. A man don't turn from *wrong* one day to *right* the next. He's playing them along for some reason. We'll see why once I get my legs back under me."

"Oh? Then how long does it take for a person to change from *wrong* to *right*? Is there some point where a person knows when another person's heart has changed?" She patted a hand on her breast. "You must tell *me*, so I will know if *I* have changed."

He sipped again and turned his eyes up to her. "You said you were taken against your will by the *comadrejas*. What changing do you need to make?"

"It is true I was taken by them. And because their ways were forced upon me, I became a part of their life in order to survive. Can you say the same has not happened to this man? Perhaps he has been part of a life not of his choosing. Perhaps he has wanted to change, and now that they have *made* him respectable, he has *become* respectable. Can this be?"

"It doesn't work that way," he said, "not for this one. He's scared and he's running, and as soon as he quits running he'll go right back to shaving cards and being a rounder."

"But he is not a bad man. You said so yourself."

"That's true." He blew on the gravy, sipped it, then looked at her and added, "I'll let him know I'm not after him, soon as the time's right." He gazed out past the spoon for a second as if considering something. "But, not just yet."

Her dark eyes searched his when he looked back at her. "But there is a child here, a young girl," she said. "The outlaw sent his *consosios* to take her to him. You cannot let this happen." Her eyes clouded as if given to some dark terrible memory.

He saw her expression draw inward and he placed a hand on her arm. "No, we won't let Red take her . . . not as long as there's a breath left in me."

While they spoke, down on the muddy trail to the west three riders slipped into town unnoticed in the pouring rain and kept to the alley behind the main street until they'd stepped their horses into the dry livery barn and closed the door behind them. "One hour," said the man, standing forward from the other two, "so don't go getting *real* comfortable here." He slapped his wet hat against his leg and put it back on.

"An *hour*?" One of the others shook open his dripping rain slicker, took it off, and pitched it over a stall door. "Come on, Rance, we've been soaking all night! Let's at least get something to drink and some hot food in us. Jack nearly *drowned* crossing that gully wash."

"That's right," the other man said. He was a younger man with one eye clouded white and blind, and he moved forward a step with water running off his hat. He spoke as the one named Rance walked along the center of the dark barn, looking back and forth. "I ain't moving from here till I dry out and get drunk."

"Yeah? So, what's this mean? You're taking over here? Running this crew now?" Rance Plum spoke back to him as he walked farther away, still looking back and forth, wondering why no attendant had come out to meet them. "Because if you *are*, Spider, I'd like to be the first to know about it." He turned, smiling, the points of his yellow mustache wet, but thick with wax and tweaked out, making his smile look even broader. His hand went to the butt of the pistol holstered high across on his stomach, and he wiggled his fingers in his tight gloves.

"You ain't nothing to me, Rance," Jack the Spider said, his right hand hanging near the pistol on his hip. The two men stared at one another beneath the beat of heavy rain on the roof and the steady splatter of it in a long stream down an inside corner of the barn.

The third man, a heavyset gunman named Doc Tyler, had stepped to the side and taken the reins to all three wet horses. "Y'all cut it out, ya hear? We've still got us some jerky left. We can eat it right here."

After a second, a closed smile stirred on Rance Plum's lips. He raised his gun hand and made a fluttering gesture like a bird flying away. "There, see? All gone now." He tweaked a point of his mustache and grinned, turning slowly and continuing to look back and forth along the barn.

Jack the Spider eased a bit, shot Doc Tyler a glance, then took out a bag of tobacco and squatted down and rolled himself a smoke. When Doc Tyler had led the horses off and reined them, he came back and held a strip of jerky down to the young gunman. Jack the Spider looked at it, snatched it from Tyler's hand, and grumbled under his breath, "No reason we can't stay here awhile."

From the far end of the barn, Rance Plum called out with a curious ring to his voice, "Doc? Come here. I want you to see this."

Doc Tyler and Jack the Spider looked at each other

in the dark light. Then Tyler grunted, standing up. "What is it, Rance?"

"It's a sign, perhaps?" Rance stood staring into a stall as Tyler walked to him.

"A sign, huh?" Doc Tyler was soaked and saddle-worn, and not in much of a mood for Rance Plum's craziness. Yet when he stopped beside him and looked into the large stall where the two horses milled close to one another against the back wall, Tyler cocked his head a bit to one side and said, "Well, I'll be strapped."

"What is it?" Jack the Spider straightened up and walked to them with his mouth working on a stiff piece of jerky, cigarette smoke curling up the back of his hand.

Now the three of them stood there looking into the stall at the white horse with the black ring around its eye. A silence passed and Jack the Spider looked all around the dark barn, and said, "You don't suppose . . . ?"

"Naw," Doc Tyler said in a quiet tone. "Bent Jackson never strays this far up." Yet on saying it his eyes went about the dark barn as well.

"But we *do agree* that's his horse," Rance Plum said, his voice equally quiet. "Perhaps he sold it?" Overhead the rain shifted side-wise on a new wind. Thunder rolled.

"Bent wouldn't sell that horse," Tyler said. "And if he would nobody'd buy it."

"And yet, there we are." Rance Plum gestured with a gloved hand. "You don't suppose someone stole it?"

"Either that or they've killed ole Bent and took it." Tyler leaned and looked the horse over more closely. "Either way, it's his horse all right."

Another silence passed, and Plum turned to Joe and

smiled, saying, "So then, Mr. Spider. It appears you'll have your wish after all."

Tyler looked at them both and said to Rance Plum, "I believe you was right to begin with. Let's go on away from here. We've got business to attend to."

"Nonsense," Plum said. "We'll stay awhile, as our Spider suggested so *ardently*. We may have ourselves a mystery here. I wouldn't sleep a wink if we rode off without solving it."

"It might be that ranger," Jack the Spider said.

"Indeed it might." Plum smiled and tweaked his mustache. "And wouldn't that be something. It would certainly explain all those dead *comadrejas* scattered across the badlands."

"If that old man's here, I don't want to fool with him," Doc Tyler said. "You wouldn't either if you'd seen what I've seen out of him."

"But think how much easier our work will be if he's around here," Rance Plum said, lifting the pistol from the holster across his stomach and checking it.

"We won't gain nothing from messing with him," Doc Tyler said. "If we're smart we'll move on—not meddle in his business."

"Aw, but you see"—Rance Plum raised a gloved finger, wagging it—"his interests and ours have *so much* in common."

"I'm not afraid of that old ranger," Jack the Spider said to Doc Tyler, dropping his cigarette butt and crushing it beneath his boot. "If you are, maybe you could stay here and hide under some straw."

"See?" Rance Plum smiled and put his pistol back in the holster, patting it. "It appears our Spider has much to prove to himself. We wouldn't want to deny the young man a chance, would we?"

"Plum," said Tyler, "I'm with you for one reason and one reason only. If you want to go getting tangled up with that ranger, you can count me out." He stepped over, threw on his rain slicker, and took up the reins to his horse. "I'm sticking to the plan. You can find me higher up in the passes if you're still alive."

"You can't leave, Tyler!" Rance Plum raised his voice above the pounding rain on the roof. He raised the pistol in his hand.

But Doc Tyler looked at it and spit. "Go on and shoot if you have to. But you'll bring in every gun in this town—*including* the ranger, if he's here."

"Let him go," Jack the Spider said to Rance Plum. "I told ya I'm sticking. To hell with that ranger, and everybody else. I'll pull iron on anybody."

"That's *real* smart thinking, Jack," Doc Tyler said reaching for the door with one hand, his reins in his other. "It'd sound good on your headstone."

Rance lowered the pistol and smiled a thin smile. "I fear you may have gotten too old and overly cautious, Doc. So go on with you. Spider and I will simply spend the evening here in these *lovely* quaint surroundings, and come morning we'll think of you over a nice hot breakfast and a warm bottle of whiskey. Eh, Spider?"

"Tomorrow *nothing*," Jack the Spider said. "What's wrong with getting something hot to eat today? Right *now*?"

"Be patient, Spider." Rance Plum smiled. "A smart man never announces himself before it's time."

Doc Tyler looked at them and shook his head. "Boy," he said to Spider as he swung open the door against the pounding rain, "you'll let this man get you killed

here, if you ain't careful. See ya both in hell before
long, I reckon." And he stepped up into his stirrups
and left, slipping back into the alley and out of sight
with his wet hat brim flattened to the back of his neck.

CHAPTER 15

Red Hollis had been standing restless on his porch, out of the rain, waiting for them with his hair slicked back and his hat hanging from his hand. He'd scrubbed his big faded bandanna and had put it on still damp around his throat. He'd even beat his hat against a post to get the dust out of it, and had rubbed a handful of grease on his square-toed boots. But when they rode into sight, he saw the look on Solomon Fish and Dick Yates's wet mud-streaked faces and spit and cursed under his breath.

"There better be one hell of a reason why that little girl ain't with ya," he called out as they stepped their tired horses to the hitch rail and swung down. The horses stood wet and straddle-legged and swung their tired heads back and forth.

"There is, Red," Solomon Fish said, stepping up on the porch, his hands spread, water dripping from his hat.

"Frank Bacon's dead," said Yates, stepping up behind him and moving to one side as Red glared at him.

"So? He never struck me as a man who'd live very long anyway." Red rested a hand on one of his crossed pistols and swung his gaze to Solomon Fish. "Now where's my little girl?"

"She ain't here, Red." Solomon Fish slumped his shoulders and shook his head.

"I see she ain't here, you idiot! But why *ain't* she?" He took a step toward Solomon Fish, then another; and Fish spilled the whole story out, stepping backward with a hand raised, changing it, lying a little, and telling him how the new sheriff came in and fouled up their whole plan, and how Frank Bacon was supposed to be watching the door but hadn't done his job. "And you can't blame us for that," he added, Red still moving in closer, one slow step at a time.

"So, you let one law-toter make a couple of sheep out of ya?"

"I swear Red I never seen nothing like this man," Solomon Fish said, his voice raised, a plea trembling in it. "And I'm one of the meanest dogs in the world. You know that!" He'd backed against the porch rail with Red Hollis staring him in the eyes. "Ask Dick! Dick, tell him! Tell him something here!" Fish's eyes swung back and forth, wide, red-rimmed, and full of fear. Red's hand rested on one of his crossed pistols.

"I hate a liar, Fish," said Red Hollis, leaning real close to his face. Fish streaked a desperate glance to Dick Yates.

"It's the truth, Red," said Yates, standing back a few feet, trying to look steady but his feet ready to bolt at any second. "He was upon us so fast, we barely got out with our lives. Hadn't been for Frank Bacon screwing things up, it mighta been different. But you know what they say—one bad apple." He offered a weak shrug.

Red snapped his head toward Yates, knowing the two of them were lying, but still not sure what he wanted to do about it. He still didn't have that little girl and he could still use these two to get her some-how. "Oh? What kind of shooting gear was this law-man carrying?" His eyes bored into Yates.

"I— Well, I never noticed, Red." Yates tried to shoot Fish a stare, but Red reached out, squeezed his face back toward him and shook it back and forth like a rag doll.

"Don't look at him. Look at me! You telling me a man's shooting at your worthless arse and you don't even know *what with*? What kind of shooting gear was he packing?" He held Yates's face squeezed tight in his gloved hand, Yates's lips twisted and puckered. When he tried to answer his voice came out all wrong, and Red looked at him with disgust and shoved him back-ward.

Red stomped back and forth on the wooden porch, his big spurs ringing out; and he screamed at them, "Look at me, just look at me! I greased my hair down and everything!" He mussed his thick greasy hair with a gloved hand and it stood up and out in all directions. "I'll be a week getting the smell of soap off'n me!" He stopped and spun toward them. "And you didn't even bring back any whiskey!" His pistol snapped out, cocked and pointed, less than a foot from Solomon Fish's chest. "I ought to kill you!" His nostrils flared wide.

Solomon Fish's breath sliced short. When Red didn't pull the trigger right away, Fish sank to his knees with his hands spread, trembling. "Oh, Lord, *please*, Red, don't kill *me!* I know you ought to—*anybody* ought to. But please don't! Kill Yates here instead!" His trem-bling dirty finger went toward Yates. "Kill him, not me! Please!"

"Huh-uh!" Yates's eyes went even wider. His feet

shuffled backward until he stopped against the rail. "Don't listen to him, Red! We'll make it up to ya! I swear we will, Red!"

Red Hollis took a deep breath and lowered the pistol and wiped a hand across his face. "I won't kill ya, not yet. But you boys better show me something from here on."

"We will, Red. That's a fact," Fish said, starting to breathe again. "Won't we, Dick?" Dick Yates just stared at him.

Red spun his pistol away, looked down at Fish, and said as he started pacing again, "Get up, you wretch."

Fish rose up, dusting his knees. "We did kill that ole man, and worked that bartender over right nice for ya."

"You don't get it, you idiot," Red hissed. "I wanted the *girl*. All this other don't matter."

"Well, that bartender wouldn't give her up no matter what. I'm thinking they might be kin or something."

"Do you now?" Red nodded his head in disgust.

"Yeah, I do . . . and I would've kilt that bartender, and the woman too had it not been for that new lawman showing up. He's bad, Red, *real* bad. He killed Fast Felton McRoy, and you know what a devil Felton was." He shot Yates another glance; Yates sneered and looked away, and Fish added, "They say Fast Felton never got his pistol up before this man burnt him down."

"Where'd you hear all this?" Red stared at him and stopped pacing. His spurs fell silent.

"Well—" Fish shrugged. "From that woman in town, right before the lawman busted in on us. She said him and Fast Felton stepped out into the street and he never gave Felton time to get his pistol out before he commenced—"

"She just said their Sheriff Elliot killed Felton, Red," Yates said, cutting Fish off with a dark stare. *Kill Yates instead? This coward* . . . "She never gave no particulars of it."

"It makes no sense either way," Red said. "I seen this Elliot around some. He ain't no lawman. I played cards with him. He's a two-bit gambler."

"Maybe he's both, Red," said Fish. "You know there's people like that, you know . . . who do more than one thing at a time."

Red settled a little, looked back and forth between the two of them, then said, "There's one bottle of whiskey left. So don't neither of ya reach for it or you'll draw back a stub." When they both nodded, he turned to Dick Yates. "If you'd looked real close, you'd seen your brother's shooting gear hanging on Elliot's hip." He watched Dick Yates's eyes for a reaction.

Yates struggled with it for a second, squinted, looked at Fish, then at Red, then squinted again and said, "You don't mean, *he* killed my poor brother Hurley?"

"He's wearing his gear," Red said in a flat tone. "You tell me if he did."

"But, everybody said the ranger done it." Yates looked puzzled.

"Maybe they both done it, Dick," Solomon Fish said. He looked from Yates to Red. "Maybe they work together?"

"I don't know." Red turned away from them and gazed out and up across the dark cloudy sky, thinking of the little girl, wondering what he might name her once he got her up here. Rain ran off the roof in torrents and splattered into a stream along the edge of the porch. He turned back to them. "What all did Frank Bacon tell ya about that ranger?"

"Huh?" Fish crooked his brow.

"He kilt my poor brother," Yates said under his breath.

"Shut up about your dead stinking brother," Red snapped. Then he turned back to Fish. "When you got here the other night you said Bacon saw that ranger shoot ole Bent Jackson. I want to know how fast he is, how he handles himself."

"Aw, Red." Fish shook his head. "Bacon said the ranger killed Bent so quick he never saw it coming."

"He's real fast, huh?" Red thought about it as Fish spoke on, telling him that Frank Bacon had seen the whole thing and that the ranger just started walking toward Bent Jackson and never stopped, not at ten yards, not at seven, until Bent had to take a step back when he drew his pistol, and by then it was too late. When he finished, Red looked at him and asked again, "I'm not asking how the ranger walked. I'm asking, was he *fast?*"

Fish scratched his head. "Well, he never said he was as far as drawing his pistol."

"Then how'd he get a drop on Jackson, sneaking up on him?"

"Naw. The way Bacon told it, the ranger had his gun already out when he got there."

"He had to draw it *sometime*," Red snapped, "unless he walks around with it in his hand all the time. Was he so fast Bacon missed it?"

"Bacon said he just come walking and drew that big pistol real slow with that list of his in his hand. Said you almost wouldn't notice he'd pulled his pistol, let alone think he was getting ready to shoot ya with it."

"That's about as stupid as anything I ever heard," said Red, turning away once more, watching the rain. Red worked a picture of it in his mind, just in case that ranger showed up when he went to town. He had no reason really to think the ranger was around, other than some dark feeling inside and the fact that his name kept coming up. Hurley's shooting gear on the gambler-lawman's hip, Bacon telling how he'd seen the ranger shoot Bent Jackson. These things came together to form a feeling low in Red's stomach, the way a scent finds its way through a wind and falls on the senses of some creature of the wilds.

"Blasted rain," Red whispered under his breath. He hated rain and he hated cool weather. But come morning, rain or no rain, he'd have to ride and get that little girl. Anybody in his way would die, and that's all there was to it. He turned, walked inside his cabin, snatched the last bottle of whiskey off the table, and sat down on a wooden stool in the middle of the floor. On the porch, Fish and Yates milled about until finally Red called to them, "All right, come on in. But don't let me catch you sheep-lickers near my whiskey."

They slipped inside like two cowering dogs and settled themselves quietly at the wooden table, shaking out their wet clothes. Yates kept his distance from Solomon Fish, and when Fish tried whispering something to him, Yates only growled for him to shut the hell up. Red sat watching them, glaring and sipping from the whiskey bottle until finally he corked it and sat it on the floor beside his boot.

"I reckon if we ride in tomorrow you two idiots will

have enough sense to shoot the town up won't ya? I mean, if I keep that big bad sheriff off of ya?"

"Red," Fish said, leaning forward on his forearm on the wooden table, "you know us. We'll do whatever you want." He eyed the bottle of whiskey on the floor. "But you got to admit, a man always works better after he's drunk himself up to it. We'd have done better today if we'd had a little time to liquor up more." He turned a glance toward Dick Yates and Yates nodded.

Red scowled at them. They were cowards and fools; but he knew that even a couple of cowards with guns in their hands could be made into dangerous men with the right person behind them, forcing them on out of fear. Most men talked a bold line, but once you got them done to it, they hadn't the guts to face an armed opponent straight up. He'd thought Solomon Fish might, but he'd been wrong. For all his hot air and bluster, Fish was turning out to be nothing but a back-shooting coward. But even that was all right, now that Red saw what he was dealing with.

He picked up the bottle and shook it in his hand. "Plenty of whiskey in town, boys." He grinned a dark grin. A coward could always be talked or shamed or pushed into anything by a man who knew what he was doing . . . and he did. Once he stuck their noses in the blood, they'd drink, whether they wanted to or not. He done it dozens of times before. He was good at it.

Most of his life he'd been a serious man, Ray Gilliam thought, *too* serious at times, his wife used to say. She had teased him about it from time to time. But now her body lay in the ground, her death giving credence to whatever dark solemnness she must've seen in him.

Life *is* serious, he could hear himself tell her, some-where back then, back when they'd first met and he'd slowly felt the changes set about him. Before they'd met he'd been a violent, dangerous man—an angry man. But she'd changed all that.

He still saw her smile sometimes. She had a real pretty smile, and thinking of her now, he smiled a lit-tle to himself. He thought of her, and of his daughter, the child they'd created between them; and his strong black hands worked deftly on part after part of his broken-down pistol atop the wooden barrel inside Decker's Mercantile. Since noon another storm had come and gone, with a promise of more rumbling on the distant horizon. Rain fell straight and steady.

He glanced up as his oily fingers stroked and pol-ished each piece of the .45, as if to bring forth life from within the metal itself; and he gazed out the window through the rain toward the saloon where Sheriff Big Joe Elliot sat alone with his thoughts. *Sheriff my arse* . . . What were the man's thoughts, Ray wondered, feeling the smooth steel on the ball of his thumb.

Did this Joe Elliot give a damn one way or the other? Did he have anything to lose, except his life? Because if he didn't, in all likelihood Gilliam wouldn't be able to count on him when it came to the showdown. And it *was* coming to a showdown. He felt it in his bones. For a second he imagined what it must feel like to have nothing to lose but his life. Wouldn't that be simple? Wouldn't life be easy?

Life is never hard on a man who doesn't give a damn about anything or anybody, he thought. Life had been that simple for *Ray Gilliam* once, back before he'd met his wife, before he'd gotten *serious*, settled down and put his drifter's ways behind him. *Those changes* . . .

He rubbed the cylinder dry on a soft cloth and snapped it in place with his thumb and spun it. He looked at the half-assembled pistol in his hand, seeing the soft shine of gunmetal in the gray light from the window. Outside, rain pelted the mud street like silver darts. Life hadn't been as hard back then, but it hadn't been as *good* either. It had been wild and reckless and free as the wind—but there'd been no salt to it, no substance about it.

For years now he'd picked in the dirt like a chicken, raising from the abandoned silver claims no more than enough dust to keep body and soul together for him and Myra. He connected the barrel, then stopped and gazed away, realizing that he would not trade one hour of scratching in the dirt for all those wild and wasted years before. Then, raising the pistol close his ear, he listened as he clicked it one notch at time, hearing the smooth inner workings of cold steel click against the softer stuff of the universe.

He hadn't had the pistol out in nearly fifteen years, since back when Myra was a baby in her crib and a rattlesnake had slipped into the house. He shook his head, thinking of the similarity between that time and this—only Montana Red Hollis was *worse* than a rattlesnake.

He hefted the pistol on his palm, opening and closing his fingers around the butt, getting the feel for it once again like the handshake of some dreaded old acquaintance. For fifteen years the big stripped-down pistol hadn't touched his hand or his life; and now, in the past two days he'd broken it down and cleaned it, twice. *Nerves* . . .

Was he still any good with it? He dared not question himself. He'd thought about trying it out, but if he *had* lost his touch with it he didn't want to know. Not now. This wasn't the time to find a flaw or weakness in himself. There was no time to wonder or second-guess his intentions. Men were coming. He meant to kill them.

"Papa?" The sound of Myra's voice startled him, but he caught himself and turned to her there beside him. He didn't realize how tight the tendons stood in his neck until he tried to speak but had to swallow first.

"Yes, child." He turned, lowering the pistol, her dark eyes on it, seeming to question it until he slipped it into his holster and held his hand in a way to shield it from her. She nudged the cup of coffee toward him and he took it and stepped back. "Thank you," he said; and he turned from her with it and stared out across the muddy street. There were things he needed to say to her but he couldn't find the right words. So silence stood between them until she spoke in a soft tone.

"You're wearing a new shirt today, Papa," she said. He felt her hand brush his sleeve.

He smiled, staring into the rain. "Yes. I'm afraid my other was beyond repair."

"And a new hat?" She picked up the black low-crowned Stetson from atop the wooden barrel and turned it back and forth in her hands.

"Yes." He turned and looked at her, and she raised her eyes to him and handed him the hat. "Miss Decker was kind enough to charge these on to my account for a while." He took the hat, brushed a hand along the brim, and let it hang from his hand.

"Why are you all dressed up?" She asked. "Because there's bad people coming?"

Her question struck him, causing him to pause

while her dark eyes searched his. Why *had* he taken on a new hat, a new shirt? He didn't know. He didn't want to know; and he turned back to the window and stared out through the rain. Across the street he saw the woman he'd met earlier. She moved across the mud street and into the saloon. Putting an arm around Myra, drawing her close to his side, he said quietly, "Yes, Myra, because there are bad people coming."

They stood for a moment until Joy Decker stepped through the curtain behind the counter and said, "Ray, I've fixed some nice hot stew and Myra and I baked some bread. Won't you have some? You haven't eaten all morning."

"Uh— Yes, thank you, Mrs. Decker." He turned and began clearing a place atop the barrel, a place to set the food when she brought it out to him. But she watched him and smiled. Gesturing him back toward her kitchen with her hand, she said, "Come on. We'll eat at the table today, Ray."

He hesitated. "Are you sure?"

"I should say so. Myra did such a splendid job helping me. She even baked the bread all by herself." She smiled, laying a hand on Myra's shoulder. "I shan't see her fine cooking served from the top of a common pickle barrel."

She and Myra turned, and Ray Gilliam followed them back through the curtain, through a narrow stockroom into the kitchen. It wasn't the first time Ray Gilliam had eaten at Joy Decker's but it was *indeed* the first time he'd ever been back here in her living quarters. She and Myra had become close over the past year and he'd eaten many times but always out front in the store, from atop the counter or the big pickle barrel.

Being back here at her table made him feel a bit awkward, dressed as he was in his new shirt and with a new Stetson hanging from a peg on the wall. There was a strange feel to it, something unreal about it, as if he were not Ray Gilliam sitting at the table, but some stranger that he watched from aside.

As they ate, Joy Decker told him about the woman who'd come over earlier, and how she seemed like a nice young lady, only strange, strange in a way she couldn't quite define. And Joy went on to talk about the weather, and about how she'd soon need to take in another quarter of beef to last her through the summer. She talked about anything she could think of to keep from bringing up Red Hollis.

Ray Gilliam finished eating before they did and tried to relax, watching Joy and Myra finish their meal while he sipped his coffee until they began clearing the table.

"Mrs. Decker?" He spoke quietly to her as Myra had taken the plates and stepped over to a wash pan with them. When Joy Decker looked at him, his eyes gestured back toward the store. He stood and swept his hat from the peg; and Joy followed him through the narrow stockroom and beyond the curtain into the store. Once there he turned, glanced back past her, then spoke to her in a low, guarded tone.

"If things go bad for me when Red Hollis and his boys get here, I was hoping—That is, Myra thinks a lot of you, and I was hoping if something happens to me, maybe you could find a place for her here? With you? We have no kin that I know of anywhere—"

"Sssh, you mustn't say such things, Ray," she said, cutting him off. "Good will always prevail over someone like Montana Red Hollis." Her hand went to his forearm. "You must have faith."

He breathed deep. "Yes. But if it should go bad?"

"Myra will always have a home with me, Ray. You have my word on that." She smiled. "Why she's practically the daughter I never had anyway."

"Thank you, Mrs. Decker." His voice was a whisper, and he started to lay his hand atop of hers. But he caught himself, smiled instead, and moved away. "I best get on over with the sheriff. If the storm breaks tonight, I look for Red and his boys to come in most anytime."

"Ray?" She called after him in a quiet voice as he stepped over to the door, putting his hat on. He turned with the door handle in his hand, and she said, "I just want to tell you what an admirable thing you're doing, standing beside our sheriff through this. I daresay you're the only man in town to do such a thing. I know he appreciates it."

He just stared at her for a moment, hearing the steady fall of rain behind him, then tipped the brim of his hat. "Yes, ma'am," he said, stepping out through the door and closing it behind him.

Beyond the curtain, back in Joy Decker's kitchen, Myra Gilliam heard the bell jingle atop the front door, and knew her father had just left. She was worried about the bad men coming to town and what they might do to her father and the new sheriff. She felt bad because she knew it all had something to do with her somehow. Although they only talked about it in veiled bits and pieces, she knew the trouble had started for her father the day the man with the red beard smiled and spoke to her on his way out of town.

She looked down at her sudsy hands in the washpan

of dishes and thought of the troubled look in her father's eyes as he'd gazed out through the falling rain. She lifted a dish and rubbed the wet soapy rag around it and dipped it into the rinse water; and she picked up the long bread knife and rubbed the rag along the blade and saw her reflection in the wet steel.

If she wasn't here, she thought, maybe the trouble would go away. She looked up from the dishpan and out the window, across the wood yard, where rain splashed and ran in thin streams along the muddy ground. But where could she go? Out there? Out into the land her father always warned her about, out there where there were snakes and lizards and many other creatures both warm-blooded and cold that could harm her? Thunder grumbled, and through the rain-bleared window she lifted her eyes to the dark gray sky and stared up into it for the longest time.

CHAPTER 16

The ranger stood at the window and watched Ray Gilliam slosh through the mud and the rain, across the mud street to the saloon. He stepped back a foot from the window when the gambler, Joe Sharpe, stepped out to the edge of the boardwalk and looked over and up toward his room. Seeing the questioning look on the gambler's face, the ranger smiled to himself, then watched the two men turn and go back inside.

"What all did he have to say?" the ranger asked, turning and looking at the *comadreja* woman, who sat on the edge of the bed drying her hair on a towel.

She lowered the towel and looked at him. "He is worried. I can tell he wonders who you are. He asked me once again how my *father* is doing. I said you are better." She looked down at the towel in her hands. "I think he is a good man. If you would tell him who you are and that you are not out to kill him, I think he would help you with this outlaw you are hunting."

"I'll tell him come morning," he said, stepping away from the window, feeling stronger now but still using the rifle as a crutch. "It'll do him good to spend the night figuring out who he is and where he needs to make a stand in life."

"You are not doing this to simply make him sweat?" She wagged a finger. "I think perhaps you are. I think perhaps you are a person who likes to see people driven to their limit just to prove something to *you*. This comes from seeing too many bad things in your life." She nodded as if accepting her own words. "Yes, I believe this is how you are."

"Oh, you think so, eh." He sat down across from her and leaned back on a pillow. "What I happen to be doing is letting him sort everything out in his mind. If he gets *too* rattled, he'll be gone come morning, storms or no storm." He smiled, leaning the rifle against the wall beside the bed. "I know his type—surprised he ain't left already. But if he's here come morning, it means he's chased off some of his demons and made the right choice."

"So, you see, you test him? You measure him by some standard of your own. This is what I'm talking about. I do not think you have the right to do this."

"Well, I'm *taking* the right then. The shape I'm in, I'll need him and the girl's father to keep Red Hollis's rats busy while *I* take Red down. The main thing is that Hollis *dies*. For everybody's sake, *especially* the little girl's. If I miss him this time I might never get another chance at him. Where will that leave everybody?"

"*If* the outlaw comes here," she said, turning, resting back beside him on the bed. "Perhaps he will not." She brought him the bottle of rye whiskey she'd gotten from the saloon. Beads of water stood on the bottle, and she wiped it back and forth on the bedspread.

"Oh, you can bet he'll be here," he said, hearing the distant growl of thunder once more on the western edge of the earth. "I can feel it." He took the bottle and pulled the cork.

*   *   *

Across the street in the saloon, Ray Gilliam had taken his wet hat off, slapped it against his leg, and dropped it on the bar top. He turned and looked at Joe Sharpe, who'd sat down at a table and let out a breath. "Wanta tell what it is about that girl and her father that has you so spooked?" Ray Gilliam asked, and stood staring at him, his eyes demanding an answer. In asking, he saw a look of resolve come over the sheriff's eyes that hadn't been there before.

"It's nothing, now," Sharpe said. "All you have to know is that I'm backing your play with Montana Red Hollis. If that's not enough for you . . . you'll have to whistle for the rest." He swiped up the bottle of whiskey from the table, started to throw back a drink, but then he stopped and looked at the bottle and sat it down and pushed it away. Above them, the storm had moved in. It pitched and tossed in a crash of thunder and a new sweep of rain. Lightning sparkled and shined.

Ray Gilliam stood watching him as Sharpe gazed off above the bat wing doors. Sharpe rubbed his palms back and forth along his trouser legs until at length he stood up, snatched his riding duster from the chair next to him, and without another word swung it across his shoulders and walked out. Gilliam moved across the floor and watched him make his way through the pounding storm and up onto the boardwalk outside the hotel.

In a moment the ranger heard the footsteps in the hall and he drew the big pistol from its holster and let it lie in his hand along his side. "It didn't take as long as I thought," he said in a muffled tone. The *comadreja* woman's eyes met his for a second, then she stood up, moved over near the window, and stood there watching the door.

When the knock came at the door, the ranger flipped the quilt over him, covering his pistol, and said, "Come in, it's not locked."

The woman saw the door open slowly, and Sharpe's eyes went to her first, then over to the small gaunt figure on the bed. The man lying there looked nothing at all like the man he'd seen shoot down the outlaws in the street. But it *was* him. Sharpe knew it. In a flash of lightning through the window, he spread his linen suit coat open, showing the empty holster on his hip. "I know who you are," he said; and he stepped inside the door and stopped. "I came unarmed. My pistol's out in the hall."

The ranger looked him up and down. "What about your *shiny* little gambler's pistol? You're not even wearing it, up under your arm somewhere?"

Sharpe let out a breath, reached inside his coat and brought out the .38 with two fingers and pitched it over on the bed. The ranger glanced at it, then looked back at Sharpe's eyes in the gathering darkness of the room.

"That the same one you meant to shoot me with a while back?" the ranger asked.

"I'd thought about it," Sharpe said. "A person thinks about a lot of things when they're stuck in something they can't get out of."

"Well . . . you'd have been wasting a bullet." The ranger raised up on one elbow, the pistol still hidden beneath the quilt in his other hand. "I wasn't looking for you. If you'd stuck around long enough, you'd know that."

"I know that now," Sharpe said, "but I didn't know

it then." Thunder broke apart above them and rolled away. "I thought you were just out to clean up your list. I didn't know what Hollis and his friends did."

"But you *did* kill Peg-Leg Molly Frome, didn't ya?" The ranger stared at him.

Sharpe nodded and hung his head. "I wished to God I didn't, but yes, there's no denying it. I'm the one who shot her. I'm ready to pay up for it."

A silence passed as lightning twisted and curled and licked a flash of light across them. "You don't owe for her," the ranger said. "You never did. It went before a territory judge and he found you innocent on grounds of self-defense. Besides, that was all outside my jurisdiction anyway. I doubt there was a lawman twixt hell and Texas who'd blame a man for Peg-Leg Molly." A grin twitched at his lips. "Damned few of them she hadn't clapped out at some time or other."

Jesus . . . Sharpe slumped his shoulders, and stared down, shaking his head. "Yep," the ranger added. "Every lawman in the country knew she was a straight-razoring whore—knew she had it coming sooner or later. You was just the first one ever lucky enough to miss the cut. You shouldn't have been so quick to bolt. Somebody probably would have bought you a drink."

"Four years, I've been running from it, always feeling I was one step ahead of the hangman. If I only knew."

"You're not a murderer, Gentleman Joe. If you was you'd have forgotten Molly Frome before she was cold in the ground. You haven't been running from *the law* . . . you've been running from your conscience."

Sharpe looked up and ran a hand across his eyes

and rubbed his temples. "I'm free of it . . . really free of it?"

"Like I said, you never was bound to it, except in your own mind." The ranger shot a glance at the *comadreja* woman, saw her caged eyes in the grainy evening light, then said to Sharpe, "What about the badge you're wearing?"

Sharpe ran a hand over the badge on his chest and as the woman moved over and lit the lamp beside the bed, he began to tell the ranger everything, about the dead lawman and Fast Felton's body he'd come upon in the desert, and the way the town had taken to him when he rode in to collect the reward. When he'd finished, he added, "But all that was for nothing. All I had to do was stop running."

"Running's a hard life. And it's a hard thing to stop once a man gets started," the ranger said. "The longer you run the more desperate life gets." He nodded at Joe Sharpe's chest. "It's brought you all the way to wearing a badge." He paused, then added, "Of course you can get shed of that piece of tin now."

"Yeah," Sharpe said with a sigh, brushing a hand across the badge once more.

"It's a heavy burden wearing one of them things, ain't it?" The ranger offered a tight smile.

"More so than I would've ever thought," Sharpe said.

"Mine weighed less than an ounce when I first cast it on my vest. Now it's up to a ton or better." The ranger cut a glance past the woman, then added to Sharpe, "I was going to *press* ya into helping me take a stand against Hollis and his rats. But I won't now. You can take the badge off . . . and go on your way."

"I know," Sharpe said. He took a step back toward

the door. "But I'd be a fool to trek out in this storm."
He looked at the woman and raised a hand to his hat
brim.

"One thing, Gentleman Joe," the ranger said, seeing
him prepared to leave. "How'd you figure it was me
up here?'

Sharpe waited for a second, then glanced past the
woman back to the ranger and said, "I just *felt* it, I suppose."

In a moment Sharpe was gone, and the ranger sat up
on the side of the bed with his pistol hanging from his
hand and turned to the woman. "You had no right
telling him it was me here," he said.

Surprise glittered across her eyes, but then she settled, and shrugged. "Yes, I told him who you are. It
was foolish to wait all night, and take a chance on his
fear forcing him to leave. I'm not sorry for telling
him."

"But you had no *right* doing it," the ranger said.

"Like you, I *took* the right." She cocked her head to
one side and placed a hand on her hip. "You need his
help."

He shook his head. "But I won't get it now. He'll be
gone come morning, for sure."

"He will be here," she said in a confident tone.

"You're a smart woman in a lot of ways, but you
sure don't know much about what fear does to a man."

"To *men*? Does fear do one thing to a man and something else to a woman? Does fear not do the same to
all, without distinction?"

He looked at her and didn't answer. "Let's get some
sleep. I've got a feeling tomorrow's gonna be a busy
day."

"You cannot tell me about fear," she murmured

under her breath, stepping over and trimming the lamp. She slipped out of her damp dress and hung it on the bed poster. Across the bed, he bunched up a pillow and lay down on his side, facing away from her with his pistol resting against his stomach. When she slipped beneath the covers and gathered them around her naked body, they lay in silence for a moment until he said, "I wish you wouldn't sleep like that."

"Oh? What choice do I have? I am a woman without a home, without a change of dress. How should I sleep, if not *like this?*"

"I just thought I oughta mention it," he said after a second when the thunder had settled above them. "Maybe I'm getting old and too set in my ways."

She smiled to herself. "Yes, perhaps that is it." And they lay facing away from one another, listening to the storm as it rumbled and flashed, until it spent itself and moved away in the night.

"You are feeling much better," she said.

"Yep. Another day or two I'll be back stronger than I ever was."

"Good." Her voice fell to a whisper as she reached out her hand and darkened the lamp beside the bed.

In the dark barn, Jack the Spider lay on a musty-smelling pile of straw and listened to the rain beat hard against the walls. He'd eaten the jerked beef and had drunk water from his canteen, and now and then before dark had gone and looked out through cracks in the wall at the saloon across the street and fifty yards away. He was restless, still hungry down deep inside, and could've used a stiff shot of whiskey. But he'd have to settle down and go along with Rance Plum for now. Rance talked a good show . . . maybe he knew what he was doing. "So, Plum," he said in the darkness toward the spot where Rance Plum had made his bedroll, "what's the chances of Doc getting there before we do?"

"So what if he does?" Rance's voice spoke as if through a hole in the pitch black. "I'm sure he'll wait for us. Besides, we all get paid equally. I'm not concerned about it."

"Just asking," said Jack the Spider; and he rolled over and cradled his head on the saddle beneath it.

CHAPTER 17

Red Hollis had saved half the bottle of last night's whiskey for the ride to town. He would ration it out to them a shot at a time every few miles, and if his timing was right, there'd be just enough for each of them to throw back a good stiff jolt of it and get their courage up, right when they moved in and made their play. Bottle brave. That's what these two were.

He glanced back at them from between his upturned collar and the low brim of his wet hat. Rain fell straight around them and slanted from time to time on the rising wind. More dark low clouds hovered in the west.

"You idiots try to keep up," he said, seeing they'd straggled behind him, crossing a narrow oxbow where a hundred feet below on either side lay the tops of sparse piñon and cottonwood; and they pressed on through the gray rain and into a snaking trail that curved in between two rising rock walls. Above them a fall of water spilled out and down with a heavy tail of spray whipping wall to wall.

"Lord, Red," Solomon Fish called out to him as Red nudged his horse into it, "a man could get washed away here if he ain't careful."

"Keep moving," he called back above the thrash and roar of water on rock.

Yates and Fish shot one another a dubious glance
and forced their horses on, seeing their leader ab-
sorbed by the heavy spray before them. "This ain't to
my liking," Yates said under his breath.

"Then why don't ya tell him so?" Fish asked, his
eyes bloodshot on whiskey, whiskey laced with fear.

"Why don't *you*? Before we get drug in any deeper."
He stared at Fish until Fish looked down and away.
"That's what I *thought*," Yates added; and he tugged
his hat down closer to his raised collar and gigged his
horse forward.

Red led them on, winding along wet switchbacks
carved by animal hooves and time through a maze of
high rockland. The thin trail lay awash in places where
water ran down and shot out of faults in the shear rock
walls. He'd spent most of the night forming some sort
of plan, and he thought of it still, pressing on.

His only interest for now was in getting the girl and
getting out with her. It would be nice to have some
kind of diversion, something to draw everybody's attention while he snatched her. But he hadn't come up
with anything yet. It would be no problem killing the
gambler-lawman—the colored bartender too, for that
matter. As far as the ranger he'd heard so much
about . . . well, if he *was* around, Red figured he'd put
a bullet or two in his head for good measure.

He'd do that just because Fish and Yates and everybody had made such a big deal of the man. It would
look good on him, he thought, seeing himself riding
up on the ranger, the ranger standing there in the
street, maybe with his feet spread, trying to look
tough. Red saw himself getting off his horse real slow
like, taking his time, letting these two idiots watch him
do it.

And ole Red got off his horse cool as a cucumber— He could already hear them telling about it, later on somewhere. *Red bit each finger of his glove until he pulled it off, then just stood there, staring at that ranger from forty feet . . .* He smiled to himself and adjusted the crossed pistols beneath his wet riding duster. Yes, sir, that would be worth doing. Shooting the old ranger would keep his name high in the wind for a long time to come. He gigged his horse on.

Everybody had been making too much of that ranger lately. Sure he'd killed a lot of outlaws; but look who they were, idiots like Hurley Yates, Donald Kurtz, a few others. It didn't impress Red Hollis. None of them boys had ever been much in his estimation. If somebody really had killed Fast Felton, that might be a man worth worrying about, but for all he knew Fast Felton might be alive and well somewhere.

You couldn't believe half the rumors you heard drifting up from the badlands. If somebody had killed Felton McRoy it wasn't that laughing gambler, and it wasn't that ranger either. He was pretty sure of that. Red was also pretty sure that ranger didn't want no part of him. If he did, why had it taken him so long to get around to it? Years ago he'd heard the ranger was looking for him. Nothing ever came of it. He was still alive and kicking high up here in his country. Hell, he always would be.

He'd put it all together in his mind last night, getting a picture of how that ranger operated. From what he'd heard, the ranger couldn't be fast on the draw—coming in that way with his pistol already hanging from his hand. What self-respecting gun handler would do that? Red figured the man couldn't be much of a shot either, if he had to get as close as Dick Yates said he did. That old man was running on luck and hot air—bet he'd never seen anything like *Montana Red Hollis*, Red thought. The sight of Red *alone* would probably melt that old ranger, Red standing there, biting that glove one finger at a time. . . . He knew Red's reputation. That by itself would stop him short and shake him to his kneecaps.

Red thought about these things as his horse moved around a sharp turn in the trail, and he came upon the rider so suddenly that both of them reeled their horses in surprise. As soon as Doc Tyler caught sight of who was before him, he made a move. One hand sawed the reins, trying to settle the horse as his other hand fumbled with his rain slicker. He'd gotten his hand inside the slicker and around the butt of his pistol. But then he stopped and only sighed a deep breath and let his hand fall, facing the barrel of Red's raised rifle and hearing it cock toward him.

Red grinned, covering the man, hearing Yates and Fish move up behind him. "Look here, boys!" Then he nudged the rifle barrel forward an inch and said in a lowered tone, "You never know what'll ride out of the rain, do ya, Doc?"

"I reckon not," Doc Tyler breathed. He slumped and crossed his hands on his saddle horn. "How ya been, Montana Red?"

"Never better," Red said. "But you sure look like you've swallowed your cud."

Yates and Fish moved beside Red Hollis and sat staring. "You got any whiskey on ya?" Fish asked and ran a wet hand across his lips.

"No, but I wish I did right now." Doc Tyler's eyes moved from one to the other, then settled on Red. "I can't complain though. I had a good run till now."

Red grinned. "Who sent ya, Doc?"

"Does it matter?"

Red shrugged, rain running off the brim of his hat. "Could make it go a little easier on ya, I suppose."

"All right, then. It was some rich feller up in Michigan. Said you done him dirt—killed his daughter. He gave us two up front, and promised three more if we brought him your head."

"*Ouch* now. Five thousand?" Red considered it for a second. "Wouldn't you done better just keeping the *two in hand*, or maybe tell him you threw me off a cliff?"

"Well, yeah, as it turns out." Doc took a deep breath and let it out, raising a hand and pushing up his soaked hat brim. "If you owe me anything from the good ole days, you'll make it quick and see my horse gets taken care of. He's a good one."

"Naw, I don't owe you nothing, Doc." Red spit out into the rain. "To tell ya the truth, you always ate too damn much to suit me."

"I wished you'd said something back *then*. I didn't mean to cut nobody short."

Red shrugged. "It's water under the bridge. Who's riding with ya?"

"Couple of Texans . . . Rance Plum and a kid named Jack the Spider. They're back there trying to scout out that crazy ranger everybody's talking about. I told them I was riding on up here where it's safer." He offered a tired smile at the irony of it. "Don't suppose I could swap sides real quick and ride for you?"

Red chuckled. "Well, I don't know. I'd kind of like blowing your head off, maybe killing that *good* horse first just so you can see me do it." He squinted, considering it for a second, then said, "What am I looking at in that town? I know Rance Plum is a fair hand with a pistol . . . what about this *Spider* Jack?"

"I ain't gonna lie to ya, Red, Jack the Spider's slick and mean. Still too young to be afraid of anything."

Red nodded, tossing the other two a glance. "Then I'll kill him first off. Who else is in town? You said the ranger?"

"That's what Rance Plum thinks. I wouldn't doubt it. Ole Bent Jackson's horse is there. We figured the ranger must've shot ole Bent and took it."

"Yeah, maybe." Red lowered the rifle an inch, his wet gloved thumb still across the cocked hammer. Rain dripped. "Who else is there?"

Doc Tyler shrugged. "That's all I know of. I cut out no sooner than we got there." A silence passed, then Doc Tyler asked, "So, what do ya say, Montana Red? You gonna shoot me or let me ride with ya?"

"You got any of your share of the two thousand left?" Red's brows raised slightly.

"Naw, not enough to mention. Plum probably does. I don't know about Jack the Spider. We'll find out though, if you let me ride with ya."

Red glanced at the other two, then back to Doc Tyler. He let the hammer down on his rifle and raised the barrel. "Why not? We can always use an extra man. I'll figure out something for you to do."

Doc Tyler let out a breath. "Glad we worked it out, Montana Red. Ole boys like us have got to stick together if we ever want to get anywhere in life, you know it?"

Red grinned. "Yeah, I know it. But maybe you oughta pitch me that smoker you got in your holster there—just in case we don't get along."

*   *   *

Before daylight the ranger awakened with the *co-madreja* woman's face on his chest, and his sleep had been so quiet and sound and taken to such a distant place it took him a moment to realize where he was and what had brought him here. When his memory drifted in and took hold just a second or so behind his opened eyes, it brought him to his proper time and place, and he ran a hand down her glistening black hair, raised her head gently, and slipped from beneath her.

Standing up from the bed, he looked down at her in the dark light, recalling the feel of her hair on his skin, as light to the touch as a handful of air. The warmth of her against him still lingered; and he covered her bare shoulder with the edge of the quilt, slipped his big pistol from beneath the pillow, and limped over to a wooden chair in the middle of the floor. He sat down, hearing the whisper of gray rain on the window until the coil of his consciousness rewound itself.

Then he stood up, and when he'd stepped into his trousers and shoved the pistol down in his waist, he went to the saddlebags on the floor by the bed and took out his razor and the bar of shaving soap and walked to the bathroom across the hall. Although he might have used the big rifle for a crutch, he decided against it. Today he would use no crutch. Today he wouldn't be seen limping in the streets. Today he would stand or fall on his own.

In the soft gold light of the lamp beside the mirror he drew the razor in long, tight strokes down his face, feeling the steadiness of his right hand and taking note of it, feeling his hand control the fine edge of steel on his jaw, and liking it. His eyes looked back into themselves from the mirror, hollow and still a bit sunken, he thought, but possessed of a sharpness familiar to him as he swished the razor in the pan of tepid water and raised it once more.

When his thoughts went to the woman he refused to accept them, and moved them instead to the faces of the woman and child given over to death at the cruel hands of a madman. Today was their day, he could feel it. Today they stood in plea before the only justice left to them. And he raised a soft towel from the shaving stand, patted his cheeks with it, searched his face for any nicks that his hand might have made, and finding none, wiped his hands dry and returned to the room.

He moved about gathering his things as quietly as he could, and yet the woman heard him and stirred and rose up on her elbows and swung her hair back from her face. He only glanced at her, then turned his eyes back down to his boots. But her eyes stayed on him as he turned each boot upside down and bumped it on the floor. His socks spilled out and as he picked them up, she said, "I washed them last night while you slept and dried them over the kitchen stove."

He only nodded, sat back in the chair, and rolled them onto his feet. She sat up on the side of the bed, gathering the quilt around her. "I repaired your trousers as well," she said.

He hadn't noticed, but now he ran a hand along the thigh of his trousers and felt the stitchwork. "Couldn't sleep, huh?"

She stretched with one arm raised and shook out her hair, then turned to him just as he'd looked back down and pulled on his boot.

"I woke up in the night at the sound of footsteps in the hall," she said. She saw him stop with his other boot raised to his foot. "But it was only the clerk. He has not left yet because of the weather."

He pulled his other boot on. "Good thing one of us had our senses about us. I never heard a thing all night."

He stood and stepped his boots into place and took the pistol from his waist and laid it on the chair while he tightened his belt. He had dropped two belt sizes, and noticing it, he shook his head and jerked the belt tight and cinched it. Her dark eyes followed his as he looked around, searching for something in the darkness. She reached out with her free hand, struck a match, lit the lamp, and raised its light into a soft circling glow. "It is here," she said, nodding to his shirt lying folded on the stand beside the bed.

He only swept a glance past her, stepping over and picking up his shirt, but in that glance he saw the lamp glow move in the depth of her dark eyes and saw it shimmer on her hair and across her bare shoulder. Stepping back, he flipped the shirt open and turning it in his hand felt the freshness of it and caught the scent of soap. "You do shirts," he said in a flat tone, putting it on, buttoning the bib up one side of his chest.

She cocked her head slightly at the sound of his words. "What do you mean by that?"

"Nothing," he said, stuffing his shirttail down in his trousers. He lifted the holster belt from off of the bed poster, swung it around himself, and closed it into place. Then he said, bending and looping the rawhide holster tie around his leg, "I don't want to see you no more today." His eyes lifted to hers as he made a bow in the holster tie and tugged it tight with his thumbs.

She only stared into his eyes, seeing them grow distant, until he turned them from her. Then she said, "I understand."

He stepped away, taking the rifle from against the wall and back over to the chair where the big pistol lay outside the circling glow of the lamp. With the rifle under his arm, he raised the pistol, checked it, took a bullet from his belt, and loaded the sixth chamber— the safety chamber. He rolled the cylinder down his forearm, let down the hammer, and fitted the pistol into his holster. He adjusted the leather to his hip and felt it come into place. Then he took the badge from his shirt pocket and pinned it on his chest.

"I'll have the clerk cook up some coffee," he said, swinging his sombrero up on his head and settling it forward. He lifted the damp riding duster and swung it over his arm.

She nodded. "When it is ready I will bring some to you."

He stopped with his hand on the doorknob and turned. "No. You heard what I told you." His voice sounded harsh to him. His eyes met hers but couldn't stay there. "Don't make it into something it's not," he said, softening his tone, looking away, away from her, away from the bed, and out through the window into the gray rising morning.

"I make it into nothing but what it is," she said; and hearing her voice without seeing her face, he nodded, opened the door and stepped out of the room. Real pretty hair, he thought to himself, closing the door and standing against it while he took a long breath and let it go. Raising the duster from across his forearm, he rolled the sleeves down, shook it out, and slipped into it on his way to the darkened stairs.

"Oh, my," the clerk said, a bit startled as the ranger

came into sight. It took a second look before he realized that this was the man who'd come in two nights
ago draped on the woman's side. He took note of the
badge on his chest, half hidden by the open duster,
and the holster belt sidled down across his waist.
"You—you must be feeling better? Your daughter
said— That is, she told me yesterday . . ." He had
raised a finger toward the upper hall, but let it go limp
in the air as it came to him that the woman was not this
man's daughter.

"Much better, thanks," the ranger said, crossing the
floor past the desk where the clerk stood staring with
his finger coming down slowly. "We'll need some hot
coffee, strong as you can make it. Take some up to her
and bring me a cup out there," he said, nodding toward the door.

The clerk moved around from behind the desk, hiking up a garter on one sleeve. "Oh, but, sir. Perhaps
your daughter— That is, the *young lady* didn't mention
it to you . . . but I'm in the process of clearing out of
here."

His eyes came upon the ranger's as the ranger
turned to him with a flat stare. "Yes, it's true," he
added quickly, nodding. "I only have a few things left
to do here . . . and of course the weather has shut me in
somewhat. But I'm afraid preparing coffee would simply be out of the question—" The ranger only stared as
he went on. "You wouldn't believe the terrible things
that have happened here." He tossed a hand. "And I
shan't bother you with them—I'm very happy to see
you're feeling better. I'm sure you understand my situation here."

He stopped and took a deep breath and ran a hand

across his forehead, and looked back into the ranger's flat, cold gaze.

"How's that coffee coming along?" The ranger asked in a level tone.

PART 5

A Killing Arcane

CHAPTER 18

"What's he doing out there?" Jack the Spider whispered, standing back in the darkness of the barn in the gray stripes of first light.

"Just standing there in the rain," Rance Plum whispered over his shoulder, his face then turning back to the crack between two boards. He chuckled under his breath. "He appears a bit off his *feed* since last I saw him."

"Yeah?" Lifting his pistol from his holster as he stepped over and raising the tip of the barrel to the crack of gray light, "Watch this," Jack the Spider said. He cocked the hammer back with his thumb.

"Don't be an idiot, Mr. Spider. You think with one simple lift of your thumb you'll become *whatever* it is you're trying to be? Is that what you think?"

Jack the Spider sighted the pistol on the ranger's spine some forty feet away. "Yep, something like that." He squinted, seeing a fine slant of rain fall steadily. "Bang!" he said in a harsh whisper.

Rance Plum just stared at him, seeing a surly smile in the striped gray light.

"But that wouldn't take much guts, shooting a man in the back," Jack the Spider said, still in a whisper as he leaned back near the crack in the doors.

"Indeed, it wouldn't." Rance Plum sighed, stepping back and across the damp straw-covered floor to their horses. He watched Jack the Spider let the hammer down and holster his pistol. "Although, *once dead*, I'm sure it would make little difference to *him*," Plum added.

Jack the Spider watched the ranger pace back and forth in the muddy street, gazing down as if judging the quality of footing for both man and horse there in the thick mire, then gazing up and out along the ridge past the north end of town. *Watching for something up there . . . ?* "Could *you* get past it, once you did it?" He asked Rance Plum, whispering from the side of his mouth as he watched the ranger.

Plum stood by his horse and hooked his thumb on the high-belted holster across his stomach. "Get past it?" His voice no longer whispered but was still low and soft there in the striped gray light. He chuckled once more and shook his head. "Dear, *Mr.* Spider . . . I have had cause to shoot *living* men of *all* variation, in the back, in the front, upside down, and sideways. The only thing to get past is whether or not they manage to *shoot back* at you." He smiled and tweaked a point of his yellow mustache. "It's the *shooting back* factor that tends to separate the kill*ers* from the kill*ees*. Were it not so, I daresay half the world would kill the other."

"Figures you'd say something like that," Jack the Spider said, stepping back from the crack of light. "Are we gonna announce ourselves and get something to eat or what? It ain't my nature to do without."

"In a moment," Rance Plum said; and he turned, walked over to the horses, flipped up the flap of a saddlebag, and rummaged through it until he drew out a small cracked hand mirror. He rubbed the mirror on his sleeve and looked into it, smiling for himself at arm's length. "If there's one thing you must learn, it's to always arrive on your schedule, not the other fellow's. Timing is everything in this business." He examined a tooth in the mirror and picked at it with a fingernail.

In the street only a moment ago, a strange feeling had run the length of the ranger's spine like a soft touch of an unseen hand. Now he passed his gaze up and out across the top of the livery barn, yet searched the weathered barn doors in his peripheral vision. Whatever had reached through and touched him had now moved back and hidden itself in the gray rain. A threat of some sort had come out at him, but now was gone—or now only watched him, he thought. As he gazed away, he raised a hand to his open duster lapel and let it slide down and stop near the big pistol. Beneath his duster the tripod for the big rifle hung from his shoulder on a strip of rawhide.

"So that's him," Ray Gilliam said to Joe Sharpe, beside him on the boardwalk outside the saloon. During the night as they'd sipped whiskey and watched the storms play themselves out, Sharpe had told Ray Gilliam everything; and now they watched the ranger step through the mud back into the middle of the street, slowly lifting his pistol from his holster as he moved, then stopping and drifting a gaze that settled slightly away from the barn doors.

"Yes, that's him," Sharpe said. They stared from a hundred feet away, watching the ranger look down at the big pistol as if checking it, his rain-streaked duster hanging wet around him. Then he raised his head and let the pistol hang in his hand.

"I've heard of him over the years," Ray Gilliam said. From where they stood the ranger looked small to him, small and frail beneath the wide sombrero and the duster hanging wet and low off his shoulders. "What's he doing out there?"

With his other hand the ranger raised the barrel of his rifle, pushed his sombrero brim up with the tip of it, then let the butt rest against his hip.

"I have no idea," Sharpe said, studying the ranger through the rain. "I'm glad he's here . . . if Montana Red comes."

"He's coming," Ray Gilliam said, turning his collar up; and he started off along the boardwalk toward where the ranger stood down in the muddy street. Joe Sharpe followed a few feet behind, knowing he'd resigned himself to staying and to facing whatever rode in today, yet hearing still within himself a pleading inner voice that kept asking him why.

The ranger's gaze only turned slightly toward the sound of their boots along the boardwalk, then moved back toward the barn. But Ray Gilliam knew the ranger had seen them, had glanced toward them. Now as they approached the ranger, Gilliam had just raised a hand and started to call out to him when the ranger's voice boomed toward the barn doors, "You in there!" And Gilliam and Sharpe froze midstep. "Make yourself known," the ranger called out. "Show yourself with your *hands* empty, or I'll kill ya where ya stand."

On the boardwalk Ray Gilliam's hand flashed around the butt of his pistol, and brought it out cocked. Sharpe saw it—*Jesus!* And his hand did the same, only fumbling a bit before clearing his holster. *It's commenced! Just like this!* One second ago he'd heard his inner voice questioning him, and now he was into the thick of it! *No way out!* In his corner vision he caught a glimpse of Ray Gilliam moving forward a step, crouching down. He did the same.

Inside the barn Rance Plum and Jack the Spider had jolted stiff at the sound of the voice coming upon them. Plum's eyes had widened. "Now what, you arrogant *fool?*" Jack the Spider hissed at him. "He heard your damn hammer cock!" His pistol flashed up and swung toward the door.

"No! No, wait!" Rance Plum stepped close and shoved Jack the Spider's pistol down. "Put it away. We're all right here! Trust me, give me room!"

On the boardwalk Joe Sharpe felt his knees go weak. He couldn't do this! He took a faltering step back even with his pistol raised and cocked toward the barn doors, even with Ray Gilliam two steps ahead of him, ready to make a stand. He swallowed hard, seeing the ranger down there in the mud, stoop-shouldered—*relaxed?*—seeming at ease there? *Jesus!*

His rifle resting out from his hip, his pistol not even raised but hanging loose down his wet duster, the ranger called out to the barn doors as they slipped open an inch, then two, then two more, slicing a slow-forming path in the fine falling rain. Ray Gilliam moved forward another step, taking aim; Joe Sharpe tried to keep from stepping over behind him for cover but couldn't help himself. "Get ready," Gilliam said, slicing his words short without looking around. "Go for Hollis! Get him first!"

Sharpe's stomach drew into a knot, but he managed to step back out from behind him on trembling legs. At the barn door he saw gloved hands reach out and wave back and forth. What was this? A trick? Montana

Red Hollis giving up? Then a voice called out through the rain. "Coming out now, Ranger. Don't get drastic on us here."

Joe Sharpe felt his pistol tremble, and he had to steady it with his other hand. From the barn a man stepped out and to the side, wearing a sheepish grin beneath a yellow straight mustache. "My, but don't I feel foolish," the man said. The ranger only stared. From the door came another pair of hands, only one of them gloved, then a younger man stepped out and over beside the first man, the glove for his gun hand tucked down in his belt. This one stood with his hands spread, glaring at the ranger with eyes full of daggers.

"Is that it, *Plum?*" The ranger stood still as stone and called out to the barn. "Just you and the youngster there?"

Jack the Spider seethed, curled his lip into a sneer, and the ranger took note of it. Rain already began darkening their hats and the shoulders of their coats. "Why, yes, Ranger," Rance Plum called out, jutting his head up with a smile, "just me and the *youngster* here."

Ray Gilliam cursed under his breath and lowered his pistol an inch; Sharpe stared, taking in the two men as they stood there, something unreal about them, as if they had only stepped in for a moment from the ether of the universe and would soon step back out. From the hotel window, the *comadreja* woman had heard the ranger's voice call out; and she'd snatched up the shiny pistol Joe Sharpe had left in the room and stood at the window with it cocked in her hand. She swept a glance back along the muddy street toward the saloon, then back to the two men down there by the barn with their hands raised.

"Why'd ya level one down on me, Plum? If ya don't

mind me asking," the ranger said, the rifle butt still at rest on his cocked thigh, the pistol still hanging loose down his side.

Rance Plum shot a glance at Jack the Spider, then shrugged and said, "Oh . . . simply some *hypothetical* situation we were discussing. No harm intended." He smiled and added, "Don't tell me you heard the hammer cock from that far away."

The ranger *hadn't* heard it, but all the same he said, "I'd have to be deaf not to hear that, wouldn't I?"

"If you say so, Ranger." Rance Plum took a step forward with his hands still out. "May we come forward? Perhaps converse in a more hospitable climate?" He gestured a hand upward toward the rain.

"Move with *care* though," the ranger said. "My hackles are still up. A slip in the mud could be mistaken . . . and you know me, once I start shooting."

"Yes . . . well—" Rance Plum stepped closer, shaking his head. "It really *is* embarrassing coming in this way—not at all what I had in mind. But I assure you, we're on *your* side."

"Asshole," Jack the Spider said in a low tone, moving forward beside him.

"Oh? What side is that?" the ranger asked, lowering the rifle barrel from them but keeping the pistol hanging in his hand.

"Why, the search for Montana Red Hollis, of course." Rance Plum slumped again, coming closer, Jack the Spider staring at the ranger, not smiling at all. "What *else* would bring you this high up? Isn't that Bent Jackson's ring-eyed barb I saw in the barn?"

"Bent Jackson no longer requires transportation," the ranger said. "And I don't want you on my side. Who are you working for anyway?"

The two men stopped a few feet away, and held their hands on the lapels of their coats. On the boardwalk Joe Sharpe and Ray Gilliam holstered their pistols. "A wealthy gentleman in Michigan has hired us," Rance Plum said. "Red killed his daughter a while back—a young school teacher *of all things*."

"I know about it," the ranger said. He turned his gaze to Jack the Spider and looked him up and down. "Let me guess. You're the one who leveled down on me, right?"

He only glared at the ranger until the ranger smiled, and added, "No need in denying it. It was you all right."

Jack the Spider glanced at Rance Plum. Plum shrugged. "All right, it was me," the Spider said. His expression was surly and cross, and the ranger took note of it, and of the glove from his gun hand shoved down in his belt.

"Wait right here," the ranger said, looking down at their feet in the thick mud. He looked all around the muddy street. Then walking over past Gilliam and Sharpe on the boardwalk, he pitched the rifle up to Sharpe and said, "Watch that for me."

Sharpe caught the rifle and looked at it in his hands. From above, the *comadreja* woman looked down through the rain; and behind Gilliam and Sharpe they heard the muffled jingle of the bell on the door of Decker's Mercantile farther up the street. Ray Gilliam raised a gloved hand back toward it as if pressing it closed from forty yards away.

From beside a vacant barbershop, the ranger pulled down a wet stack of walk boards and picked out one four feet long and examined it in his hands. He sloshed back with it, holding it out before him. Rance

Plum and Jack the Spider looked at one another. Plum smiled and looked away. And Jack the Spider said to the ranger when the ranger drew closer, "What're you gonna do with that?" He glanced down at the mud.

"I'm gonna wear ya out with it," the ranger said in a quiet tone.

"Hunh?" Jack the Spider snapped his eyes up from the mud in time to hear the whooshing sound and see the dark blur coming toward him, but not quick enough to get out of the way.

The *comadreja* woman turned from the window and shook her head. She uncocked the shiny pistol and walked over to the cup of steaming coffee the clerk had brought her.

"All I'm trying to convey to you, gentlemen," Rance Plum said, shrugging, "is that we happen to be at a point in the road where your interest and mine have come to a juncture. We'd be less than wise to simply ignore it. With this many of us, we simply ride up and take Montana Red down. I have a man already scouting ahead for us."

He stood in the center of the saloon floor with his thumb hooked high on his holster, his tight-gloved fingers tapping out nervous energy on his pistol butt. His thumb and finger went to the point of his mustache as he glanced at Sharpe and Gilliam—their expressions seeming to agree with him—then to the ranger as the ranger stepped around from behind the bar with a wet rag dripping in his hand.

Rance Plum's eyes were on him as the ranger stopped and tossed the rag down to Jack the Spider, who sat dazed. "Here," the ranger said, "a little cold water might help the swelling." A trickle of blood ran down from the large knot on the side of Jack the Spider's forehead. Without turning to Rance Plum, the ranger said to him, "I told ya, I've got all the help I need. You're both lucky I didn't flush you out of that barn and kill you."

"Are you going to *dwell* on that all day?" Plum tossed a hand and rolled his eyes upward. "You must look at the logistics of the situation. If Montana Red Hollis rides in here, he's bound to have a few of his followers with him! They'll shoot this town into the dirt, take what they want, and ride out. What you must do is launch an attack against him . . . strike him up there where he lives."

Plum passed a glance across the other two men, hoping to sell them on his idea as he spoke. "And to do that, you *need* the strength of numbers, sir!" The black man only stared with a grave expression, but Plum could tell he was being swayed; the other man—this young *sheriff* with the look of a cardsharp—appeared too stunned to *think* one way or the other.

"How much is he paying you?" the ranger asked Plum, but as he spoke he watched Jack the Spider press the rag carefully to his forehead.

"What?" Plum's brow narrowed; he spread his hands. "I hardly see what *that* has to do with *anything.*"

The ranger turned to him with a slight smile. "I believe my men here would like to know how much their share would come to for riding up there and helping you kill Red Hollis." He scratched a jaw. "I'm kind of interested myself."

Plum wagged a gloved finger, smiling a tight smile. "No, no. Let's back up for just a second here." His finger moved toward Ray Gilliam. "You said this gentleman is here protecting *his daughter*. The other is a law-man like yourself—it's a matter of sworn duty. How could you possibly expect me to share the reward with you?"

"Because when men side together, they have to throw everything they've got into the same pot and draw from it equally," the ranger said. "If you came offering to fight for us *here* for *righteous* reasons, you'd get out of it what we get. If you expect us to go riding off to fight for *you*, we'll have to get from it what *you're* getting. Make sense to you?" His eyes narrowed on Rance Plum's.

"Frankly, no. Not in the least. But let's not bicker, let's put it to vote." He looked at Ray Gilliam. "What say you, sir? Do you want to face Montana Red here with only the three of you . . . or would you prefer to go up there boldly, *five men* strong and cut him to ribbons?"

Ray Gilliam let out a tight breath, looking at the ranger. "He's got a point. We don't know how many men Montana Red will have with him. Even if he's alone, he's not to be taken lightly." His eyes searched the ranger's for a second, then he shook his head slowly and added, "I've got to think about my daughter's safety."

"Of *course* you do, sir. You have more to lose here than any of us." Rance Plum tossed a hand again, then turned back speaking to the ranger. "You see? What sense does it make to turn me down? So what if my payoff is in cash, and this man's payoff is his daughter's life?" He took a step closer to the ranger. "We're after the same thing here. You just happened to get here first and stumble onto the right bait."

"Why you—" Ray Gilliam started to step toward Plum, but Sharpe's hand caught his forearm.

"Stay out of my way, Plum," the ranger said. "You ain't riding into my business at the last minute, sticking your nose in and changing things." He shot Ray Gilliam a glance, then said to all of them, "He's right about one thing, the girl *is* bait. Let's just get that said right now."

Ray Gilliam's face and neck drew tight, and the ranger raised a hand toward him. "I didn't plan it that way, God knows. But like it or not it's a cold, hard fact. If you want to ride off with Plum, go ahead." His eyes swept them slowly each in turn. "But you could spend the next six months searching for Red Hollis up there in his country, and *still* not find him." His eyes fixed on Ray Gilliam's. "Meantime, your daughter will be here unprotected. You want to risk it? You want to *give her* over to that monster?"

Gilliam just stared at him, his eyes flat, his neck tight, a vein standing out on his forehead. Sharpe looked from one to the other, not understanding why the ranger had to be so coarse abut it. He could use a little more tact, a little more sympathetic tone. Couldn't he see what poor Ray Gilliam had going through his mind? *Jesus* . . .

"So, there ain't going to be no *vote* here," the ranger said, turning slowly. "Everybody's free to do what suits them. But for me, I ain't going to *think* about nobody's *daughter*, how young and pretty she might be, how gentle and sweet she might be, or how cute she mighta been as a baby—I don't *want* to think about her in any way!" He swung an arm, his eyes gone to a swirl of fire. "I'm here to kill a beast and nothing else." He stood for a second with their eyes pinned to him, then added in a level tone, "She *is* the bait, and I plan to wait for the beast right here . . . where I know he'll come to *feed*."

A dark, tense silence gripped the room. Sharpe saw Ray Gilliam's lips seem to go dry and parch before his eyes. But then Gilliam swallowed hard, and with a fierce stare fixed on the ranger he said to Plum, "I'm sticking *here* with the ranger."

"Me too," Sharpe said in a low tone.

"You're—?" Plum shook his head as if to clear it. "Fine then," he said after a second of pause. "Spider and I will be on our way." He gestured toward the door. "Come along, Mr. Spider. I trust you've had more than your fill of this place."

Jack the Spider stood half up from his chair with the wet rag to his face, then froze in place as the ranger said, "You're not leaving here, Plum."

"I beg your pardon?" Plum looked at him with a flat bemused smile. His tight glove wrapped around the pistol across his stomach.

"You heard me," the ranger said, lifting his pistol so casually that it was out and cocked before Plum realized what he was doing. "You had your *vote*, such as it was. Now sit down and make yourself to home. I ain't having nobody out there fanning the trails until after he gets here and I finish with him."

Plum took a step toward him, but dropped his hand from his pistol. "I told you, I have a man out there scouting for us! What am I supposed to do, forget him? Leave him to Red Hollis?"

"Who's the man?" The ranger stared at him.

"Well . . . it's Doc Tyler. You know him. He threw in with me for the reward."

"Yeah, I know him." The ranger shook his head. "He

used to ride with Red Hollis." Before Plum could answer, the ranger shook his head, adding, "Plum, you
must be as stupid as you look. You can't trust a man
who's rode for Red Hollis."

Plum's face reddened. "He knows the country up
there! He has a better chance than anyone of finding
Hollis."

"Yep, and if he does, he'd throw back in with Hollis
in a second if the going got tough."

Plum swung back and forth in place, wanting to
blow into a rage, but he was held in check by the
ranger's big pistol hanging there in his hand. "You
can't hold us here against our will! For how long?
What if Montana Red doesn't come here at all? You
could be wrong!"

Jack the Spider slumped back down in his chair,
dropped the wet rag on the table, and glared at Plum.
"You never said Tyler used to *ride* with him."

"It's not important!" He swung back toward the
ranger.

"I'm not wrong," the ranger said, "I can hear him
coming."

Plum settled, raised his brow, and spread his hands.
"Oh? You simply *hear* him coming?"

"That's right—" The ranger offered a thin wry smile.
"The same way I heard the youngster there cock a pistol on me." He nodded toward an empty chair beside
Jack the Spider. "There's a lot of things you don't
know, Plum. Now sit down and keep quiet before I
take a board to you."

Plum seethed, but sank down in the chair beside
Jack the Spider. "You're a fool to treat me like this,
Ranger," he said with a hiss. "When this is over, you'll

to have face me. We'll have to set things straight between us. You know that don't you?"

"I hadn't thought about it, but now that you brought it up"—he took a step over to them, raised the big pistol, and tapped the barrel on the table—"maybe you and the *youngster* better lift your shooting gear with two fingers and lay them right here for me, friendly end forward of course."

"What? You can't mean—"

The ranger tapped the barrel a little bit harder. "Way to go, asshole," Jack the Spider hissed at Rance Plum as together they lifted their pistols with two fingers and dropped them on the table.

The ranger picked them up one at a time and without turning his face from Plum and the Spider, pitched them back to Joe Sharpe at the bar. "We'll let the sheriff hang on to them for you till you're ready to leave." He grinned, leaning down to Plum. "What about that little smoker you carry in your boot? Think it'll cause any problems?"

Plum glared at him, reached down, and raised a small pistol from his boot on one finger and let it fall on the table. "You know you've just signed our death warrant when Montana Red gets here."

The ranger picked the pistol up, looked it over, and shoved it down in his waist. "Now listen good, Plum, so we both understand one another. Once I lay Red Hollis facedown, I don't care if ya tote his head out of here or not—don't care how much you get paid for it neither. But until he's *dead*, he's *mine*. I don't want no mix-ups and no misunderstandings about what's going on here. This is going *my* way."

He leveled the cocked pistol six inches from Rance Plum's chest and pulled the trigger. Plum's face went chalk white and blank as the ranger's thumb snapped across the hammer and caught it the split second it fell. "This is serious business, boys." He flipped the big pistol around and shoved it down in his holster. "Let's not have no *accidents*."

CHAPTER 19

"Keep an eye on them," the *comadreja* woman heard the ranger say to the others; and she stepped back from the bat wing doors and to the side with the coffeepot in her hands as his boots sounded across the floor. She saw a flash of pain on his face as he pushed through the doors and stopped, lowering a hand to his wounded thigh. The big rifle bobbed under his arm. Then his face hardened as his eyes flashed up at her. He straightened and stared at her, seeing from the look on her face that she'd been standing there awhile.

"I—I brought you coffee," she stammered, holding the pot forward an inch. Fine rain beaded in her hair, on her face.

He sliced a breath through his lips, and gazed away, then back to her. "I can't have this," he said, shaking his head. "I told you to stay away—"

"You must have something," she said, cutting him off, nudging the pot forward. "At least something hot to drink."

He looked back over his shoulder past the bat wing doors, then back to her, seeing once more the look in her eyes. "It's my *job*," he said. But she only stared at him, and he added, "Take your *coffee* and go. Stay away from me, woman." He shooed his hands toward her, but she stood firm.

"You are ashamed? Ashamed for me to see how you bully, and push, and frighten people—even those on your side? Yes, I heard how you spoke of the man's daughter right in front of him, as if she means *nothing* . . . as if she is some kind of lamb, some sort of mindless creature to be staked out for a crazed animal—"

He squinted, ran a hand across his brow beneath the brim of his damp sombrero, and stepped back and leaned the big rifle against the front of the saloon. "You, don't, understand, *ma'am*. This is law work, it's *ugly*, I know it is. But you're fooling where you don't belong! You're gonna get us killed."

Her dark eyes turned caged and cold, and she stepped forward, shoving the coffeepot to him, making him take it. "No. I do not understand. I do not want to understand. *Ugly*? I have seen *ugly*. Enough of it to last a lifetime." She spun and started off the boardwalk into the mud and the fine gray rain.

"Wait." He grabbed her arm, causing her to spin back to him; and dropping the coffeepot, he caught her and held her before him. "Don't do this to me, not now. This is not the time or the place for me to *care*, not about his daughter or *anyone* else." He glanced over his shoulder and pulled her to the side. "*He* sees that, why can't you?"

She shook her head. "He only accepts it because he knows that he must go along with you—"

"And that's good enough for now. That's all I require of him. There's no time to think of *nicer* ways to say it. Red Hollis is a straight-up monster . . . if we can't get down to his level and his thinking when he gets here, he'll have that little girl for supper. That's as coarse and ugly and real as I can say it." He let go of a tight breath and relaxed his grip on her shoulders. "Now . . . I want you to go stay with the woman and the girl until this is all over."

"You see him coming, don't you?"

"He's coming," he said, looking away.

She turned his face back to her, feeling the scar on his weathered cheek. "But, you see him somehow?"

"No, but I *feel* him . . . and he feels me waiting here. Don't ask how."

She didn't. She looked away and settled, and looked back into his eyes. "I have a name, you know."

"What?" He looked at her.

"Yes, I have a name. You call me *woman*, or *ma'am* . . . but I have a name. Like everyone else has one"—she jutted her chin—"so do I."

"Well, I never doubted that you did." He blushed, looking down.

She raised his face with her hand. "It's . . . Maria," she said.

He could tell by the way she'd said it that it wasn't really her name; but he smiled. "Yeah? Well, that's always been a favorite of mine—a really pretty name, *Maria*."

"Oh?" She looked at him closely, checking his eyes, his expression. "So, from now you will call me by my name."

"Of course, Maria." He drew her against him and ran a hand down her damp hair. "Now, I want you to go back to that store and stay there. Will you, please, Maria?"

She gestured a hand down at the coffeepot lying on its side on the boardwalk with its lid flipped open.

"You have wasted the coffee, and the clerk said he has let the stove go out."

"It's all right, we'll fix some later. Now go on." He smiled as she turned.

She stepped down and started off through the rain. "Maria?" When she stopped and turned with a hand shielding her eyes, he said to her. "Do they have any dresses in that mercantile?"

"I am sure they do."

"Then you pick one out, like I promised you."

"You do not have to." She shook her head, looking back at him, stepping on through the mud.

"I know it, but I *want* to."

She nodded and said, "Then I will," and moved on through the rain.

"Tell her I'll settle up with her later today." He smiled. "Tell her I'll need a *receipt*."

He watched until she stepped up on the boardwalk across the street and moved inside the door of Decker's Mercantile; and he took note of the narrow alley beside the store, then moved his eyes slowly along the street through the rain, along rooflines, into alleys, judging, considering. He looked from one end of the town to the other, measuring the length in his mind, not walking it off the way he'd measured the width of it earlier before he'd been interrupted. If he were Red Hollis, how would *he* play this? He wondered, taking in the town.

If he were Red Hollis he wouldn't come riding in down the middle of the street—not if he wanted that little girl. He would slip in, get her, and be gone before anybody knew what had happened.

His eyes swept upward north past the livery barn, out across the ridgeline three hundred or more yards away, the edge of it not much more than a gray blur. On a clear day, he'd get there and look the town over. But not today. Today he would move closer down, stop somewhere just in sight, check things out, look for the little girl.

No matter where the ranger looked, his eyes seemed drawn back to the narrow alley beside the store. He stared, adjusting the steel tripod up under his duster. What stood out about the place? Something . . . what? What was it that made him feel it would attract Red Hollis? His eyes drifted along the roof lines once more and it came to him. Only one building in the town had smoke curling from its stove pipe. He smiled. *Always the little things that you miss at first* . . . Would Red Hollis know the girl was there? Was he smart enough to see it? How sharp are your senses, Red Hollis?

He smiled a thin smile to himself. *Sure. You'll see it, won't ya, Red? Of course you'll see it. You'll take note of that low curling smoke—you'll know she's there, I know you will, I'm giving you this much, I'm sending this much to you. Can you hear me up there, Red?* His eyes searched the gray ridgeline once more and lingered there. If *he* were Red Hollis and he'd been watching that little girl, thinking about that little girl, *wanting* that little girl so badly . . . he would know.

Muddy water rose in a spray from the horse's hooves as they pounded across the flatlands. Red Hollis held the lead. The other three struggled to keep up with him, but spread wide and abreast, they fell behind in the last mile. Red pushed his horse hard through the gray drizzle and cut a wide circle around the flatland before slowing at the rock pass and heading on toward the town.

When he stopped the horse a hundred yards back from the ridgeline, the big stallion stomped and blew and shook himself out and stepped high-hoofed back and forth until the others came splashing to a halt. Their horses were docile and spent, just the way Red wanted them.

Red grinned and wiped dark specks of mud from his face with the corner of the drooping bandanna around his neck. "What took yas so long?" Streaks of gray-brown mud covered Red's legs and his horse's sides. Steam curled from the stallion's muddy flanks, and he spun a circle in place, Red checking him down and staring at the others. "I was beginning to think you bottomed out in a hole somewhere."

"My horse is plumb blown now, Red," Solomon Fish said, himself breathing hard and wiping a hand over his muddy face. "That's a good way to kill a horse in weather like this."

"If ya ask me," Dick Yates said, "we oughta rest these horses off and maybe hit that town once it dries up some."

Fire streaked behind Red Hollis's eyes, but he pulled it back, smiled a tight smile, turned from Yates, and said to Doc Tyler, "You sure you want to throw in with a bunch of complainers like this, Doc? I couldn't blame ya if you didn't."

Doc ran the wet sleeve of his muddy slicker across his chin, looked at the other two, then at Red. "One bunch is the same as the other, far as I care."

"That's right, Doc," Red said, chuckling. "And you two idiots can learn something just watching this man." Doc Tyler leveled his broad shoulders a little as Fish and Yates turned their wet faces to him. "Back when me and Doc rode together, weather never stopped a man from doing whatever he wanted to do."

"Us neither, Red," Yates said, his face reddening. "Alls I meant was, these horses are near blown on us." He ran a wet glove down his horse's withers.

"Shut up, Dick," Solomon Fish hissed beside him.

"Well then, boys, let's step down and rest 'em a little. I ain't hard to get along with here." Red grinned, swinging down from his saddle and stretching his back. Doc Tyler's eyes went across the three of them and he thought for just a second about kicking his horse out and making a run for it. But his horse was as tired as the others, and he had no pistol, no way to fan these men off his tail. "Ain't you gonna join us here, Doc?" Red grinned up at him, pulling the bottle of whiskey from inside his coat.

Doc Tyler made himself smile. "You bet I am." And he swung down from his saddle and led his horse over beside Red Hollis with his reins hanging from his hand. "Whew. I haven't had cause to push this horse that hard for a long time."

Red pulled the cork from the bottle with his teeth, chuckling, and spit it away. He handed the bottle to Doc Tyler. "To be such a *good* horse, he don't seem to have a lot of spring to him. Look at my stallion, he's wanting to run some more."

"He sure does, Red, I admire that stallion," Doc Tyler said. That was Red all right, the way Doc remembered him—strongest horse, fastest gun, always the one carrying the bottle, keeping control of everything and everybody. Doc took the bottle and threw back a shot, Yates and Fish leaning, watching the bottle rise and fall, their eyes working as one like a two-headed snake.

Doc passed the bottle into Fish's wet gloved hand and said to Red Hollis, "We're getting pretty close to that town, ain't we? Suppose you'll be giving me back my pistol before long?"

Red didn't seem to hear him. He'd turned and looked through the gray steady rain toward the edge of the ridge, where a loft of silver fog drifted. "You know that ranger, don't ya, Doc?"

"Wouldn't say I know him, Red—*nobody* knows him. But I've seen his work many times. Saw him take down Clarence Duvall and Bobby Roundtree outside of Abilene years back. One shot each with that big pistol, like swatting a couple of flies. And Duvall and Roundtree weren't nobody to fool with, you know that."

"Yeah, they were good boys all right." Red squinted, scratching his beard with a wet glove. "Now, let's see. That must've been twenty, twenty-five years ago?"

Doc thought about it. "I reckon so, every bit of *twenty*, at least."

"How'd he handle them?" Red asked without facing him, still gazing over at the silver rise of fog along the ridge above the town.

Doc shrugged, chuckled a little. "Hell, Red, we're going back a long time. He just faced them off in the street and shot them down."

Fish and Yates looked at each other, Yates finishing off the bottle of whiskey and running the back of his hand across his mouth. Was Red worried here? This was the second time he'd asked about the ranger in the past two days.

"So, you don't remember how he done it?" Red turned to Doc Tyler, drawing one of his crossed pistols from his holster and twirling it. "Can't recall how he threw down on them? How far away they were? Nothing at all?"

Doc eyed the twirling pistol, glanced at the other two, then back at Red Hollis, feeling a little edgy. "Well—That is, he wasn't far away from them, I remember that much. Seems like he was not more than a few feet from them. They made for their pistols and he swung his up and dropped them, bam-bam, just like that."

Red nodded, stopped twirling his pistol and slipped it back into his holster. "Didn't draw on them then? Already had his pistol out and ready?"

"Yeah . . . come to think of it." Doc breathed a little easier now that the pistol was back in Red's holster. He scratched his head beneath his hat brim. "Now that I think about it, I've never seen him draw on a man. He's always out and cocked, come to think of it."

"That's what I thought." Red grinned. "Nobody's ever seen this man draw his pistol, but he's always *shooting* somebody. Can you figure that out? How the *hell* does he keep getting the drop on everybody?"

"Never really thought about it," Doc Tyler said. "Seems like he's just always *got the drop* some way or another."

"Boy, oh, boy." Red Hollis shook his head. "It amazes me how stupid everybody is. He's kilt off enough good ole boys to keep hell half full over the years, and nobody's *ever* called him out to a straight-up gunfight that I know of. Ain't that right?"

Doc Tyler gazed down, studying it for a second, then, "Well, I'll be," he said, raising his eyes to Red Hollis. A light seemed to have come on for him, and he smiled. "Red, you're saying . . . ?"

"Yep." Red shot a glance at all three of them, hooked

his thumbs in his gun belt, and looked away. "All this time, that ranger's been bluffing himself along . . . coming upon folks all at once and not giving them a chance to get things settled in their mind. He keeps them off balance with the blasted list of his, then before they know it they've got the devil down their shirts."

"He kilt my poor brother with a rifle though," Dick Yates said, "from a long ways off."

"That's because your *yellow* brother turned tail and ran like a coward. Anybody with one eye and half sense can kill a man with a rifle," Red said. "But nobody till me has had the nerve to make the first move on the man." He laughed under his breath. "And you bunch of *sheep-lickers* call yourself outlaws."

Fish and Yates nodded, a little baffled, but laughing along with him just the same, feeling the whiskey surge and glow inside them. Doc Tyler shook his head, going along with anything Red Hollis had to say until he could manage to get his pistol back and make a run for it. "I've got to admit, Red, I feel a little foolish not figuring it out first. But *you're* right. Now that I realize it, that ranger has never been *anything*—just one more lousy arse lawman when ya get down to it."

Red chuckled and wheezed; and he ran a finger under his nose and stepped over close beside Doc Tyler and threw his arm up across his shoulders. "Ain't it a kick, Doc?" He jostled Doc's wet shoulders back and forth, then sighed and said, "Now here's what I've got planned. Since Plum's down there and knows you, I want you to be the one who rides in and tells everybody I'm coming. Will ya do that for me?" He turned his face close to Doc Tyler's and stared into his eyes. Doc could smell his breath and his wet beard, strong and foul.

Doc smiled. "You know I will, Red. Can I have my pistol back now?"

"Sure." Red nodded, still close, his face only inches from Doc Tyler's. He hugged him and slapped his wet glove on Doc's back. "You've been concerned that I wasn't gonna give it back to ya. But to be honest I feared you might take off once you got a chance. You won't, will ya?"

"Hell no, Red. I wouldn't miss you shooting that ranger for the world."

"That's what I thought. That's why I'm sending you down to let them know I'm coming." He grinned, still close against him, took up Doc's pistol from his waist, poked it into Doc's big belly, and said, "Here now, just like you left it."

Doc glanced down at the pistol jammed in his belly, then eased down when Red chuckled and flipped it backward and handed it to him. "Now I don't want you changing sides again once you get down there, ya hear?"

"That's no problem, Red." He smiled, took his pistol, and slipped it down into his holster.

"I know it ain't." Red squeezed him close again, slapped his back once more. "We've known one another a long time. I trust ya, Doc—" His voice lowered barely above a whisper. "Not like them two idiots, eh?"

Doc nodded, ready to pull away, get out of there. But Red still hovered and said in his lowered voice, "Know how far I trust ya, Doc?" He grinned. "I trust you from ear to ear."

"What—?"

Doc felt his chin snap up as Red grasped his bandanna from behind and yanked it back hard. He heard
the sound of the blade go across his throat, a flat soft
sound that he seemed to hear from inside himself—he
felt the deep cold chill, the warm rush that followed it.
And he sank to his knees grasping his throat with both
wet gloved hands as Red stepped back, smiling down
at him through a gray wavering veil.

"I hate a glutton," Red said, bending down before
him, Doc rocking back and forth on his knees on the
wet ground, struggling for breath, finding none. Red
picked up the fallen hat from the ground, wiped his
blood-streaked knife blade on it, and shoved it back on
Doc's quivering head. He leaned close again, grinning,
and said in the man's stiff face, "Now go on to hell,
Doc, save a place for me."

Solomon Fish and Dick Yates stood watching, wide-
eyed, until Doc toppled over in the mud. "Lord, Red,"
Fish said in a tight breath. "You—you've kilt him?"

"Yep." Red shoved the knife back into its sheath behind his back and walked over to the two of them.
Rain dripped from their hat brims and ran down their
coats. "I killed him just for *thinking* about cutting out
on me." He stared at them. "Imagine what I'll do to
you two idiots if you try *doing* it."

CHAPTER 20

Joy Decker had shown the *comadreja* woman her late husband's pistol, and the *comadreja* woman had patted her side, where beneath her ragged dress lay the shiny pistol she'd brought from the hotel room. The two women nodded at one another as Joy Decker slipped the pistol back beneath her apron. She turned and walked from behind the counter, over to the front window where Myra Gilliam stood staring out toward the saloon.

"Come away now, you poor child, your father is all right." But when she took Myra by the forearm, the young girl did not budge. The *comadreja* woman saw the girl stiffen at the touch of Joy Decker's hand, and she moved from the counter over to them.

"It is true," the *comadreja* woman said softly, standing near her with a flowered cotton dress draped over her arm. "Your father is a brave man and he has other brave men with him." She laid her free hand on Myra's other forearm and coaxed her back a step with Joy Decker's help. She smiled at the girl. "Besides, I must have you help me decide which dress I should choose. You will help me? Please?"

Her eyes met Joy Decker's as the girl looked at the dress and moved back with them. Joy said, "Your father wants you to stay back from the window . . . back here with us." She gazed past Myra and at the *comadreja* woman. "You know, I believe that dress might fit Myra, do you think?"

"Yes. You are right," the *comadreja* woman said. She held the dress up against Myra Gilliam, judging it for size. Myra looked down and ran a hand along the fabric, smoothing it to her side.

Joy helped her size the dress to herself and said to the *comadreja* woman, "I used to make a few of these each year for travelers passing through—women with no free time to make their own? It was silly, I suppose." She shrugged and smoothed a sleeve along Myra's arm.

The bell above the door startled them and the *comadreja* woman's hand went to the shiny pistol hidden inside her ragged dress. Then she eased down when Joy Decker looked at the hotel clerk and said, "Newton! For heaven sakes. Don't you realize everyone's a little pensive today?"

"Sorry, Mrs. Decker," he said, standing there with a sheet of canvas draping down from atop his head. He held the canvas gathered at his chest with one hand and held a folded piece of paper in his other. "May I come in? I want to settle the hotel's account with you before I leave."

"Of course, come in." Joy Decker smiled. "And take that canvas off your head. I daresay, you look like the angel of death shrouded that way."

"Oh"—his eyes darted up to the canvas—"yes, certainly." He took it off and shook it and laid it over the wooden barrel beside the door. Smoothing out the rain-dampened piece of paper in his hand, he glanced at the *comadreja* woman. "You haven't returned the coffeepot yet, you know."

"*Sí*—I mean *yes*, I know. But I will bring it soon."

He nodded and turned to Joy Decker with the piece of paper. "It looks like the hotel owes you fourteen dollars . . ."

On the boardwalk across the street the ranger had tensed, watching the man come out of the hotel with the sheet of canvas covering his head and shoulders and shielding his face; but he'd settled once he caught a glimpse of the clerk's face, and now he leaned back against the front of the saloon. As he studied the street through the gray rain, Joe Sharpe stepped out of the saloon, glanced at the fallen coffeepot, picked it up, and without commenting on it stood it near the front wall and turned facing the north end of town.

"Shouldn't we have a guard posted?" he asked the ranger without looking at him.

"We do," the ranger said. "I'm it."

Sharpe looked at him, noting his flat expression. "I meant up there somewhere, near the edge of town."

"No. That would just tip our hand. We sit tight here." He nodded toward the drift of fog at the north end of town. "You figure that's the way Red Hollis will ride in?" The ranger pushed forward from the wall and gazed in that direction.

"I—I didn't mean to question how you run this—"

"I know it," the ranger said, cutting him off. "But I'm curious why you'd think he's coming from the north."

Sharpe let out a breath and shoved his hat brim up with one finger. He shrugged. "I wouldn't give short odds that he's coming at all. But if he does, I figure it'll be from the north. He lives up there somewhere . . . it's the most logical."

The ranger smiled slightly—"So it is"—and let his gaze drift back to the mercantile store and to the alley beside it. After a second of pause, he added, "I was surprised seeing you still here this morning. Think you'll stick for the whole show?"

"I'm trying to." Joe Sharpe studied the ranger's face. There was nothing cynical or offensive in the way he'd asked, just something blunt and real, a question for more than merely the question's sake. He shook his head slowly, staring into the ranger's eyes. "But I won't lie about it. I'm scared to death . . . can't promise a thing. When those two bounty men came out of the barn, I nearly lost it and ran."

The ranger nodded. "That's good to know. I rather you tell me that than to put up a false front."

"Well, I wished I could say you can count on me." He looked down at his boots. "But I'm just taking it one minute at a time. It's all I can do."

"Gentleman Joe Sharpe," the ranger said; and he stopped for a second when he thought he'd heard the sound of a horse off to the north in the gray drift of fog. But he listened, heard nothing more, then added to Sharpe, "I've built a career of law enforcement *one minute at a time*." He grinned, his senses still honed toward the north end of town. "Any lawman tells ya he ain't afraid is either a liar or a fool."

"You mean . . . you're just as afraid as I am?"

The ranger spoke as he listened toward the fog. "No. I meant any lawman *except* for me." He stared at Sharpe with his flat expression. "Now, am I *lying*, or am I a *fool*?"

Sharpe didn't answer, instead he said, "Well, all I

know is, I've ran so long and so hard from *nothing*, it's time I stand for *something* and really mean it."

"You stood toe to toe with Red Hollis, didn't ya?" The ranger looked him up and down, wanting to hear his version of it.

"Yep . . . but that wasn't really me. It was just a *scared gambler*, on a spot, with nothing else to fall back on but the air behind me. That's all I had. That's all I've *ever* had, when it comes down to it."

"When it comes down to *it*, that's all any of us have." The ranger took note of the sheriff's badge on Joe Sharpe's chest, and of the fear lying one layer beneath the surface of his tired, tortured eyes. "Welcome to the club," he added; and he turned toward the north end of town, hearing something there, something too faint for the human senses, but something there all the same. He knew it, he felt it.

Inside the saloon, Rance Plum had risen up from his chair and moved over to the bar, Jack the Spider watching him from the table with the wet rag against his face. "I know who *you* are," Plum said, stepping a foot back from the bar, where a sawed-off shotgun lay cocked and pointed at him. Ray Gilliam's broad hand rested on the shotgun, one finger curled into the trigger guard.

"You don't know me," Gilliam said in a low tone—a warning in there behind his words.

Plum smiled a thin smile beneath his pointed mustache and nodded slowly. "It's taken me a few moments, but yes, indeed . . . years ago." A gloved finger raised and pointed. "I *know* you."

"You'll do well to *not* know me," Gilliam said, his hand tightening a little on the shotgun. "Now sit down or I'll powder your chest."

Plum moved back a step, gesturing a hand toward the front of the saloon. "Does he know?" When Gilliam only started at him, Plum broadened his thin smile, saying quietly, "Oh? He doesn't, you think?" He leaned forward, almost in a whisper now. "He knows everything . . . *eve-ry-thing*." He straightened. "And yet you back his play? What about afterward? Once it's over? What then?"

Ray Gilliam raised the shotgun. "I said *sit down*, Plum."

"Yeah, Plum," Jack the Spider said. "If he shoots you I'll get splattered here. Sit down and stop aggravating."

Rance Plum, moving back, still smiling, eased over to his chair and sat down slowly, staring at Gilliam and saying to Jack the Spider, "Shut up, Mr. Spider . . . soak your wretched face."

Outside, the ranger heard it again, this time more clearly, this time seeing by the look on Joe Sharpe's face that he'd heard it as well. "It's them!" Sharpe's voice sliced low in his throat and he took a step back.

"Easy," the ranger said low, clamping his gloved hand on Sharpe's arm, "one minute at a time, remember?"

Sharpe checked himself down and stared off with the ranger toward the drift of fog. The gray rain had stopped and silence stood beneath the slow dripping of rain from the rooflines and the sound of water trickling into rain barrels from metal downspouts.

From Decker's mercantile, the *comadreja* woman felt a jolt in her stomach, gazing over and seeing the ranger step down in the mud with his duster thrown open. "They are coming!" She spoke back over her shoulder, watching the ranger kick open the steel tripod and stick it down into the mud. "Take the girl into the back and hide her! Quickly!"

The hotel clerk panicked in place. "Oh, goodness! I—I suppose I should stay here and protect—"

The *comadreja* woman grabbed him and shook him. "Do you have a gun? Do you know how to kill?" Her voice rasped in his face. He shrank back from her.

"No! That is—I don't! I mean I've never—"

"Then go! Leave us! What good are you to us? Go find shelter from it!" She shoved him to the door as Joy Decker dropped the piece of paper and the money in her hand and snatched Myra's arm and pulled her beyond the curtain.

"Bu—but!" He stammered; she shoved him harder, and he fumbled and found the door handle and swung the door open. She turned, glanced back at the swaying curtain, raised her ragged dress and jerked out the shiny pistol. Her hand was tense but steady.

"Do you have the pistol loaded and ready?" She called back through the curtain to Joy Decker.

"I do—I do!" Joy Decker answered in a trembling voice.

"I'm telling both of you idiots right now, I'll be on your heels once we start in. Either one of you tries to cut and run, you're dead!" He glared at Solomon Fish and Dick Yates from atop his big stallion, and both of them cowered back from him and held their horses in check. "Do like you're told and at least you'll have a fighting chance." A streak of Doc Tyler's blood still glistened wet down Red's chest.

"We won't, Red," said Fish, "and I swear to it."

"All right then." He pulled his stallion to one side and swept them forward with his bloody gloved hand.

"Get in front of me and stay there. Ride quiet till I fire a round, then hit 'em hard before they know what's happening." He grinned a nasty grin. "Doc Tyler's down there getting them ready for us."

Solomon Fish swallowed hard. "Red? What if the ranger ain't there?"

Red Hollis just stared at him for a second until Fish looked away and over at Dick Yates. The whiskey hummed in both of their brains, just enough to keep them steady. They stared at one another, then heeled their horses forward at a walk, down from the edge of the ridge, toward the gray halo of fog between them and the town below.

Red Hollis lagged behind for a moment on the ridge. Above the halo of fog he could see through the top of the mist the thin curl of smoke rising from a rooftop—from only *one* rooftop in the whole town. Wasn't that something, he grinned. He ran a hand down his damp beard and gigged the big stallion on.

Down in the mud street three hundred yards away, the ranger had walked up on the boardwalk, picked up the big rifle from against the wall, and stepped back down with it. Again the sound of the horse came from the fog. He looked up at Joe Sharpe on the board-walk and said, "Well? Go tell him they're here."

Sharpe shook his head to clear it, and turned to call out across the bat wing doors. But Gilliam had already picked up the shotgun and started around the bar with it. "Red Hollis is here," he said, walking quickly across the saloon floor without a glance back at Plum or Jack the Spider.

"Red's here?" Plum looked astonished. "I didn't be-lieve he'd do it!" They stood up as Ray Gilliam left, and before the doors had stopped flapping back and forth, Plum was at the bar with his pistol in his hand. From the fog came the blow of a horse, clearly now even from inside the saloon.

Jack the Spider came shouldering in beside him, snatching his pistol up from the bar top. "Nobody smacks me in the head and gets by with it!"

He'd turned toward the door when Plum grabbed his arm. "Wait, you imbecile! He's *giving* us Montana Red's head!"

"I don't give a da—"

"Check your pistol, then!" Plum raged and shook his pistol in his face. "They're empty! He unloaded them!"

"That dirty—" Spider snatched bullets from his belt and shoved them into his pistol. "He was going to let us charge out there with unloaded guns?"

"Shut up, Spider! That was just in case we made a play for them." Plum hurried, loading his pistol as well. "Can't you see our situation here? I didn't think Red would come! But he *has!* All we have to do is hang back here. He said we can *have* Montana Red when he's finished with him."

Jack the Spider slipped the last bullet in his pistol, checked it, and spun the cylinder. "What if they don't kill Red Hollis?"

Plum shook his head. "Then *we* will, wake up for crying outloud! We'll ambush him on his way out. Come on . . . the back way, before the shooting starts."

Outside, the ranger had fanned Ray Gilliam across the street with his big rifle barrel. *Stick close to the store-fronts,* he'd said. Sharpe was down in the mud street now, watching the fog for any sign, and as the ranger reached down and snapped the big rifle to the tripod,

Sharpe sliced out a breath—"There they are"—as a horse stepped forward within the silver gray swirl.

The ranger straightened, squinted toward the horse as it stood there tired with its head low and a hoof scraping the mud. "All right, spread away from me," he said, shoving Sharpe to get him moving. Gilliam moved forward on the other boardwalk, his back near the storefronts, his pistol raised and cocked.

Sharpe glanced back at the ranger as he spread wide of him. The ranger reached down to the rifle on the tripod and swung it around until the barrel faced away to the south. *South? Jesus!* Sharpe just stared at him. "Go on," the ranger said, turning, drawing the big pistol, "let's see how they're gonna try to play this."

Sharpe moved forward step by step, every inch that widened between him and the ranger feeling like a mile of cold death. What now? Just keep walking? Closer and closer? Until somebody put a bullet in him? *Aw, Jesus, this was a mistake!*

He stared ahead at the horse, the horse standing sideways to him now, the rider just sitting there shrouded in a swirl of fog, something not right about it. Something not right about the way the rider sat there. A trick? How many guns lay waiting behind the rider, deeper in the mist, waiting for him to come closer, Sharpe wondered. He glanced back and couldn't see the ranger behind him. He glanced over at Ray Gilliam as Gilliam moved forward on the boardwalk.

Closer up, Gilliam stopped, already seeing this wasn't what it looked like. This was a dead man sitting there—not Red Hollis, not any of his men. Tricked! He flattened his back against the wall behind him, his pistol up beside his face, the shotgun hanging in his hand. *A mistake! Myra!* He never should have come this way.

He should have stayed at Decker's with his daughter . . . made Red Hollis pry her from his dying hand—not this! He looked back, saw the ranger falling back, slipping into an alley across from the mercantile store. Gilliam breathed a tight breath. Okay, the ranger saw through the trick. The ranger had things covered, for now anyway—until he could get back to her.

He'd started to ease back a step when a few feet ahead of him he heard the creak of a plank inside a doorway. He froze, then moved toward it with his pistol leveled. Before making his move, he took a deep breath, then stepped out onto the boardwalk, swinging the pistol around, cocked, the hammer ready to drop; and he saw the man's face two feet from the pistol barrel, saw the eyes thrown open wide, saw the mouth fly open in a shrill scream. "Doooon't Shoooot!"

Aw, Lord . . . Gilliam slumped and staggered back, his pistol nearly going off as he jerked it up. The hotel clerk bolted past him, waving his arms, still screaming, across the boardwalk and down into the mud. He hit the hitch rail at waist level, flipped over it and into the mud in a brown spray, then screaming yet, crawled and clawed to his feet and ran until he disappeared, *still* screaming, past Joe Sharpe and into an alley.

Sharpe wiped a hand across his muddy face in the hotel clerk's wake and moved over near the boardwalk and bent down there and looked back for the ranger. In the alley across from Decker's Mercantile, the ranger had bent down out of sight. When the screams of the hotel clerk faded, he leaned forward and looked off up the street at Ray Gilliam, who'd collected himself and moved into the doorway. "It's a trick," Ray Gilliam called over to Sharpe in a sharp whisper.

"What?" Sharpe whispered back.

"A trick!" Gilliam rasped.

The ranger shook his head, spit, ran a hand across his mouth, and gazed back across the street, into the alley, the alley that had been calling to him all morning. "Where are ya, Red," he said aloud to himself in a low tone. "Let's get this little dance over with."

CHAPTER 21

He was here and he wasn't leaving, Joe Sharpe thought, starting to like the feel of it. Live or die he would stick here today. If there were to be a *tomorrow* in his future, it would be his actions *here*, *today*, *now*, that made that future worth living. Something about seeing the terror in the clerk's screaming face made Sharpe realize that there was nothing worse to face in life than *overpowering* fear.

Something clicked in his mind as the man crawled and scrambled and screamed his way through the mud and out of sight. Watching him, it came to Sharpe in a flash that no fear, including the fear of death—perhaps *especially* the fear of death—should reduce a person to such a state. He moved forward in a low crouch, took cover behind a rain barrel at the edge of the boardwalk, and stooped down there, staring out at the horse and rider in the mist of fog. The rider wobbled and swayed lifeless atop the worn-out horse.

A trick. A stupid, foul trick, designed to do what? Was it supposed to strike terror in their hearts—send them screaming away like the hotel clerk? Maybe yesterday it would have, he thought, but today? Today he saw how small and terrible and pointless Red Hollis really was, intimidating, bullying, brutalizing decent folks. For what? Just to keep alive some sick rage within himself?

To hell with you, Montana Red, *to you and your whole bunch and whatever small mindless game you came up with*. Today they might kill him, but they wouldn't see him run . . . they wouldn't see his fear. He wouldn't give them that satisfaction. From deeper in the fog he heard the pistol shot, followed by the pounding of horse's hooves.

"Come on, Red Hollis, you coward!" He yelled out, half standing from behind the barrel, feeling a strange feeling of strength well up inside him.

"Get down!" Ray Gilliam shouted at him from across the street. Gilliam shot a glance toward the sound of the horse's hooves and flattened himself against the building behind him. This was a mistake! Red Hollis had something more than this in mind. Gilliam knew it. Myra! This dead rider was only a decoy, something to draw their attention. As the hooves pounded closer, he looked back toward the ranger, only seeing the tip of his hat brim. Did the ranger see it? Did he know? The hooves pounded closer; a cold sweat beaded Ray Gilliam's brow. He couldn't risk it!

A long yell came out of the fog above the pounding hooves. A pistol shot exploded. Gilliam caught the orange-blue flash of it as he sprang from the board-walk. He raised the shotgun, fired it into the fog, and raced toward Decker's Mercantile. Sharpe saw him running back. *Jesus!* But now the riders broke from the fog, coming toward him like demons out of a night-mare, a high pitch of mud from their horse's hooves. He fired twice as the tired horse and its dead rider fell to one side; and he saw a shotgun raise up and explode toward him. He ducked down and felt the rain barrel jolt against his shoulder, taking the impact.

In the street, Gilliam spun and dropped the shotgun as a pistol shot nipped his leg. He got a shot off with his pistol and saw the horse sway, letting out a scream. He saw the rider struggle to right the horse, but the horse had gone too deep to one side, lost its balance, and went rolling over against the boardwalk as the rider hit the mud in a high spray. Gilliam fired again, this time at the second rider, whose shotgun had just blasted a round at Sharpe behind the rain barrel.

Down the street, the ranger came forward at the sound of battle. Had he been wrong . . . had he misjudged Red Hollis? The second rider charged past Sharpe, Sharpe rising up with his pistol pointed. Two shots exploded and the rider stiffened in his saddle. He reeled back as Sharpe's second shot hit him, but his shotgun exploded in his hand just as Ray Gilliam rose up from the mud and shot him in the chest.

But the blast of the shotgun caught Ray Gilliam high in his right shoulder, flipping him backward. The ranger's big pistol swung up as the wounded rider tried to right himself, his tired horse still pounding forward. One round from the ranger sent the man up and backward, out of his saddle and sliding in a spray of mud. As the horse pounded past him, the ranger hurried to Gilliam, with his pistol raised toward the drift of fog. *Where's Red Hollis?*

Sharpe stepped out into the street with his pistol up, both hands training it toward the fog. Solomon Fish had managed to crawl off through the mud, away from his downed horse, and made his way beneath the boardwalk. The ranger took Ray Gilliam by his arm, dragging him. "Come on, let's get out of the street."

He swung a glance at Sharpe and called out to him as he dragged Ray Gilliam through the mud, "Where's the other man? Where's Red Hollis?"

Sharpe looked around, saw the smear of mud where Solomon Fish had dragged himself under the boardwalk. Before he could swing and fire, Fish had raised his pistol and got off a shot. The bullet sliced through Sharpe's side and spun him down. The ranger saw Sharpe fall, and he dropped Gilliam at the edge of the boardwalk and had started forward. But Gilliam's bloody hand caught his trouser leg. "No!" His breath heaved. "Hollis . . . back there." His eyes darted toward Decker's Mercantile.

Gilliam tried to rise up and make his legs work; they wouldn't. The ranger shoved him back against the edge of the boardwalk. "Stay here, cover the sheriff," he said; and he turned and ran limping through the mud, back to his spot across from the mercantile. Behind him he heard another shot from under the boardwalk and he glanced back to see Sharpe crawl into cover behind the rain barrel. There was nothing he could do for them now. Sharpe would have to take out the gunman.

Ray Gilliam was right. Red Hollis had sent in the dead man, caught their attention, then sent in his two flunkies as a kicker. But Red himself wasn't with them. His plan was to hit while their backs were turned. The ranger ran it through his mind, getting the picture. He'd had Red figured all right, but not tight enough. Red had slipped one extra play in the game sending in these two, giving them up to get what he wanted.

As he slipped quickly back into his spot, out of sight, he knew Red would be coming into the alley soon. And he'd be ready. From this spot, one clear shot

and it would all be over. But as he turned his gaze back
to the alley beside Decker's Mercantile, his breath
stopped in his throat. There in the narrow alley stood
a big mud-streaked stallion, its breath blowing in and
out like a bellows, its reins hanging loose in the mud.

No! No! Not this . . . The ranger's eyes scanned the
storefront. *Nothing moving in there. Nothing!* He
glanced back past the big stallion, down along the narrow alley—Red's clear shot out of town. With the girl
as hostage, what would stop him? He glanced up the
street where Ray Gilliam lay struggling to raise himself up. He leaned and saw Sharpe, pinned behind the
barrel, covered with mud and squeezing a hand to his
wounded side.

He heard a muffled scream from inside the store, followed by breaking glass and a pistol shot—a small pistol. The ranger swallowed a breath, raised his pistol,
took aim, and felled the big stallion with one shot. He
looked away as the animal went down on its front
knees, then toppled over on its side. He called out
along the muddy street to Sharpe and Gilliam. "Both
of ya, get behind the store! Red's in there."

A shot exploded from beneath the boardwalk as
Sharpe leaned out to call back to the ranger. He
ducked back behind the barrel and yelled, "We're
pinned here!"

"Kill him, and get back there, *now!*" the ranger
yelled. Gilliam pulled himself up onto the boardwalk
with his good hand and clawed his way up a post until
he stood on his feet, leaning there. Sharpe raised up to
get a shot toward Solomon Fish beneath the boardwalk but a bullet rang out off the steel band of the rain
barrel and whistled away. *Aw, man! Kill him now? Get*

back there now? Sharpe lay against the rain barrel, scraping mud from his hands and from his pistol.

"Walk him *down* and *kill him*," the ranger called out. "Or we'll lose everything."

Sharpe saw Gilliam stagger from the post to the front of a building and steady himself there. *Walk him down and kill him?* He saw Gilliam check the muddy pistol in his hand. He swallowed hard, and called out, "Ray? Are you able to get—"

"I'm done in," Gilliam called back in a fading voice, cutting him off. "Kill him, quick . . . before I'm gone." With his pistol pointed down at the boardwalk, where beneath it lay the outlaw twenty feet ahead, Gilliam staggered forward, blood dripping a steady stream down his arm and off the tip of his pistol.

"Come and get me then," Solomon Fish yelled, sobbing; and as Joe Sharpe stood and moved forward firing, he saw splinters fly up around Ray Gilliam's struggling feet as the outlaw's pistol exploded beneath the boardwalk.

Inside the livery barn, Jack the Spider turned from the crack of light and said to Rance Plum, "That's it. I'm going out there. I'm not missing out on this."

"Stand down, Mr. Spider," Rance Plum said. "This is how our dear ranger wants it . . . let them have at it. We'll still get paid once it's over."

"Got to hell, Rance. I want a hand in it."

Inside Decker's Mercantile, Red Hollis reached out a bloody gloved hand and yanked the curtain down. He looked out across the counter, across the store, and through the window. He caught a glimpse of the gray sombrero as the ranger drew back into the alley beside the saloon. "Oops," he said. "Bet that's the ranger I've been hearing about."

He chuckled and turned back to the two women as he shoved the wadded-up curtain inside his shirt against the gunshot wound in his left shoulder. With his other hand he raised the shiny pistol, let the bullets drop from it one at a time, then pitched it to the *comadreja* woman's feet. "Lucky you didn't hurt somebody with this," he said.

Blood ran from the corner of the *comadreja* woman's mouth, her breath raced in and out. She stood four feet from him, clutching Joy Decker's bloody face to her breast. "You pig!" She spit at him, swinging away from Joy Decker and lunging at him with her fists. "I will kill you—"

A glancing blow caught Red Hollis across his chin. He chuckled and shoved her back. She sprang again, this time clawing at his face with one hand, her other hand reaching for one of the crossed pistols on his stomach. "You are a feisty one!" He shoved her back far enough to get off a hard left. It connected and sent her against a shelf full of canned goods. She staggered there, wrapped a hand around a can, and hurled it at him. It missed; and he snapped out one of his pistols and pointed it at Joy Decker's head.

"You're starting to make me mad here," Red hissed, cocking the pistol with the flick of his thumb. "I'll blow her *brains* all over ya."

The *comadreja* woman froze. "No wait!"

"Wait?" Red grinned. "Now why would I do that? To tell the truth ain't neither one of you ladies done like I've asked ya to." He lowered the pistol an inch, and Joy Decker's face turned up to him, her eyes wet and pleading. He chuckled again, glanced around the store and out across the street, then back to them. "You know what I'm after . . . now where is it?"

"She's—she is not here, we told you," the *comadreja* woman said. "Do you think they would leave her here, knowing you were coming?"

He started to speak, but the ranger's voice called out from the alley, sounding distant through the building. "Red Hollis . . . give it up. I shot your horse, we've got ya covered. Throw out your gun, and walk out behind it."

"My horse, huh? I wondered what that shot was." Red grinned, reached out, and snatched the *comadreja* woman by her new dress as she stepped over to Joy Decker. He pulled her against his side. "That was a good horse in case you're wondering."

"It's over, Red Hollis," the ranger called out.

"It's *Montana* Red Hollis to you," Red yelled.

"No. It's just Red Hollis to me," the ranger called out. "You never was nothing special."

"What? What's that?" Red raised his pistol and fired three shots out through the big window. Glass crashed and fell. "Now then, I can hear ya a little better," he called out. "Nothing special, eh? Well ask these women if there's anything special to me *killing* them both."

"Both, huh?" The ranger listened to what he said, trying to piece together the situation in there.

"Yep, both of them. I make *one* kill the other, then *I'll* kill the one that's left." He laughed long and harsh. "How's that suit ya?"

"They won't let ya make them do that, Red. They'll die first. You're used to dealing with riffraff like yourself. But that's all over now." The ranger's voice fell silent for a second, then he added, "Kill whoever you're gonna kill in there, Red, so you and me can wrap this thing up. I can't wait on ya . . . there's some *real dangerous* people out there, I need to attend to."

Red Hollis gritted his teeth, the ball of fire spinning in his forehead. The *comadreja* woman saw the ranger's words had struck a chord, and she followed up, saying, "Yes, get it over with, so he can kill you like the coward you are."

Red snapped her out arm's length and cocked his pistol an inch from her forehead. She saw his knuckle turn white on the trigger, but she held her dark eyes steady on his. He started to shoot her down; but he stopped, shoved her away, and snatched Joy Decker by the front of her dress. The gingham fabric tore as he pulled her close, her white breast exposed as she tried to throw a hand over it. "Where's the girl?"

His breath blew harsh and sour in her face. She wanted to scream. She wanted to plead. But she'd seen the way the *comadreja* woman had stared into his eyes without faltering, and with all the power within her she swallowed the tremor in her throat and forced herself to do the same. "Then kill me, you *low trash*. You'll *never* lay hands on that child! Our *sheriff* will kill you."

He felt the ball of fire spinning hotter, but he held himself in check, smiled a crazy smile, and said, "Your *sheriff*? You mean the laughing gambler? That pimp? The whoremonger? *He'll* kill me?"

She seethed at his words and hissed. "We'll *all* kill you!"

"Wrong there, lady," he said, leaning even closer to Joy Decker's face. He reached out with his pistol and backhanded it across the *comadreja* woman's jaw, knocking her backward once more against the shelf. This time she crumbled to the floor. He holstered the pistol, holding Joy Decker close with his bloody gloved hand, and reached back and swung the big knife from its sheath behind his back. "Come on, honey, let's go. I'll send ya out to your *sheriff*."

He slung Joy Decker from the stockroom and against the counter. She gasped. With a slash of the blade he cut away the front of her gingham dress and tore the rest of it off her back as she tried to spin away from him.

Outside, from across the street, the ranger saw them moving about in the store. He raised to fire, but it was too risky. Down the alley, he saw Joe Sharpe move into position with his pistol up. He glanced down the street to where Ray Gilliam leaned against the front of a building, the body of the outlaw halfway out from under the boardwalk, facedown in the mud. He cut his glance back to Red and the woman, trying to get a bead on Red but the woman coming between them. "Turn her loose, you lousy, rotten—" He'd stood and started forward, then crouched and tensed as Red Hollis shouted from inside. "Anything you say, Ranger . . . one *woman*, coming out."

CHAPTER 22

The ranger raised up once more, leveling his big pistol, trying to take aim as Red came laughing toward the broken window with Joy Decker's naked body over his shoulder. The ranger raised his pistol, knowing he couldn't risk a shot. All he could do was watch and grit his teeth as Red hurled the woman out the broken window and onto the glass-covered boardwalk. She rolled through the glass, off into the mud, and lay there still as stone, her face turned toward him, a long gash down her cheek spilling blood. Her lips moved but no words came from them. "There's a little *appetizer* for the laughing gambler," Red called out, his voice in a raging fit of dark laughter.

The ranger turned his eyes from her white naked body as Red's voice fell back deeper into the store. Something moved in the street to his left, and the ranger swung and almost fired before he recognized Jack the Spider running toward him through the mud, crouched with his hands spread before him. "Don't shoot, it's me. I want in on this."

He slid in down beside the ranger and looked across at Joy Decker's body in the street. "Good God," he whispered; and he snapped his eyes up to the ranger's.

The ranger lowered his big pistol, nodded across at the woman lying naked in the mud, her head raising a bit now, but only for a second, then dropping back down. "On *this?* You want in on *this?*"

"I meant— Maybe I can help, some?" He lifted his pistol from his holster, checked it, and trained it on the big empty window frame. Red's raging laughter resounded out of the broken dark opening where shards of broken glass stood like jagged teeth; and as Jack the Spider studied the front of the store, the ranger looked at him, at his bare head, and at the knot on it the size of his fist. He spit, shook his head, and ran a hand across his mouth.

From inside Red called out, "Got another one coming right up. I'll skin this one for ya first!"

"So, what's our plan?" Jack the Spider fidgeted in place like a young colt.

"Plan?" The ranger looked away from him, down the alley where Joe Sharpe had taken cover behind a stack of walk boards, and signaled by waving his pistol back and forth. "No *plan*, other than to go in there and try to turn this thing around, get it going my way. Right now it's his show till I get a chance to kill him."

"But, how many are in there with him? He'll kill them all! Can't we all rush him?"

"I've got one man down and one wounded. Red would love for us to rush him. A good old-fashioned shoot-out is his best chance at getting out of here."

Jack the Spider bit his lip. "Damn it! I ain't just sitting here doing nothing."

"Where's Plum?" The ranger's eyes searched the muddy street.

"He's in the barn, with the horses."

He looked back at Jack the Spider. "Suppose he'd shoot Red for us if I pushed him into his lap?"

Jack the Spider grinned. "I bet he'd love to, in the *back*."

The ranger nodded. "All right. That's what I'll keep in mind if it comes to it. If you want to help, get around behind the store and back the sheriff till I get Red out on the street."

"What about you? Shouldn't I cover you while you move in?" Jack the Spider looked at him.

"No. Get going—if he kills me, just make *sure* he dies. Don't let him get away."

"I won't." Jack the Spider shook his head, drew back a few feet, and slipped away, off along the boardwalk until he cut across the muddy street in a full run and into the alley beside Decker's Mercantile.

Inside the store, Red stood looking down at the *comadreja* woman. She'd come awake and managed to pull herself across the floor and up against the kitchen cabinet; but she'd fallen back down on the floor as Red came across, walking over to her. "Now, then," he said, grinning, the big knife in his hand, "let's start all over. Where's the girl?"

She didn't answer, but only shook her head. "All right, then!" He picked her up by her arm and slung her toward the stockroom. "We'll start with your ears and work our way down." He stepped toward her. She'd caught her balance in the doorway to the stockroom and leaned there against the frame. "Come here, *hon!*" He grinned, reaching for her.

But she didn't cower away. Instead she flung herself at him, her hand going down inside her torn dress and coming up with the bread knife she'd found on the baking cabinet. She stabbed him hard in his thick chest and felt the blade bend and break off. He grunted and staggered back, his big knife flying from his hand. His eyes wide in surprise.

She moved forward, quick, before his hand could go to his pistols. She stabbed at his face with the broken blade, keeping his hands busy trying to ward off her blows. She found one of his pistols with her free hand, but fumbled with it and felt it drop to the floor. It went off, the explosion sounding loud in the small area.

A scream came from the doors of the baking cabinet and the sound of it seemed to strengthen him. He took a stab to his face as he swung wide and sent her tumbling over the kitchen table. "There's my girl!" He tore off the cabinet door and dragged Myra Gilliam out by her thin arm. She screamed again, kicking at him as he raised her from the cabinet and slung her up under his arm. Blood poured from the stab wounds in his face, from the jagged broken blade sticking out of his chest.

"*Noooo!*" The *comadreja* woman dived across the overturned table, her fingers spread like claws, nails going into his face. Red side-armed her away, and laughing and turning, he headed toward the front of the store with Myra Gilliam kicking and screaming under his arm. At the front counter, the *comadreja* came onto his back, beating him with her fists, screaming, cursing him. His free hand went to his nearest holster but it was empty. Damn! What a fracas!

He laughed and slung the *comadreja* woman away. By the time he struggled and ran his hand beneath the struggling girl and drew his other pistol, the woman was gone. The girl under his arm kicked and bit at him. He squeezed her hard and heard her scream end in a sharp yelp, and she went limp. Now then. He'd go out there, shoot that nosy old ranger, anybody else that got in his way, and he'd get himself a horse and be on his way.

He grinned, feeling the blood run down and drip from his nose, feeling a long streak of it running warm down his belly. This would sure be one to talk about. *Yes sir!* He bet the boys up at the line camps would get a kick out of this. It was better than his Mexican bloomers story, *or* the one about ole Bert learning to fly!

He stopped at the counter in the store and looked back along the stockroom floor for his other pistol. He didn't see it. He shrugged. Well, he'd just take the one the ranger carried after he killed him. Under his arm the girl regained her breath and struggled again, this time not as hard. But he jiggled her roughly, laughed, and had started on to the door when he saw the silhouette of the ranger step into the gray light with the long pistol hanging down his side. "Put her down, Red. She ain't a part of this," the ranger said in a low steady voice.

Red swung the girl up in front of him, turning sideways to the ranger, cocking his pistol against her head. He chuckled. "I bet when you was a kid, you kept all the other kids from ever having any fun," he said. "Now get back or I'll splatter her all over the place." He took a short step forward; the ranger took a shorter step back.

"You ain't leaving here with her, not until you kill me, not until you and I finish our waltz." The big cocked pistol hung there, relaxed, the ranger's shoulder appearing a bit stooped from the weight of it.

"You don't want no part of me, Ranger. If ya did you'd come looking long ago."

"I've been busy, Red, and you never was *that* important. You've just become a nuisance . . . a bug that needs swatting. Now come on, let her go. You know I'm gonna kill ya." The ranger smiled. *Smiled!* Had the nerve to smile, Red thought, the ball of fire starting to spin faster.

"I'll kill her, then you," Red hissed.

"You can't kill us both at once, Red." The ranger smiled again.

What was wrong with this old fool? Was he crazy? Before Red could say anything more, the voice of the *comadreja* woman spoke behind him from the stockroom. "And no matter who you shoot, I will kill *you*, you pig."

He glanced back, moving more sideways, flashing his eyes back and forth, the girl still in front of him. "So there's my missing pistol. I'll be wanting it back you know." He grinned, taking a short step closer to the door. The ranger took a short step back, letting out a breath, not expecting the woman to come into the play. Now he had her to think about.

He looked past Red at the *comadreja* woman. "This is between Red and me. Why don't you back off and let us settle it." He cut his glance to Red, still smiling. "I hate it when everybody wants a piece of the play, don't you?"

Red snarled, his hand going tighter around the pistol. "You think I won't kill her?"

The ranger shrugged. "Sure, Red. I figure you're *stupid* enough to kill her—to kill your only chance at getting out of here. But once you kill her, what's this whole thing been worth to ya?"

Red stared, his eyes an angry swirl. "Back out of here," he said to the ranger. "You've got something you want to finish with me? All right, we'll do it. Hit the street and holster that pistol."

The ranger cast a glance at the *comadreja* woman and backed out, one slow step after another, Red moving forward the same way. The *comadreja* woman followed, the pistol out arm's length before her and steadied in both hands. The ranger knew she would pull that trigger—he hadn't the slightest doubt—but he wondered, as he moved back, if she realized what would happen if her aim was off an inch. He wondered if she knew that even if her aim was perfect, the impact of the shot could cause Red to pull the trigger and kill the girl.

When he'd backed to the edge of the boardwalk, the ranger stepped down and glanced at Joy Decker, lying there naked, bleeding, sobbing quietly, pulling herself forward inch by inch through the mud. Red had stepped out and backed away a few feet, grinning, holding the girl tight against his chest, the girl's eyes lost in shock. He glanced at the ranger's big rifle set up out in the middle of the street and said, "What's that all about?"

"That's for you, Red." The ranger shrugged. "I figured you'd turn yellow before it was over and I'd have to shoot ya on the run."

Red's eyes lit hotter. When the *comadreja* woman moved out of the store with caution and down near the ranger's side, the ranger gestured toward Joy Decker with his pistol barrel and said in a quiet tone, "Get that poor woman covered, and out of here? Red and me will be finished in a minute or two." Then he smiled at Red. "Shame on you, Hollis, carrying on this way." And he shook his head taking a step forward.

"Hunh-uh! Hold it!" Red jiggled the pistol against

the girl's head. "I told ya to *holster* that pistol. This ain't going to be the way *you* want it." He watched the ranger's eyes, looking for something there, something to tell him he'd been right about this old man—had him figured, knew his edge and wouldn't give it to him.

"What?" The ranger looked confused. Red saw a flash of doubt there before the ranger caught it and hid it behind his eyes.

"That's right, Ranger. If you want to *waltz*, we're doing it my way." He chuckled, seeing the ranger swallow a lump in his throat.

Behind the ranger, Joe Sharpe and Jack the Spider stepped out of the alley. Sharpe bent down to Joy Decker with one hand pressed to his wounded side. The *comadreja* woman had Joy by an arm, raising her from the mud but keeping the pistol aimed toward Red Hollis with her free hand.

"You rotten lousy—!" Joe Sharpe stood up, stepping forward. "Let the girl go! I'll take you! I'm holstered!" He stepped wide of the ranger, one hand pressed to his side, his other flexed near the pistol on his hip. The ranger saw the look in Red Hollis's eyes, saw things ready to spin out of control. Fanning wider into the middle of the street, Jack the Spider lowered his pistol into his holster and stood with his feet spread. Red's eyes flashed back and forth.

"Hold it, *everybody!*" The ranger shouted. He raised an arm, holding Joe Sharpe back. Red took a step back; the ranger stepped forward with him. "I told Red this was between him and me. Everybody give us some room here. You've got no business on the same street with me and *Montana* Red Hollis." He watched Red's eyes settle, knowing he liked hearing it. Then he

added, raising the big pistol and slipping it down into
his holster, "Okay, Red, you've got it all . . . let her go.
Let's get to it." He moved a step closer.

"Stay put, Ranger." Red chuckled. The ranger had
played it up bold, but Red saw through it. He backed
off another couple of steps, clasping the girl more
firmly against him. "We'll do it when I say we'll do it."

The ranger stood still as he backed farther away.
He had the ranger pegged all right. He even thought
he'd seen the ranger's trouser leg tremble just a bit as
he put the pistol away. "I like a little bit of ground,
don't you, Ranger? Makes it more interesting."
Again he saw the ranger swallow, seeming to struggle with it.

He stopped thirty feet back, his pistol coming
down from the girl's head. She stood dazed and
docile against him. Across from them on the boardwalk, Ray Gilliam raised his head from his chest and
saw them through a blur—his daughter out there? In
the street? With *Montana Red Hollis*? It made no sense
to him. He tried to call out to her, but his voice
wouldn't leave his chest. A pistol lay near him in a
puddle of his blood. He wanted to pick it up. Why
couldn't he?

Red hiked the girl to one side and swung the pistol
up into his holster. He grinned looking at them, all of
them there, *scared*, scared to death of *him*, the ranger
looking like he'd just swallowed his watch. Red had
him. He knew he had him. Behind him another twenty
yards lay the livery barn. He'd make it there with the
girl as a shield after he burnt this old fool to the
ground. "Ready when you are, Ranger," he called out.

"Then let her go," the ranger called back to him. "It's
just you and me—"

"Naw, naw." Red cut him off. "She's *fine* here, if you're any shot at all." His hand spread, flexed near the pistol butt. "Now let's do it up!"

"Aw, Red." The ranger sighed and shook his head, his shoulder slumped. "I thought I could trust ya here—thought you'd decided to be a man for once in your cowardly miserable life . . ."

The ball of fire spun hotter and hotter in Red's forehead, and even as the ranger spoke on in a level tone, Red shouted, "*Coward?* I'll show you *coward!* I figured you out! You ain't *fast* and you *can't shoot.* You're just one more *stupid* lawman—"

"Myra . . ." Ray Gilliam had rolled down onto his side and called out to her as his hand slid through the blood to the pistol butt. In Red's ranting toward the ranger his grip around the girl had lessened; and at the sound of her father's voice, she seemed to snap out of the shock. "Myra," Ray Gilliam cried out again and her eyes went to him, saw him lying there, saw his blood-covered chest.

"Make your play, Ranger!" The ranger was still talking, saying something there. Red's hand went for his pistol just as Myra Gilliam spun away from him screaming and raced across the mud toward her father. *Damn it all!* Red's eyes cut from the ranger to Myra Gilliam for just a split second as his hand came up instinctively, cocking the pistol on his way. His eyes cut back to the ranger. But somewhere in that split second the ranger's big pistol had come out of his holster, had cocked, and was once again hanging at his side. *What?* The ranger's lips were still moving. A piece of paper in his other hand? The ranger still talking?

The pistol just hanging there! Why? Red's pistol was out, up, and the shot firing, but all this had rattled him—had thrown his concentration off. His shot caught the ranger high in the left shoulder and knocked him back a step. But the ranger was smiling! Smiling? Coming up with that pistol real slow, stepping toward him, the paper raised in his hand as Red's second blast whistled past his head. *No, no, no! This was crazy!*

"Dead or alive." The ranger's words stopped as he stalked closer. Red wanted to call out that this wasn't right . . . that the little girl had caused it . . . that, okay, maybe he was wrong about the *fast* part. *What was this?* Nobody was *that* fast! He didn't even see it! He backed off a step as the ranger kept coming—not *wanting* to step back but doing it anyway! Why? And in moving back his next shot went wild, kicking up a splatter of mud. *Damn it all!*

Behind the ranger, Red saw the others moving forward, spreading out as they came. A shot rang out from the boardwalk; Red cut a glance, saw the black man there, bloody, the pistol wavering in his hand. Now that one on him too? This wasn't right! "Ayiii!" He screamed, faltering back a step, another of his shots going wild past the ranger, people ducking away, the ranger grinning now, his eyes ablaze.

"Red, you can't seem to hit anything," the ranger said. "But I figured you couldn't." The big pistol exploded; Red felt himself flip backward and land facedown in the mud. He was down, his pistol still in his hand, the ranger still coming. This wasn't right! Couldn't they see it wasn't right? Mud filled his eyes, he swiped at it with his trembling hand, trying to see. How did they expect him to shoot when he couldn't—

Another shot exploded. Red felt his body buck up and slam back in the mud. *Damn it to hell! What was—!*

His body bucked again. He raised his face an inch from the mud, seeing the ranger real close now, seeing his boot soles rise and fall, coming right up to him. All right! Now he had him! He struggled to raise his pistol. One more shot—he had this old lawman! But he saw the wet muddy boot sole come down on his hand and stop there, pressing it into the soft mud. "It— it . . . ain't right," Red gasped, looking up at the open end of the smoking barrel, inches from his eyes.

The ranger's smile turned tight, staring down at him. "Oh? What part of it aren't you happy with, Red?"

"I'm . . . faster," Red gasped. "I'm faster . . . and better . . . and I—I—"

The ranger stood reloading his pistol, letting the spent shells fall in the mud near Red Hollis's face. "Naw, Red. Like I told ya, you never was nothing. Nothing but an idiot, like the idiots that rode with ya. All you ever had was a few poor souls more stupid than yourself."

"I—I gave you the hardest time . . . you ever had." Blood rolled forward from his lips and spilled down his muddy beard.

The ranger stooped down beside him with his boot still on his gun hand. "No, you didn't. Only thing hard about this was the ride up here." He leaned closer. "I'll make it known that you couldn't hit nothing here at the end . . . that you begged, and cried, and pleaded like the coward that you are."

"Why, you . . . dirty . . . sheep-licking . . ."

He ranted under his breath as the ranger stood, kicked the gun away—but left it an inch from his hand—reached inside his duster, took out a pencil stub and whispered under his breath as he ran a line through Red Hollis's name. He smiled, put the list and the pencil stub away, and gazed off toward the others as they moved up to him. From the livery barn, Rance Plum stepped out with a long carving knife and feed sack hanging from his hand. "You said I could have his head, Ranger," Plum called out.

"So I did, Plum." The ranger gestured him forward, looked down at Red Hollis, and added in a low tone, "Better buck up a little, Red, you've got company coming."

CHAPTER 23

"Hey you . . . up there," Red Hollis said, feeling himself become smaller and smaller somehow down there in the mud, seeing the long dark shadows stir above him, surrounding him. A face would appear atop one of the shadows for a second and speak in a long slow voice. Then it would blur and turn dim. Why wouldn't they listen to him? Why didn't they pay attention here! *Sheep lickers* . . .

At first his fingers had crawled to the butt of his pistol, where it lay in the mud; but once feeling the cold steel at his fingertips, his hand went slack. An empty bag dropped in the mud near his face, and he saw the long knife hanging from the hand of one of the long shadows. The ranger was there among the shadows; Red knew it—he could see his muddy boots. He said something to the ranger, and the ranger didn't even look down. But that was all right, Red thought, he'd show them. Once he got rested here, once his hand started working again, he'd fix *him* . . . he'd fix them all.

One of the shadows had moved down now, and Red felt a wet gloved hand raise his face a few inches from the mud. Now the hand had moved and taken a firm grip on his hair. *One damned* minute here! He tried to shout something, but somewhere beneath his beard he felt a deep burning shiver run across his throat, then felt it moving back and forth.

Another shadow moved down, only inches from Red's face—the face of a woman, her dark eyes burning into his. As the shiver ran back and forth on his throat, the dark eyes bored deeper into him, the lips pursed slightly. A kiss? No, he didn't think so. And when he felt her spit in his face, the ball of fire inside his head tried to spin, but couldn't. Instead, his eyes drifted from shadow to shadow to shadow. Dim light flashed on and off inside his head, at first flashing red, then blinding white, then gray, then black, pitch black . . . so black he couldn't see a—

The *comadreja* woman stood up, wiped a hand across her lips, and glanced around at the others. "That was for all of us," she said. They stood staring past her at the ground where Rance Plum stood with one boot pressed down on Red Hollis's back. He twisted and wrenched, and having pulled the head free, with his muddy boot toe he rolled it into the bag, hefted the bag with both hands, and smiled as dark muddy water ran down in a stream. "There now, that wasn't so bad," he said.

The ranger looked around at the others. Ray Gilliam stood against Joe Sharpe with his good arm looped across Sharpe's shoulders. Gilliam's daughter stood at his other side with her arms around his waist. Sharpe's free hand pressed against the wound in his side. "This is one *rough*-looking bunch," the ranger said.

A pistol shot rang out and they all turned to where Jack the Spider stood over the mud-covered body of Solomon Fish with his smoking pistol pointing down. Dick Yates lay facedown, half sunken in mud in the middle of the street. Above them a sliver of sunlight stood long and slanted from within the parting gray sky. "We'll have to get them up before the ground starts drying," Joy Decker said, "or else they'll be stuck there half the summer."

They all looked at her. She stood wrapped in a blanket beside the *comadreja* woman, and when the ranger asked if she shouldn't be inside getting her face attended to, she'd said yes, she was going, but that after all they'd been through, she wouldn't have missed *this* part for the world.

"Yep—" The ranger nodded as the *comadreja* woman raised an arm around Joy Decker's shoulders and Joy Decker in turn put a bloody arm around the *comadreja* woman's waist. "A rough bunch all right." And when she'd gathered the blanket at her breast with her free hand, the ranger walked with the two women toward the mercantile store while the others stepped along through the mud behind them.

"There's something I need to tell you, ranger," Ray Gilliam called out behind him in a weak voice.

"No there's not," the ranger said back to him without looking around. "What you're wanting to *tell* me happened a long time ago. I'm sure *that* man's been dead for years."

As the ranger stepped away from the women and walked over to his rifle in the street, he called out to them as the *comadreja* woman helped Joy Decker up onto the boardwalk. "Ladies," he said. They turned facing him. He tipped his muddy sombrero. "Remind me to never make either one of you mad at me."

"*Sí*—I mean, yes," the *comadreja* woman called back to him, lowering her eyes with a trace of a smile. Behind them, Joe Sharpe and Ray Gilliam stepped up out

of the mud and Myra moved forward ahead of the rest
and swung the door open.

The ranger picked up his big rifle and swung it up
under his arm. Then he picked up the tripod, kicked it
shut, and carried his weaponry toward the livery barn.
Everything would have to cleaned now, cleaned and
oiled and checked, and put back in their places until it
was time once more to bring them into play. Above
him another streak of sunlight sliced down on the mud
street. He looked up at it and shook his head and
walked on with the wound in his shoulder not bothering him at all.

Neither the fresh wound from Red Hollis's pistol,
nor the healing wound from the *comadrejas'* poison
arrow, or any of the older wounds, the ones that
marked his time and place—the ones from a day long
past—none of these bothered him.

There in the sunlight he walked straight forward in
his mud-streaked duster. A breeze blew in and pressed
his damp collar up against the scar on his cheek. He
walked on. The breeze lifted the front brim of his sombrero until he reached up and took it from his head
and ran his fingers back through his damp hair and let
the breeze blow cool against his brow. No. These
things did not bother *him* . . . these things were a part
of his job.

A week would pass before the ranger stepped up in his
saddle atop the white barb with its black-circled eye.
By then the sun had baked the street into fine brown
powder, and what the rain had turned dark green for
a time along the distant ridges now stood pale and dry
and wavered in dusty heat as if no rain had fallen. And
by then the white barb had filled out in its flanks and

turned surly and bold, and had taken to nipping and lunging at all who came near it but the ranger himself.

"Easy, Black-eye," he'd whispered, collecting the big horse taut in its reins and pressing his knee to it as it high-stepped quarter-wise out into the sunlight. He straightened it and heeled it forward into the street.

A few townsfolk who had left were back now, seeming to rise up from the mud as the last shot still rang in the street. They'd invited him to stay awhile longer, but *no* he'd told them, he'd best be getting on. Now they stood on the boardwalks with dust on their shoes, watching the big horse sway beneath him and shake out its mane. Their eyes moved with him as the ranger kept the restless horse settled and looked straight ahead.

By the third day, word of the killing had spread, and miners began drifting in two and three at a time. They swilled beer and rye and smoked thin cigars. A newcomer would ask was there any whores here, and someone would tell him no, but there's an outlaw's head out behind the saloon—well worth a dollar a look.

They would go there with their mug frothing in their hand and sure enough, back beside an abandoned old jake, Rance Plum had stobbed a sharp stick in a soft spot of ground and had sunk Red Hollis's head on it. When Plum and Jack the Spider got falling-down drunk and knocked it over, they charged the same to see the head on the ground . . . until sometime in the dark of night *someone* or *something* had slipped in and carried the head away.

"What about the rest of our reward?" Jack the Spider asked in a whiskey slur.

"You've got a lot to learn, *Mis-ter* Spider," Plum

replied, gazing out across the garbage dump through bloodshot eyes as if Red Hollis's head might yet be there. "There are still a few pleasures money simply can't buy."

"Oh? Like hell there are." The Spider sneered.

"Like hell *indeed* . . ." And they bickered back and forth.

The ranger glanced alongside the saloon and saw the two of them arguing there. He tipped a finger to his hat and rode on as they raised a hand toward him. On the boardwalk, Ray Gilliam stood with his daughter beside him, his pistol holstered low on his hip, and his wounded arm in a sling across his chest. "Wish you'd stay awhile," he called out to the ranger.

The ranger smiled, took note of the deputy badge on Gilliam's chest, and told him *thanks* but he best be getting on. Then he added, looking back at him, "Who's tending bar while you help uphold the law?"

"Newton, the hotel clerk," Gilliam called out. "This badge is only temporary . . . while our *sheriff's* on the mend. I'm no lawman, Ranger," he added as the ranger rode on.

"Don't you listen to him," Joy Decker said from across the street outside the store. "Now that this town is coming back, our sheriff will need a good man at his side." She stood against Joe Sharpe and smoothed a hand down his freshly pressed shirt. The ranger looked over at them, turned the white barb toward them, and the horse stepped through the dry, fading impression Red Hollis's body had left in the street.

"She's right," Sharpe said. "Between Ray and me, we'll keep this town on the square." He stepped forward, down off the boardwalk with the small bag in his hand and handed it up to him. "There you are, double-wrapped for a long ride, just like you asked. Wouldn't thought you'd have a sweet-tooth."

"It's for a friend." The ranger smiled a little, took the bag of rock candy and put it inside his duster. He pushed his sombrero up with the tip of his gloved finger, looked down at Joe Sharpe's fresh clean shirt, and said in a quiet tone, "She a good woman, ain't she?"

Sharpe's face reddened. "Well . . . she's been good to me, in spite of knowing who I *was* and *why* I came here."

"Takes a certain kind of woman to stand beside a lawman," the ranger said. "Think you'll stick here, give that badge a good name?"

"I can't promise yet. Law work's a shaky business, but I'm gonna give it my *best try* . . . day at a time, minute at a time . . . who knows, maybe I can string enough days and minutes together to make a life here."

"I hope ya do, *Gentleman* Joe." As he spoke, the ranger looked around for the *comadreja* woman but didn't see her.

"*Gentleman* Joe?" Sharpe smiled and rubbed his chin. "Let's see, I've heard that name. Gambler wasn't he? Died out on the badlands? *Comadrejas* got him, I heard."

"Yep, I heard that too," the ranger said, still glancing around, seeing no sign of the *comadreja* woman. "You might want to go over and check on Plum and Jack the Spider. They're pretty drunk, arguing. They lost Red Hollis's head someway—coyote carried it off more than likely. You'll probably have to wear them out with a pistol barrel and let them sleep it off."

"We'll see," Sharpe said. "You leaving or not?"

The ranger looked down at him, nodded, and

chuckled under his breath. "All right then, I ain't telling ya how to run your town." He glanced around one last time for the *comadreja* woman, didn't see her, then heeled his horse forward. "*Adiós,* Sheriff *Elliot,*" he said.

Joe Sharpe brushed a hand along the white barb's side as the ranger rode away; and he walked back up onto the boardwalk and slipped an arm around Joy Decker's waist. "He's something, isn't he," he said to her, watching the ranger ride toward the end of town.

"Yes, he is. But so are you, and so is Ray Gilliam. The ranger didn't do anything you wouldn't have done, did he? I mean if it had been another way? I'm proud of everybody here. We all did what people must do."

"But there was something about him being here . . . just *being* here," Sharpe said; and he wanted to let it go at that.

"You would have shot Red Hollis yourself . . . I know you would have." She ran a hand across his shoulder and picked at a piece of lint.

He glanced down at her, knowing there were things about this that she wouldn't understand. "Yeah, sure," he said.

Down the street at the edge of town, the *comadreja* woman stepped out of a shadow with the reins to Rance Plum's horse hanging from her hand and one of Red Hollis's pistols in a holster up high across her stomach. "So . . . now you leave without saying good-bye?"

He stopped the white barb and looked down at her as the barb milled in place. "I looked, didn't see you nowhere."

"And of course you would not *ask* where I might be?"

He squinted at her, took note of the pistol on her stomach and the bedroll behind Rance Plum's saddle. "I travel alone, if that's what you're thinking. You'd find scarce comfort striking the trail with me."

She put a hand on her hip, lifted her new low-crowned Stetson, shook out her hair, and put the hat back on. "If it had only been me against Red Hollis, I believe I would have killed him all the same."

He raised a gloved hand. "All right, I won't argue that with you. But you didn't listen to a word I said, didn't do like I asked ya to. I ain't forgot it." He eyed the horse behind her, and added, "Where'd you get the horse, ma'am?"

She tossed a hand, and without answering about the horse she reminded him that from now on her name was *Maria*, then went on to say that had it not been for her, he probably, *no*—she raised a finger and shook it at him—*he would have*, died out in the badlands and had his bones picked clean while the *monster*, Montana Red Hollis, ran free. . . .

From the boardwalk, Joe Sharpe stood watching them at the edge of town, seeing their shadows stretch long across the ground through the wavering heat as the woman shook her finger at the ranger and the ranger leaned and swiped a hand back and forth as if brushing her words away. In a second the woman turned, stamped a foot, then swung up on the horse and heeled it alongside him.

Beside Joe Sharpe, Joy Decker leaned and visored her hand above her eyes and looked their way. "Isn't that . . . ?"

"Yep, that's her," Sharpe said. "Looks like she's going with him."

"Oh. Well, then. I shall miss that young woman."

She squinted and studied them as the ranger and the *comadreja* woman rode away. "That horse she's riding, it belongs to Mr. Plum doesn't it? I'm certain it does."

She tugged at Joe Sharpe's arm until he turned and looked out with her. "There now," she said, "isn't that Mr. Plum's horse she's riding?"

"What horse?" Joe Sharpe looked away, and across the street where Ray Gilliam and his daughter stood looking back toward them. He nodded at Ray and Ray nodded back and smiled and turned and walked away, his arm across his daughter's shoulders. "I can never see a thing in the sunlight this time of day," Sharpe said. He smiled to himself as a wake of dust rose up behind the ranger and the woman until in a moment they'd faded into the land. Yes, he thought, turning his smile back to Joy Decker and running a hand down the front of his clean shirt, there were things she wouldn't understand, because it all had to do with men like the ranger, and Ray Gilliam, and himself—it all had to do with their sacred *law* . . . with *law*, and *lawmen*, and the dark stuff that bound them together.

EAGLE
by Don Bendell

Chris Colt didn't believe in the legendary Sasquatch, no matter if witnesses told of a monstrously huge figure who slew victims with hideous strength and vanished like smoke in the air. But now in the wild Sangre de Cristo mountains of Colorado, even Chris Colt, the famed Chief of Scouts, felt a tremor of unease in his trigger finger. The horrifying murderer he was hunting was more brutal than any beast he had ever heard of, and more brilliant than any man he had ever had to best. Colt was facing the ultimate test of his own strength, skill, and savvy against an almost inhuman creature whose lethal lust had turned the vast unspoiled wilderness into an endless killing field. A creature who called himself—Eagle. . . .

from **SIGNET**

THE DAWN OF FURY
BY RALPH COMPTON

Nathan Stone had experienced the horror of Civil War battlefields. But the worst lay ahead. When he returned to Virginia, to the ruins of what had been his home, his father had been butchered and his mother and sister stripped, ravished, and slain. The seven renegades who had done it had ridden away into the West. Half-starved and afoot, Nathan Stone took their trail. Nathan Stone's deadly oath—blood for blood—would cost him seven long years, as he rode the lawless trails of an untamed frontier. His skill with a Colt would match him equally with the likes of the James and Youngers, Wild Bill Hickok, John Wesley Hardin, and Ben Thompson. Nathan Stone became the greatest gunfighter of them all, shooting his way along the most relentless vengeance trail a man ever rode to the savage end ... and this is how it all began.

from SIGNET

Prices slightly higher in Canada.   (0-451-18631-1—$5.99)